WHEN WE
WERE GODS

A Novel of CLEOPATRA

WHEN WE WERE GODS

A Novel of CLEOPATRA

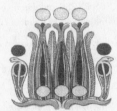

COLIN FALCONER

THREE RIVERS PRESS
NEW YORK

This book is for Helen.

Published by Three Rivers Press, New York, New York.
Member of the Crown Publishing Group, a division of Random House, Inc.

www.randomhouse.com

THREE RIVERS PRESS and the Tugboat design are
registered trademarks of Random House, Inc.

Originally published in hardcover by Crown Publishers in 2000.

Map illustration by David Cain

Printed in the United States of America

Design by Lauren Dong

Library of Congress Cataloging-in-Publication Data

Falconer, Colin, 1953–
When we were gods : a novel of Cleopatra / by Colin Falconer.—1st ed.
p.   cm.
1. Cleopatra, Queen of Egypt, d. 30 b.c.—Fiction.   2. Antonius, Marcus,
83?–30 b.c.—Fiction.   3. Egypt—History—332–30 b.c.—Fiction.
4. Queens—Egypt—Fiction.   5. Caesar, Julius—Fiction.   I. Title.

PR6056.A537 W48 2000

821'.914—dc21   00-022572

ISBN 0-609-80889-3

10 9 8 7 6

ACKNOWLEDGMENTS

My THANKS TO Tim Curnow in Sydney for his faith in me and this book; and to Jane Gelfman in New York for finding Cleopatra a home in Manhattan. I would also like to thank my London agent, Anthea Morton-Saner, for once again helping me with the research, and to the travel writer Michael Haag for his insights into the history of Alexandria. To Jan, Cathy, and Vicki for again helping me find the books I needed. And to my wife, Helen, my first critic and editor, for so much help and encouragement through the first drafts.

I shall be forever grateful to Ayesha Pande, at Crown, the kind of editor writers dream about, who worked so hard to make this book sing; and to Rachel Kahan, whose passion for this novel kept me from despair and showed me there are at least two truly wonderful editors in New York.

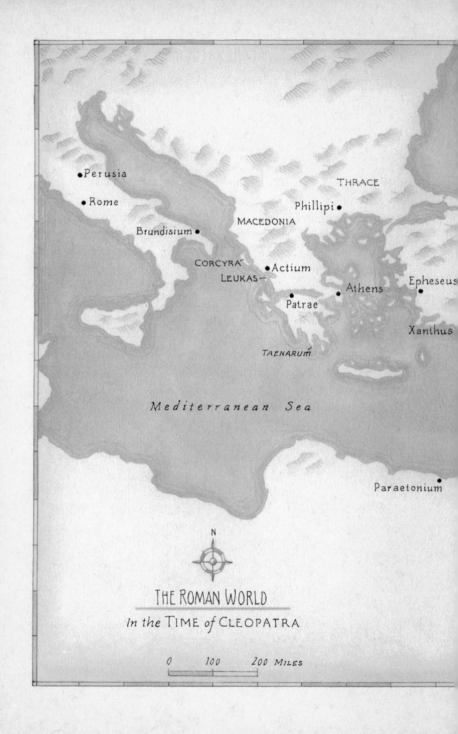

• Perusia

• Rome

THRACE

Phillipi •

MACEDONIA

Brundisium •

CORCYRA

LEUKAS—

• Actium

Athens

Epheseus

Patrae

Xanthus

TAENARUM

Mediterranean Sea

Paraetonium

N

THE ROMAN WORLD

In the TIME of CLEOPATRA

0   100   200 MILES

PART I

. . . the most complete woman ever to have existed,
the most womanly woman and the most queenly queen,
a person to be wondered at, to whom the poets have
been able to add nothing,
and whom dreamers find always at the end of their dreams.

THÉOPHILE GAUTIER, 1845

PROLOGUE

DARKNESS, COLD STONE under her fingertips, shadows dancing on the walls, torches flickering in the downdraught of the tunnels. So cold, and damp as death down here, and it was long moments before her eyes became accustomed to the darkness.

She heard them before she saw them, their sinuous coilings and cold slithering, as they retreated before the light of the torches. She felt her muscles freeze. She was unable to look away, her limbs paralyzed by the horror in the pit below. There were hundreds of them, countless deaths sliding upon and under, eyes glinting like chips of garnet. The executioner's storehouse.

There an asp, its tongue flicking in and out of its slit mouth in agitation, sensing their presence. Its bite caused agonizing pain that spread to the whole body, and the affected limb was soon covered with ugly purple blotches and swellings. Its victim soon began to retch, and then lost control of bladder and bowels. An ugly death, reserved for criminals who were to be doubly punished.

And there, its slender body banded with yellow and brown, the hooded cobra, the divine symbol of Upper Egypt, the royal emblem of pharaoh and Ptolemy alike. The Greeks called it basilisk, or little king. In the Book of the Dead the hooded cobra was the symbol for everlasting life.

Its bite was deadly but relatively painless. After a short time its victim's eyes began to droop, and then they fell quickly into a deep sleep from which they did not return. The fangs left two small marks from their bite, but there was no other disfigurement to the body, granting dignity in death. It was the way chosen for her older sister, Berenice, after she had rebelled against her father and tried to usurp his throne.

Now her father put his mouth close to her ear, she felt the wiry hairs of his beard tickle her face. "This is the world you have inherited," he whispered to her. "Every palace is filled with snakes, twice as deadly as these. You will live in such a nest all your life and you must learn to be as sinuous as these serpents, use your venom as wisely, and to strike without hesitation if you are to survive. Do you understand?"

"I understand," Cleopatra answered.

She was ten years old.

1

ALEXANDRIA-BY-EGYPT

Egyptian month of Phamenoth,
fifty-one years before the birth of Jesus Christ

HER FATHER, PTOLEMY XII, the Piper, the Bastard.

When he died, he left her alone in the inky darkness of the future, and even from the moment of his final breath she could hear the slithering of cold bodies and the baring of fangs.

She stood by the bed, staring down at him. His eyes were closed, the lips composed in a beatific smile; the parting with life had been gentle. Her father, yet not him. The skin was gray, like melted wax, the muscles without the tension of life, so that his features were the same yet only distantly recognizable.

She wondered when the grief would come, why she could not cry for him. But at that moment all she felt was a tingling in her belly, a thrill of fear. She was on her own now. For the last few months she had ruled as his coregent, but now, with his passing, the life for which he had so long prepared her had begun.

From this day and to all the world she was Cleopatra the Seventh, Queen of the Two Lands, Upper and Lower Egypt, Philopater Philomatris, Father-Loving Nation-Loving God. But in her heart she knew she was no such thing. She was eighteen years old, just a girl, without experience, without help, and without friends.

❧   ❧

Help me, she wanted to say. I am not ready for this. But he was gone, death had relieved him of the burdens of power and survival. Only death could relieve her of these same burdens now.

He had called himself the New Dionysus, the savior who would rescue the East from the tyranny of Rome. He'd had the Bacchic ivy leaf tattooed on his body, had been initiated into the secrets of wine and music and abandon. They had laughed at him, and called him the Piper because of his fondness for the Rites. Others called him the Bastard and sneered at his efforts to stall the Romans.

And this was his legacy, this glorious white city—the Brilliant City, as the Romans called it—the gypsum-plastered palaces and shaded groves glittering in the spring sunshine, running right down to the water, clinging to the beautiful curves of the Lochias peninsula. A fresh breeze, rich with the smell of the sea, whipped the silk hangings in her father's room, ghosts dancing her father's last revel. The palaces of Brucheion crowded down to the royal harbor, broached by the arched causeway, the Heptastadion, dividing it from the Harbor of Good Return to the west and the forest of masts of the merchantmen clustered by the docks there. Alexandria-by-Egypt, also a Roman name, had one of the great harbors of the world. The warehouses down by the docks were creaking with the wealth of Egypt and its hinterlands, ivory tusks piled up like cypress logs, pearls tossed in jute sacks like pine nuts, tottering bales of silks and muslins, and great mountains of pungent spices, henna and cardamom and rich cinnamon.

It was the foremost city in the world for culture and for learning. The famous Library contained more than 700,000 *volumen,* cylindrical scrolls containing treatises on mathematics and philosophy, medicine and astronomy, anatomy and geography. The Museion boasted some of the finest scholars in the world, who lived at the state's expense, in return for having their knowledge at the queen's disposal. From the marble halls came victory odes, medical prescriptions, and engines of war, whatever the Ptolemies required. It was here that Eratosthenes calculated the circumference of the earth, by comparing the length of shadows at midday in Alexandria and at Aswan. It was where Aristarchos demonstrated that the earth went around the sun, where Euclid formed the first school of mathematics in the reign of the first Ptolemy.

Yet Alexandria, for all its glories, was a bitter legacy, for such a jewel was lusted after by the whole world.

The city had been named after Alexander the Great, who defeated the pharaohs three centuries before and installed his own line of Greek kings, the Ptolemies. His descendants had controlled vast tracts of land, won by his conquests, but over the centuries they had been chipped away, Syria, Cyrenaica, Cyprus, until they were all gone.

The Mediterranean belonged to Rome. When a monarch or satrap or prince heard the stamp of the legionaries' boots, they knew, too, that the census takers, the tax farmers, the engineers with their roads and aqueducts, would be following close behind, to trample their traditions and culture underfoot. The whole world was becoming a province of Rome.

Only Egypt was left, the greatest emporium in the world. But there were no great generals like Alexander to defend it now, just a rabble of pirates, escaped slaves, and outlaws Ptolemy was pleased to call an army, ruled by a court made up of Greeks, Syrians, and Jews whose idea of a good dinner was to poison all their guests. The population consisted of a metropolis of excitable Greeks and Egyptians whose only loyalty was to their purses and whose first reaction to any crisis was to storm the palace, and a hinterland of Egyptian peasants who prayed to crocodiles and still believed their overlords were pharaohs.

And yet, and yet, she loved Egypt, as her father had. Philopatris, Philomatris; Father-Loving, Nation-Loving. They were traditional titles but ones of her own choosing. She had chosen them as her watchword.

She kissed the Piper's hand for the last time, laid it cold on his chest. She would save Egypt, as he had designed, and she would avenge Dionysus for every private joke they had enjoyed at his expense.

"I have given orders for him to be borne to the Monument," a voice said. "He will lie there along with his ancestors and Alexander."

She turned around. There he was, a great slab of Macedonian lard with oiled ringlets and too many lapis and carnelian rings on his fat fingers, and the sort of superior expression all Greek secretaries seemed to acquire with their robes of office. He had been a privy councillor of the House of Adoration, one of her father's closest advisers, and now that the king was dead, a dangerous man.

"That is for me to command, Pothinus."

"It is proper. I seek only to lighten your burden at this hour of grief."

"I am sure that was your intention."

The Piper was right. The rustling of the vipers had already begun, this one slithering out eagerly from its hibernation. They give orders which they know I will not rescind, and so already they start to chip away at my power, before my father's body has cooled. From this moment there is to be no respite.

❦ ❦

The Regency Council filed into the chamber, her younger brother Ptolemy pushed ahead of them, like a prisoner. Arms no thicker than spear shafts, scowling and surly, an unpretty youth, she thought. They had dressed him in the chlamys of a man, although he was yet to sprout a beard.

What am I to do with him? Pothinus has filled his head with mischief, no doubt. One day when he truly is a man he will no longer be my brother, but my enemy. She indicated a gilded chair on the dais, and Ptolemy came to sit beside her.

The Regency Council sat on a bench, richly gilded, but their heads below hers. There was the unctuous Pothinus, head of the Regency Council and officially Ptolemy's *tropheus*, his Foster Father; beside him was Theodotus, Ptolemy's tutor, another functionary she would trust only after he was dead and his head thrown to the fish; and Achillas, an Egyptian and Captain of the Royal Guard, still loyal to her—for the present. Her *dioiketes*, Hephaestion, her prime minister of the moment, was also there, she knew by his perfume. And of course her sister, Arsinoë. Just fifteen years old, her lovely fair hair tied on her head in a chignon, swathed in silk, her haughty, threatening beauty so lovely and so dangerous. Last of all young Antiochus, still a child, in a short white tunic, a perpetual look of pale apprehension on his face.

Not a soul in the room she trusted, least of all her family. But it had always been this way with the Ptolemies. The third Ptolemy had been murdered by his son for the throne, the eighth Ptolemy had murdered his nephew and then married his own mother in a grab for power. Here was her father's snake pit, her kin her keenest rivals, for they alone could replace her as Egypt. Even the Piper had blood on his hands; he had married his own stepmother and murdered her when his position was secure.

She gazed up at the fretted gold ceiling, the vast fresco of the god Dionysus surrounded by his adoring maenads. She imagined her father's face behind the flowing beard, and she silently asked him: Did you really love me more than them or was this yet another game you played?

She returned her attention to the court: the Kinsmen in their headbands, all of them, even the few Egyptians among them, dressed in Greek chlamys, loose-fitting gowns fitted at the shoulder with a gold clasp; the First Friends in their rich purple robes; the chief priests of Isis and Serapis, with shaved heads and white linen robes; farther away, clustered in knots around the Great Hall of Pillars, the aristocrats, officers from her Household Guard, a few Gauls and Germans of the Roman contingent, as well as a few wealthy Syrians, Jews, and Egyptians. Immensely tall Nubians from her private body-guard, almost naked, had been posted around the perimeter of the court, clutching ceremonial spears.

All of them waiting to see what she would do. Her first big test.

The formalities were dispensed with quickly. Pothinus was eager to be down to business. "We must move quickly to arrange your marriage to your brother, Ptolemy," he said. "It will allay the fears of the population. And we must have an orderly succession so that we do not arouse the interest of the Romans."

"You think the succession has not been orderly, Brother?" she said, using the honorific that was his due from his lofty position at court. She tilted her head, as if observing some curious object she did not fully understand.

"Indeed it has, Majesty," Pothinus said, with an oily smile. "I merely point out the wishes of the people. I believe it is imperative you uphold the tradition without delay."

The tradition. The pharaonic practice, adopted by the Ptolemies, of royal brother marrying royal sister, a sop to the priests and the fellahin, the masses. Her father had married his own sister, and Cleopatra's two older sisters, now dead, had issued from that marriage. This barbaric practice was supposed to ensure the purity of the royal line. She did not believe that was the Council's main concern in this instance.

"When our father became ill . . ." she began, the royal prerogative of speech sitting uncomfortably with her. I cannot do this, she thought. They all see through me. I am just a child myself. "When our father became ill, he arranged for our coronation as his coregent to ensure an orderly line of succession. In our view, the wishes of the people and the needs of state have been served already."

The smile did not leave Pothinus's face, but his eyes were hard. "You do not intend to rule without a king, surely?"

"It is not as if Ptolemy is a foreign prince come courting. You are not hoping for issue from our loins, are you, Brother?"

She saw Ptolemy blanch at this. She smiled and felt a little better for having asserted herself in this room of enemies.

"Pothinus said I should be king," Ptolemy blurted out.

Did he, indeed? Outrage took the place of her fear. "You are still a boy," she snapped at him. "That is why these men have appointed themselves your Council."

He scowled back at her.

And so the argument went back and forth, couched in the polite language of the court. She had no intention of giving ground on the issue, and she knew they could not force her to do so, outside of outright rebellion. They would not risk that with the Romans watching for any opportunity to intervene.

"It was your father's wish," Theodotus said to her.

She smiled to cover her anger, something she had learned to do well as a Ptolemy princess. "He did not express such a wish to us." It is *your* wish, Theodotus, she thought. If I were to marry Ptolemy, I would become his queen and subordinate to him, or in this case subordinate to you and the rest of the Regency Council. You think me a green girl and suppose that you can bully me into giving up the power for which I was born to my surly, ignorant brother and to the three of you—a dusty scholar, a bully two generations out of the field, and a shrill-voiced fat man with nothing between his legs but scallops of fat.

Well, I won't. I may be young, and I may be yet a girl, but Isis will help me somehow, and I will defy you somehow.

"Surely your accession was but a temporary measure?" Theodotus ventured.

"Do you presume to question your queen?" she said back to him with a thundering heart.

To her relief, Theodotus subsided like the lamb he was, head bobbing. If these others were not here with him, she thought, he would not dare to speak up in our presence. . . . *In our presence.* How quickly she might become accustomed to the trappings of power. She must stop thinking of herself as Cleopatra the girl and assume the authority of Cleopatra the queen.

A long silence followed, as she stared them down; all but Pothinus, who glared back at her from beneath black, heavy-lidded eyes. It was Hephaestion who broke the tension. "There is another matter," he said.

She felt herself relax. To her astonishment, she had won this first encounter, had proved something to herself as much as to them.

"Rome is on the brink of war once more. Julius Caesar vies with Magnus Pompey for power there. This Caesar has defied his own Senate and thrown Pompey and his armies out of Italy. Pompey has sent to us for our help in the conflict."

Such a request came as no surprise. Pompey had been her father's ally, and the Piper owed his throne to him. Now Pompey would expect their help in return.

"We must ignore this request," Pothinus said.

"Ignore it?" she said. "And how will that benefit us?"

"We are not slaves to the Romans. Should this Caesar gain victory, will you provoke him by supporting his enemy?"

"And if Magnus Pompey should prevail?"

Pothinus did not answer her.

So, her first decision on foreign policy. But she knew her own mind on this; for years she had been impatient to have her say. Her father had called her opinions unschooled. For her own part, she thought him too timid. "My father owes this Julius Caesar nine talents of gold," she said to them. "If he wins, he will be here to claim it. You still wish to see Magnus Pompey defeated, Brother?"

"He asks for sixty ships and three hundred soldiers."

"Then we shall give them to him."

"They will say you are a lover of Romans!"

Cleopatra stared at him. So, that is the rumor you intend to spread about me. At least you did me the honor of letting me hear it first. "They will say many things about me before I am dead."

Pothinus gave her a look. It said, Oh, you think it will be that long before you join your father in Alexander's Monument?

"Do as we command," she said, and her mouth felt suddenly dry. She stood up and swept from the room.

She sat alone for a long time in her private apartments, her limbs still trembling with anger and nervous exhaustion. She was as lonely as she had ever felt in her life. All around her, the susurration of vipers. She would pray to Isis for strength.

The richness of the room, the tortoiseshell inlaid into the doors, the rich Cappadocian carpets, the carnelian-encrusted chairs, did not console her at all. In her mind this was still her father's room and this pomp and splendor seemed to belong to him, not to her. Despite all the training he had given her, she did not now feel like a queen, but an impostor, impossibly young, impossibly green.

She heard a noise behind her and she started, for she had thought she was alone. But she relaxed when she saw that it was just Mardian, her own *tropheus,* and her tutor since childhood. The closest thing she had to a friend. He was fat, as many eunuchs were, fatter even than Pothinus. His blue chlamys was as voluminous as the royal pavilion, and his face as crumpled as a discarded gown, all folds and creases.

"That Pothinus," he said. "He has the intelligence of a roof lintel."

"Will they stand against me, Mardian?"

"While Achillas is on your side they cannot move against you."

She brooded on this.

"Of course, all Alexandria is against you. They disapproved of your father's policies toward Rome. Yours as well. They think you are pro-Roman."

"How can we be against the Romans unless we have an army like theirs? I am just being practical."

"Also, Pothinus and the rest are out to line their pockets. Every merchant and middleman in the bazaar would rather have a milksop like Ptolemy on the throne and under the thumb."

She felt her shoulders sag. She closed her eyes. "I have no support, I run a nation of shopkeepers and slaves who riot in the streets if the sun goes behind a cloud, I have the Romans breathing down our necks looking for one opportunity to ransack the Treasury. What am I to do?"

Why had her father left her so young? A few more years as his coregent and she might have been able to consolidate her hold on the throne, would have known what to do. But then she knew that was not true, for while she had brothers, she would never be considered queen in her own right, she would always be subordinate to their claims. And there would always be a Pothinus to exploit her weakness.

2

THE TEMPLE WAS on the promontory of Lochias, overlooking the open sea. It was a private sanctuary, reserved only for members of the royal house, a place where she could be alone with Isis, the Goddess of Ten Thousand Names, Shelter and Heaven to Mankind, Protector of Women, Word of God, Great Mother of all Nature.

The salt wind whispered through the columns, sand filtered along the marble tiles with the sea smells. Cleopatra fell to her knees, waited for her eyes to become accustomed to the gloom of the sanctuary. Isis gazed over her head toward the ocean, the feathers of justice on her head above the silver disk of the moon, the sacred knot between her bare breasts, a jug containing the waters of the Nile in her left hand, a snake entwined around her right arm, a crocodile docile beneath her left foot.

From somewhere close by she heard one of the priests singing a hymn to the goddess in a high-pitched voice.

She laid the offerings of fruit and flowers at the foot of the statue, silently asking the Great Mother for her help.

When she had finished her devotions, she walked back through the palace gardens, now brilliant with the white flowers of spring, and was told that the Apis bull had died.

⟐ ⟐

Cleopatra lay naked, facedown on a smooth bench of alabaster, while Iras, her Nubian, massaged balsamic oil into her back and shoulders. Another slave rubbed her hands with almond cream, while yet another massaged her feet with mint water. Charmion brushed through her long dark hair with a tortoiseshell comb.

She had sent for Mardian, but had not bothered with the fretted cedarwood screen for the interview. She never minded him seeing her immodestly. He was practically her mother. There was no one who knew her better, and besides, all masculine feeling in him had been razored away when he was ten years old.

The fleshy jowls danced as he walked, like dewlaps on a bull. Which was exactly what she wished to speak of. "Majesty," he said, fell heavily to his knees, and touched his head to the floor. "You have doubtless heard the news. The sacred Apis bull has died."

The Apis bull was thought to be the incarnate of Ptah, the god of Memphis. The Apis bull was always chosen for its characteristic markings, black, with a white diamond on its forehead, a crescent moon on its right flank, the mark of the scarab on its tongue. It was pampered as no other animal on earth, and when it died it was mummified and placed in a special tomb with its forebears, like a pharaoh. The funeral was followed by an elaborate ceremony to consecrate its successor, which was escorted on a barge down the Nile to its new home in the Temple of Ptah.

The death of the bull so soon after her father's death was considered a bad omen; all Alexandria was abuzz with the news. In the marketplace they were saying it was a sign from the gods that they were unhappy, that a queen should not rule Egypt without a king at her side. No doubt Pothinus had helped spread the rumor.

I will show them I am not some empty-headed girl to be manipulated by eunuchs and bullies, she thought. I will turn this omen around to my own advantage. I will use this occasion to cultivate a power base of my own, away from Alexandria and these scheming Greeks and Jews.

"I have decided to attend the funeral service myself," she said.

Mardian blinked in surprise. For once, she had her tutor at a disadvantage, and she felt a glow of satisfaction. "At Memphis?" he said. "No Ptolemy has ever paid court to the Egyptian gods."

"Then this will be the first time," she answered him sweetly.

"I see," he said, his face a hieroglyph for bewilderment.

She settled her chin on her hands. Perhaps I can do this, she thought. If I can outwit my own tutor, perhaps I can outwit the Council also. "Ask the *dioiketes* to prepare the state barge. We are going to pay our last respects to the Apis bull and welcome the next."

"Is it wise, Majesty?"

"They do not love me in Alexandria, Mardian. But I am not queen of just this one city. I am Mistress of the Two Lands, and I intend to show the Council that I will not be besieged in my own palace. How do you think the priests and the people of the *chora*"—the peasant fields—"will react when they see their queen, in the body of Isis, the Great Mother, greeting a fellow god in his own temple? Will they not love us then?"

She smiled, closed her eyes, and surrendered herself to the ministrations of Iras.

❦   ❦

Mardian spared a glance at the hard, brown body on the alabaster table before he departed. Such a tiny body and such a fierce determination. Hard to think of her as a woman, but you could not deny the evidence of your eyes. They have all underestimated her, he thought, except for me. He had known, since she was a child, that she was different from her brothers and sisters, and quite a different proposition from her father. Pothinus, Theodotus, none of them really understood what they were dealing with. She was stubborn and willful, but with a fierce intelligence. No other Ptolemy had taken the time to learn the language of the people they ruled. The tongue of the court was Greek. To his knowledge, she was the first to learn the common language. If Isis had decided to return to Egypt, it was his belief that the goddess might indeed have chosen little Cleopatra for her incarnation.

❦   ❦

They were in an Egypt utterly unknown to the Greeks and Jews of Alexandria, of mud villages clustered under dom-palms, donkeys pulling creaking *sakkiehs*—water wheels. In Alexandria the colors were the blue of the sea and the white of the buildings, and there were so many different nationalities that the whole city might have been a bazaar; here the colors were brown and green, and every face the same, hooked nose, nut-brown. They had left the capital in the middle of a rainstorm; here the Nile was placid and blue, the skies clear and endlessly warm.

It was only the second time she had left the city to come to the *chora*. The first had been the occasion of her coronation just a few months before, as regent beside her father. Every king since the very first Ptolemy, in Alexander's time, had chosen to be crowned first in Alexandria and then a second time at Memphis, where the ancient pharaohs had held their coronations.

On that day in Memphis, a shaven-headed priest had handed her the royal crook, scepter, and flail, and crowned her with the double pharaonic crown, the cobra diadem of Lower Egypt and the white bulbous-tipped vulture headdress of Upper Egypt.

"Life is a pageant," her father had said to her once. "The people do not wish to know of you, the girl with the lustrous dark hair and long Egyptian nose and olive Macedonian skin, of her fear of snakes and the darkness, or of her fondness for olives; they wish for a queen and a goddess, with none of the faults of nature that were given to them. You must be beyond their reach for them to love you."

So now she reclined on a couch on the cedarwood deck of the royal barge, shaded by a golden-fringed canopy of pure silk, surrounded by Nubian slaves with long-handled jeweled fans. Her long dark hair fell around her shoulders in tapering ringlets, and on her hair she wore a golden band with the two feathers of justice. Above her brow a round disk that shone like a mirror, the silver face of the moon. Her pure white linen gown was knotted at the center with the sacred knot, her bare breasts painted blue. There was a golden snake coiled around the flesh of her right arm.

The silver-tipped oars sparkled as they dipped and rose. With every mile small children ran from the mud-brick houses, and farmers with sun-browned skins and white loincloths ran to the banks to gape at the goddess queen returned.

Is it really our queen, here in the *chora*? Is it really our Isis?

Cleopatra fidgeted in the desultory heat of the canopy, raised a languid hand to the faces packed on the riverbank, gawking. Even the slight movement of the boat on the river made her nauseous, and the linen gown was uncomfortably heavy.

But this piece of theater was vital to her destiny, she knew, and the uncertainties that had plagued her after her father died seemed to slough away the farther they sailed up the great Nile. She experienced an elation with herself, a powerful conviction of her own destiny. I can do this, she told herself. I can prevail in my father's palace of serpents.

She was borne on a litter past the sacred pool, down a paved avenue lined with sphinxes to the Temple of Apis. She heard the dismal music from the temple, the sour-sweet smell of incense drifting on the still, hot air. The priests poured from the temple to greet her, their heads shaved, dressed in the blue of mourning.

First to greet her was Pshereniptah, High Priest of Memphis.

"Dread Queen," he murmured, "you do us great honor."

"On the contrary, I am here to honor Ptah," she said, and saw from his expression that she had chosen her words well.

The great complex of Saqqara, she knew, was one of the most revered sites in all Egypt. They passed the great stepped pyramid of Zoser with its massive limestone wall, the mastabas of long-dead priests and viziers, shimmering in the bleak desert heat. She attended the funeral rites for the dead bull at the temple, and then followed in procession to the great catacombs nearby.

At the entrance they passed a semicircle of statues of Greek poets and philosophers, Homer at the center, Pindar playing the lyre, Plato expounding on the soul. Her father's work, she remembered. He had given generously to the priests to restore their temples and sacred places. It was he who had taught her that she must not be just a Greek princess, but an Egyptian pharaoh as well.

They followed a ramp down into the bowels of the desert, dark and breathlessly hot. The priests chanting their dirges, the smoke from the torches burning her lungs, she followed the procession down the long underground gallery, past the enormous black sarcophagi, covered with hieroglyphics, the mummified remains of other Apis bulls from a thousand years past.

The air down here was thin and fetid with age and dust; it smelled of heat and decay. A scorpion scurried across the sand, darting into the shadows away from the light of the torches.

At last the mummified bull was borne on a litter along the narrow corridor by a sweating phalanx of slaves. They gasped under their load, their grunts of protest drowned by the funereal hymns of the priests.

It was huge in death, wrapped tightly in its white bandages so that only the horns protruded, huge canopic jars bearing its viscera and other vital organs. The bull litter was lowered onto a bed of white alabaster inside a vast sarcophagus of pink granite, and then the great stone lid was levered into position.

The sacred Apis was finally at rest, ready for his next incarnation.

That night, at the feast held inside the temple to commemorate the passing of the Apis, Pshereniptah leaned toward her and whispered: "Your presence here today will never be forgotten. To the priests and the people here, you are no longer just Cleopatra. Now you are Isis herself."

3

To be a queen, she quickly learned, was to become the overseer of drudgery. Each day was an an endless round of Council meetings; statecraft involved the daily mastery of detail, making countless decisions on dredging irrigation canals, the proper administration of import taxes, the appointment of minor officials.

With her prime minister, the *dioiketes,* beside her each morning, she interviewed or sent directives to the functionaries, the *strategioi,* who were responsible for each *nome,* or district. But as pharaoh she also had to be accessible to the common people, so afterward she held court in the great Audience Hall, receiving petitions and requests in her own hands, dispensing justice in person. And of course she knew she must never fail to inquire after the health of the new divine bull, Apis, from the chief priest.

She had inherited far more problems than she had realized. The country was paralyzed by its vast bureaucracy, nationalism was rampant in the *chora,* many fellahin had fled their fields— unwilling or unable to pay the increased taxes raised by her father—and the onset of another famine had even led to uprisings in Upper Egypt. This last problem she addressed immediately; more princes were unseated by hungry mobs than invading armies. So she had astonished Pothinus and the rest of the administration by announcing she would devalue the currency by one-third, thus increasing exports and making more money available to the Treasury to buy grain from abroad, while at the same time instituting a strict program of rationing throughout the country.

For the time being the prospect of mass starvation was allayed.

Meanwhile, they all waited for news from Greece on the outcome of the conflict between Caesar and Pompey. Everyone believed that Pompey would surely defeat the upstart general, despite Caesar's string of military successes in Gaul. For her own part, Cleopatra was sure her decision to send Pompey soldiers and supplies would be vindicated. That would teach Pothinus a thing or two about diplomacy.

Her feelings of terror were gone. She no longer felt like an impostor when she sat on the throne of Alexander. I had underestimated myself, she thought.

But then the two Roman envoys were murdered by some drunken legionaries in a camp outside the city, and her newfound confidence evaporated like the mists over Lake Mareotis in the morning sun.

The whole of Alexandria was celebrating. You would think we had just defeated the crack Mars legion and sacked the Forum, Cleopatra thought. It wasn't even Egyptians who had killed them.

The two men were both sons of the Roman governor of Syria, Marcus Bibulus. They had been killed by Roman legionaries stationed outside the city, loaned to her father by Pompey eight years before to protect him against an uprising. Well, hardly Roman, she thought. The soldiers were mostly Germans and Gauls with foul breath and lank beards, who drank too much and looted the bazaars in the city whenever it took their fancy. Many of them had found wives of equal ugliness in Rhakotis, and some had even fathered hordes of brats.

The Syrian governor now wanted this ragged and unruly bunch back, to help him fight the Parthians, but it seemed they had grown overfond of life in Alexandria and did not relish the thought of being soldiers again. A few of them had gotten drunk on hearing the news from Syria and decided, in their dense and provincial way, that the answer to their problems was to murder the messenger. In this case, Marcus Bibulus's sons.

And now the problem of what to do about this affair is mine.

The court, as usual, was a colorful and elaborate affair, Greeks in purple chitons, Persians in coats and trousers, Judaeans in long white robes, Egyptians in traditonal *kalasiris*. Her prime minister was there, with his *oeconomi,* in their Greek robes and wreaths, the officers of the Royal Guard distinctive in the wide-brimmed felt hats, the small oblong mantles and high-laced boots of a Macedonian country gentleman. The Chief Huntsman, the Chief Physician, and the Chief Cupbearer were resplendent in diadems and gold brooches.

Cleopatra was dressed in the formal robes of state, a pectoral of gold and ivory, lapis and carnelian, a thick belt of heavy gold, her arms and ankles adorned with bracelets and anklets of gold and lapis. She held the crook and flail of the Great House of Egypt; on her head, the vulture headdress and golden *uraeus* of the Two Lands.

Charmion had spent long hours applying her cosmetic, paying especial attention to her eyes, which were accentuated with black kohl and green malachite. Her mouth had been reddened with a special ointment made from ram's fat mixed with red ocher, and her hair gleamed with a special ointment of oil and juniper juice. Her hair had been braided and decorated with gold ornaments. The figure who stared from the throne was not an eighteen-year-old girl but a goddess.

An Egyptian scribe in a kilt sat at her feet beside a scholar from the Museion in a Greek robe, ready to record the proceedings in Egyptian and Greek.

A deadly hush had fallen over the Great Hall of Pillars as she entered. Now she spoke: "Would someone like to explain what happened in the city yesterday?"

A fidgeting silence. It was Pothinus who finally spoke up, that same insulting look in his eyes. "Majesty, the Roman soldiers were ordered by two envoys to accompany them to Syria to assist the governor there in his petty wars. They refused to go."

"And so they murdered two defenseless men?"

"They were Romans!" Pothinus almost spat the words.

"These troops have settled here now," Theodotus said, more soothingly. "They are simple barbarians from Gaul or Germany and have taken wives and mistresses for themselves. Many have families from local women. They have no love of Rome."

"They are Roman soldiers nevertheless."

Pothinus seemed to glow with pleasure. Perhaps it was he who engineered this crisis, she thought. It has his hallmark on it. He would make her choose between antagonizing the Romans and fomenting the disgust of her own people. How like him. "Well, it is done now, Majesty," he said.

She looked around the court for the third member of the Council, the Captain of the Guard. Achillas was of the highest rank in the court, a Kinsman. "Brother," she said, "you have not given us your opinion."

"Dread Majesty, as Pothinus says, they are just Romans."

Oh, just kiss his fat backside and be done with it, she thought irritably. Does he own all of you?

She turned finally to her prime minister, standing beside her throne: one Protarchus, who replaced Hephaestion after he had completed his year's tenure at the post. "What do you think of this matter?" she asked him.

"Majesty, they are Romans, as the Captain of the Guard says. And they have broken Roman law. Therefore it is my opinion that they should answer for their actions to Rome."

She turned back to the court. "That is our opinion also. Therefore we command that the murderers be found and handed over in chains to the Roman governor in Syria for judgment."

Achillas took a step forward. "Majesty! Is this just? Should we grovel to the Romans? We might as well lie down at their feet and let them march into Alexandria!"

"Well, if they wished to, you and your army could not stop them!" It was the truth, and it silenced him immediately. He stared at her, white-faced. I believe I have just lost my last ally in the palace, she thought, appalled at her own impetuosity.

"Majesty, will you humiliate us before the Romans?" Pothinus asked her, more gently.

"If Egyptian soldiers murdered your sons in Rome, would you not expect them to be handed back to you for justice? Though I admit it is not a likely event, in the circumstances."

The barb hit home and Pothinus's cheeks suffused with purple. But he persisted. "The people will ask if we are ruled from Alexandria or from Rome."

"We have no authority over people's questions, only their actions, Brother. Find the men who murdered the envoys. Bring them here."

Pothinus dared for a moment to glance around the room at Ptolemy. The boy stared sulkily at the floor. It will not be long, she thought. I believe he will decide to challenge me soon enough. But not today.

She looked back at Pothinus. "Do as we command," she said.

4

EGYPT WAS KNOWN among its own people as the Black Land because of the ribbon of rich, black soil left behind by the Nile after the annual floods. It was this sediment the people of the *chora* depended on each year to feed their crops.

All along the banks of the Nile were domed mud-brick buildings called Nilometers that were built over underground chambers specially constructed to measure the height of each flooding. There were gauges on the walls to calibrate the level of the river. If the river rose too high, the dikes were washed away and the fields were flooded and ruined. But if the river did not rise enough, the fields would not be watered and the soil would be too thin for next year's crops. There would be famine in the year ahead.

Death, it was said, could be measured on the walls of a Nilometer in cubits.

For the second year in succession the Nile rose below the Cubits of Death, and this time she was powerless to prevent the oncoming disaster. In the *chora*, the children died first, and then the sick. There were riots in Alexandria, uprisings reported in the Upper Nile. Thousands of fellahin were abandoning their villages. The perfect climate for treachery.

❧ ❧

Mardian came in the middle of the night, out of breath from his rapid shuffling along the echoing corridors of the Lochias palace. His long gown flapped around his ankles.

Cleopatra had not yet retired to her bed. She sat at her work desk, her most treasured possession. It was made from a solid slab of lapus lazuli supported at each corner by basalt sphinxes inlaid with gold and coral. They said it had once belonged to Alexander himself.

She worked with wax tablet and stylus, scrolls spread across the pale blue bench. A crisp sea breeze, scented with jasmine from the garden, stirred the curtains in her apartments, setting the lamps on the brass standard guttering.

Again and again she had gone through the figures supplied her by her *strategioi*. The grain reserves in the warehouses at the docks were dangerously low. Most years they had enough to feed not only Egypt, but half the Mediterranean. This year thousands of her own people would die of starvation, no matter how many times she stared at the figures in the ledgers and reports in front of her.

Mardian did not wait for permission to speak. "Majesty," he gasped, "you are in danger."

She laid down the stylus and stared at him. Just one look at his face and she knew. It had happened at last. She heard her father's voice, heard again the susurration of reptiles in the long-ago cell below the palace.

Every palace is filled with snakes, twice as deadly as these.

"Pothinus?"

He nodded. "Achillas has been persuaded to support him."

She jumped to her feet in fright, then crossed quickly to the doorway. The two Macedonian guards who stood sentry outside her apartments each night were gone. The empty corridors mocked her.

"You have no friends left in Alexandria, Majesty. Except myself and Olympos, your doctor. And I am afraid neither of us would know which end of a sword to hold."

She and Mardian had prepared secretly for this moment for months, ever since she sent the two Romans in chains to Syria. In her pride and her arrogance, she thought she could outwit Pothinus and his cronies. Now she knew how foolish she had been.

She could hear her father's voice: *I warned you.*

Mardian had smuggled money and jewels down the Nile to Thebes and Philae in Upper Egypt. The priests had helped her; not all Egypt was against her, at least. Her visit to Hermonthis and her dedication of the sacred bull had proved her lifeline.

She reminded herself that it would not be the first time a Ptolemy must fight for the throne. Her father had spent time in exile, with Pompey, who had helped him win back his throne. Yet the thought gave her cold comfort.

At once she fought the urge to throw herself on the couch and weep. Tantrums are for children, she told herself. Yet here she was, as she had been when her father left her, eighteen years old and friendless. The night was suddenly chill as the grave, and she wanted only to hide in the corner like a child and cover her face.

"We must leave now, tonight," Mardian breathed, his voice shrill with agitation. "Your executioners may already be on their way through the corridors."

She turned away from the window, searching desperately inside herself for the strength and the resolve she needed now, like a gambler who has lost all his money, fumbling deep inside his purse for the one gold coin that might yet keep him in the game.

"The boat is ready at the landing," Mardian said.

She did not trust her own voice. She nodded silently and hurried past him, her throat so tight she could scarce breathe, an iron band around her chest. The future was as dark and forbidding as the ocean below the steps. No time to think of that now. Stay alive. Keep one step ahead of the asps and their venom.

ψ ψ

A small boat was waiting at the foot of the palace steps; Charmion and Iras clambered aboard after her. Mardian had summoned slaves, and her jewels and chests of clothes had been loaded on board. He was last into the small boat.

They slipped silently through the Heptastadion into the Harbor of Good Return, and through the canal under sleeping Rhakotis into

Lake Mareotis. There they transferred to the dhow that would carry them up the Nile to Thebes and safety.

The last time she had visited the *chora*, it was as a goddess, in a royal barge, shaded by silk canopies and fanned with peacock feathers. Now she would return as a frightened young girl, with the stench of the bilges in her nostrils, a veil thrown across her face, hunched in the hold like a criminal.

5

Roman month of Septembris,
forty-eight years before the birth of Jesus Christ

CAESAR WATCHED THE galley draw alongside his flagship. A great silk-robed barrel of pork was helped out of the galley and onto the deck. It was painted and perfumed in the manner of a Damascan tart, and now awaited his pleasure, grinning like a slave hoping for betterment. Two Nubian servants stood behind him, almost naked, their black skins glistening with sweat.

The emissary's name was Theodotus, apparently.

The dangerous shore was like a line painted on the black border of the sea in uneven kohl by some nervous girl. The slap of the waves against the ship, the strong breeze guttering the torches. The soldiers gathered on the deck were nervous, alert for treachery, faces cast in shadow by their helmets. The whip of canvas in the yards.

"Greetings, Noble Julius Caesar," the emissary said in a shrill voice that grated on the general's nerves. "On behalf of the Regency Council, I welcome you to Egypt as a guest of the great Ptolemy the Thirteenth, King of Egypt, Master of the Two Lands."

Caesar kept his hand on his sword hilt and said nothing. His eyes went to the wicker basket one of the Nubians held in his arms.

"We bring you a gift, Noble General."

Caesar nodded his assent. One of the Nubians placed the basket on the floor and took out an object, which was wrapped in cloth. The fabric was white but had a brownish stain.

The other Nubian spread a small carpet on the deck beside it. The two then placed the object on the carpet and began to unwrap it. There was another cloth under the first, this darkly stained also. They peeled it away to reveal a human head.

The head had been separated from its owner some time ago and was unrecognizable. The flesh had turned black, and it stank like a barrel of squid in the sun. This treat was presented to him on a silver platter. Theodotus, holding a scented handkerchief to his nose, came forward and held out a signet ring. Caesar recognized it. It was Pompey's.

"What have you done, you fat pansy?" Caesar growled.

Theodotus took a step back, as if struck. "He offended all lovers of peace," he squeaked. "Our king's sister had set herself up against you, had sent him ships and soldiers. We did it for you."

"For me?"

"Dead men don't bite," Theodotus said.

So. They thought he would be pleased. This gypo thought he would commend them for murdering and butchering a fellow Roman. Caesar took a step forward and grabbed him by the throat. Only the intervention of his own officers prevented him from throttling the man then and there.

6

MOUNT KASIOS, EAST OF PELUSIUM

A HOT WIND shifted across the desert. Two months they had waited by the wells, her army sprawled in ragged tents under the palm trees. If army it might be called; a core of enthusiastic but ill-trained Egyptian fellahin recruited from Middle and Upper Egypt, augmented by a few hundred Nabataean mercenaries she had enrolled into her army at Ashkelon.

Achillas, meanwhile, was secure in his fortress at Pelusium, blocking the way to the capital, his own ragged army of purse snatchers and brothel guards bolstered by veteran legionaries, the Gauls and Germans who had refused to go to Syria.

A stalemate. She could not go on, they would not come out.

Everything she had feared for Egypt had come to pass in the year she was away from Alexandria. The Roman general, Julius Caesar, was now invested in her palace on the Lochias promontory. Against the odds, he had defeated the great Magnus Pompey at Pharsala in Greece, and pursued him all the way to Egypt. The Regency Council had thought to placate him by offering him Pompey's head.

It seemed the ruse had not worked.

A shameful episode, in her youthful opinion. Her father owed his throne to Pompey. If that proud Roman had expected loyalty or gratitude from Ptolemy's descendants, he had badly miscalculated. Pothinus had instead decided to play the Roman and set a trap for him. As Pompey waded ashore, Achillas stabbed him and then hacked off his head. They left his body to rot on the beach.

Caesar had shown his gratitude for their perfidy by installing himself in the royal palace and holding Pothinus and Ptolemy virtually as hostage. He was behaving not as a foreign ambassador, but as the city's conqueror. He'd had Theodotus banished for his part in Pompey's murder, and now claimed the right to arbitrate between herself and the remaining members of the Regency Council in the war.

The mob had behaved predictably; there were riots in the streets and some of Caesar's soldiers had been killed. Caesar was now himself besieged in the palace, beset by the populace and Achillas's soldiers.

For months it had gone on, and she thought she might die here in this white and empty wilderness. And then Caesar's freedman rode out of the desert.

❧ ❧

"My name is Rufus Cornelius," the man said. "I bring a message from Imperator Julius Caesar."

Caesar. She felt her heart leap to her throat.

Rufus Cornelius had removed his Roman helmet, with its decorative brush, and placed it under his left arm. He was resplendent in red cloak and enameled breastplate. He had about him that air of confidence all Romans possessed—not the snot-nosed arrogance of some of her own Greek ministers, but the absolute confidence that went with membership of the most feared army in the world.

She felt her throat tighten. Here I am, a brigand girl queen with a ragbag army. What must he think of me, this Roman? Sharing my silk pavilion with snakes and lizards, the sweet sandalwood incense barely disguising the stink of the camels and sand in everything?

I wonder how I might impress him? "What does your lord have to say to Queen Cleopatra?" she asked him.

Rufus Cornelius bowed. "He is much grieved by the situation he finds here in Egypt, Your Majesty. Rome enjoyed friendly relations with your father and with Egypt, and he is most concerned to find the nation racked by war."

"This war was not of my doing. I was deposed unlawfully by the Regency Council."

"As you know, your father made a will that was vested in Rome, stating that you and your brother were to rule jointly."

If there is such a will, she thought, this is the first I have heard of it. But I suppose my father might have signed anything to squeeze more money out of the Romans to get his throne back.

"Imperator Caesar is aggrieved to find your brother in contravention of his father's will and has taken it upon himself to decide the matter."

So, she thought, this Caesar is now not only king, but kingmaker. There is no end to the arrogance of these Romans. And yet his arrogance is not entirely misplaced, for I am a queen without a country, and though he is yet just a magistrate, he is a Roman magistrate, and his armies hold sway over us all.

"It is Caesar's wish that you come to Alexandria so that he might broker a solution to Egypt's problems."

"If I could come to Alexandria, I should not need Caesar."

The Roman had the temerity to smile at that. "The offer stands."

"And I thank him for it. Tell him I shall consider it."

7

SHE SAT ON the throne, stiff-backed, staring into space, long after Rufus Cornelius had gone. *I put on a good show, I think. My whole life is theater now. If they knew how weak and afraid I really feel, I would not have a friend left in the world.*

Mardian was watching her, his doughy, hairless face blank, but his eyes telling a different story. *He must be as frightened as I,* she thought. *If I win, his future is assured. If I lose, he is dead too.*

"What do you think of this, Mardian?" she said finally.

"Trust a Roman and you deserve whatever misfortunes result. Those bastards would penetrate their own grandmothers if there was profit in it."

"Yet what choice do I have?"

"None. It is impossible to get into Alexandria."

"Perhaps that is the whole point of his summons. It is a test."

"A foolhardy one."

"I win nothing here. We cannot mount a siege of Pelusium. Achillas is content to let us camp here until I run out of money or our Arab mercenaries lose heart and go home."

"But should there be a way of getting you into the city, you would only become Caesar's prisoner."

She closed her eyes. *I cannot just sit here in the desert, day after day. I would rather die. A year in this desert and I feel like a dried-up old woman. I have to do something.*

If only she knew this Caesar, knew what he was like. "What do you know about him, Mardian?"

The eunuch puffed out his cheeks. It was a sign he did not approve of the man who held their destiny in his hands. "He is a great soldier. He routed Pompey at Pharsalis, and that mean-tempered bastard was considered Rome's best general. He is married to a woman called Calpurnia, a political union, of course. He is a renowned lecher. They say he has bedded every one of his friend's wives and that not a divorce takes place in Rome without Caesar's name mentioned."

Cleopatra felt a thrill of fear. She might pretend to the throne of Egypt, but she could not compete with such a man. She was certainly no warrior, and she was yet a virgin. The thought of dealing face-to-face with this Caesar was intimidating, at the least.

Mardian was watching her. His thoughts were written plainly on his face. He was thinking the same thing.

"Is he very handsome?"

Mardian hesitated, the question rousing his suspicion. "Not particularly. My spies say he has a problem with baldness, about which he is particularly sensitive."

"We shall have to find a way to impress him," she said.

"It would seem very little impresses Caesar."

"Oh, there must be something."

Me, perhaps.

It was an impertinent thought. But to test it, first she would have to gain entry to Alexandria. It would have to be done by subterfuge, for not even Caesar could guarantee safe conduct through the battle lines. He was as much a prisoner as Ptolemy and Pothinus. Cleopatra doubted that even Rufus Cornelius and his escort could find their way back into the city now.

But it had to be done. She would not sit here in this stinking tent a day longer.

"Does Caesar favor Ptolemy against me, Mardian?"

"If he is a Roman, he favors whoever suits his purposes best at the moment."

"Then why should he love my little brother when his prime minister and his general both make war on him and want him out of Alexandria?"

"You would invite the Romans to stay in Alexandria, in place of your brother? It is like inviting a crocodile into your house if he promises only to eat the corn."

"At this moment, Mardian, I am queen of nothing. Before I can reorder our country's destiny, and my own, I must have the power to do it. I must be Queen of Egypt again."

Mardian was silent. Outside she heard the camels cough, and the hot desert wind whipped the silk of the tent. "You are right, of course," he said finally. "But it is a gamble. I fear for you."

"This invitation is nothing else but a challenge."

"Or a trap," Mardian said. "Even should you find a way into the city, once you are there, you are virtually his prisoner, to do with what he wills."

"What do I have to lose?"

"Your life, Majesty."

"My life! A renegade living in the wilderness."

Mardian gave a small shrug of his shoulders, mouth twisted downward in a bow.

"You disagree?" she asked him.

"The Romans are all bastards. I would rather place my buttocks in a vat of boiling pitch as trust any of them."

"I do not intend to place my trust in this Julius Caesar. I put my trust in my own ingenuity. And yours." Brave words, she thought, if only I believed them. What has my ingenuity won me so far? I have just one thing that Caesar might want. It was something she could offer that she could truthfully say no man had ever owned before. But whether it might be considered worthwhile to a man of so much experience she could not say.

"To get inside the city," Mardian was saying, "your disguise will have to be absolute. For you were queen and princess there, and everyone in the palace knows you as well as they know their own mothers. You will need a disguise of great cunning."

"Perhaps I can hide inside something. A crate of figs, perhaps."

"That may only get you as far as the kitchen, Majesty." He stood for a long time staring at the carpet.

So how? she wondered. She knew Mardian was right. If she went in alone and in disguise, or perhaps with two or three bodyguards, she might get past the gates and into the city; but how could she get inside the palace, and into Caesar's presence?

Mardian suggested the sewer, and she imagined standing in front of the greatest and most powerful Roman in the world, stinking of Alexandrian turds and asking him to make her Queen of Egypt.

And what if she did get inside? She would be alone and cut off from her own army, at his mercy. What if he wanted her only to force Pothinus to make a deal: You give me nine talents of gold and I will give you Cleopatra.

Once inside the city, what power did she have to save herself?

It was a risk she would have to take. "There must be some way into the palace," she said.

"Every gateway is bristling with soldiers. Pothinus has thrown underwater chains across the harbor. I believe it was done as much to keep Caesar in as to keep you out."

"Yet you have that look in your eye. You say all this but you have thought of something."

Mardian sighed. "You are committed to this course of action, Majesty?"

"Have you ever known me to change my mind?"

"If you must throw your life away in this reckless manner, then as your friend and adviser I suppose it is my duty to help you." The hurt was etched into his jowls and the small black eyes. He was dismayed not that she might die, but that she had chosen to disregard his counsel. "There is someone who can get you into Caesar's palace. A spy who moves freely in and out of the city."

"I wondered how you knew so much of Caesar's affairs."

"He is a Sicilian, a merchant. It was his ship that took us to Thebes the night we fled the palace."

"Is he trustworthy?"

"I would trust him with my life."

"It is not your life that is at risk, it is mine."

"He will not fail you, Majesty. He is my brother-in-law, my sister's husband. His name is Apollodorus."

8

"APOLLODORUS," SHE SAID.

"Majesty."

He bowed but there was something almost insolent in his expression, an arrogance she had noticed before in men without a country. His face had been burned by salt and sun, like rock weathered over time into something formidable rather than pleasing. Dark eyes blazed beneath thick lashes. He had the air of a man more accustomed to giving orders than receiving them. Mardian said he was thirty years old.

Apollodorus was dressed in the Greek style, his chlamys fastened at the shoulder by a large emerald, his sandals of the finest tooled leather. There was a golden ring in his left ear, which gave him a rakish look, but otherwise he wore no jewelry.

"It seems you have been in my service for some time and I did not know it," she said to him.

"Mardian pays me well."

"Not too well, I hope."

"I am worth it."

She resisted a smile. She found his arrogance not unpleasing. For the task she had conceived, she needed a man with more than the usual share of confidence.

"Mardian says you move in and out of Alexandria with ease."

"I own a score of ships, perhaps twice as many barges. They move freely in and out of the harbor and the lake. If I wish to go into the city, I go. If I wish to leave, I leave."

"Your boats are never searched?"

"I have a safe conduct pass," he said, reached into the purse, and took out a gold coin. "It is signed by the God of Greed and is good for all cities everywhere."

"I have many such passes, but they have done me no good at all."

"Boundaries are for princes and soldiers, Majesty. Not for merchants."

"Has Mardian told you what I want you to do?"

The lazy half-lidded eyes stared back at her unblinking. Yes, if anyone could carry it off, it was this man. "He has."

"And you will do it?"

"My part is easy. If I may speak freely, Majesty?" he said, and there was absolutely no humility in his voice as he made the request.

She gave an almost indiscernible nod of her head.

"I shall sail into Alexandria with a hold full of Syrian carpets, as I have done a hundred times before. My role requires no courage. It is you who must be brave."

She admired his boldness in saying so. But after all, it was boldness she was paying for. And he is right. Do I have the courage to do this?

If courage it is, she thought. This last year of exile I have grown bone weary, and even fear loses its hold over the soul when it is a constant companion. I have lain awake every night seeing Pothinus in chains and feeling the cool breeze of the royal harbor on my face, the salt smell of the sea in my nose, and not the bad breath and fetid stink of the camels. I wish for my destiny like a thirsty man dreams of water. I am too tired, too full of anger and hate to recognize my own fear tonight.

"My courage is my own affair. All I need to know is how you intend to fulfill your role."

Apollodorus shrugged his broad shoulders. "Caesar has taken up residence in the palace on the northern tip of the Lochias promontory, near the Temple of Isis." My former apartments, Cleopatra thought bitterly. "To get there we must sail into the royal harbor and make a landing at the palace steps. However, as your brother Ptolemy and his minister Pothinus are also in residence, the situation inside the palace is confused. There are Macedonian guards inside the grounds as well as Roman legionaries, so you will not truly be safe until you are inside Caesar's palace itself."

"*My* palace, Apollodorus, but let us not quibble over terms."

He bowed his head in graceful acknowledgment. "My safe conduct pass will see me to the palace, but should any of Ptolemy's Macedonian Guard see you, I fear that will not be enough."

"So what do you plan to do?"

He smiled. "That, Majesty, is what you pay me for."

♈ ♈

She had her women prepare her as best they could for the interview with Caesar. It would be the most important audience of her life and she wanted to appear at her best.

Iras massaged her with oils of almonds and then rubbed balsam into the skin of her face and neck as protection against the hot desert wind. Charmion worked her hair into thin plaits crowned with a high chignon. She applied antimony to her eyebrows and eyelids, brushed ocher onto her lips, and then dyed the soles of her feet and the palms of her hands with henna. She would not go to Caesar looking as if she had just crawled out of a well.

As they worked, she studied her reflection in the bronze mirror. What she saw was a haughty young girl with olive skin and high, patrician cheekbones. Her great-grandmother was a Syrian princess with Persian blood in her veins, and it was to her that she doubtless owed the darker tone of her skin and her black eyes. She knew there were some who called her beautiful, and others who found her features too strong and commanding for a woman. She did not have the cherubic beauty of her sister. But she had wit and charm to burn, she had the tight little body of an Asian princess, and she had a great sense of theater. It would have to do.

"Charmion, have you ever lain with a man?"

Charmion seemed startled by such a question. She was, after all, just a slave. "No, Majesty."

"The truth? I am not trying to trick you."

"It is not that I have not the desire," Charmion said, but would not catch her eye in the mirror. "But there has seldom been the opportunity and I do not have the courage."

Cleopatra felt a welling of frustration. Surely she would not have to ask Mardian? "I wish to know more about such things. If we were in Alexandria, I might do this myself. I do not want to talk to such camp followers as the Arabs might use. Do you know someone who might help me?"

Charmion glanced up, and their eyes met in the metal mirror. "There is a woman. She lives in Ashkelon, she has retired there. She was well known at the court, among the men. A *hetaira*. In her day she was very expensive."

"Send for her. Pay whatever she asks. I leave here in two days. I must see her before then."

Charmion hurried away. Cleopatra closed her eyes, listening to the wind whip the silk of her tent, the stale breath of the desert camp carrying through the entrance, overcoming the perfumes of the Arabian incense. She was relieved to finally be away from this place, to have her future decided for better or ill. Caesar would decide it, and when she was face-to-face with him, she wished to have at least some knowledge of what he already knew too well.

9

HER NAME WAS Rachel, and she was a Jewess. Unusual for a professional courtesan, a *hetaira*. She looked much younger than the forty years she admitted to, with jet hair and fine bones and pampered dusky skin. She wore a tunic of fine rose silk that seemed to shimmer as she walked, fastened by a brooch of pure gold. There were gold bangles on her bare brown arms and a small gold ring in her hooked nose. Her fingernails had been powdered with mother-of-pearl, and there was a jeweled diadem in her hair. She dressed like a princess. She had done well at her trade.

Her dark eyes glittered with amusement and knowing.

She looked around the royal pavilion, at the diaphanous curtains sewn with gold and silver thread, the thick woolen carpets in gold and peacock blue, the cushions in red hand-tooled leather.

Cleopatra lounged on cushions while a slave—a deaf mute, the only other person present—fanned her with a large ostrich feather to cool her and keep away the desert insects. She tried to appear at her ease, though her emotions were a churning and entangled mess. She was acutely aware of the disparity in her experience and this woman's. *This Jewess has more the bearing of a queen than I do.*

"They say you were a *hetaira* for many years," she said to the woman.

Rachel's deep brown eyes flashed. "The best there is. I am retired now, in Ashkelon."

"In some luxury, they tell me. Did Charmion tell you why I asked you to come here?"

"She only said that my services were required. She was very generous or I would not have come."

The woman watched her, hands cupped in front of her, one knee bent. *A courtesan by nature and not just by birth,* Cleopatra thought. *She seemed hardly as intimidated as Cleopatra would have liked. Why should she be? The court of a bandit queen is not the palace at Lochias.*

"How many men have you lain with?"

"I never counted them. One man is much like another."

"Hundreds?"

"Certainly that many."

"Charmion says that you once commanded a high price in Alexandria. That you have a reputation."

The woman only smiled. Such a small and secret smile that it might even have aroused Mardian.

"For myself, I have never known a man in that way." She waited, but Rachel's expression was unfathomable. "I should like to know your secrets."

"I can tell them to you in an hour, Majesty. But . . ."

"But?"

"Their application requires more than simply learning. If you understand."

"Yes, I do understand. That is why I allowed Charmion to be so generous. And I will be more generous still. I wish you to show me."

Rachel tilted her head to one side. "Show you, Majesty?"

"You have not retired entirely from your activities?"

"Indeed, I have not. I am a married woman now. I just perform my duties much less frequently."

"Could you be persuaded to return to your previous occupation for an hour?"

"Two hours, Majesty," Rachel corrected her gently, "and that would depend on the amount of persuasion I was offered."

Cleopatra held out a set of earrings. Red Sea pearls and fearfully expensive.

"Is this man so displeasing to the eye?" Rachel asked.

"Indeed, he is not. If I was any other woman, I might wish for him to teach me himself. But that is not possible."

Rachel took the earrings and cupped them in her palm. "I will perform for you, Majesty. If that is what you wish."

ψ ψ

The oil lamp flickered, throwing shadows on the silk roof of the tent. A blind slave crouched in the corner of the tent, working a fringed canopy that stirred the air, hot and thick as molasses. It rippled the curtains that divided the room, each of the finest silk, to deter the insects.

Cleopatra sat on a high-backed chair behind one of these diaphanous curtains, her presence concealed by the shadows. The lighting inside had been so arranged that she could see into the tent but remain an anonymous observer. A stylus and wax tablet was poised on her lap. She was determined to learn how to please a man, as surely as she had learned oratory from Mardian and geometry and mathematics from her tutors at the Museion.

She saw the tent flap part. Apollodorus. A bonus for him, he had been told. A gift from the queen.

She felt her stomach muscles tighten, and it was suddenly hard to breathe. She wondered at her own reaction, her own thoughts. I should gain no pleasure from this, she thought, this is purely a matter of instruction. I cannot go to Caesar completely unarmed.

Rachel lay on a simple bed in a corner of the tent. She wore a short, fringed tunic that revealed the long line of her thigh muscles, rippling with sweet-scented oil. She had darkened her lips with a bluish powder to make them appear fuller and heavier, and had accentuated the corners of her eyes with touches of vivid vermilion. Her breasts were bare, covered with a transparent gauze veil. Her nipples had been brushed with carmine, a swollen bloodred.

Apollodorus stepped into the tent, dressed only in a short white tunic. Rachel rose slowly from the bed. There was a short, murmured conversation. Cleopatra smiled, despite herself. She remembered that the Sicilian was a merchant, first and foremost, and he was probably eager to confirm that he was not expected to pay for this.

Satisfied, he reached for her, but she slid away from him. A pitcher of wine and two silver goblets had been laid out on a folding cedarwood table, inlaid with ivory. Beside it was an hourglass, filled with sand. Rachel turned it over to set the sand filtering to the bottom chamber, then poured wine into one of the goblets and brought it over to the big Sicilian. He stood there, eager, but uncertain about his own role.

She took his hand and led him to the bed, sat him down, held the wine to his lips and made him sip it. Then she took his head in her hands and kissed him on the lips. Apollodorus tried to grapple her onto the bed, but she pulled away, whispering to him to be patient. Then she knelt between his legs and told him to take off his clothes.

Cleopatra felt her fingers tighten around the stylus. Her mouth was suddenly dry and she felt a bead of sweat make its way down her spine between her shoulder blades.

Apollodorus removed his tunic. He was built like a gladiator, his muscles hard and pronounced, and his chest and belly covered in a pelt of dark hair. His face was flushed, and he looked as if he was in pain. Cleopatra leaned forward, her face touching the silk of the curtain, straining for a better view in the smoky, lamplit gloom.

As if she knew what her pupil was thinking, Rachel moved to the side, the perfect tutoress, and Cleopatra could now see the reason for her Sicilian's agitation. The Jewess was holding the length of him in scarlet-painted nails, and Cleopatra puffed out her cheeks, repelled and fascinated. Impossible that such a small thing could grow so large. Could it ever fit inside such a small woman without tearing her?

And now what was she doing?

When she saw, the queen, the virgin, dropped the wax tablet on the floor, where it fell soundlessly on the thick carpet. That a woman could do that with her tongue and her mouth! She was not sure if she could ever do it herself. Apollodorus was thrashing wildly about, as if he were being whipped. His expression was that of a man under extreme torture. Yet he had Rachel by her hair now and he held her there.

I can see why she could not make me understand such a thing by telling it. The woman's hands and her tongue seem to be everywhere at once. Apollodorus was groaning aloud, his voice eerily like the chanting the priests made inside the temples.

Rachel suddenly stood up, turned toward the curtain, and walked slowly to the table. She took another draught of wine, looked directly into the shadows, where Cleopatra was watching, almost as if she could see her there. She smiled. The little witch is enjoying this, Cleopatra thought. Like every great performer, she craves an audience.

She walked slowly back to the bed, where Apollodorus lay sprawled like a sacrifice. She leaned over him and kissed him again, dribbling the ruby red wine into his mouth. Then she stood up and removed her tunic. She was naked beneath it.

Her body had been carefully oiled and it glinted in the candle-light, accentuating the sinuous curve of her spine, the rounded swell of her hips. She let her Sicilian kiss her belly and small breasts. He took a hard brown nipple between his lips, and she uttered a little cry like a wounded bird.

Cleopatra swallowed hard. Her hands were shaking. She felt as if she had despoiled a temple, was watching something both sacred and profane. It was not as she had imagined at all, something that could be learned by instruction, as men went to the Gymnasium to learn to wrestle or throw javelins. She had seen the mating of horses and cattle and had imagined it was simply a matter of technique. Yet here she realized there was something more; a theater of submission and passion.

There was an urgent warmth in her belly, wetness between her legs. She put a hand to her mouth, her teeth sunk into the flesh of her palm.

The Sicilian had the *hetaira* pinned beneath him on the bed, and Rachel writhed her hips in rhythm with him, her hoarse whispers and sharp cries punctuating each thrust. The strings on the narrow cot creaked in cadence; scarlet fingernails raked the skin of his broad back and the clenched muscles of his buttocks. The Jewess threw her head back, her mouth open. But then she turned her head to the side and smiled into the shadows. Rachel, for all her feigned submission, was still in control.

Perfect love, perfect theater.

Cleopatra felt a burning heat in her own loins, a deep ache in her belly. She felt physically sick with her own desire. She did not think she could watch anymore.

Rachel now sat astride her lover, riding him, letting his hands roam across her oiled body. But she seemed to know the time, for suddenly and without warning she lifted herself away and held him in her hands as the seed spilled out of him, onto his belly. He lay gasping, his mouth open, his fists clenched.

She rose from the bed and went to the table to fetch more wine. She tapped the great hourglass beside the wine flask. The sand had run only half through. It seemed there was yet more of the performance to come.

But Cleopatra knew she could watch no more. She stood up and rushed from the pavilion.

10

A FINE-GRAINED AND violet dusk had fallen over the coast as they rowed out to the galley. It was one of the Sicilian's merchantmen, on the way down from Syria. Farther to the west, in the quickening haze she could see the great fort of Pelusium and the campfires of Achillas's soldiers.

They reached the galley, the tiny craft wallowing in the gray chop until rough hands hauled her up as if she were some castaway found at sea rather than Queen of Egypt.

❦   ❦

They weighed anchor and made their way out to sea for the final leg of the journey down to the Delta and Alexandria. She was terrified. Though she had convinced herself there was no other way, now that the danger was real and imminent, she felt betrayed by a small but strident voice that told her life, any kind of life, was more precious than duty and pride.

But she would not let her weakness show. Instead she hid her terror behind the haughty mask that had served her so well until now.

Apollodorus stood with her at the prow. She could not look at him. Remembering what she had seen that previous night, she was overwhelmed with shame. She could have chosen any other man for her lesson with the Jewish *hetaira*. Choosing the Sicilian had been an unpardonable indulgence, an attempt to answer a longing in herself that she could never express in any other way. The truth of the matter was that she would never be free to choose the path of her own desire.

But the irony. Her master spy, himself revealed to his depths. And yet there was still so much she did not know about him, and it was to this man she had entrusted her life.

"You are married to my tutor's sister," she said, keeping her eyes on the coastline, quickly fading to black.

"These ten years, Majesty," he grunted.

"Where is your wife?"

"I do not see her very often," he said indirectly. "The demands of my business take me away much of the time."

"She is not in Alexandria, then?"

"No, Majesty."

His sullen demeanor angered her. Did he think because she no longer occupied the Lochias palace that he was free to be so insolent? She wanted to shake him from his arrogance. "How did you enjoy your whore?"

He was silent a long time, and she thought he had not heard her. Finally, he said: "You are very generous. I thought I had already been paid."

"A little bonus. You are away from home so much of the time," she added, mocking him.

"I would rather it had been my wife."

"Of course. But if there is a bargain to be had . . ."

"I love my wife. With my life."

She could not see his face in the gathering darkness, but his answer did not surprise her; all men were liars, her father had told her in one of his more lucid moments. They even lie to themselves. That men took other women did not shock her, it was the way of men. Even for those without noble blood, marriage was often no more than convenience, an alliance between families. But it galled her that this Sicilian should say he loved his wife when he still had the scent of another woman on him.

"Of course you love her. When you are with her, anyway."

"Do not dare to judge me!" he hissed under his breath. "You may be a queen, but you are just a girl and you do not know everything there is to know about life!" He turned away from her and went to stand alone at the stern. Cleopatra huddled inside her cloak against the bitter night wind. If I win Caesar, I shall have you whipped, Mardian or no, she thought, her heart hammering with the force of her anger. I will not be spoken to like a servant! Abandoned, betrayed, and forced to sneak into my own palace like a thief, I am yet Queen of Egypt, the reincarnated Mother, and I shall be till the day I die!

⚬ ⚬

She discovered, not for the first time, that she was prone to seasickness. She spent the entire day hunched over the stern, paying her respects to Neptune, as Apollodorus said. She learned that the proudest will is prey to the motion of a small boat. When there was finally not even bile enough left to vomit over the stern, the Queen of Egypt lay huddled in the scuppers like the poorest beggar in Rhakotis.

❦ ❦

She had never seen her city as most Alexandrians had seen it, from the horizon, from the sea. The impossible Pharos rose from the black sea, immense, Zeus standing astride the great tower, above the vast beacon of flame, waves breaking like phosphorus below the colonnades of the court below.

Apollodorus roused her from where she squatted miserably at the stern, to see this spectacle. She held weakly to the rail, her knuckles white, to watch the blessed landfall. Alexandria, her city, the white palaces and temples ghostly against the star-chipped night sky. It was breathtakingly beautiful, but she felt so wretched she would have been as pleased to see the Land of the Dead.

❦ ❦

From the shore came the stench of the dock front, the spices in the warehouses, the sour sea-smell of the fishing boats, the piquant aromas of the food stalls. Her stomach rebelled at the heady cocktail. She kept her gaze fixed on the dark shoreline, too ashamed to look at the sailors and at Apollodorus, knowing they had seen her at her worst. Her limbs were shaking uncontrollably from the violence of the nausea. This lack of physical control horrified her. They will think I am afraid, she thought.

Lamps were twinkling in the Brucheion palace, the place she had been born and had spent her whole life until this last year. But now it seemed as cold and dread to her as any enemy fortress.

❦ ❦

The carpet was brought out and laid on the deck. It was one of the finest she had ever seen, a gift fit for an emperor, not just a Roman magistrate. It had been woven in Cappadocia of the finest wool, the pattern a rich scarlet and blue of Tyrian dye.

"You must get into the rug," Apollodorus said.

Cleopatra took a breath. Few of us have the privilege of being mummified while we are yet alive, she thought. She felt the eyes of the sailors watching her. She wondered if she could go through with this.

"Hurry," Apollodorus urged her.

Steeling herself, she lay down on the carpet, folding her arms over her chest. Even before she gave the signal that she was ready, three men had darted forward and begun to roll her inside the carpet. Already weak and nauseous from the seasickness, the sensation of spinning over and over was unbearable and she cried out, but her moans were muffled by the rug.

When it was done, she lay there, unable to move, fighting down a wave of panic. Like being buried alive. The smell of wool and dust was suffocating. She was helpless, unable even to move her arms or legs. I am going to choke in here! She felt herself being lifted and lowered into the small rowing boat alongside the galley. She could feel the pitch and roll of the boat, and swallowed down another wave of nausea. Vomit in here, and you might truly die. Was this the glorious death the gods planned for you?

"Courage, Majesty," she heard the Sicilian whisper, his voice muffled. "I will see you safely into the great Roman's presence."

She could hear her own heartbeat. *I can't breathe!* She forced herself to be calm. Breathe slowly, gently, or you will faint. Have courage, Cleopatra. You will not have to endure this for long. Before the sun rises again you will be dead or you will be before Caesar.

❧ ❧

She heard the muffled shouts of fishermen in the harbor. Then other voices, gruff, their heavily accented Greek unmistakable. Her own Macedonian Guard. The boat nudged a pylon, scraped against the wharf. Apollodorus shouted a greeting. They knew him here.

"What have you got there, Sicilian?" she heard one of the guards say.

"A carpet. It is for the young prince. It cost more money than you'll ever see in your whole life, you fat donkey's ass. Want to see it?"

There was some more ribaldry and she felt herself being lifted out of the boat. Her spine was twisted by the sudden movement and her body was almost bent double. It was impossible to breathe. She thought she would faint.

Then she was lifted onto the shoulders of the two slaves Apollodorus had brought with him in the boat. Moments later she heard the heavy clanking of an iron gate. They were inside the palace.

Thoughts she had previously discounted now clamored again for her attention. What if this Apollodorus betrays you? How much would your head be worth to a humble merchant? Mardian says he is loyal, but every man has his price.

Can you even trust Mardian?

Another exchange; they had reached another checkpoint. These guards were Roman, judging by their accents, but with the words muffled, she could not hear what was said. The carpet was slung between the shoulders of the two slaves, bowed under her weight, pressing her face against the fibers. She tried to twist her head around to get more air, heard the two slaves grunt in protest at the shift in her weight.

From what seemed far away, she heard the creaking of a heavy door as it swung open, then the sound of music and voices. She felt herself dropping heavily to the floor, and her head took a solid bump. The world turned black and there was no air.

✾ ✾

"What is this?" Caesar asked.

"It is a gift to my lord Caesar," Apollodorus said. "From the Queen of Egypt."

Caesar turned to one of his officers, Decimus Brutus. "Too large for a head. Perhaps this time they have sent us the whole body. Who could it be? Cicero, perhaps?"

Decimus touched Caesar's arm. "Be careful, Imperator. It could be an assassin."

"You unroll it, then."

Decimus drew his sword and made Apollodorus and his two slaves stand back. He kicked the carpet with his foot several times, rolling it out across the marble floor.

"Caesar," he said. "There is indeed a body in here."

Caesar's sardonic mood sloughed away and with a glance he signaled his bodyguard to draw their swords. Three of them formed a tight circle around Apollodorus and his slaves.

There was a heavy silence. Decimus Brutus gave the carpet a final kick.

"By Jupiter's hairy balls!" Caesar muttered.

Cleopatra lay prone, her hands at her sides, not moving. Apollodorus made a move toward her, but Decimus pushed him back. "It may be a trick."

Apollodorus looked up at Caesar in genuine alarm. "I fear she may have suffocated!"

"Who is this?" Decimus shouted.

"It's her, you fool," Caesar muttered. He strode forward and bent down beside her. She looked so small, like a broken bird. He scooped her up easily in his arms and carried her to the couch.

❦   ❦

It took some moments to remember where she was. She opened her eyes and found herself staring at a pair of heavily muscled legs, encased in thick leather shin protectors. She heard a man's voice say, in Latin, "She's a pretty piece."

"Do you think she meant to come here, Decimus, or did someone send her over as a sweetener for a deal? You know these gypos, they'd sell their own grandmothers."

"They'd sodomize her first," the other one said, and they both laughed.

"Gentlemen," she murmured, in Latin, "that is no way to talk about my family."

She had not meant to declare herself so soon. But the one called Decimus heard what she said and stopped laughing. Then the other one—she assumed it must be Caesar—stopped laughing too. But his expression was still one of amusement. Not a trace of guilt or shame there. "You understood what was said?"

"My grammar is rusty . . . but I know that in one sentence you have insulted not only my entire nation, but also my grandmother, who was a Syrian princess related to the King of Parthia."

"We have got off to a bad start," he said. "Can we start again?"

"Then let us start in Greek," she replied, reverting to the more familiar language, "it is easier for me to follow." She tried to move, but her head was spinning. Strange, for her mind was as clear as a crystal pool.

"Of course." He clapped his hands for the servants. "Fetch me some wine to revive her."

From where she lay he looked like a giant. She tried again to sit up, found her muscles would not respond, and the sudden movement made her head spin. She thought she was going to pass out again. But the wine revived her; he held the cup to her lips as if she were a child and then held out his hand. She took it, a grip like iron, and he helped her to sit. His hands held hers a moment longer than was necessary; they were huge hands, a heavy gold signet ring on the third finger of his right, thick veins like rope beneath the surface of the skin, fine golden hairs. His palms were callused and hard from holding a sword and the reins of a horse.

Everyone was staring at her: Apollodorus, Decimus, the slaves and servants, even Caesar's bodyguard standing there openmouthed, like provincials at a theater. Caesar was suddenly aware of them also.

"Out," he said, shooing them toward the door. "All of you. Out!"

꙼ ꙼

So this was the Julius Caesar she had heard so much about, the great general, the man who defeated Pompey. She had imagined a giant, an Alexander, but his physical features were disappointing. He was tall for a Roman, and perhaps he may have been good-looking once. But he was past fifty, and bald, with a fringe of short-cropped golden hair going to gray. As Mardian had told her, he must have been uncomfortable about his receding hair, for he wore a laurel crown to conceal it. His features were brown and deeply lined, as hard and leathery as a well-worn saddlebag. But as Mardian always said, it was power that afforded attraction to a man and not beauty. His face had been carefully shaved, betraying a fondness for the barber she would not have expected to find in a warrior.

What Caesar did possess was an authority that she found unnerving. He had the most penetrating black eyes she had ever seen, and now they studied her in a detached, objective way, as if he might haggle for her at the bazaar.

She was suddenly aware of how she must look; she wondered what use her kohl and face powders were now, after hours rolling around in the rug. She smoothed down her hair, straightened her clothes. What a mess. But Caesar did not seem displeased.

"So. You have accepted my offer to visit me," he said, apparently recovered from his surprise.

"I am not a visitor. This is my palace."

"That has yet to be established." He turned away and slumped into a heavy, hard-backed wooden chair. Abruptly, he grinned. "You are resourceful. Pothinus will shit himself when he finds out what you have done."

She looked around the room. She recognized it with a pang. They were in her father's former apartments. She saw the table of carved ivory where he had worked at his papers, the vase of lapis lazuli that had been a personal gift to her from the King of Punt. Now these strangers were sprawled across the rich couches as if they were their possessions. This was the room where she had sometimes taken her own meals before Pothinus and his gang had expelled her. Less than a year, but it seemed she had been away a lifetime.

"So. You are Cleopatra."

"And you are Caesar. I have heard much of your deeds."

He smiled at that, but not in a way of modesty. It was the smile of a man immoderately well-pleased with his own accomplishments. It should have irritated her, but instead she felt curiously attracted to him.

"You are very beautiful," he said.

Cleopatra felt herself flush. It was true what they said about him, his lust for women. She could see it in his eyes.

This was the man she'd had in her mind to persuade, to influence, perhaps to seduce. What had seemed so logical in the bleached desperation of Mount Kasios now seemed absurd. Like a piece of driftwood thinking it might influence the waves around it. In the end the sea would toss it where it would.

Mardian was right. She was naked, utterly defenseless.

His smile faded and the look in his eyes turned suddenly hard. "Nineteen years old, a queen, and beautiful. So why did you send soldiers and supplies to my enemy, Pompey?" This delivered in the tones of an interrogator.

"My father was in his debt. It was a matter of loyalty."

"And yet now you wish me to arbitrate in this matter between you and your brother?"

"It was at your suggestion, not mine."

"You set your sails according to the wind, I see."

"It is called seamanship."

He laughed at that.

"I was unlawfully deposed by Pothinus and the Regency Council. I look to you for justice." It was her case, as she saw it. But even before she had finished, she realized how hollow it sounded.

He grimaced as if he had a bad taste in his mouth. "There is no such thing as justice. There is only power and how you use it."

I am nothing more than a young girl to him, she thought. Another ruler to toy with. I would be foolish to bluster and bluff with this man, for I have no sway over him. "And how do you intend you use your power?"

"I have four thousand legionaries and thirty-five ships. Achillas has twenty thousand men camped outside the city, and the Egyptian fleet is on the other side of the Heptastadion. What power do you *think* I have?"

"*You* offered to mediate."

"Because that is much easier than vanquishing Achillas's army. You do take my point?" He got up suddenly and came to sit beside her on the couch. Without preamble, he picked up her hand, turned it palm upward, and kissed it gently.

"You did not marry your brother, then, after the custom?" he murmured.

"Not my type," she managed.

"And no other prince was proposed for you?"

"Who would have me?"

"Only a blind man would not feast his eyes on you."

"I doubt that."

"Do not doubt my word. I am something of an expert in these matters."

Suddenly it was difficult to breathe. "So I have been told."

She thought of Rachel and the *hetaira*'s instruction in these matters. Did she really think to mesmerize this man? What arrogance. She felt absolutely frozen with fear. You really will have to do better than this, my girl, she told herself. It is obvious what Caesar wants, and that he is intent on taking it, whether it is freely offered or not. Like Gaul.

"Will you help me, then?" she whispered.

He answered her with a smile. "That, my kitten," he murmured, "entirely depends on you."

11

This was not as she had imagined it at all. She had planned to be in control, like the Jewess with Apollodorus, but her nerve had failed her. How could she impress someone like this Roman, who had lain with so many women? It was one thing to watch a performance, another entirely to emulate it. She had always considered herself precocious; now she felt as hopeless as a child. Caesar was not about to make it easier for her; he stood there, by the candle, holding a goblet of wine, watching her.

He had, of course, appropriated her own bedroom. The soft glow of candles in their lanterns of colored glass reflected like dull gold on the onyx floors and ivory-paneled walls. The curtains, finest Arabian silk, billowed and fluttered in the night breeze off the harbor. From below the windows, the rhythmic beat of the sea.

The bed had been carved from ebony wood, brought up the Nile from lands beyond the cataracts, and inlaid with ivory. The coverlet was dyed with Tyrian purple. She slipped out of her clothes as quickly as she could and climbed into the bed, pulling the coverlet to her shoulders. She felt his eyes on her.

Caesar finished his wine, then undressed, with a casual assurance. He unhooked the clasps on his general's purple cloak, unbuckled the finely worked enameled breastplate, the leather shin protectors and heavy leather sandals. Still wearing his tunic and underclothes, he slipped into the bed beside her.

This was not how she had ever imagined her first introduction to love. A Roman had never figured in her young girl's dreams. Even trembling in the carpet she had thought to retain some power over her position here, to make Caesar wait. But it seemed Caesar was not accustomed to waiting for anything.

He pulled her toward him. His hands were rough and callused. The things she had learned from watching the Jewess were no use to her now, for Caesar was not to be gentled or commanded. She could only lie there and let it happen. As he kissed her for the first time, she was aware of the warm, slightly spicy smell of his breath, and his hands squeezing her breasts, hard, almost as if he wanted to hurt her.

She was too fearful, too aware of the importance of this moment to her very survival to feel anything pleasurable. He buried his head between her breasts, licking and biting. He perhaps misinterpreted her groans of discomfort for pleasure, for he only did it the harder.

She stared into the darkness, her body tense, rigid with apprehension. She wondered what he was thinking. *Caesar conquers Egypt.*

He eased himself between her legs and she held her breath. Then he thrust inside her, quickly and very hard. She bit her lip, stifled a gasp of pain, felt hot tears in her eyes. She had not imagined it would hurt so much the first time.

It was over very quickly. After what seemed like just a few moments, he went suddenly rigid and she felt the weight of him slump on top of her. She lay there for a long time, his body crushing her, feeling the wetness on her face from her own tears. There was wetness between her legs also, blood and seed.

And this was all. He kissed her gently on the cheek and murmured some endearment. But she did not hear it. She felt suddenly sad and defeated and achingly lonely. She turned her face to the window. A crescent moon hung over the lighthouse, a sliver of inverted silver in the shape of the horns of Horus, the symbol of fertility.

All she could think was: *Another conquest for Caesar.* He had invaded and he had possessed. Perhaps that was sufficient for him. If she was to hold him to her, it was not with that organ that all women owned. She would have to use that which no other woman possessed—Egypt.

❧ ❧

"You must be hungry," he said. He threw open the door and roared for his slaves. When he came back into the room, he was smiling. "I was told you were resourceful. Was it your idea? The carpet?"

No, but you don't want to hear that. "If I had known how disagreeable it would be, I would have thought of some other way."

"Yes. I imagine you would." He sat down, and she felt his eyes inspecting her carefully, as unabashed as if he were at a slave market. "You are very young to be a queen."

"That depends on the situation in which the queen finds herself. For instance, the inside of a carpet is no place for an old woman."

"Nor would Caesar be as delighted to find an old woman brought to his apartments at this time of night."

"Precisely."

This, she thought, was like being swept along in a raging flood. She had imagined that losing her virginity to this man would have been the climax of the evening, but instead it seemed to have sapped his energy not at all. He had enjoyed her favors, and still she commanded his rapt attention. She wondered if she really understood exactly what he wanted from her.

She also wondered if she knew what she wanted from him. She had been prepared to be repulsed by this Roman, this barbarian general, but she found him like no other man she had ever met. But then she supposed no other man of her acquaintance had ever truly felt himself qualified, physically or otherwise, to be the lover of a Ptolemy princess.

Her body felt bruised from the battering it had taken inside the carpet, and from Caesar's robust affections. Her mind and heart were in turmoil: How to reconcile this intimidating man with her first experience of loving? His presence thrilled her, yet the physical act of love had been nothing as she had imagined. She thought there would be tenderness, and there was none. The crushing sadness she felt at so foolishly wasting her currency with this overbearing Roman had been replaced by bewilderment at discovering that she evidently possessed other riches that Caesar seemed eager to explore.

It was as if she had been initiated into a conspiracy rather than inducted into the secrets of love.

The food arrived on a silver platter: ewe's milk cheese, Rhodian raisins, some fat dessert grapes. It was set out on the table in front of her. Caesar poured more wine into a jasper goblet and went to stand by the window.

"You will not eat?"

"Food does not interest me overmuch."

She found, to her surprise, that she was hungry. Her misadventures on the Sicilian's galley had left her stomach empty, and her rigorous introduction to the interests of a Roman magistrate had left her feeling weak. She attacked the food with abandon.

Caesar watched her, apparently delighted with this diversion. "So, this is the exiled Queen of Egypt."

"I hope you are not disappointed."

"I am not disappointed at all. Neither in your company, or the manner of your arrival."

"I come like a supplicant, seeking your help."

"You might find that help is freely and happily given."

"I have to first understand why you would wish to help me."

"Even Caesar does not always understand himself."

He had the habit, she noticed, of referring to himself as some other person, in the manner of a king. Or as if he were a detached observer, watching his own life, curious to see what he might do next.

"You know what they did to Pompey?" he asked.

"Pompey had been a friend to my father," she said. "He had the right to expect better treatment." Well, perhaps. Pompey was also just another pompous, greedy Roman. But murdering him was a gross tactical mistake. I wouldn't have been that stupid, she thought. No doubt Pothinus and the rest thought they were being clever. With that misguided piece of pork as his tutor, no wonder Ptolemy turned out as he did.

"Can any man trust such people?"

"You would have a far stauncher ally in me, General," she said.

He looked thoughtful. "That is yet to be seen," he said. "For instance, you were once ally to Pompey."

"As I have said, he was a friend of my father's. You do not betray your friends."

"Besides, he must have seemed a better gamble at the time."

Oh, what was the point? She smiled, and he smiled back.

"I would have done the same, in your position," he said, more gently. "But we will talk more about this later. First you must tell me how you came to be living in the desert."

"There was a plot against me. My Captain of the Guard betrayed me. When he saw I did not intend to marry my brother, in the traditional way, he allowed the Regency Council to buy his loyalty. I had to flee the palace in the dead of night."

He frowned. "You would really marry your own brother?"

"As we are gods on earth, we can only mate with each other. It has always been the way in Egypt, since the pharaohs. We Ptolemies adopted the custom in order to assuage the priests. In usual times it is not consummated."

She knew what he was thinking: *barbaric*. Perhaps he was right. Arsinoë and Antiochus were the product of her father's dalliance with one of his sisters.

"I would not assume the ancient tradition," she told him, "that was the difficulty."

He winced. "Through delicacy?"

"Because my brother is an idiot. I am the only one who has the wit and the determination to save Egypt. My father knew it. I know it."

He grinned. "You are a tigress."

"I know what I am."

He sipped from the goblet, his eyes watching her intently, his gaze unsettling. "I am listening."

"The morning after I left Alexandria, the Regency Council assumed power in the name of my brother."

"By the Regency Council you mean this fat pansy boy called Pothinus with a voice like a badly fitted cartwheel?"

"Yes, *that* Pothinus."

"And so you fled to Mount Kasios?"

"Not at first. I have much support in the *chora,* the lands of the Middle and Upper Nile beyond the Delta. The priests of the old religion are still very powerful there, and they promised to help me. I have always shown respect for their religion, and they repaid me with their loyalty."

"I believe it is a little more than just respect," he said. "I am told you are a follower of this god of theirs, Isis."

"Isis, Aphrodite, she speaks for everyone."

He raised an eyebrow at that. "Please. Go on with your story."

"I stayed in Thebes for many months, raising an army, but then Pothinus issued a *prostagma*—a royal decree—in my brother's name. It forbade the transportation of grain to anywhere except Alexandria, threatening death to anyone who disobeyed. They meant to starve me out. I could not let the *chora* suffer anymore for my sake, so I decided to leave Egypt altogether."

Caesar smiled. "Besides, they might have handed you over themselves when their bellies started to growl."

"I didn't want to find out."

"Very wise."

"By now I had a small army raised in the *chora,* I had guides and porters, and the treasure that I had moved to Thebes months before the rebellion as insurance against Pothinus."

"I am impressed."

"We sailed north again, aided by the downstream current, took the easternmost branch of the Nile. Finally we left the barges and followed the Necho canal on camels to the Red Sea. We crossed the border at a place called the Sea of Reeds. It is a flat, depressing piece of marshland, subject to the tides. It is the place where the Jews escaped from Memphis many years ago with the renegade Egyptian, Moses. When the pharaoh's soldiers tried to follow them, the tide rose again and they were trapped in the marsh and many of them drowned."

"I have heard Herod tell me this story."

"Is he a friend of yours?"

"A client," Caesar corrected her gently.

"Well, the story is true. The waters there are treacherous, and foul. You can smell them from miles away. Some of the Egyptian porters would not go with us. They believe the stench is the breath of Seth, their god of evil."

"But you got across?"

"In boats made of reed. The guides led the camels across on foot, through the shallows. I still remember the heat and the stench of that crossing, all the time wondering if I would ever see this palace again." She smiled. "They put poor Mardian in one of the boats and it almost capsized with the weight of him."

"Who is Mardian?"

"My adviser. He has been my *tropheus*—my tutor—since I was a child."

Caesar was smiling. "And so there you are in the middle of a swamp, without a country and with just your teacher for guidance."

"We found sanctuary at Ashkelon. My father is well-remembered there."

"So how did you gather this army?"

"As my father did. I recruited a number of Nabataean Arabs as mercenaries, offering them money I did not have if they would help me recover a throne. Of course, the promise of money costs twice that of real money."

"Indeed. Money is the greatest expense a man may have in his lifetime."

"Still. Gold alone is worthless unless it can be parlayed for power."

He raised an eyebrow at that. Doubtless his own thoughts on the subject. "And you really intended to fight?"

"I had no choice. We marched on Pelusium, but Achillas would not come out to face us and we did not have the equipment to lay siege. And so this is how I have lived these last months."

"What if Achillas had come out to fight? What if you had lost?"

"If I lose, I die. I cannot change sides like a common soldier."

"Indeed. A remarkable story."

For herself, she did not remember that period of her life with anything approaching the same degree of amusement. The months of exile were an unremitting horror. But the experience had hardened her, and she learned she had the ability to endure hardship and reverses, and that in turn had given her confidence. She was not the pampered girl who had been driven in terror from the palace, and she had learned she could not be easily defeated. But she also felt scarred, and feared that she had lost the patina of royalty. She was the rebel now, without a true power base of her own, just her name and birthright to live by.

"Is there anything else I should know about you?" he asked her.

"I speak eight languages, including Hebrew and Aramaic. I can read the price list in a Syrian *taberna,* or ask a Phoenician sailor what cargo he has in the hold of his ship, and insult a Jew in his own language. I have read Homer's epics, as well as the histories of Herodotus and the tragedies of Euripides. I can play the seven-string lyre, I studied rhetoric, astronomy, and medicine at the Museion, and my tutor says that I have a great natural talent for mathematics and geometry. And I can also ride a horse passingly well."

Caesar's smile slipped away. "Is there anything you cannot do?"

She decided to be honest. "I cannot rule Egypt without you."

He nodded thoughtfully. "I already knew that. But thank you for being honest with me."

Those black eyes bored into hers. She felt as if her heart was in her mouth. Somehow she felt compelled to trust this man, and that was dangerous ground indeed.

12

SHE FELL INTO the blackest of sleeps, to be woken the next morning by the sound of screams. She sat up abruptly in bed and saw Ptolemy standing in the doorway gaping at her, Pothinus beside him. It was her little squirt of a brother making all the noise. Caesar was standing by the window, dressed, dipping a crust of bread into a glass of wine for his breakfast.

She realized immediately what Caesar had done. Bedding a queen, after all, was a political act first and foremost, and therefore a pointless exercise without witnesses. It occurred to her that he might perhaps have even summoned Pothinus and Ptolemy to his bedchamber as soon as he rose. If she was to play the harlot queen, she would not shrink from it. She allowed the sheet to slip from her shoulders to her lap, baring her breasts. Then, on an impulse, she stuck out her tongue at her little brother and made a face. She immediately regretted her impetuosity. It was childish and petulant, unbefitting a queen. But it served its purpose. Ptolemy started to cry.

Stupid boy.

"What is *she* doing here?" he howled.

Caesar raised an eyebrow at him. "What does it look like she is doing?"

Ptolemy's face was screwed up, like a raisin in the sun. He stamped his foot. Ah, little brother, if you want Caesar to take you seriously, you should never stamp your foot. He will swat you around the head and send you off with his Roman boot up the skinny crack of your behind.

"This is your fault!" he screamed at Pothinus, and ran from the room.

Pothinus looked at Caesar in anger and bewilderment. But he saved his special venom for her. Thankfully, she thought, men cannot transmit poison through their eyes. He then departed after his protégé. Caesar nodded to the lictors who stood waiting by the door. "Get after them. Bring the boy back here."

Then he turned and smiled at her. "It is going to be a wonderful day," he said, and returned his gaze to the blue harbor and the gentle whitecaps on the ocean beyond the Pharos lighthouse.

13

CAESAR ORCHESTRATED IT perfectly. He received them in the House of Adoration, the throne room, the great pillars of purple-veined porphyry reflected in the shimmering marble floor, a vast chamber that rendered those standing at the foot of the dais almost insignificant. Caesar wore a fringed *toga virilis* with the purple stripe of a Roman senator, and sat on a throne resplendent with yellow jasper and carnelian stones the size of pigeon eggs. Cleopatra, in a robe of shimmering gold, was seated on a similar throne beside him.

Pothinus and Ptolemy stood before them like supplicants, rather than the regent and prime minister of the wealthiest country on the earth. Caesar was letting them know precisely what he thought of them.

Ptolemy's eyes were swollen from crying and his hands were shaking. His father's son, only more so, she thought sadly. If he had anything like his father's temperament, he would shield himself from life's later disappointments by cloaking himself in wine. Poor father.

Poor little Ptolemy.

Pothinus, greasy foot-kisser that he was, his curls stiffened with some expensive pomade, was trying to conceal his loathing of the Roman general behind an unctuous grin.

"Is the Crown Regent feeling better?" Caesar asked, his voice acid.

Pothinus's head bobbed and nodded like a parakeet's. "He is much recovered from the shock he received, thank you, Imperator."

"He behaved as if he had lost an entire legion and had a strapping Gaul standing on his foot. He should learn self-control if he is to be a king."

"His youth betrays him. When he is a little older, he will prove himself as fine as Alexander."

"Alexander," Caesar murmured, as if a blasphemy had been spoken. It was no secret that Caesar aspired to one day be as great as the legendary Macedonian general. His lips curled into a sneer and he repeated the name, wonderingly, under his breath. "Alexander!"

She wondered what was about to happen. Although Caesar had made it appear that she was now his cohort, she had been summoned as peremptorily as her brother, and Pothinus and Caesar had so far said nothing to her of his plans for her future. She was utterly in his power. Whom would he favor? Her—or that stupid boy? She did not delude herself that she had tamed him with one night of love; love was easy currency for such a man, he took it as he liked and valued it not at all. She hoped only that her arguments of the previous night had stirred his stern Roman soul.

"As you know," Caesar was saying to Pothinus, "it was the former king's will that Egypt be ruled jointly by Ptolemy and his sister, Cleopatra. It grieves Rome greatly that there has been discord between them. As you know, their father was a friend and ally of the Roman people."

Indeed he was, she thought bitterly. And he had squandered most of the country's treasury for the privilege of such a title.

"Caesar's only desire is that Egypt be at peace once again. Therefore it is Caesar's wish that the prince be married to his sister immediately, in the Egyptian way, so that they can fulfill the last desires of their beloved father."

So that was it. Caesar was going to make her marry her brother.

Well, of course. He did not want justice, he wanted peace. She stared fixedly ahead, not wishing to betray her disappointment at this news. She waited for Caesar to announce his price for setting them all back at each other's throats again.

"You will take advantage of the peace that Caesar has created to repay your father's debts to the Roman republic, a debt which I have assumed." So that was how he planned to turn a profit out of this. She saw him watching her for signs of her disgust and anger; he seemed disappointed when she did not afford him any.

And besides, do I have any cause for anger? she thought. Has he not done everything he promised? I am back on the throne. Caesar gets what he wants, I get what I asked for. At least I do not have to share the desert with the flies and the lizards.

Ptolemy looked as if he was once again about to burst into tears.

Stupid, stupid boy.

"Is there something wrong?" Caesar said.

Ptolemy was about to answer, but Pothinus silenced him with a look.

"I have made arrangements for the marriage to take place immediately. I am sure all of Alexandria will share with you your joy in this arrangement."

"Thank you, my lord," Pothinus said, but he sounded as if he was choking. He all but pushed Ptolemy out of the room.

14

CLEOPATRA STUDIED HER reflection in the bronze mirror. Strangely, this was exactly how she had imagined her wedding day; the sky a gray overcast, a dull feeling of dread in the pit of her stomach, the dismal prospect of preparing herself for a bridegroom unsuited to her in every way except for the demands of the state. She had always thought it would be some foreigner too old or too young or too boorish to ever make a suitable companion.

She had always feared it might be Ptolemy.

She wondered what her father would say if he were alive to see this moment. Probably too drunk to make any sense. Would he have been disappointed in her? He had always told her she could outwit them all, but it seemed he was wrong.

To her astonishment she found herself wondering what it would be like to marry Caesar. Until now her fantasies had been of politics, not her personal pleasure. She had nurtured dreams of restoring Alexander's empire, making his city the foremost in the world, perhaps—impertinent thought!—of making her own name as famous as his. But imagine if this day were to make me Caesar's queen. We would have the greatest empire in the world, perhaps the greatest in history. And, she thought, staring hard at the mirror, I might even learn to be happy with it.

Charmion had softened her skin with an ointment of oil and cyprus grass, and removed the paste with cucumber juice. Now it glowed like marble. She began to prepare her hair, carefully plaiting it on top of her head into a "melon" chignon.

"There is a rumor," Charmion said.

The palace was full of rumors. They said it was why they made the corridors so long and straight, so people could rush along them faster to find an ear to whisper into.

"Where did you hear it?"

"Caesar's barber, Majesty."

Cleopatra replaced the mirror on the table in front of her and raised an eyebrow to establish her interest. The Imperator's *tonsore* was regarded as Caesar's unofficial legislator, disseminating all the information he could not make known officially.

"What is this rumor?"

"That Pothinus has told your brother to bed you, as in the old days."

"What?" The idea was so absurd she was not sure whether to laugh or rage.

"So that if you have a child, you cannot claim it is Caesar's."

"Ptolemy is a boy! He thinks his pistle is just for passing water!" Listen to me! she thought. A few days ago I was a virgin. Now I sound like a streetwalker from the docks at Canopus.

"Pothinus has told Ptolemy that his life depends on it."

"A eunuch advising a child to bed his sister? What the Romans must think of us!"

But the news agitated her. She leaped to her feet, tipping one of Charmion's little pots of cosmetic onto the floor. She was taller and stronger than her brother. He would not dare!

But then the thought struck her: Caesar's child! Is it possible, after just one night? And if not, perhaps she should arrange things to give herself better opportunity. Pothinus had just cause for apprehension. A child, a son, by Caesar, would change everything.

〜 〜

All Alexandria attended the wedding: the scientists and mathematicians and physicians from the Museion, the white-robed priests of Isis and Serapis, the captains of the Household Guard in their white Macedonian boots and flat caps, Caesar's senior officers in their red cloaks and leather kilts, the treasurers and courtiers and scribes in their purple.

The pillars in the ceremonial hall had been twined with garlands of green silk, and a thick carpet of rose petals had been scattered across the marble floors. It was a scene of breathtaking richness and colors, the purple-veined marble forest rising to a sky of massive cedarwood rafters, the vaulted roof gilt in shimmering gold.

Cleopatra entered the hall through great doors of ebony fretted with ivory and as tall as a giraffe. Trumpets announced her arrival and a hush fell over the thousands gathered in the great hall for the spectacle.

She wore a gown of diaphanous blue Cathay silk, of such texture and exquisite workmanship that it seemed to ripple, some said afterward, as if the queen were wearing water. She wore a prince's ransom in Red Sea pearls on her fingers, at her throat, and richly plaited into her hair. As she crossed the floor her braided silver sandals crushed the bed of rose petals, releasing a rich, heady scent.

She looked around the great hall. She saw her other brother, little Antiochus, his face a mask of fear and bewilderment, Arsinoë beside him, beautiful and venomous. Pothinus, his hair curled with hot irons, earrings hanging from his ears like ripe figs. And then Ptolemy himself, a gold fillet on his head in the style of the pharaohs, and the double diadem of Egypt ornamented with the sacred cobra. The collar of his pleated linen robe was set with lapis and carnelian stones, and there were golden sandals on his feet.

He looked utterly ridiculous.

Caesar was there to order the whole affair, magisterial in a fringed *toga virilis* with purple stripe. Olympos the physician and his general,

Rufus Cornelius, were standing by to act as witnesses to the marriage.

The ceremony was to be enacted by the high priest, Pshereniptah.

Caesar did not look at her, gave no sign of recognition at all. He gave a slight nod to the High Priest, the signal for him to begin. Pshereniptah uttered a few sentences in demotic Egyptian and it was done.

~ ~

Caesar turned to the entire assembly and announced in a loud voice that Queen Cleopatra the Seventh and King Ptolemy the Thirteenth had settled their differences and were now reconciled and would rule Egypt with one voice.

The crowd cheered on cue, but with little genuine enthusiasm, Cleopatra thought. At a rehearsed signal, more rose petals were thrown.

Cleopatra turned and stared down at her new husband. She brought her lips close to his ear. "Lay a finger on me, tonight or ever, and Pothinus shall wear your privy parts on his fat ears as decoration. Do you understand me?"

Ptolemy stared back at her, his face riven with fear and loathing. Yes, he understood. Stupid boy.

~ ~

The banquet had been organized by Caesar himself, and he had spared no expense, for it was not his money. There was purple shellfish, roasted kid and wild duck, sea urchins in mint, mushrooms and sweet nettles, Attica honey. The best Falernian wine spilled from golden goblets, thickly encrusted with coral and jasper. Afterward the guests were entertained by Nubian dancers, their black sinewy bodies oiled and glistening, who danced to the savage beats of tambours and the clapping of a thousand hands.

Caesar, a garland of cornflowers and roses draped around his neck, stood up and raised his cup in the direction of herself and Ptolemy, and proclaimed that there was now peace in the land.

An ordinary-looking man, except for those eyes, she thought. Yet now, when she looked at him, she felt a tightness in her chest that she could not explain. She kept wanting him to look in her direction, give her some sign, silent assurance that he was on her side, that what she had done was not a terrible mistake. She realized that for the first time since her father's death she had placed her trust in another man.

But he studiously avoided her eyes.

"As a measure of Rome's goodwill to Egypt and its new coregents," he now announced to the assembled guests, "Caesar bequeaths the island of Cyprus to Egypt, and proclaims that its new governors shall be the royal princess Arsinoë and her brother, Antiochus."

Cleopatra caught her breath, saw several of the Roman officers glance up at him, their faces betraying their consternation. Cyprus had become a Roman province by force of arms during her father's reign. The Piper had given it up without a fight, a matter that had caused a great deal of resentment in Alexandria. It was not in Caesar's power to return it to Egypt, or so she had thought, but it seemed he now believed himself powerful enough to speak for Rome itself. Did he hope to placate Pothinus and Achillas and the rest of the nationalists?

"As to the matter of the late king's debt to Rome, I am prepared to accept a settlement of ten million denarii."

It was less than half the full amount of the claim. Perhaps Caesar thought he was being generous. Only the Romans will see it that way, she thought. There is not a man in all Alexandria who would pay a single dinar of my father's bill for reclaiming his throne, particularly now that he is dead.

As the toasts were drunk, Cleopatra looked around at the faces in the room and wondered if Cyprus for ten million denarii would be enough to calm the outrage of Pothinus and his followers.

Somehow she didn't think so.

15

LIFE IN THE palace took on the manner of a dream. After the marriage ceremony, Ptolemy was banished to another palace of the Brucheion, while Cleopatra took up residence in her former apartments with Caesar. There, he was attended by his staff officers and protected by his own legionaries, while she—abandoned by much of the royal court, and with her own advisers cut off from her at Mount Kasios—lived virtually as his queen. Ptolemy and Pothinus kept themselves apart, attended by their own enclave of supporters and fellow conspirators, protected by the Macedonian Household Guard, themselves kept under watch by a cohort of Roman soldiers.

And here am I, sleeping with the enemy, at war with my own people. She was at once the betrayer and the betrayed. She had learned to detest Rome since she was a child, seeing the Romans as barbarians, watching them humiliate her father, her whole family. She had pledged herself to break their hold over Egypt, and now she was on the other side of the barricades, while her people flung themselves at the legionaries' spears.

And here I curl under the protective wing of this Caesar, laugh at his jokes, listen to his stories, willingly take his seed. I wonder if I am just my father's daughter or if I will ever be my own queen?

She waited and watched for Pothinus to make his move. If Egypt won, she would be destroyed. If Caesar won, she would survive. Each side waited and watched. The tension in the Lochias was palpable.

Only Caesar seemed oblivious.

❦   ❦

"It seems your army is intent on war," Caesar was saying to Achillas, as cheerfully as if he was commenting on a chariot race or the Games. "The question of the succession has been resolved to everyone's satisfaction and yet they have marched on Alexandria and laid siege to the city."

"It was not done on my order," Achillas said.

Achillas must be nervous, she thought. His skin is gray and there is sweat on his forehead the size of dewdrops. His smile was meant to placate Caesar, but it had the effect of making his head appear like a death mask.

At Caesar's insistence they all dined together each day, but the food that Pothinus provided was not the kind to stir the juices, just moldy corn bread and small, greasy fish caught in the harbor. Instead of the gold service, the food was served to them off wooden plates; Pothinus claimed he had to melt down the table settings to repay Caesar's claim of ten million denarii.

The wine she would not have served to a thirsty dog.

They ate in the traditional Greek manner, the couches arranged around three sides of the dining tables. Little Antiochus, being yet a child, took his place on a stool.

Only Caesar appeared to have an appetite, which Cleopatra knew to be an act because Caesar had no interest in food. He rarely sat down to eat like this, preferring to tear off pieces of bread and cram them in his mouth while studying charts with his generals. Decimus Brutus said he once picked up a piece of asparagus that had, by mistake, been covered in skin ointment instead of sauce and ate it without a murmur.

She watched Achillas pick without interest at his fish. Arsinoë and her tutor Ganimedes exchanged glances and mouthed silent comments to each other across the table. Ptolemy, for his part, ignored the food altogether. He had his head down and there were tears streaming down his face.

Pothinus saw this and shot a look of pure hatred at Cleopatra. Well, there is no need to stare me down in such a fashion, you piece of camel dung, she thought. You cannot blame me for the poor boy's disposition.

"The mob again tried to storm the palace today," Caesar said to Pothinus.

"The actions of a few merchants and sailors are beyond my authority, Imperator," Pothinus said.

"It is more than just a few merchants and sailors."

Pothinus shrugged his shoulders. "The presence of Roman soldiers is a goad. I am sure the situation will settle once they are gone." When

Caesar did not reply, he added, "Now that the matter of the succession is settled, you will not want to waste any more time in Egypt when you must have more pressing matters to attend to elsewhere."

Caesar regarded him steadily with those cold, black eyes. A look like that, she thought, it was like a sentence of execution. "It is for Caesar to decide which matters press upon him and which do not."

He bit off a hunk of bread with his teeth and washed it down from the wooden goblet at his right hand. How he could drink the vinegar that Pothinus had supplied them was beyond her.

Achillas could keep his silence no longer. "The talk in the bazaars is that Caesar is keeping the royal family hostage," he said.

"Perhaps Pothinus can talk to the rabble," Caesar said. "Calm the situation."

"I do not think the people will listen to me. You cannot blame me for what people say to each other when they are buying fish."

"A strange situation. The mob doesn't seem to listen to you or anyone else. Even the king here." He looked around and seemed to notice Ptolemy's unhappy demeanor for the first time. "What is His Majesty sniveling about now?"

Pothinus's voice showed the strain. It was all he could do to keep the smile in place. "He does not like the food, Imperator."

"Well, it is his own soldiers who keep him from his shellfish and game birds. If they would relieve the siege, he could dine on roasted giraffe if he wished." Caesar put his hands on his hips. "I don't understand why he makes such a fuss. When I was on campaign in Britain, we chewed on nettles and drank water scooped from rock pools."

"Like your ancestors?" Arsinoë said sweetly.

Caesar smiled, but his eyes were hard as flint. Oh, my pretty little sister, Cleopatra thought, with your fair hair and cornflower-blue eyes you could play Caesar like a fish on a line if you wished. But instead you behave as if you are sharing the table with an alley dog. Yes, the Romans are barbarians, but this one has at least some refinement, and if battle was one of the arts, then he would have no scholar his equal in the Museion.

"You have no appetite either?" Caesar said to Arsinoë.

"There is a bad smell in the room," she said.

Caesar sniffed the air, with the lavish gesture of a man in a garden of roses. "All I can smell is the sea. You do not appreciate the smell of salt? For myself, I find it invigorating. In Rome the sea is too far away."

"I would rather share my meal with a dog than with a Roman."

His smile vanished at this deadly insult. "Then perhaps I may grant you your wish," he said.

Arsinoë got up and swept from the room.

Caesar went to stand behind the stool where Antiochus ate with his head down, fearful of the hard voices and angry looks. "If only all of Ptolemy's family had his youngest son's sweet disposition," he said, and tousled the boy's hair.

She saw Achillas and Pothinus exchange a look. They all knew that Antiochus was merely scared, not mellow. If he ever grew to be a man, Caesar might see a different side to him. There were no sweet dispositions at the palace at Brucheion, and there had not been for centuries.

❦ ❦

"The thing I enjoy most about dining," Caesar said to her after the others had left, "is the conversation." He poured himself a little more of the vinegary wine and drank some without wincing.

"Among my own family," Cleopatra said, "it was considered a good dinner if no one was murdered before the entertainments."

"I have tasters to make sure the wine is not poisoned."

"You mean it isn't?" she said, tossing the remains of her glass out of the open window.

He shrugged his shoulders. "I am a soldier. I will drink anything. If Pothinus thinks to wear me down by starving me of luxury, he does not understand Caesar." He regarded her thoughtfully. "Tell me, that man who was with Arsinoë. Is that her lover?"

"She is a princess of a royal house. How may she have a lover?"

"He seems very familiar with her."

"He is her tutor. Ever since the first Ptolemy, the daughters of the royal house have had exactly the same education as the boys."

"Extraordinary."

"You think a woman might not have the same wit as a man?"

"I think it would have to be an extraordinary woman."

"Then our family has always had extraordinary women, for no Ptolemy princess has ever struggled to keep pace with her brothers.

Each of us has a *tropheus* who tutors us in the arts and sciences, and later, if they are trusted, they may become advisers also."

"And not lovers?"

"Lovers?"

"What is so amusing?"

She smiled. "It is not possible. Ganimedes is a eunuch. Like Mardian."

His expression changed. He had until that point thought her naive. Now his face betrayed both his disgust and embarrassment.

"It seems there is much Rome does not understand about the East."

"Why do you look like that?" she asked him, genuinely puzzled at his reaction.

"You and your animal gods and *eunuchs,* and your preoccupation with death. My gorge rises in revolt at such practices."

"It makes perfect sense if you—"

"A woman ruling men who have had their manhood razored away! It is . . . barbaric!" He slammed his goblet on the table and stormed out of the room.

10

WINTER STORMS LASHED the Pharos, there was white water even in the harbor, and the skies had turned the color of lead. The streets by the docks were swept with lashing rain and salt spray. Caravans from Punt and Arabia still filed through the Gate of the Sun, but the merchant galleys were anchored in the Harbor of Good Return and Alexandria was effectively cut off from the Mediterranean until the spring.

The Egyptian army—as Achillas was pleased to call his band of pirates, freebooters, convicts, and runaway slaves—was now camped outside the city. Twenty thousand of them, backed by two thousand native cavalry. Perhaps Pothinus and Ptolemy thought that Caesar could be intimidated into capitulating to them by this show of force. But Caesar did not seem much concerned. "After all," he told her, "I have over three thousand veteran legionaries, and eight hundred Celts as cavalry, as well as fifty triremes at the foot of the Lochias steps—and four royal hostages."

It was the first time he had admitted she was no longer his guest.

Typical of him, she thought. His easy charm made all in his privileged circle feel they were uniquely special to him. And each time she felt herself—yes, admit it, girl—falling in love with him, she was reminded of his utter ruthlessness and drew back. And yet despite her position, she remained yet a woman and found him utterly compelling. She did not trust herself when she was with him.

She suspected he knew that, that he was counting on it.

The mob had built triple barricades of stone blocks in the streets, so the Canopic Way was no longer passsable, nor the Street of the Soma. Caesar had likewise fortified the palace, and set up his headquarters in the banqueting rooms, spreading out maps on precious ivory and rosewood tables, the alabaster floors resounding now to the stamp of boots as centurions and officers ran in and out all day and night with reports or to attend hurried conferences.

Caesar seemed to treat the whole thing as a game.

〜 〜

The wind roared and buffeted the palace walls, the glow of the great fire inside the Pharos the only light on this bleak and winter night. She had expected Caesar to take her, as he often did, with the same ferocity, but tonight, as if in response to the ferocity of the gale, he was gentle and took his time.

Often she felt as if she had left her own body to watch their coupling from a high corner of the bedroom. She saw their bodies entwined under the leopard skin covering on the bed. Their silhouettes seemed to shimmer and dance in the flickering light, as the lamps guttered in the draught from the doors and windows.

She saw his naked shoulders and his back, scarred by old wounds, raised above her like a lion contemplating prey. Her heels wrapped themselves tightly around the base of his spine, rising to meet him. He began to move, a gentle cadenced rhythm, waiting for her to respond.

But tonight was different from every other time; suddenly she was no longer watching, apart, she felt the tantalizing sensations of her own body, a surprising warmth rising up from her calves and thighs to the pit of her belly. She closed her eyes and now was no longer watching but part of the shadowy ballet, as a roseate glow grew like an unchecked fire inside her body. As she edged toward this unknown longing, she began to buck against him, her hands balled into fists in the coverlets. Her back arched and the muscles in her thighs cramped as the need became strident, and her body and spirit were overtaken by unbidden spasms.

Then it was as if the darkness exploded into light, like a little death, surrender utter and complete, and she experienced an intense and breathless sensation of pleasure and release such as she had never known. As he finished, she clung to him like driftwood in a boiling ocean, her heart thundering, mouth gasping for breath. Afterward her body seemed to glow like the charcoal in the brazier in the corner of the room, and when she closed her eyes, there was no darkness, just a thousand colors, like the shimmering of silk. And she slept.

⚘ ⚘

She woke suddenly, remembered where she was, what had happened. Caesar was asleep beside her, his arm flung carelessly across her breast, his head against her shoulder. As she looked at him she felt a sudden upwelling of tenderness, and she despised herself for it. The treachery of the heart.

"Julius," she whispered, and ran the tip of her forefinger along his cheek. I am so weak, she thought. This is not what I intended.

But then, outside in the gardens, she heard shouts, the clash of metal, running boots. There was a terrible scream. She realized it was these sounds that had woken her. Caesar was instantly awake, a soldier's instincts, and he leaped out of bed and went to the window, naked, staring out into the darkness. Cleopatra felt her heart thumping painfully in her chest. Perhaps the rabble had broken through the barricades.

"What is happening?" she asked.

"It is nothing," he said. "My men are attending to it." Almost at once she heard boots running along the corridor toward their bedroom, a fist pounding on the door. Caesar seemed quite unconcerned at this alarm. He unhurriedly slipped on his tunic.

"Enter," he said, and crossed his arms.

A centurion strode in, holding a small sack. Its contents were dripping onto the carpets. Caesar nodded, and the man unwrapped the sopping bundle. It was a head, although scarcely recognizable. It was drained of all color and life, and blood still leaked from the severed neck veins.

Caesar turned to her. "Do you know him?" he asked her casually, as if it were some foreign dignitary he had spied at a state banquet.

"It's Pothinus," she said. And then, because Caesar did not respond, she added: "He's lost a lot of weight."

Caesar threw back his head and laughed, delighted at this remark. "Yes. And he used to be much taller also." A slight nod of the head and the man threw the head back in the sack. "Thank you, centurion. You may give it to the dogs."

"There was a problem, Imperator," the centurion said uneasily. "Their general, Achillas. He was nowhere to be found."

"Unfortunate. He must have been warned."

Caesar dismissed him with a nod. The soldier saluted and left.

Caesar turned to her. "Tonight, while we slept, there was an accounting. I would have preferred to have crushed the whole nest, but there you are."

He planned this from the beginning, she thought. From the moment the Regency Council decided to kill Pompey, their fate was sealed. Caesar was no doubt privately pleased that the Council had done his work for him, but he was always going to be a Roman about this. He would take revenge in the name of Rome and then claim the victory as his own.

"You never had any intention of letting him live," she said.

"Of course not. It's a pity about Achillas, though."

His ruthlessness did not horrify her, but struck her with awe. He had dealt with his enemies without rancor, without signaling his intentions. It was doubtless why he had become so powerful, and so feared in Rome. I wonder if I could learn to be this pragmatic?

"And what do you intend to do now?" she asked him.

"I am too busy to fight Egyptians. Perhaps now that Pothinus is taken care of and Alexandria has a new king and queen, we can all get on with our daily business."

"And me?"

"You have what you wanted, kitten. I have done your dirty work for you. I am sure you can handle young Antiochus now that we have disbanded the Regency Council." He gave her a wry smile. "Can't you?"

You have what you wanted, kitten. He might as well have plunged a knife into her belly. *You have what you wanted.* Like he had thrown her scraps from the table. She thought he had finally accepted her as his lover and his ally, and now he treated her like some underling.

The truth of it was that from that very first night with Caesar another desire had sprung unbidden inside her. On reflection it made good political sense: I can be good for you. You can be very good for me.

You have what you wanted, kitten.

No, Julius, not everything I want. I want you.

17

A COLD BUT bright winter morning, clouds like mare's tails racing across the sky, waves beating against the rocks below the Pharos and sending plumes of spray high into the air. Over in the western harbor, the big cargo carriers, the *barides,* wallowed at anchor. Below her, close to the Brucheion and alongside the wharves opposite the island of Antirhodos, were Caesar's Rhodian warships, fifty Roman triremes, riding the chop. Over by the warehouses and granaries were over threescore of her own warships, biremes and triremes with two or three banks of oars, her navy now turned against her, masts bristling against the sky.

Cleopatra stood at the window of her bedroom, Caesar's heavy cloak, leather and lined with bear fur, wrapped around her shoulders.

You have what you wanted, kitten.

Why did you do it? she wondered. Why did you take my part in this? From the moment I set foot inside the palace I was utterly in your power. You could have tasted a little of Egypt and betrayed me anyway, kept Ptolemy as a client king, without recourse to war. Pothinus would have agreed to repay my father's debt in return for your help in getting rid of me.

Was it, as you said, because of what they did to Pompey? Or was it simply a whim? You seem to me the sort of man who allows himself many indulgences simply because you can. You do precisely as you please and nothing stops you.

I should like to think you did it because of some fond feeling for me, but that is a vain hope. Perhaps you did it for political reasons, out of pragmatism. You are planning something. I wonder what it is?

꒰ ꒱

A blue and cold day in Alexandria. A good day to be alive and plotting, Caesar thought. He stood on the terrace, braced against the driving wind, the cold burning his cheeks.

The great curve of the mainland swept around the harbor to the arcaded breakwater, a great arch affording passage to the western harbor. And there, beyond the massive pylons of the Isis temple, rose the wonder, Pharos, Zeus standing astride the circular tower, silhouetted against the sky. It was an awesome sight, a square blockhouse of limestone, an octagonal castle of pink marble above it, topped by a tower of purple granite from Aswan. It seemed to change its color through the day, a pale pink at dawn, the color of blood at sunset.

Behind him, rising above the roof of the palace, a square tower with conical roof, the tomb of Alexander himself. The gypsum and marble of the Brucheion was so white it hurt the eyes and he had to turn away.

A marvelous city, he thought. It makes Rome look like a village of mud bricks.

The palace itself had proved a delight; chairs of ivory and ebony wood, coffers encrusted with gold, incense of Arabia in tripods of bronze and silver, floors marbled with red and black porphyry. It was a city not just of indolence, as a man might think, but of learning, with its vast Library, every important book ever written, everything that a man of culture and refinement might wish for in his repose.

And indeed, until the grand entrance of their beautiful little queen, he had been content to assert his authority among these gypos and enjoy a sojourn after the endless campaigning, first in Britain, then Gaul, and finally the great gamble against Pompey.

But this dark-haired little adventuress had given him other ideas.

Apart from the obvious pleasures, physical and psychological, of bedding a young and vital Oriental queen, there was a political advantage to be had here, if he proceeded carefully. An alliance could bring the granary of the world under his personal control.

It had been obvious from the start that Pothinus was not one to bend to the wind. He was one of those most dangerous of all creatures, an ardent nationalist. That his head would have to bid a fond *vale* to his body had been inevitable.

Now he had the situation better under his control. He would certainly need Egypt's support if he was to pursue his aims in Rome. Pompey's supporters had not been totally defeated; his sons had retreated to Africa, where he would have to follow in time. To do that he would need money, and what was Egypt if not a vast treasure house?

Cleopatra, he was sure, was the key. And such a softly pink and fragrant lock for the turning.

🐏 🐏

For years Cleopatra and her sister had been unable to exchange anything but the smallest pleasantry without bitter recrimination. It was now their habit to speak only when necessary, and even eye contact was painful.

They had not seen each other alone since the day of her coronation. But one day, soon after Pothinus's death, Cleopatra saw Arsinoë sweeping toward her along the palace corridor, all silk and perfumed condescension. Her *tropheus*, Ganimedes, was with her.

Cleopatra was prepared to ignore her, but to her surprise Arsinoë stopped her, evidently wishing to talk.

"Sister," Cleopatra said, wondering what she wanted.

Arsinoë gave her a chill smile. "So. You did it. You finally fucked a Roman."

Cleopatra was shocked. Not even a small comment about the weather first. What bad manners.

Ganimedes's face was a study. He tugged at his charge's sleeve. "My lady, let us not do this," he whimpered.

"Don't presume to tell me what to do, you old bitch," Arsinoë said to him.

Barely eighteen years old, Cleopatra thought. What a little snake you have become.

"You are just like Father," Arsinoë went on. "You have lapped at their feet for so long, it was only a matter of time before you bent over for them."

There is no point in wasting my breath on her, Cleopatra thought. If her sister could not see the point of what she was doing, she would not explain it to her. You did not send the enemy your battle plans in advance.

Ganimedes again whispered to his charge to come away.

"May you suffer a thousand deaths," Arsinoë hissed and turned on her heel, Ganimedes shuffling along behind her as she walked away. Cleopatra shook her head. If hate were a salable commodity, her family would not have enough warehouses in all Alexandria to keep it under lock and key.

18

THE WINDOW HANGINGS, white silk and almost transparent, billowed and danced in the night breeze along the moonlit colonnades. The afternoon's storm had again raised the waves on the ocean, and the sound of the sea beating against the reef sounded like distant thunder.

The onyx floor was cool beneath her feet, and Caesar did not hear her enter the room. Her shadow fell across the table where he was writing and he looked up in surprise. She was naked.

She held out a goblet of wine, but he pushed it away. Wordlessly, he laid down the stylus, stood up, and came toward her.

But this time she had resolved that she would not let him take control over her. Tonight she would prove to be his gentle master here, assert at least a little of the natural power she had in being a woman, put some of the *hetaira*'s lessons to good use.

As he reached for her, she took his wrists and forced them down by his sides. He resisted at first but then allowed her game.

"Take off your clothes," she whispered.

She was nervous. This was something she had never done before, had never imagined herself doing for any man.

But, intrigued, he did as she ordered.

There were many scars on his body, puckered, ugly memories from a hundred battles. Despite his age, his stomach was still as hard as rosewood, his chest and shoulders heavily muscled. There were no hairs on his chest or even his thighs. Mardian had told her it was rumored he had them singed off with red hot walnut shells.

His penis was already engorged. Caesar, she thought, god of fertility, like Osiris. Now she, as Isis, the hawk, hovered over his body, to accept, and to succor.

She had never imagined that she would kneel before any man. But she did so now, as Rachel had shown her to do. She began tentatively, but encouraged by his groans, she forgot for a moment that she was a queen and he was a barbarian. He may be above me, she thought, as supplicant and god, but for now I have Caesar in my power.

She stopped, suddenly, as she remembered Rachel had done, and eased him gently onto the bed, on his back. She found the goblet of wine and held the wine in her mouth, cold and slightly acid. She leaned over Caesar and kissed him again, dribbled the wine into his mouth, felt it spill onto his chin.

She sat astride him and eased him tentatively inside her, fighting his urgency. He held her hips now, moving her in time with his own rhythms, and Cleopatra groaned aloud as she remembered Rachel had. But it was not all theater, for she experienced again the same deep, wonderful sensations that seemed to warm her whole body. His movements became faster, more desperate, and in the moonlight she saw the look on his face, a look of surprise and disappointment and release, as she had seen before on the faces of men as they died.

But there was one lesson she did not take from the Jewess. At that final moment she did not lift herself away from him. Instead she let him plunge deep into her, and willed his seed to find her womb.

⚜ ⚜

It happened without warning.

They were alone in their apartments one evening when Caesar gave a small cry and fell heavily to the floor. He lay rigid, his face blue, a bloody froth on his lips, his limbs twitching.

She stared at him, horrified. Someone has poisoned him, she thought. *Achillas!* He had outmaneuvered her!

She realized with a thrill of fear that if Caesar died at this moment, her life might yet be worthless. She still needed his soldiers, his influence, to protect her, not only from Achillas, but from Rome.

Caesar was lying on his back, his breath gurgling in his chest. She ran to the door and screamed at the startled guards to fetch a physician.

She ran back into the room and held Caesar in her arms. *Don't die, please. I have gambled everything on you. Don't die!*

Caesar's aide, Decimus Brutus, ran into the room and crouched down beside her. "What happened?"

"He just collapsed," she said. "His whole body was rigid and shaking. He is coughing blood."

Decimus shook his head. He seemed almost relieved. "It is just the falling sickness," he said. "Look. He has bitten his tongue. Help me carry him to the bed. This will pass."

⚜ ⚜

Decimus sent the guards out of the room, their eyes wide. He looked up at her, cradling Caesar's head in his lap. "The falling sickness touches those who are inhabited by gods. It is a sign of his greatness."

"He has not been poisoned?"

Decimus shook his head. "He will recover. When he wakes, he mumbles things no one can understand. It is the gods speaking. After a while they leave him and he will be himself again."

It happened just as Decimus said. After a while Caesar opened his eyes, mumbling incoherently, did not even recognize her when she tried to hold him. Decimus spoke to him softly, rocking him in his arms, and finally he slept.

When he woke the following morning, he got up and went to the antechamber, called for his slaves to bring him wine and bread for his breakfast, as if nothing had happened.

She stood at the doorway of the bedchamber, watching him. "Last night," she said, "something happened to you."

There was a sudden wariness in his eyes. "Did I fall?"

"I thought you had been poisoned."

He looked away. "So. Now you know Caesar's secret."

He finished a perfunctory breakfast, called for his *tonsore* and his dressers.

"Decimus says some think you are a god."

Caesar smiled and shook his head. "Fortunately, I do not believe such stories," he answered, but he said it lightly, as if he allowed for the possibility. "You are not to speak of this."

She understood. But for the first time it occurred to her that Caesar might be more than just a Roman Consul and Imperator. Perhaps he, too, was a god, not a barbarian after all. Perhaps Isis had found her Osiris, her mate and bull.

19

THE STREETS OF Alexandria were still dark when she woke. She heard the noise, rose from the bed, and went to the window. The Romans were pouring out of the palace gates, the stamp of their boots echoing on the cobbled streets along with the jangle of armor and leather strapping. All the legionaries were carrying torches, and their progress was marked by a sinuous column of smoke and flame.

She heard the sound of the fighting along the darkened waterfront as the soldiers crashed through the barricades and made for the docks.

Caesar came to stand beside her at the window.

"Come back to bed," he whispered. "It's just a skirmish. It will be all over in an hour."

A roseate glow, a false dawn, appeared over the western part of the harbor, followed by trails of orange sparks and a plume of black smoke against an indigo sky. Flaming hulks drifted across the inner harbor into the docks, Caesar's own Roman galleys, ablaze. She saw one of them drift among the Egyptian warships, the conflagration spreading among them also.

"What is happening?" she whispered.

"Achillas has been trying to board my ships and I do not have enough men to defend them all. So I have ordered sixty of my ships to be fired and sailed into Achillas's fleet anchored at the docks. My soldiers are also throwing brands on board from the wharves. That should solve the problem. Meanwhile, if you look out to the promontory, you will see my men boarding the rest of the galleys to cross to Pharos. They will take the lighthouse and from there we can govern the straits entering the harbor. Then Achillas cannot force our position. This little skirmish at the docks not only serves a useful purpose in handicapping our enemy, it is also a diversion for our true aim."

The fires had caught quickly among the fleet at the cramped wharves and was spreading rapidly from ship to ship. In the gray light she saw men leaping into the water from a quadrireme as the fire licked hungrily along the pitch used to caulk the decks. The flames had even spread to one of the warehouses.

"War is a beautiful thing," he whispered. "It exercises both the body and the mind. You outwit your enemy and then you outfight him. It is almost art. Now, come back to bed."

He took her then, with a soldier's roughness and appetite. She gave herself with a hunger that matched his own. It was more than just politics now; it always had been. Her head thrown back on the coverlet, teeth bruising the hard muscle of his shoulder, she saw the glow of the fires throw a pink stain across the cedarwood beams of the ceiling. He violates my city, he violates me, she thought. And still I cannot find it in my heart to hate this Roman who destroys my beloved Alexandria.

20

THE OIL LAMPS had been lit and Caesar worked quietly at his desk. He was writing his memoirs of the campaign in Gaul when he had defeated the Gallic chieftain, Vercingetorix. Cleopatra watched him work, the stylus scratching the papyrus, her mind and soul filled with a restless energy. For the first time in her life she was bored.

When she had taken the regency after her father's death, she spent long hours of every day either closeted with her ministers and advisers, or at endless meetings with her *strategioi* discussing everything from dredging the canals to the more effective administration of import duties. Even in exile she had dedicated herself to the business of government, questioning Mardian's spies, planning strategies, raising loans, and recruiting mercenaries for her army.

Now at last she was once more Queen of Egypt, but Egypt's borders extended no farther than the palace, and its government was Caesar's affair. She was queen in name alone; was, in fact, Rome's prisoner. There was absolutely nothing for her to do except provide for Caesar's pleasure, and though that had not proved as onerous a duty as she might have once imagined, indolence and slavery did not sit well with her nature.

Achillas's attempt to seize the harbor had failed when Caesar set fire to his fleet as it lay at anchor in the docks. He had now fled with what remained of his fleet into the western harbor. Meanwhile the Romans had secured the lighthouse and the straits that governed the royal harbor, and their position seemed secure. It would now take a frontal attack to dislodge them.

By way of retaliation, Achillas tried to interrupt their water supply. Their drinking water came from underground channels that diverted the Nile through the city. Achillas had managed to interrupt the flow, instead pumping seawater into the wells on Lochias. For a few days Caesar's soldiers were reduced to drinking wine.

"The Celts among them will find that no hardship," Caesar announced, laughing, but that night he sent out a party of men to dig wells along the beach, and by the next morning they had located a new source of water.

And so it continued, a war of nerves, Caesar content to wait and to plan, treating the whole thing as if it were a game.

🙰 🙰

Cleopatra roamed the room, patrolling the borders of her luxurious confinement. She summoned a slave to play dice with her but sent her away again after just a few games. She summoned Iras, but when she arrived, Cleopatra dismissed her immediately. She stood by the window, but the view of the harbor was now as dismal to her as the bars of a cage. She sighed heavily.

Caesar looked up from his desk. "You are unhappy?" he said to her.

"I have nothing to do."

"Call the slaves for a massage or a bath."

"It is not my body that needs fulfillment, it is my mind."

He looked at her as if she had spoken to him in Egyptian. It seemed to her that he could not become accustomed to the idea of a woman being his intellectual equal. An extraordinary man, but in many other respects he was just a typical, provincial Roman.

"A Roman woman is never bored."

"What do Roman women do?"

He looked away. "I don't know. They seem content enough."

"Is Calpurnia *content*?"

It was the first time she had spoken of his wife in his presence. She waited for a reaction from him, but was not afforded one. "If I tell her to be," he replied.

This answer spoke eloquently of Romans, she decided. She decided not to bait him further. "What are our plans?"

"For what?" he answered, mildly irritated by her constant interruptions.

"For Achillas."

"Our plan is we have no plans, kitten." Kitten. It made her teeth ache to hear him call her that, but for the moment there was nothing she could do about it. "I am waiting for the Thirty-seventh Legion to come down from Rhodes. Mithradates, a client of mine in Syria, is sending more troops by land; Malchus, in Nabataea, has promised me cavalry. When my reinforcements arrive, we shall see about your Captain of the Guard and his army of ruffians. Until then we remain here in the palace and wait."

Wait, she thought. Wait! For how long?

He laid down his stylus and gave her a familiar smile. "Come here, kitten."

So that's what he thinks I want. As if I have been waiting all day for him to finish work just so he can pleasure me. "I think I shall go for a walk," she said, and swept from the room.

She sat for a long time on the lonely, windswept rocks of the promontory. Toward evening she went alone to the Temple of Isis, to consult the Protector of Women and ask for her guidance on her troubled heart and divided soul.

21

CAESAR LOUNGED ON a couch, studying a report from one of his commanders. He looked up from the wax tablet in his hand almost as if he was surprised to see Ptolemy standing there. Even though he had sent his own guards to fetch him.

The stupid boy looked utterly miserable. Pothinus had led him deeper and deeper into this morass, and now the fat fool had taken the easy way out by letting Caesar's soldiers decapitate him. Life really wasn't fair.

"Your Achillas is advancing on Alexandria," Caesar said to him.

No tears today, he was pleased to see. Ptolemy was sullen, his thick lips holding a grim and stubborn line, his eyes on the carpets. "Achillas is acting on his own orders. I remain loyal to Caesar and my coregent, my sister."

Caesar nodded as if this made perfect sense to him. "Well, I am pleased I find you in such a frame of mind. Your other sister does not show the same admirable loyalty."

Ptolemy looked up for the first time, allowed the surprise to show on his face. Had he really not heard the news? No Pothinus, no spies. The boy was as helpless as a lamb.

"It seems she and her . . . creature, Ganimedes, have gone to join Achillas. She has proclaimed herself queen. Egypt is indeed a fortunate country. Most countries count themselves fortunate to have one monarch. Egypt now has two queens and a king."

Ptolemy looked utterly lost. I wonder if he has worked it out, he thought. If Arsinoë wins, does he think she will share her power with him? This idiot boy has been thrown around like dice, everyone has tried their luck with him, and now he has been left alone in the palace with the roll call of the dead and missing growing by the day.

So now he clings to Caesar.

"Fear for nothing," Caesar said. "I shall protect you."

The look on his face. He should have liked to have had it immortalized in a mosaic on the floor of his villa on the Palatine. The boy must have known from that moment that his days were numbered, heard Anubis the jackal, God of the Underworld, laughing and cackling out his name.

⚜   ⚜

Caesar returned to his desk to continue his account of the Gallic wars. And so the question of Egypt had been decided. Now that he had gotten to know the Piper's family a little better, it was clear in which direction the future lay.

22

SHE COULD SEE the progress of the battle from the palace roof. She wrapped a cloak about her in the chill light of the predawn, shivering against the cold, and a second cloak around her shoulders, wanted no one to see her trembling and perhaps misinterpret it as fear.

"I have said a prayer to Isis to protect Caesar today," a voice said.

She wheeled around, recognizing Ptolemy's high-pitched voice, though she could not see his face in the darkness. Even now it had that wheedling tone that so irritated her.

She returned her attention to the events unfolding on the far side of the harbor.

The plan had seemed so simple when Caesar described it to her. The Thirty-seventh Legion had arrived with a fleet of warships, and Caesar immediately announced that he would put an end to the "skirmish," as he called it. His ships would strike at the Egyptians in the western harbor, blockading the arches in the Heptastadion so they could not escape. Meanwhile, reinforcements from the Thirty-seventh would land at the western end of the Pharos island, where they would link up with the troops who now fortified the lighthouse. Joining forces, they would strike out from the island along the Heptastadion, securing control of the harbor.

From her position on the terrace she could see only the distinctive red cloaks of the Roman legionaries on the distant island, hear the clash of weapons and armor carried to them on occasional gusts of wind. In the distant harbor Caesar's galleys and Achillas's warships were grappled together, but they were too far away and the dawn yet too dark for her to see what was happening.

⚜ ⚜

"You have gambled everything on this Roman," Ptolemy said to her.

She could not bear to look at him. She kept her eyes on the breakwater and the island around the lighthouse, looking for a flash of purple, the general's cloak Caesar wore with such pride although it also made him a distinctive target. It was getting lighter now, and she could see that the Romans were winning, as Caesar had said they would, for the battle lines had retreated farther toward the causeway.

If Alexander rose from that great crystal coffin, she thought, and came to stand beside me now, here on this chill and blustery terrace, what would he think of his distant daughter taking the side of an enemy against her own? Would the master tactician understand this act of expediency, know that she would play the fawn only until she had the chance again to show her claws?

"I am Caesar's ally as much as you," Ptolemy said.

"Just leave me alone," she said, but he stayed, wondering what the goddess of Fortune would decide for them this cold and blue morning.

❦ ❦

The Romans were distinctive in their scarlet cloaks and iron helmets, Achillas's ragged army in makeshift costumes of every kind. She had been watching from the terrace for hours; now the sun had climbed almost to its zenith, and still the battle raged. The Romans had fought their way along the Heptastadion, almost to the midpoint, almost directly opposite the palace. In the distance smoke rose from the burning hulks of Roman and Egyptian ships in the Harbor of Good Return.

And there he was in the midst of it, Julius himself, in his purple cloak. Suddenly it was hard to swallow, even to breathe. She was overwhelmed with relief that he was alive, sick with dread that she might see him fall. As of now her destiny rested with him. If he died, she died with him.

❦ ❦

It was apparent that Caesar had miscalculated. She felt a chill of fear in the pit of her stomach. There were Egyptian soldiers on the causeway, cutting off his retreat. One of the Egyptian triremes had broken away from the battle in the western harbor, barging through the burning hulks to land more troops at the base of the island. The great general had been outmaneuvered.

He was cut off now, pressed on both sides. A captain on one of the Roman Liburnians saw what was happening and brought his ship close to the causeway to try and rescue the soldiers cut off there. She saw legionaries leaping onto the deck of the little galley, which rocked alarmingly in the water.

But she could see that it was futile. On this occasion the fabled Roman discipline had broken, and now the Egyptians were swarming onto the Liburnian, making escape impossible.

The galley started to capsize.

The unthinkable was happening in front of her eyes. The invincible Romans were being cut down by her former army, the ragged band of mercenaries she had once derided in front of Achillas and her whole court.

She turned around. Ptolemy was watching her. There was a wolfish smile on his face. "I have always hated you," he murmured.

"And I have always despised you. If Caesar dies, do not think I shall fall on my knees and beg you for mercy."

"They say our sister lost control of her bowels at her execution. Our father chose to have her throttled. You didn't know that, did you? He told you it was the cobra. That would have been a kinder death. But Pothinus told me what really happened. He said the stench was appalling. I wonder which death I shall choose for you?"

She saw a flash of purple as Caesar leaped from the Liburnian and began to swim across the harbor. The closest Roman ship was perhaps the distance of one stadion. There were heads bobbing everywhere in the water now, and she lost sight of him. The Egyptians were crowding around the capsized Liburnian, hurling spears into the waves. Impossible to tell now whether he was alive or dead.

"I think I should like to see you throttled," Ptolemy said. "The stink as you died would be as sweet as roses."

She ignored him. She could not believe destiny had kept her alive these last three terrible years to fail her now. He had to be alive.

He had to be.

23

HIS FACE WAS gray and his shoulders hunched in exhaustion. He looked older than she had ever seen him. His sparse hair was plastered to his head, and his tunic was ragged and wet. There was blood on one arm, down his wrist and to his fingers, from a sword slash. He seemed unconcerned.

He had commandeered a banqueting hall as his headquarters, where they dragged her father's ceremonial table to the window for better light, a rare treasure made from the trunk of a single tree from the Atlas Mountains in Mauretania, the legs on each corner made from elephant tusks. Maps had been thrown across it as if it were a wooden bench. Roman boots had left mud prints across the shining alabaster floors.

Caesar was surrounded by a coterie of his commanders, studying charts of the palace and harbor, laying new plans. They had captured the island and inflicted heavy damage on Achillas's navy, but the Romans had lost four hundred legionaries on the causeway, a heavy defeat.

"Imperator," Ptolemy said as they entered. "We are relieved to find you safe."

Caesar turned around. The shadow of a weary smile curled the corners of his mouth. "I can see you are, my boy."

"You risk too much on our account."

"No doubt you would be happy to see me leave."

"For ourselves we do not wish it. But it is clear that all Alexandria is against you. Your life is in constant danger." It seemed absurd, this boy using the royal prerogative, she thought.

Cleopatra smiled to herself. Well, you will not have me throttled just yet, little brother. While Caesar lives, you can keep the executioner's fingers off my neck.

"Caesar's life is in constant danger," he said to Ptolemy, "no matter where Caesar goes. But I am sincerely humbled by your concern for my well-being."

With a nod of his head, Caesar sent his officers out of the room. A hard stare let Ptolemy know he wished him to leave also. He left, if reluctantly. What is my brother playing at? Cleopatra wondered. Does he think to appease our Julius, *my* Julius, with his oily smiles and fawning words? Does he think, perhaps, that if he bends over far enough Caesar will steer the throne of Egypt inside?

The great doors closed behind the guards. They were alone.

"I thought you were dead," she whispered.

"And that would concern you?"

"You have become precious to me," she said. Not an outright lie, either. What is happening to me?

He grinned. "Come here, kitten." He held her. He was shivering, his tunic cold and still wet from the harbor.

"You should change out of these wet clothes," she whispered. She ran a finger along the wound in his left arm. A gaping slash, caked with dried, black blood.

"They fought well," he said. "It seems my sojourn in Alexandria is going to be longer than I anticipated." He smiled, but his eyes betrayed how he truly felt. He had been shaken by the events of the day. Achillas's ragbag army were a more formidable foe than he realized.

Yet despite the near disaster, if anything his legend had been augmented by what happened on the Heptastadion. He had himself cheated death by swimming in full armor the distance of almost one stadion to another Roman ship, while keeping one arm clear of the water to keep his battle plans from getting wet. Apart from the arm wound, the only other injury was to his pride, for he had lost his precious purple cloak, his personal emblem of rank.

He let her take him to bed, an act of possession and affirmation rather than passion, for his body was cold as a corpse, and he lay beside her there, curled in her arms like a baby, and slept. She stroked his thinning hair and whispered "Julius" over and over, imagined Ptolemy's executioner with his great hands around her neck, and to dispel these dark dreams she summoned again her own desperate conviction in her own destiny, beyond Caesar.

🙰　🙰

Caesar picked idly at his breakfast, some bread and a little ewe's cheese, a flask of water.

As he ate he interviewed several of his staff officers, while Cleopatra had two of the palace slave girls attend her toilet in the next room. Neither was as skilled as Charmion or Iras, but they would have to do for now. Her own servants, along with the rest of her retinue, were still stranded in the desert at Mount Kasios.

Then she heard another voice in the next chamber, and recognized it immediately. "Ptolemy," she hissed, and got to her feet, pushing the slave girls away.

⬬ ⬬

Caesar reclined on a couch, examining a report from one of his officers, the wax tablet held idly in one hand. He looked hardly the Imperator now, just a man idly disturbed at his reading, dressed in a simple white tunic. Her stupid brother stood in the doorway, ridiculous in a brocade gown threaded with gold, his hair pomaded and in ringlets. Sixteen years old and he already played the part of an Alexandrian fop off to the theater.

"Ah, Your Majesty," Caesar said, his eyes still on the wax tablet.

"You requested my presence," Ptolemy said. He looked up, saw her standing in the doorway of the bedroom, and gave her a smirk. He had started the day with the resolve to stand his ground against Caesar. There had been another riot this morning on the Street of the Soma, and no doubt the yells of the mob at the gates had puffed him up with a sense of his own importance.

"Caesar has welcome news for the King of Egypt."

Ptolemy's air of perfumed arrogance slipped away. What a shallow mask it was.

"I wish you to go to your sister Arsinoë," Caesar said.

Ptolemy let his jaw fall open, a trap for the flies and midges.

"Don't look so surprised. What better emissary can Caesar have than her own kin?"

"You wish me to leave the palace?"

That will be a shock for him, she thought. Had Ptolemy ever been outside the Brucheion? she wondered. She doubted if he had ever ventured farther than the gardens on Lake Mareotis.

"You will be accompanied by a squadron of the Palace Guard as escort."

Cleopatra watched the play of emotion on his face. Disbelief, panic, fear. Without Pothinus he was lost.

"But why?"

"You think Caesar enjoys being cooped up here? You must broker a truce so that I and my men can board our ships and go back to Rome in peace."

Cleopatra felt the blood drain from her face, unable to believe what she was hearing.

"But I do not wish to leave the palace," Ptolemy was saying.

For the first time Caesar showed a flicker of irritation. "What has it to do with what you wish? You have a duty as a king! If this war continues, your city is going to be destroyed, do you not care about that?"

No, he doesn't, Cleopatra thought. You can see that. It is written on his face as clearly as the hieroglyphs on Alexander's tomb. He does not realize that you are giving him back the throne, that you are set on betraying me. Yet what should I have expected from a Roman? Mardian told me as much.

"Your sister has murdered Caesar's envoys," he said to Ptolemy. "She has even quarreled with her general, Achillas, and her eunuch has had him murdered. You alone they will treat with reverence, for you are their king. You will broker this peace for Caesar so he may return to more pressing matters in Rome."

Achillas, murdered? Why had he not told her about this? Of course. Because after the defeat on the Heptastadion, he had decided to abandon her. She could not believe he could be so timid. Was this how the legend had been carved?

She looked back at Ptolemy. Even in her dismay she could feel almost sorry for him. She knew what he was thinking: How would Arsinoë receive him, as her sibling and her king or as her deadly rival, and immediately have him killed? His lower lip quivered, as if he'd been smacked by his tutor for slowness; which, in a way, he had.

And in this way, she thought, Caesar sets both our destinies.

She stood mute in her humiliation, staring back at her brother, who seemed almost to be looking at her for guidance. She could not comprehend this Roman's treachery. But she would not give way to anger—it had no point and was beneath her dignity as a queen. Why should Caesar protect her, after all? He had allowed himself to be drawn into a conflict for which he was totally unprepared. Perhaps he had fallen victim to overconfidence after his defeat of Pompey. He no doubt intended to return to Alexandria with a more significant force at a later date and settle scores with the Egyptians. By then she would be dead, if Arsinoë had her way.

"The arrangements have been made," Caesar said to the boy. "You will leave at noon."

But Ptolemy just stood there.

"Do you not wish to hurry on your way?"

"I like it well enough here," Ptolemy said, fear making him bold.

"I have told you, what you like is of no consequence." His voice grew stern. "You have your duty. A king does not skulk around his palace when there are matters of state to be performed. Now go."

She thought Ptolemy was going to cry. He seemed about to say something else, but Caesar dismissed him with a wave of the hand. Ptolemy gave her a last look, as if she could somehow rescue him from his fate, then rushed from the room.

〽 〽

Perhaps Caesar knew she was standing there the whole time, for as soon as Ptolemy was gone he looked up at her and smiled. "Good morning, kitten."

I will not give him the pleasure of seeing me grovel or rage, she thought. I will be calm, even in this betrayal. "Did the Imperator sleep well," she said, "untroubled by his conscience?"

"Indeed he did."

"You know my brother won't be back?"

"Of course."

She watched his face, searching for the clues to his intent. Clearly, he was not going to explain himself further. He wanted her to fathom it for herself.

He was still smiling, as if he thought himself inordinately clever. Well, he undoubtedly was. She forced herself to think deeper about what she had just seen and heard. Perhaps she had been too quick to judge him.

After a while it came to her. "You have sent him to his death," she said.

Caesar nodded as if humbly acknowledging the applause of the Senate.

She realized she had underestimated the mendacity of this Roman. He was playing a double game; if Arsinoë had Ptolemy murdered, then she, Cleopatra, need no longer share the throne with her difficult brother. She would rule alone, as Caesar's client. If Arsinoë was unable or unwilling to murder him, then Ptolemy would no doubt seize the opportunity to ride ahead of the ragged army assembled outside the gates. And Caesar himself would then kill Ptolemy as a rebel.

Further, he had led Ptolemy to believe that he wished to quit Egypt, that he was at a disadvantage; a weakness her brother would think to exploit. The heart of it was, Caesar wanted Ptolemy to attack him so he could in turn have just cause to kill him.

"You want to control Egypt, but you have to be able to justify your actions in front of the Roman Senate," she said.

"Your tutor was right about you when he said you had a quick mind. You learn very fast. I shall have to take care you do not overtake me one day."

"You still have to defeat his army."

The smile fell away. It was clear that his pride would not wait long to be avenged. "I will not be caught on the Heptastadion a second time." The wolfish smile returned as quickly as it had faded. "And what about you? Will you play the widow and throw your jewels on his pyre?"

"He is only a boy," she heard herself say.

"Who, if left to nature and his own devices, would one day grow up to be a man and a prince of Egypt. If he had any sense at all, he would know he has to die."

She closed her eyes. I wonder if I could learn to be this ruthless? Something in her nature rebelled at this final, brutal, necessary act. "I wish this were over," she said.

"It is never over, kitten," he said to her, his voice suddenly gloomy. "If you wish to order the affairs of the world, it is never, ever, over."

24

CANDLES FLICKERED ON the finely carved candelabra. The wall drapes, dyed with Tyrian purple and edged with gold brocade, shivered in the draughts. Outside in the darkness the waves crashed against the rocks, the wind moaned and howled around the palace walls.

Caesar tapped a finger on the map spread on the table in front of him. "My Syrian ally, Mithradates, has taken Pelusium and now marches to the Delta. Your sister and her pretty boy general Ganimedes have taken their forces to face him."

"You will wait for him to relieve the siege?"

Caesar's lips curled in contempt. As if he would endure such ignominy as to wait to be rescued by some primped foreign satrap, half Greek, half Gaul. "When the weather breaks I shall take the Thirty-seventh Legion and sail east to join with Mithradates just beyond the farthest branch of the Nile, near the Sea of Reeds. Your sister and her ponce will meet their accounting there."

And so it will end, she thought, with Roman soldiers again marching into Alexandria. Her father had paid for his throne, and Roman force of arms had secured it for him. Now she had been forced to play the same game. If Caesar wished, he could reduce Egypt to a Roman province like Greece or Syria or Judaea.

No wonder her father had spent most of his life in the service of Bacchus. Perhaps he was disappointed with himself and his own timidity, or else he understood the futility of being a prince in a world of Romans, and wished only for the world beyond.

This Julius Caesar was everything to her now, her savior, her lover, her enemy, and, though he did not yet know it, the father of her child.

She had known it these last few weeks, known it in her heart even before the bleedings stopped and she felt the tenderness and swelling in her breasts. She had to remind herself that it was what she wanted, that the child growing in her belly was the political solution she had set her sails toward. Her son—it had to be a son—would be half Rome, half Egypt, the only bloodline that could secure her throne and her country's future. But there was also an abiding sadness in her now. The scepter of Isis was a heavy burden for the Cleopatra who was also woman and mother. That woman was a frailer, simpler creature, a woman who wanted only for the father of her child to love her and protect her. And at that moment it seemed a more forlorn wish than the mere survival of Egypt.

Caesar threw himself down on a couch, citrus wood inlaid with yellow jasper and red carnelian stones, draped with Indian silk. A flaxen-haired German slave scurried across the room with a footstool. Cleopatra noticed that the hardened veteran of a hundred battles was becoming accustomed to the little luxuries of the Brucheion.

"What news from Arsinoë's camp?" she asked him. She hated this utter helplessness, having to rely on him for all her news of the outside world. She was trapped here on the Lochias without her advisers, without her spies, without power to act against her enemies or assist her supporters. All she could do for the present was wait and hope that Caesar was triumphant.

If I survive this and regain the throne of Egypt, she promised herself, I will never again allow another man to decide my fate. Especially not a Roman.

The cold blue eyes settled on her. "You will be pleased to hear that the son of Egypt is safe. My spies report that your sister's loyal troops carried him through their ranks on a litter. He has denounced Caesar, his dearest friend, as a barbarian, and you, his own flesh and blood, he labels a whore and a traitor. But you look surprised."

"I thought Arsinoë would have him killed, like Achillas. She is not as murderous as I thought."

"It is good when our family surprises us."

"They must know they cannot win."

"Or else they are prepared to die for their principles."

"Are you saying I have none?"

"I am saying, what good are they? Speaking for myself, the question of principle has never bothered me. Ask any of my friends, their bankers, or their wives. They will tell you."

Was it a slur? Did he think of her merely as an opportunist, a time server? Or did he seek to compliment her, had he seen in her the same penchant for ruthlessness that proscribed his own character? "You underestimate me if you think I do not love Egypt," she said.

"Egypt is just a desert with a river running through it. Love yourself. *Your* contours are far more interesting."

She was not in the mood for his wit. She went out onto the terrace, hugging his bearskin cloak tightly around her body. The northern gales were sweeping across the breakwaters, foam shining like phosphorus on the rocks below. Another massive wave hurled itself against the rocks at the base of the Pharos, throwing up a great wall of spray as high as the marble colonnades. Winter, and beset on all sides.

If the weather did not break soon, Caesar might yet be deprived of his victory.

He came to stand behind her. "What is on your mind?" he said.

"There is something I have to tell you."

He waited.

"I am going to have a child. Your child."

A raised eyebrow. Was this the only reaction her news warranted from him? She waited for something better.

He put a finger to his lips, as if deep in thought. She wanted him to hold her, like an ordinary man holds his woman at such news, but that was not his way. The only time he ever touched her was a prelude to taking her.

She imagined she knew what he was thinking. He had only one heir, a daughter, Julia. There might indeed be a horde of other spawn, as Mardian had once put it, left around the palaces of the Mediterranean like bodies after a skirmish. But this was different. If she, the Queen of Egypt, had a son by Caesar, such progeny might not as easily be ignored, dismissed as collateral damage after a battle. After all, a son by her and Caesar would be heir to Egypt, and perhaps, conceivably, heir to Rome also.

"A gift from the gods," he murmured finally.

"Indeed," she said. "A gift of the gods, for the gods."

Hold me, she thought. Show me some sign that this news is a joy to you. She wanted to weep from frustration, but her pride would not allow it. He would never see her pain, she had promised herself that much. It was her only power over him.

He stood there on the terrace, wearing only his tunic. It had started to rain, the drops hurled with force by the wind like a shower of stones. But he did not seem to feel the cold, this man. "You think I am a god?" he said.

"I know that *I* am."

"You have given me something to think about, kitten."

"Do you not wish to hold me?" she murmured.

He hesitated. For a moment she thought he might be about to soften. But then he said, "Your condition is delicate," and turned and went back inside.

25

Egyptian month of Phamenoth,
forty-seven years before the birth of Jesus Christ

OVER THE GLARING white of the palace roofs, she could see the people streaming toward the city gates. Three centuries after Alexander, the city had a new conqueror. All along the Canopic Way the mob that had hurled insults and stones from the barricades through the long winter now knelt in submission under the great marble colonnades as Caesar rode back into the city at the head of his legions. He was met with the silence of the defeated, just a few moans of despair to be heard over the rhythmic tramp of heavy Roman boots.

The city elders met him at the Gate of the Sun, barefoot and dressed in the blue linen robes of mourning, throwing dust over their heads as a sign of their contrition. They chanted the dirge of the defeated: "Mercy O Son of Amun! We submit, we bend our necks and backs before you, Mighty Conqueror!"

Good to see these Greeks grovel, she thought. Even the courtiers, the Kinsmen and First Friends and the rest of the backstabbers, had their faces in the dirt. The fat merchants, their fingers bulging with jaspers and emeralds, were there, too, down on their knees alongside the Egyptians and Syrians and Phoenicians and the rest, the mud wallowers and embalmers, goldsmiths and bakers, barge captains and glass blowers. Only the

Jews were not required to bend their necks. Their quarter had stayed quiet during the war and they had smuggled food into the palace for the Romans. Caesar had rewarded them with the freedom of the city.

Caesar, as always, had been lucky. Tyche, Goddess of Fortune, must have fallen for his charm, as so many other women before her. The weather had broken for him, sun and clouds bending before the will of a god, allowing him to sail his fleet out of the harbor as he had planned. But he had not sailed to meet Mithradates, as he told Cleopatra he would. Knowing Arsinoë's spies would be watching his departure from the city, he had sailed east, as if making for Pelusium. But under cover of darkness he had ordered the fleet to turn around and instead landed his legion west of the city. He then force-marched them to the south, encircling the pirates and ruffians that Achillas had once called an army. Caught between Mithradates's levies and Caesar's legions, the mercenaries tried to flee through the papyrus swamps and were ruthlessly cut down in the mud, their bodies left as bloody feast for the crocodiles. Ptolemy's boat overturned and he sank, drowned by the weight of his own gold armor.

❦ ❦

He reached the palace at twilight.

She was waiting for him in the courtyard behind the Hall of Pillars, surrounded by her new bodyguard, Roman legionaries of Caesar's own choosing, in their distinctive leather armor, short stabbing swords in scabbards on their belts, red scarves knotted at the neck below their helmets.

The only sounds were the crackle of the torches, the murmur of the fountains in the court.

Caesar was riding at the head of a cohort of his bodyguard, astride a white stallion. He wore his ceremonial armor, a gold breastplate engraved with past deeds, the purple cloak of Imperator, a laurel wreath on his head. He looked down at her and smiled. She returned the smile, surprised at how relieved she was to see his face again.

Soldiers with long spears and large, rectangular shields marched beside a cart, drawn by two oxen. The metal-rimmed wheels rumbled on the stones.

Ptolemy lay in the back of the wagon, his body uncovered so all Alexandria could see that he was dead and no pretender could ever arise from the marshes of the Nile and claim to be heir. Her little brother was pale and bloated like a fish, eyes half lidded as if caught asleep. Mud and slime oozed from his nose. There was a rank smell about him. The body would not last much longer.

"He died well," Caesar said to her.

She looked up. He was standing beside her, his face thrown half in shadow by the torches. How can a man die well? she wondered. Death is death.

"In the end he put on armor and tried to fight like a man," Caesar said.

He put on the armor because it was gold, she thought bitterly, and he did not want to lose it. But she said nothing.

She had played dice with him as a child in this courtyard, she remembered. He had always cheated. She made the effort now, but discovered she could not summon grief for her brother. As Ptolemies, they had been born as adversaries, not as kin. She had despised him in life; in death, she despised him still.

⚭ ⚭

And now for Arsinoë.

She was dragged into the Hall of Adoration by two legionaries, screeching like a cat. Caesar had summoned the court to watch this, the Greeks in their fine robes, the shaven-headed priests, the secretaries and schemers and treasurers, all herded into the hall like goats to witness the final humiliation of the Ptolemies. Cleopatra was seated beside Caesar on the dais, on a throne of ivory and ebony covered with a purple cushion.

Arsinoë twisted and spat, her screams echoing around the great marbled hall. She was barefoot, her wrists chained in front of her, her face spattered with dried mud. Her sister, whom Cleopatra had always feared and resented for her beauty, now looked as filthy as any crone in the markets selling her husband's fish.

Her clothes were ragged and stinking. Even the Nubian guards twitched their nostrils at the stench. Some of the pretty boys went so far as to cover their faces with their hands.

Ganimedes was with her. He, too, was almost unrecognizable, his finery lost under a thick layer of fetid swamp mud.

Caesar turned to Cleopatra. "Your enemies," he said.

She felt nothing. She is not my family, she thought. My family is Egypt.

Ganimedes, on his knees, dried black blood congealed over an ugly gash across his forehead, stared resolutely at the floor. Arsinoë was made of sterner stuff.

"You whore!" she screamed. There was a fleck of spittle loose at the corner of her mouth. "You have betrayed Egypt to this Roman!"

"As you can see, your little sister has missed you," Caesar said.

Cleopatra realized he was enjoying this. It was his moment, after all. For her own part, she felt nothing for her sister, as she had felt nothing for Ptolemy's corpse. She was queen now, without dispute. Caesar had committed himself.

"You stinking whore!" the mud-spattered creature at her feet screeched up at her.

If I am ever brought to these straits, Cleopatra thought, I shall never beg or rage like this. What good does it do? You have gambled and you have lost, sister. I thought you should bear your defeat with better grace.

"Take her away," Caesar said to his guards, and Arsinoë was dragged, frothing and screaming, from the chamber. Ganimedes followed, as compliant as a lamb.

26

MARDIAN REGARDED HER in the manner of a tutor with a pupil he had once despaired of, who had finally shown the application and aptitude he knew all along was there. He approached the throne and touched his head to the marble. A slave helped him rise.

His chiton was filthy and he had lost weight. No skeleton, to be certain, but still a shock to see him so reduced. She wondered what privations he had endured since the last time they had seen each other, before her departure from Mount Kasios.

They were alone in the private audience chamber of the apartments she shared with Caesar. Her poor *tropheus* looked shabby and frankly out of place among the jeweled couches and Arabian silks.

"Majesty," he murmured.

"I am happy to gaze on your fat chops once more, Mardian."

"And I am relieved and overjoyed to find Your Majesty . . ."

"In one piece?"

"In good health."

"Your brother-in-law gave me good service."

"There have been so many rumors. Many times they said you were dead."

"Well, I have survived and I remain in the good graces of Rome. It seems Isis has smiled on our endeavors."

"I never thought to see this day." He hesitated. He raised his eyes to hers, as if looking for some evidence of change.

Oh, I know what this fussy old hen is thinking, she thought. "Say it, Mardian."

"I do not wish to presume."

"Presume anyway."

A deep breath, and then, in a mumble: "They say Caesar is in love with you."

"Whenever Caesar is in a room with a woman, he is in love. But I think I have impressed him more with my intelligence than any of those parts of a woman's body that can be bought for a few coins in Canopus." He colored at this indelicacy, which delighted her. "You survived the rigors of the desert."

"But barely. The Nabataeans deserted a few days after you left. Then your own irregulars started to drift away. Seeing us reduced, Achillas finally emerged from his fort. We were forced to flee farther into the desert. I thought I should die there."

Poor Mardian. Before this, his idea of an emergency was to run out of his favorite perfume.

"Well, you are here now," she said to him. "So now we must get to work. Summon the litters. We shall inspect our city and see what has to be done after these wars."

❧ ❧

The extent of the destruction was heartbreaking. Caesar had said once that there was a beauty to war, but it seemed to her that war, like fire, could only be thought lovely from a distance. At close hand there was nothing splendid about it.

Her beautiful Alexandria lay in ruins. The facades of the great buildings along the Canopus Way had been torn down to build barricades. The mob had vandalized the Museion, even the Temple of Neptune. The great porticos of the Gymnasium, with their gold-fretted roofs of massive cedarwood beams, were gone, too, torn down by the mob for use in the barricades.

The waterfront where Caesar had fired Achillas's ships was a mass of charred timbers and rubble. Thousands of *volumina* in one of the warehouses, intended for the Library, had been caught in the conflagration and were destroyed.

In the Brucheion itself the pristine gypsum walls of some of the palace buildings had been blackened by smoke, and the stables, baths, and cisterns had all been damaged in the fighting.

She felt depressed. They could rebuild but not replace what had been destroyed, such as the long timbers that had graced the porticos of the Gymnasium. They had been fashioned from cedarwoods in the Lebanon and the Atlas Mountains in Mauretania, trees that no longer grew to such fantastic girth and height. Those massive and unique beams had gone up in flames in one of the street riots.

These Romans. They left behind a trail of ruins and ashes wherever they went, as if the world had an inexhaustible supply of beauty for them to despoil, as if beauty itself could go on and on forever.

※　※

For the first time since his arrival in the autumn of the previous year, Caesar was free to visit the city he had conquered. His first request was for her to take him to Alexander's tomb, beneath the gleaming white marble dome of the Soma.

She had always found it a frightening place, that long descent down echoing stone steps into the vault, where the smell of mold and decay was unmistakable beneath the sweet layers of incense. The mummified body of the Invincible lay in a domed crystal sarcophagus, the oil lamps surrounding the tomb reflected in his golden armor. All around the sarcophagus were banks of votive offerings, wine from the rich, bread from the poor, masses of flowers, some withered with age, others still freshly blooming.

The Great One could have been a statue. His hands were crossed on his breast, his golden hair spread around his head like flax. The skin had been highlighted with cosmetics, to give it a more natural hue, but beneath the embalmer's artistry the skin was like parchment. One of the nostrils was gone, knocked off by accident, it was said, by one of her ancestors.

Caesar was overwhelmed by what he saw. He had taken no more than a few steps into the chamber when he gasped and fell to his knees.

She was astonished. It was the first time she had seen him in awe of anything. He is human after all, she thought. And what he most reveres is my own bloodline. Perhaps I have a greater hold on this man than I believe.

For a long time he did not speak. Finally, he said: "He was far younger than me when he died, and yet he had conquered half the world."

"You are greater than he is," she whispered.

"How can I be greater? When I compare myself to him, I have achieved nothing."

"But you are still alive. Alexander is dead."

That seemed to cheer him slightly.

"Any Roman who wishes to call himself great must emulate Alexander. He must go to the East and conquer Parthia, as he did."

"That is a fool's dream."

"No," Caesar said to her. "Babylon is Rome's destiny."

At the time, she thought nothing of what he said. She shivered in the chill of the tomb and longed for the light. But there would be many moments in the years to come when she would think again of what Caesar said to her that morning, and finally the prophetic words would return to haunt her.

Any Roman who wishes to call himself great must emulate Alexander. He must go to the East and conquer Parthia, as he did.

〜 〜

When they left the tomb, Cleopatra ordered that their litters return to the palace by way of the docks at Rhakotis.

"There is something I wish to show you," she said to him.

Despite the damage from the "Alexandrian wars," as Caesar now called them, most of the warehouses along the harbor front remained intact, guarded from the mob, even at the height of the fighting, by a detachment of the Macedonian Guard. They were the property of whoever ruled Egypt. Achillas might have allowed the rioters to tear down the Gymnasium, but he was not about to let them destroy the prize he was fighting for.

They descended from the litters and, their bodyguards and retinues trailing after them, Cleopatra showed him the treasures of Egypt.

Caesar followed her through one cavernous warehouse after another, like a man in a trance; first the granaries, with their thick limestone walls, heavy iron doors locked and bolted from the inside, the interiors in a permanent twilight of choking golden dust, veritable mountains of wheat or barley or millet piled to the ceilings, guarded from the mice and rats by an army of cats. It was as if the cat-goddess Bastet peered down at them everywhere, from the rafters, from the corners, golden eyes gleaming in the darkness.

She watched his face. Every year Rome had to import wheat, it never had enough to feed its own people. Here there was enough to feed the entire Mediterranean.

Afterward she showed him the spice warehouse, a great square building with heavily armed guards posted at the doors and at every ventilation vent. Inside, sunlight pierced the gloom in narrow yellow shafts, the air a golden haze piquant with choking, overpowering aromas. Even Caesar gaped at the magnitude of it, the countless wooden crates containing cardamom, cinnamon, and pepper, the bulging jute sacks of saffron, cumin, turmeric, aniseed, and coriander. She watched his face, knew what he was thinking: an unimaginable fortune just in this one building.

There were separate warehouses for the oils, inside each one rows and rows of amphorae, like fat old women, snug in their beds of straw; sesame oil, linseed oil, and of course olive oil, used everywhere in the world for cooking and in lamps.

"As queen I hold the monopoly for all of this," she whispered to him as they returned to the sunshine. "It is the queen who tells the peasants how much to plant, and the products are pressed in my factories. All that oil is mine. It is Cleopatra's grain that feeds the Mediterranean, and the tax on wheat is twenty million bushels a year. And there is so much you haven't seen. My papyrus plants make paper for the whole world. I have a monopoly on wool, a quarter share on all fish and honey sold in Egypt, a third share of all the grapes. I have salt and natron pits. I have gold mines in the south. I take a twelve percent duty on all goods that go up the Nile—"

"Stop," he murmured, overwhelmed. "Why are you showing me all this? Do you think there are not Romans enough who covet Egypt already?"

"I am not concerned with other Romans," she said. "Just the one who would be like Alexander if only he had the money to do it."

He stared at her. There was a new respect in his eyes, and for the first time something else: fear. Until now, despite all his ambition, he had yet remained a Roman. Now she had offered a glimpse of something more. The reason Egypt had alone stayed free of the Roman yoke was that the Roman Senate would not allow any one man control over Egypt, for that Roman might then no longer need Rome. But now here was Egypt herself, no longer resisting, but lying down and parting her thighs for him, whispering to him to forget Rome and do as he wished.

❦   ❦

"There should be a new coronation," she said to Mardian.

He looked doubtful. "You have already assumed the throne, Majesty, in the Serapion and at Memphis."

"Then a wedding."

"A wedding?"

"We must tie our Caesar a little more tightly to Egypt."

"Are the Romans not already close enough?"

"What the mob in the city sees right now is Caesar as our conqueror. What they hear in the *chora* is the tramp of Roman boots. We must rebuild Cleopatra as we have set to rebuilding Alexandria. They must see me as his consort, not his dupe. It is the one advantage I have over my father. He could not marry a Roman general."

"He could think about it," Mardian murmured. The Piper's fondness for catamites was not unkown. She rebuked him with a glance.

"We must put on a show, Mardian. The world loves a theater. In this theater, I shall be Isis and Caesar shall be Amun, the bull-god, the god of fertility. In Rome, no doubt, they will see Caesar as my patron and Cleopatra as his client queen. But here in the Two Lands we must be gods, Mardian, for that is what the people want, and that is what they must see; Isis and Amun come together to bring a new era of prosperity to Egypt. We will take our little theater to the *chora,* and then we will never again have to spend another night in a tent!"

"You will not fool the mob in the street or the Kinsmen at court."

"I do not care to. I have Caesar's legions behind me now, so they will not dare challenge me again. And with the *chora* and its granaries in my hand, they will court me even if they do not love me."

Mardian looked at her as if seeing her for the first time. "It is a bold vision, Majesty."

"I know my destiny, Mardian. It is not just to change Egypt. Cleopatra is going to change the world."

Mardian gave her the patronizing smile she had seen her father's secretaries bestow on him countless times. He did not believe she could do it, could not even conceive of what she planned. Well, he would catch up with her one day, that fat brain huffing and puffing behind her.

She knew what Caesar planned, a pliant queen, his own private fiefdom, a proxy rule in Egypt, playing her off against his own Senate. Caesar believed in destiny; it had persuaded her also. But although she now saw her destiny as inextricably linked with his, her vision was not quite the same. She knew that she now bore, in her womb, not just a child, but a dynasty. If Mardian knew what she was thinking, she imagined he would have swooned away.

27

SHE WAS SURE that Caesar, for all his fifty-one years, had never sailed on a boat such as this. The *thalamegos,* the state barge of the Ptolemies, was as large as a quadrireme warship, half a stadion from the sweetly curved stern to the bow, which itself was carved from Lebanese cedar into the shape of a lotus flower. There were six banks of oars, banqueting salons, even a garden. The cabins and bedrooms had been paneled with sweet-smelling cedar and cypress woods, there was a banqueting salon, shrines to Venus and Dionysus and, of course, Isis. Although the furniture was Greek, the walls were painted with murals in gold leaf and lapis lazuli after the Egyptian style, featuring many of the old Nile gods, Sobek and Bastet and Cleopatra's personal symbol, Horus and Isis.

Out of respect for Caesar's feelings, however, she had the bedroom she would share with him repainted, choosing a frieze depicting scenes from Homer's *Iliad*. The apartment was richly appointed with gilt-edged polished mirrors, coral- and carnelian-encrusted chairs, a cedarwood table inlaid with ivory, and a bed of precious ebony, trimmed with gold leaf and with a coverlet of purple silk.

They set out from Lake Mareotis, and it seemed that almost the entire population of Alexandria lined the docks to watch their departure. Today, she thought, is my true coronation. From this moment it is clear to everyone that I am the true Queen of Egypt once more, and my patron the most powerful man in the world. With Ptolemy dead and Arsinoë in chains, there will be no more challengers for the throne of Egypt.

The dangers for me now lie across the ocean, in Rome.

〜 〜

The sails whipped in the desultory river breeze as the royal barge glided through the moist green heart of the Delta, past the waterwheels and vineyards, mud banks and bullrushes, fields green with barley and beans, the flat-roofed mud-brick villages baking under the date palms. The backs of the Nubians shone as they bent over the great ebony oars, their silver tips flashing in the sunlight. Behind them was a massive caravan of four hundred Liburnians, the greatest fleet perhaps the Nile had ever seen, carrying their escort, two of Caesar's legions.

People streamed from the houses to stand knee deep in the redblack mud at the riverbanks to watch this once-in-a-lifetime spectacle, the passing of the great gods Isis and Amun, reclining together on golden couches under a fringed silken canopy, attended by servants wearing the fillets and kilts of the ancient times, beautiful naked boys with jeweled fans.

A show of force, a theater of splendor. Look on me, Egypt, and see how powerful I am now.

⟐ ⟐

They left behind the endless, verdant green of the Delta, and the valley became a strip of green ribbon on either side of the river, the bleached wilderness of the desert sometimes far in the distance, other times reaching within a stadion of the river itself.

Everywhere there were people, staring in awe at this astonishing spectacle. Unlike cosmopolitan Alexandria, here the faces were all alike, the same hair, the same clothes, the same nut-brown, hawklike faces.

They moored at the riverbanks near Memphis, watched the sun dip below the violet rim of the desert and the great white wall of Zoser's temple. Caesar gazed in awe at the great stepped pyramid of Saqqara, silhouetted against a deepening sky, and asked her who had built such monuments. The pyramids were as old as Egypt, she told him, as old as time itself. Like the desert and the mountains.

She had thought the journey and its shared triumph, the knowledge of the child she was bearing, would bring her closer to him. Instead it served only to drive a schism between them. Her condition was not yet evident, but even the gentle rocking of the barge often left her weak with nausea and confined her belowdecks in solitary misery. Worse, she no longer trusted her own emotions and was subject to bouts of weeping, which she endured in the privacy of her cabin.

I will not let that Roman see me cry.

⟐ ⟐

As they traveled south, huge cliffs rose from the desert, ash-white in the heat of midday, purple at sunset. They reached the ancient town of Thebes, the City of a Hundred Gates, where the ancient pharaohs had sculpted their tombs from the searing rock. As the barge drifted past, they saw a hippopotamus watching them from the water, just its ears and pig snout above the surface. Behind it the pylons and lotus stem colonnades of ancient temples rose above the dom-palms. Women swayed along dusty paths with water jars on their heads, crocodiles slept on sandbanks or slithered splashing into the blood-warm water, alarmed and excited by their approach.

When they left Alexandria the weather had been cool and mild, the sandalwood braziers still burning in the palace at night. But as they sailed farther upriver the days became searing hot, the skies a fierce and unending blue.

As night fell, the mists rose from the papyrus marshes and thousands of insects darted about the oil lamps. The temperature dropped rapidly and the brilliant stars were cold. Cleopatra stood with Caesar on the deck of the royal barge, shivering inside her cloak.

Caesar seemed unperturbed by cold or heat. He had on the same tunic he had worn through the miserable heat of the day, brown arms and legs bare to the elements. He seemed consumed by his own thoughts.

That day, they had been met at the landing by priests from the local temple, brown heads shaved, wearing the white robes of Isis. The landing and the avenue to the pylons of the temple forecourt had been thronged with people, ordinary fellahin as well as Nubians, Arabs, even a few Greeks. As she stepped off the royal barge, they fell to their knees and touched their heads to the ground. She had been borne on a litter along an avenue of sphinxes to the dirge of the priests and the rattle of a thousand systrums.

The day's events seemed to have moved him. So, we have finally impressed Caesar, she thought.

"Today, when we arrived here, they treated you as if you were a goddess," he said.

"As Queen of Egypt, I am a goddess. Perhaps not in Alexandria, but here in the *chora,* and to the priests, I am the incarnation of Isis herself."

He frowned. Such sentiments did not sit well with his Roman upbringing. Yet she could tell that there were aspects to it that deeply attracted him. "Men cannot be gods. Nor women, either."

"That is not what they believe. They say you are the incarnation of Amun, the god of fertility."

He smiled at that. "None of my wives think so. I have been married four times and I have just one daughter to show for it. Hardly divine."

Indeed. But in my belly perhaps I have the son you must crave. He will wed me to you, one way or another. Both as a prince and as a man. "You are fertile enough in Egypt. Perhaps rich seed needs rich soil."

He made no answer to that.

"I imagine you would like to see all Rome drop down on their knees for you, as the priests did for me today."

"That is sacrilege."

"But it is tempting, isn't it?"

He turned away from her, refused to be drawn on what he was thinking. The mud-brick dome of a Nilometer rose above the black outlines of the palm trees. Beyond it was the dark shape of another island, beyond Philae, the pylons of another temple silhouetted against the night sky.

"What place is that?" Caesar asked her.

"That is Biggeh, where Osiris is said to be buried. He is brother to Isis and also her husband."

"So that is where you get such . . . practices." There was contempt in his voice.

"An Egyptian will say: 'If it is law for the gods, why cannot it be law for us?'"

"You believe that?"

"I believe that if a Ptolemy is to rule Egypt and help her regain her glories, then that king or queen must first make Egypt a part of themselves. You think too much like a Roman to understand Egypt."

"You are not Egyptian either. You are Greek."

"My blood is Greek, but my family has ruled here three hundred years. Part of me is Egypt now."

His face was like stone. "Tell me the story of these gods."

She took a breath, wondering where to begin. The gods were not easy to understand. "Osiris was once a great king," she said. "He brought writing and agriculture and the arts to the earth and transformed humanity from barbarism to civilization. He won mastery over all the lands of the earth, not with arms and war, but with persuasive discourse, and song and music. His wife Isis was renowned for her fidelity and self-sacrifice. But their brother Seth was jealous of Osiris and murdered him. Then he cut his body into fourteen pieces and scattered the parts all over Egypt. Osiris's wife, Our Lady

Isis, scoured the land to find the pieces of his body. She found them all except one, the phallus. By piecing them together she bestowed on her husband the gift of eternal life. She spent just one last night with him before he traveled to the underworld, and from that magical union she conceived a child, Horus. When Horus grew up, he took revenge on Seth, and killed him, and took back the throne of Egypt. Now Osiris rules the realm of the dead, but Isis remains the giver of life, the Great Mother, the goddess of love and compassion."

"How can a man give a woman a child without his manhood intact?"

"He was a god," she answered simply.

She wondered if he could understand. There were temples to Isis in Rome, of course. Like most Romans, he no doubt considered the Great Mother just a goddess for women, her temples sanctuaries for prostitutes and love trysts. His gods were Jupiter and Mars, the gods of valor and war. Could he understand redemption and resurrection? Could he understand that to the Egyptians he himself was now Osiris incarnate?

"So now she has a temple next to his burial place," he said.

"Every ten days the golden statue of Isis we have just seen is ferried over in a sacred barge to visit her beloved husband."

"Her brother," he murmured. His voice was heavy with contempt and revulsion.

"Not all the world can be as pure as Rome," she said, and by the look on his face she saw that she had made her point.

He was quiet for a long time. She listened to the boom and tonk of the frogs in the marsh. Then he said, abruptly: "Have you considered marriage?"

She stared back at him. Her heart leaped in her chest like a girl's. Ever since she knew his child was growing inside her, she had considered nothing else. She composed herself before replying, hoping she had not allowed her eagerness to show itself.

"Marriage?" she said, trying to sound disinterested. Somewhere a night heron cried in a thicket of papyrus reeds.

"You were right what you said, that Caesar thinks too much like a Roman. I must think like an Egyptian, like you. So it seems to me that to keep the people from becoming restive, you should marry young Antiochus. That is the Egyptian way, is it not?"

Oh, you steaming heap of crocodile dung. You are going to betray me yet again.

"Antiochus is only twelve years old."

"It hardly matters. It will prevent other young bloods from setting their eyes on you and on Egypt."

"I do not need Antiochus to rule here."

"But you have just told me that marrying one's brother is the way of the gods, so how can it not be the way for you? A queen cannot rule alone. Without a husband, foreign princes will come courting you."

"I am carrying your child!"

"You think people will suspect it is your brother's?"

"I think everyone in Alexandria knows why my belly is full!"

He smiled, the easy smile of a man who thinks he has found the solution for all his problems. And, of course, he had. Why was she surprised by this latest ploy? Marrying an Egyptian queen would complicate his life needlessly. This was the simplest solution, for him.

Besides, had she not got what she wanted? Would she behave like a spoiled princeling, like Arsinoë or Ptolemy, and stamp her foot because her life was not perfectly ordered? Caesar was merely protecting his investment as he saw fit.

For her, the baby in her belly was the chance to create the greatest dynasty the world had ever seen. For him, it was just another bastard offspring.

"So, that is settled," he said.

What choice was there? She could defy him. And he could as easily make Antiochus his creature here in Egypt, instead of her. He had still given her no clue as to what he felt about the child she carried for him.

I adore this man and he does not care for me at all.

"Are we agreed?" he repeated.

"If that is what you would have me do," she answered coldly.

"You may take lovers as you wish, of course."

"The Queen of Egypt may not disport herself as recklessly as a Roman general."

"One of your pretty slave boys, perhaps?"

"Unlikely. Whenever I call for one, they are playing the catamite to a centurion."

"You have a wicked tongue."

"But I live a blameless life. That is the difference between you and me."

She was rewarded with a smile. And that was all.

⌇⌇   ⌇⌇

Long after Caesar had retired for the night, she sat alone on the deck, listening to the slap of the water against the sides of the barge. She felt the stirring in her womb. She watched the stars tilt above the earth and wondered again at how Caesar had outmaneuvered her. *Marry Antiochus!*

She had much to learn from him.

Perhaps a compromise would have been enough for her father. It always seemed to be. She had her throne, albeit she must share it with her younger brother, and she had the protection of Rome. Of course, she did not yet know what Caesar's patronage would cost her, although she could guess. No doubt when Caesar brought his legions east to invade Parthia, following in the steps of Alexander, Egypt would be asked to pay for Caesar's glory.

Yes, the Piper would have settled for that. But I am not my father, she thought, I will be Queen of Egypt by my own right, not just by Caesar's. He still thinks me just a flighty girl, a willing vessel for one man's seed, a banker's chest for his aspirations. But I will yet save Egypt from this bastard's designs.

Oh, he has had many women as he has had me. Married four times, by his own admission, each time for reasons either of money or political alliance, according to Mardian. Well, he does not yet know it but I shall give his ambition the thickest stand of any of them, for when Cleopatra opens her legs, she has Egypt between them and the fruit will be the whole world.

I have held this man's balls in bed. One day, she promised herself, I shall hold them in fact, and the juice I squeeze from them shall feed the thirst of my family and my Egyptians for peace.

⌇⌇   ⌇⌇

But as she lay in her bed that night, she found herself tossing and turning in her quest for sleep. In the darkness it was harder to hold her grip on the purposeful and vengeful queen who would use any weapon to save her nation and her ambition. A mosquito whined endlessly about the silk curtain around her bed, as persistent and elusive as the voice in her head, wailing like an untried girl: *Why won't he love me?*

28

ON THEIR RETURN to Alexandria there was urgent news waiting for Caesar. He spent all day locked away with his officers, receiving messengers, reading reports. The news, she was told, was all bad. Well, she thought, bad news for Caesar is not necessarily bad news for me. She herself was kept busy with Mardian, locked away in her private audience chamber, choosing her new ministers and secretaries, preparing to once again assume the government of Egypt.

That evening she found Caesar in the banqueting room he had commandeered for his personal use during the siege, seated at the long ivory and rosewood table that had once been layered with charts and maps. A table lamp had been lit, the tiny lamps on its bronze arms throwing his face into mottled shadow. There were scrolls scattered across the table and littering the floor at his feet. He looked desperately tired.

A cool breeze off the sea billowed in the silk curtains and sent the flames in the oil lamps guttering. From somewhere in the palace came the sound of soft music, flutes and lyres, an evening symposia in progress. Beyond the windows the bright beacon of the lighthouse reflected on the rippled waters of the royal harbor.

He looked up as she entered. "Caesar is gone from Rome for a few months and the entire world convulses."

"You have to leave?" she asked him. She was surprised at her own reaction, a surge of relief but also of disappointment. *Why do I feel this way? Is this not what I wanted, to take control of my Egypt again without this manipulator and bully in the way? To her disgust, she suspected that this worthless Roman bastard* had charmed her. And the woman in her wanted him there when she presented him with his son. It had to be a son!

"I have already stayed too long," Caesar was saying. "The Thirty-seventh Legion that came to my aid from Pontus was my salvation but the people's ruin. The inhabitants there have taken advantage of the legion's absence to slaughter the entire Roman population. Meanwhile Pompey's sons gather on the shores of Carthage to make more mischief for me. Even in Italy there is trouble. The veterans have mutinied in the country, while Marcus Antonius sits on his ass and watches the mob rioting in the Forum. So you see, I am much criticized for idling here while the empire falls to pieces around me."

"I would you did not have to go," she said, and it was almost true.

"I shall leave three legions here under Rufus Cornelius to protect you."

To protect me? Or to keep me under your thrall? I imagine it does not matter how this Roman characterizes it. He knows I need him as much as he needs me.

"I shall assemble the Sixth Legion and sail to Pontus as soon as practical."

"Will you miss us?"

He shrugged his shoulders. "Alexandria is pleasant enough."

The casualness of his response goaded her, as perhaps as it was meant to do. "Is that all?"

"Your Egyptians have too much fondness for death. Everywhere there are tombs and the stink of embalmer's fluid. I shall be glad to have it out of my nostrils. And these courtiers. I never know if I am talking to a man or one of your . . . pretty boys."

"You mean eunuchs. Like Mardian."

"What is a man if he does not have that which makes him a man? I shall never understand it. It is barbarity."

Caesar is going to lecture us now on barbarism? "I am told you took ten thousand men prisoner at Uxellodunum, during your Gallic wars, and had their hands cut off so they could no longer hold a sword against you. And you call us barbaric?"

His eyes flashed and she saw that she had gone too far. "That was war," he growled.

"It was necessity. As our eunuchs are necessary to us."

"For what purpose?"

"You think a king or queen could trust his *dioiketes* if he thought he might one day covet the throne for himself?"

"And because a man has been introduced to the razor you trust him more?"

"A king or queen must have heirs. The first duty of a royal person is to govern, and the second is to make more kings and queens. Without it, you are just a—" She was about to say "tyrant" but stopped herself. She would make her point presently but did not wish to demean him.

"And so you have pretty boys instead?"

"Eunuchs like Mardian are chosen from our best families. As children they display exceptional abilities in the arts and in their schooling. If they wish to rise to greatness then the operation is necessary. It is also voluntary."

"And how old are they when they choose this drastic course?"

"Usually it is at ten years."

"And you call that voluntary? They do not even know what they agree to! I still say it is barbarism!"

"Yet you do not think of yourself as a eunuch?" she said softly.

He stared at her, his eyes blazing. But this time she did not back down.

"Think about it. You are king of Rome in all but name. And why are you not king? Because neither your sons nor your daughters can follow you to greatness. No matter how the world trembles when Caesar passes, you are still just a man and you will die and be forgotten. So you see, in Egypt we would call you a eunuch. That is what your beloved Rome has made of you."

She thought for a moment he would strike her. His face had drained of blood. She had goaded him beyond the mask of the civilized man. Here was the real Caesar.

"Get out," he hissed.

"If you hate me at this moment," she whispered, "it is because I have told you the truth."

Had she said too much? Let the dice fall as they may. She had not regained her Egypt to be just another Roman's fop. It was the first time she had stood up to him, but now she could afford to, for there was no Ptolemy, no Arsinoë with whom he could replace her. Besides, he had showed her what it took to persuade others to do as you wished, and it was a lesson she would not easily forget. As she had pointed out to him early on in their acquaintance, her tutors had always said she was quick to learn.

〜 〜

The next day, as Caesar's last act before leaving Alexandria, Cleopatra was married for the second time to one of her brothers. Little Antiochus did not seem to understand what was happening to him. Indeed, it seemed the terror in which he lived for the last four years had left him a little simple. Pshereniptah again officiated at the ceremony, asking them if they had come willingly to the marriage, then invoking Isis to bless and preserve the union. They made the usual vows of fidelity and then the priest proclaimed young Antiochus as Ptolemy the Fourteenth of Egypt.

She caught Caesar's eye and wondered if she saw some satisfaction in his face as Pshereniptah spoke the words. They had barely spoken since their quarrel of the previous day, and when, later, he came to bid her farewell, it was done in the formal language of the court. There was not even a moment for private embrace.

But she did not regret what she had said to him. She knew her words would burn inside him for months, perhaps years, until again they met. He would not forget Cleopatra of Egypt now.

29

ISIS, THE GREAT Mother, her face serene. The rich scent of camphor, the regular cadence of the waves beating against the Lochias shore, the wailing of the priests, the rattle of systrum. Cleopatra, on her knees, staring up at the smooth white marble of the goddess's face, the headdress of vulture feathers with the silver disk and the horns of Hathor the cow-god. A goddess. But also a woman like me.

The stone of the shrine was well worn, countless knees had polished this stone, wailing their troubles to the goddess; make my daughter well again, send my husband safely home from the sea, keep my rebellious son away from his pretty boys in Canopus, make the harvest a good one. At the Great Mother's feet lay the offerings of a thousand hands, flowers now long since dead, bread moldering where it had been left. The urns of goat's milk the priests would keep for themselves.

In her arms Cleopatra held a stone jar containing the finest Attica honey and a garland of roses. "Isis, Great and Compassionate Mother," she murmured, "make my child a boy. Let me give Caesar a son. A son that will save Egypt and save Asia."

She left the honey and the flowers at the goddess's feet and made her way back to the palace, Charmion and Iras supporting her. She felt the infant move in her womb.

Please, let it be a son.

〜 〜

The child was born in the summer, when Alexandria was warmed by pleasant breezes and the harbor glittered like mercury under the Mediterranean sun. Cleopatra wrapped the birthing ropes tightly around her wrists and strained against them as another pain began. She closed her eyes and balled her hands into fists, felt the sweat running in rivulets down her naked body, heard the exhortation of her midwives from the end of a long and pain-bright corridor. She writhed and screamed, only dimly aware of Charmion wiping her face with a cool cloth.

Finally the child was delivered. It was a difficult birthing and the ropes had burned weals on her wrists. The midwives had to physically prize loose her fingers, which had clenched in rictus around the cords. Then they carried her to the bed, where the child was washed with warm rosewater and placed at her breast to suckle.

She was unprepared for the upwelling of emotion she experienced as she looked down into the child's face for the first time. *I will make you a promise, my sweet. You will not struggle with your siblings as I have, you will not curse your brothers and sisters as rivals. I will give you everything I have not had, and the crown when you receive it shall not be a poisoned cup.*

"It is a boy," Charmion whispered in her ear, and Cleopatra wept with relief. A boy. Caesar had his son. Egypt had its heir.

❧ ❧

Mardian crept into the room, his face as excited as a child's. You would think he was the father, she thought. He peered into the crib, parting the coverlet for a better view of the sleeping infant.

"He looks just like you," he said.

"He looks like a sea cucumber. Let us see who he resembles when he has teeth and hair."

Mardian ignored the rebuke. He was accustomed to her moods and her mordant wit. He had known her long enough. "You have a name for him?" he asked.

Cleopatra did not answer right away. She closed her eyes, and imagined she saw Mother Isis, and she was smiling, knowing what she was about to do. A humid breeze stirred the curtains, and across the harbor Pharos glowed like butter in the late-afternoon sun.

"Majesty?"

"I intend to name him . . . Ptolemy Caesar."

A moment of stunned silence. Mardian closed his eyes and emitted a soft groan. "I beg you to reconsider, Majesty."

She bit her lip to stifle a smile. She felt an odd sense of pride about this most commonplace of achievements, the birth of a son. But this was different, this boy was Caesar's. No Roman woman had ever managed it. And he had given them enough opportunity. Let them talk about that in the Senate. "Why should I reconsider, Mardian?"

"The reasons are legion, not least of all is the approbation that shall fall on all our heads."

She pretended not to understand. "Is he not Caesar's living son?"

"Does Caesar acknowledge him?"

"He acknowledged him to me. Who else could be the father? Do you impugn my character, Mardian?"

The poor man blanched. "Dread Queen, that . . . that is the last thing I should ever do," he stammered. "But unless you have Caesar's acknowledgment of paternity, you cannot use his name."

"He is the father of the child. I do not need his permission to acknowledge it."

"Roman law forbids it."

"This is not Rome, this is Egypt. Julius Caesar is my child's father and the world will know it."

He stared at her, his face betraying both awe and dread. Once again he had underestimated her. They had all underestimated her. This was the moment she would show them all she was a queen in her own right, and not Caesar's dupe. All Alexandria had seen until now was a silly young girl throwing herself at the feet of a Roman general in order to win back her throne from her brother. But the infant was another matter. Caesar may have thought that he possessed her. But now she had his son, and the slave now also possessed the master.

30

IT WAS THE new year of the Egyptian calendar, and once again the Mother Nile had betrayed her. In the first two years of her reign there had been drought. Now the waters they had been denied those two previous harvests were sent in one season. The Nile broke its banks, swamping fields and washing away the dikes that had been built to control it in kinder years. Every day, all over the country, her *strategioi* descended the wells of the Nilometers to peer anxiously at the markings on the walls. Within the month the waters had risen higher up the gauges than anyone in the *chora* could remember.

The whole of the country was converted into an inland sea, the villages and towns built on higher ground appearing like islands in a vast, glittering ocean. All along the great valley of the Nile the mud-brick houses of the fellahin were crumbling into mud, the crops in the fields disappearing under the floodwaters. Now they would have famine as well as the extra devastation wrought by the flood. The floods brought with them other plagues; first of insects, then of mice, then snakes, and finally disease, as the floodwaters putrefied.

Cleopatra called an emergency council of her ministers. "Any grain that can be saved must be transported to warehouses away from the river. Build new ones if you have to. And we must again set up a rationing system. I want you to appoint officers to oversee the procedures. If any of them attempt to profit by it, they will answer to me, and I shall not be merciful." She looked around the room. "In good times we take their grain in taxes, in bad times we must help them or one day they will have all our heads."

"But even with rationing we do not have enough grain to feed everyone," Mardian protested.

"Then we shall have to buy it from wherever we can."

"It will drain the Treasury. The famine has driven up prices for wheat and barley all around the world."

"Do whatever you have to, Mardian."

She saw the troubled look in his eyes. But she remembered how the priests and the fellahin of Upper Egypt had helped her once before when Pothinus had plotted against her. She owed them a debt. And now the time had come to repay it.

🌱 🌱

Cleopatra, as had become her habit, worked long into the night, poring over reports from her *strategioi*. It was winter now, and a gale had blown in during the evening. A cold draught made the embers glow in the brazier in the corner of the room.

In front of her were reports from Mardian's spies in Mauretania. Caesar was about to confront Pompey's sons, Gnaeus and Sextus, and the fanatical Republican, Cato. After Pompey's defeat at Pharsalus, they had fled to Africa and allied the remnants of their legions with Juba, the King of Numidia, in order to continue the war against Caesar. Caesar had forged his own allegiances there, with two Mauretanian kings, Bogud and Bocchus. True to his nature, it seemed that Caesar had already cuckolded one of them, bedding Bogud's queen, Eunoe. Mardian had edited the reports, and tried to couch his agent's references to the Mauretanian queen in the most guarded of language. But the inference was clear.

My Julius, she thought. If he is not waving his sword at his enemies, then he is waving his prick at the wives of his friends. No wonder he has bodyguards everywhere he goes.

Right now I could stick a knife in his ribs myself. Here I cradle his son in my arms, and he is cradling another woman in his. Some decorative Arab tart with eyes like a doe and the intelligence of a bath tile. He chooses her over Cleopatra?

Eunoe only has what every woman has between her legs, she thought. When I part my thighs, I can offer all the riches of the Nile and the wealth that goes with it. It was not a woman that stood between her and Caesar, it was the Roman Senate. And also, perhaps, the fragile bonds that tie a man to the earth.

The prospect had to be faced. What if Caesar should die on this campaign? She doubted that his victory over Pompey's heirs would be as easy as his victory at Pontus. *Veni, vidi, vici* indeed. What would happen to her if he died on his African adventure?

Let the dice fly high. She had chosen her lot with the stars. Now it was in the hands of Isis to keep him safe and deliver Egypt from her enemies.

꒰ ꒱

Over Mardian's initial objections, the boy became known to her, to the servants, to the whole household, as *Caesarion*—"Little Caesar." Cleopatra set a room aside for him, filled with scented rushes from Lake Gennesareth, where he could lie in his cot and smell the salt of the sea and hear the crashing of the waves on the breakwater and watch, mesmerized, the whipping of the silk curtains at the windows.

Yes, he was like Caesar, she thought. He had the same black and piercing eyes, the same hair—though more of it, already—the same curve to his jaw. My little Egyptian god, she thought. My Ptolemy, my Caesar.

He had Caesar's constitution also. He was indifferent to food, more intent on play. He suffered not a single croup through the long Alexandrian winter. His body grew brown and sturdy.

But still no word from his father. She had sent him letters, telling him of the birth, that it was a son, describing the boy to him.

Not a word.

The days went by, rolling into weeks and months, an endless round of work. Caesarion had taken his first, tentative, steps when she had news of his father once more. He had defeated the remnants of Pompey's army at Thapsus. Fifty thousand had been slain in the rout, and Cato and Juba had fallen on their own swords. Caesar now ruled all of North Africa, save for Egypt. Caesar effectively ruled the whole world west of Parthia.

31

MARDIAN BROUGHT HER one of the newly minted coins she had ordered struck with a likeness of her as Isis holding Caesarion as the child Horus in her arms. The intimation was plain; if she was Isis, then Caesar was Osiris, joint ruler of Egypt, and Caesarion was plainly his heir.

On the Upper Nile stonemasons were already busy in the temples carving reliefs depicting Caesar in a pharaonic crown, sacrificing to Osiris and Horus. In the *chora* they now believed Caesarion was the result of a divine union. In Egypt, Cleopatra could not be just the mistress of some adventurous Roman.

She smiled as she weighed the newly minted coin in her hand. She wondered what they would make of it in Rome. She turned it over. On the reverse she was in profile, looking more fearsome than Caesar himself.

"You look formidable, Majesty," Mardian said. "Rome will tremble."

"What would you have me do? Look like a simpering girl? Already your spies would have me believe that my reputation in Rome is halfway that of a dancing girl and a prostitute."

"They will surely wonder if Caesar was not quite mad, spending so much time with such a harridan."

"My Julius would spend the night with a crocodile if it would be compliant to his wishes. But tell me, what do your spies tell you is happening in Rome?"

Caesar was returned to his capital now, had arrived there in the Roman month of Quintilis. Only now it was to be renamed Julius, it was said, after the month of his birth.

"Caesar has been feted like a god since his return. He has no rival for power. Even Cicero and the other old men in the Senate cannot challenge him."

She had, finally, received a missive from him, couched in the most formal language, advising her of his victory against Cato and congratulating her on the birth of her son. My Julius. Always the politician.

"And what are they saying about me?"

Mardian would not meet her eyes. "I get reports of various ribaldry in the Forum."

"I am still the subject of their gossip? Should I be flattered?"

"It is the same here in Alexandria. People gossip about everything."

"In Alexandria they have respect for their queen. Do they show the same respect for Caesar?"

"You know what men are like, and Roman men are just more so. They encourage it." Mardian pursed his lips reproachfully. From some of the things he said, it seemed to her that he regarded himself more as a woman than a man. Indeed, he rarely spoke kindly about the sex he had been born to.

"I want to know what they say."

"It is disgusting."

"I am no longer a little girl, Mardian."

There was color in his plump cheeks. "They make fun of our disasters. There is a graffiti in the Forum. That the Nile rose six inches in a night and so did Caesar."

Cleopatra smiled. "Was it only six inches? It seemed much more."

Mardian seemed shocked by this.

"What else?" she asked him.

"The common people have made up a song and they sing it in the streets. That Caesar spent two weeks up the Nile and two months up the queen." She realized how appalling and ridiculous such ribaldry must sound to a man with no feelings for women. "They laud him for it. To them you are just another conquest he has made. If he paraded you through the Forum, they would doubtless cheer."

"And what of Caesarion?"

His manner changed abruptly. "There are certainly no songs about your son, Majesty. He is merely whispered of in the Senate and the highborn talk of him in the baths. But with Caesar's reputation . . ."

He did not have to finish. With Caesar's reputation, Caesarion was just another bastard. But surely the existence of the boy must make them nervous. It must make them think.

No, Caesarion was not just another bastard. Even Caesar must see that, must see the significance of his son by Egypt. "I do not want little Caesarion to bear the same yoke I inherited from my father," she said. "We gave the world mathematics and astronomy and the greatest library in the world. What good is all this learning to us? Still we wriggle under the boots of the Roman."

"We cannot match their armies."

"Blood does not have to be spilled for freedom. It can be joined."

"With Caesar?" He looked at her as if such a thought had never occurred to him. Why not? she thought. What is so outlandish about the idea? Was Caesar not just another eligible foreign prince?

"He is a Roman. Just a soldier. He is not worthy of you."

"You mean the Senate would not allow it."

His eyes were wide as dinner plates. "It would give him too much power."

"When was too much power enough for my Julius?"

"He has no royal blood!" Mardian said indignantly.

"Then I will lend him some of mine."

"Majesty, it can never happen."

"It can, and it will. Be patient, Mardian. I do not think Julius is a dull man. He will see the benefits of it. You will see."

〰 〰

His name was Quintus Dellius and there was something of the weasel about him. He strode into the Hall of Audience, his metal-studded boots echoing around the chamber. He wore the distinctive armor of a Roman officer—a cloak of red leather and a decorated enameled breastplate—his red tunic and the leather thongs of his boots reflected in the polished marble. He bowed and then looked up at her down the length of a fine Roman nose.

"A message from Julius Caesar, Consul of Rome, to the Queen of Egypt, his friend."

His eyes were moving rapidly around the chamber, taking in everything. He seemed a little surprised to find her court like any other in the East. He had spent too much time listening to the gossips at the baths on the Palatine. Perhaps he had expected to find her half naked, in the cobra headdress of a pharaoh, eating the mummified remains of her father.

Instead he found himself surrounded by fat, hook-nosed Greek functionaries and Roman legionaries from Calabria. The Nubian guards with their shiny black skins, and the shaved skulls of Pshere-niptah and his retinue, was all that distinguished today's audience from any other Hellenistic court.

"What message does he send?" she asked him.

"He hopes to find you in good health and congratulates you on the birth of your son."

It was still *your* son, she noted. Not *our* son. These Romans and their games.

"You may tell him our son is in the best health. You may also remind him that he is almost eleven months old and that his felicitations are a little tardy."

This Dellius was stalled by her forthrightness. Did everyone grovel before these Romans?

"He is pleased to announce that the Conscript Fathers of the Senate have granted him the right to hold four Triumphs and he invites you to come and share in his celebrations."

"The Queen of Egypt congratulates Caesar on his glories and is honored to be invited to Rome. We shall think on this and give you our reply."

"Caesar expressed the wish that you are present at the triumphs to demonstrate to all that you are not Rome's enemy," Dellius said.

"Thank you, Quintus Dellius," she said. "You have made yourself plain." She dismissed him.

To demonstrate to all that you are not Rome's enemy. She wondered at this implied threat. He could not order her to go to Rome. She was not a vassal. Or was she? She had to do what she was told if she wanted Caesar's patronage, and without it she might still be lost. Freedom had its price, if she did not want to go the way of the others.

And there was no question that she would not go to Rome. It was what she had prayed for. The fact that he had seen fit to order Dellius to induce her to come, even with veiled threats, was somehow gratifying. Perhaps the man had finally come to his senses.

PART II

Count no man happy until he is dead.

SAYING IN ROME,

EXTANT AT THIS TIME

32

CITY OF ROME

*Forty-six years before the birth of Jesus Christ,
in the newly inaugurated month of Julius*

CLEOPATRA HAD NEVER seen pine trees before, was both fascinated and repelled by their dark green foliage, somehow fore-
boding and gloomy. They left sharp brown needles in the grass
and nothing grew below them. Like the Romans, she thought.
Tall and dark and imposing, but allowing for nothing to flourish
in their shadow.

Caesar had lodged her in his own villa on the west side of
the Tiber, on the Via Campana. Surely, she thought, a statement
in itself. It was comfortable enough, though without the light
and air to which she was accustomed in Alexandria. It was constructed from pale creamy stone, the pillars festooned with
roses, wisteria, and clematis. Marble busts flanked the atrium at
the entrance; there was Venus, as Isis was known to the
Romans, whom it amused her to learn Caesar claimed as an
ancestor; there were likenesses of Alexander, of course, and several of Caesar himself, fashioned in a younger time. She wished
she had known him then, when there would have been more
time to map a future.

Beyond the atrium was a small courtyard with an inward-
sloping roof, which the Romans called an impluvium. A passage
led away from this to the bedrooms and dining rooms. At the
rear of the house was an elaborate garden court, surrounded
with colonnades, around a piscina, a fish pond.

The interior walls had been painted the same green as the
pine leaves, their somber tones enlivened with colorful friezes of
flower garlands. The main living and dining rooms had delicate
mosaics on the floor, country scenes, nymphs dancing around
an arboretum. A possibly decadent choice for a sober Roman
senator. The furniture was spartan for a man in his position, she

thought, but it fitted with his character; a few brass lamp stands with small lamps hanging from their branches on slender silver chains, some tables inlaid with ivory and tortoiseshell.

Her bedroom, she was assured, had once been Caesar's. It was a grim affair, scarcely large enough to flog a slave in, as Mardian remarked. A large bed, carved from oak wood, with coverlets of wool and silk, took up almost the entire space.

It was soldiers' quarters compared to her palace at Alexandria, and yet, as it was Caesar's principal residence, it was no insult, either. In fact, if he wished to advertise his relationship with her to all of Rome, he could not have chosen a better way to do it.

The villa was surrounded by vast gardens, overlooking the Tiber and the city of Rome. The gardens were like none she had ever seen. Elms, planes, and cypress trees had been planted in regular order, like legionaries at the drill, and there were great walls of clipped yew hedges as well as box, bay, and myrtle. From the shade of the banks she could watch the barges creep from Ostia on their way upriver to the Probus Bridge and the Emporium, the vast indoor market that she could smell when the wind was in the right direction. Across the river the great sprawl of the Aventine was spread out before her, the five- and six-story red-brick apartments that the Romans called *insulae* shouldered like eager schoolboys up the hill.

Several days had gone by since her arrival, but as yet Caesar had not come personally to greet her. She wondered if he had brought her here as his guest or as his hostage. She supposed she would discover that soon enough.

He sent Quintus Dellius—whom Mardian now persisted in calling "Caesar's Ferret"—every day to send his felicity and inquire of her needs. But it seemed Rome's foremost citizen was too busy with the preparations for his glorification to see her. Well, she thought, what did you expect?

She did not delude herself that he might have missed her. But she had hoped he would want to see the Queen of Egypt, and she had also hoped that the great Caesar might also be curious to see his son. After all, to her knowledge, young Ptolemy Caesar was the only heir he had, and certainly the only one to bear his name.

✤ ✤

"So, Mardian, what news from your ears in Rome?"

Mardian did not like Rome. He disliked his quarters, which were altogether too cramped for his tastes compared to his sumptuous villa on Lake Mareotis, he disliked the weather, which was too hot, he disliked the Romans themselves.

But somehow he knew more of what happened here than perhaps even Caesar himself. "Majesty," he said, "it would seem Caesar is now not only Consul of the Republic, he has been voted Prefect of Morals and Dictator of the Roman People for the next ten years. It is an honor without precedent among these Romans. Truly, your Caesar is eclipsing even the great Pompey in power."

"Pompey's head ended up on a plate. Not a difficult feat to eclipse. He just has to stay alive."

Mardian made a face. "This is Rome, Majesty. As in Alexandria, staying alive is no small achievement."

✤ ✤

She wondered if he would come at night, in a carriage or borne in a curtained litter. It would have told her all she needed to know of her position. But no, Caesar came the next morning, in daylight, on the back of a white horse. Ahead of him marched twenty-four lictors, the symbols of his power as dictator of the Republic, each carrying a fasces—a polished axe bound with fir branches and tied with a silk ribbon.

There were two centuries of soldiers with him, his bodyguard, and as he dismounted they hurried to take their positions around the gates and the gardens, as if deploying themselves for an expected attack. It seemed that even in his own capital Caesar did not feel safe.

Perhaps *especially* in his own capital.

She received him in the large room that overlooked the impluvium. She positioned herself on several different chairs and couches before finally settling herself for his entrance. Her heart was racing. The bastard had made her wait. Now he could cool his heels in his own atrium until she was ready.

But as hard as she tried, she could not summon the same anger she had felt the day before. She was far more eager to see him than he was to see her. Well, she would not let him see that eagerness.

So much depending on the outcome of this. Will he ask to see Caesarion? Or will he treat me just as any other foreign dignitary? It had been more than a year since she had seen him. *Would he play the perfect Roman, turn his back on the opportunity she had offered him?*

This waiting was making her nervous. She nodded to her chamberlain, the signal for him to usher Caesar into her presence.

🙟   🙟

"Greetings, Most Exalted Majesty," he said in elegant Greek.

"Greetings, My Lord General. It is a pleasure to look on your face again."

"I believe it is a trifling pleasure compared to mine, for your face is fairer than any I have seen in Rome."

Ah, Caesar the diplomat, she thought. *Caesar the lover and liar.*

"Fortune has been kind to you since last we saw you," she said, and that, too, was an elegant lie, for in truth he looked tired and drawn. The endless campaigning had taken its toll.

"Yes, the Goddess of Fate played her part. But good tactics played a role also."

Well, he was never one for too much humility.

"It pains me I have not been able to come to greet you before this," he said. "I have been busy organizing the Triumphs." When she did not respond, he said: "I trust you find the accommodation here to your liking."

"It is a little cramped."

He looked around the room, at the slaves, the waiting women, the courtiers, advisers, and ministers; flaxen-haired Gauls and Germanics, ebony-skinned Nubians, bearded Greeks in flowing bright-colored chitons, Jewish *oeconomi,* even her priest Pshereniptah. She could see him thinking: *Jupiter, she has brought all Alexandria with her.* "I had not expected such a large retinue."

"Any invitation to Cleopatra is an invitation to Egypt."

A shadow of a smile. "I take it you have erected the pyramids in the garden?"

"Of course not," she answered, straight-faced. "Only the light-house."

An awkward moment. He gazed around the room as if looking for something, or someone, he had hoped or expected to see. "You have brought your son?"

Ah, she thought. Finally we come to the business at hand. So, you are not made of stone after all. A wave of relief swept through her. What would she have done if he had left without asking after little Caesarion? "He is in the nursery."

"May Caesar visit him?"

She did not want to appear too eager, though it was the moment for which she had waited for over a year. Finally, she murmured, "This way," and rose from the silk-embroidered couch and led the way through the villa to the room she had chosen as her son's nursery. There was an art to being a queen, as she had discovered, of keeping a regal bearing and an imperious expression while your heart hammered against your ribs and it was difficult even to breathe.

❦   ❦

They entered the room alone. Caesarion lay on a fur rug, a sleek, black panther skin. He was a docile child and was playing quietly with a wooden toy horse that Charmion had given him. My son. She experienced a familiar surge of pride, as she did whenever she looked at him. So many hopes and dreams invested in this small, brown creature.

Cleopatra watched Caesar's face. No clue there to what he was feeling. He was content just to stare, and she wanted to scream at him: *Pick the child up! Hold him! He is yours!*

Finally, Caesar crouched down beside the child. He tentatively held out a finger, which the boy took gratefully and immediately started to chew on, biting down hard with his pointed little teeth. Caesar laughed and snatched his hand away.

He stood up, smiling. "You have a fine son."

His indifference made her furious. Your blood is in that boy! "We both have a fine son."

It was as if he had not heard. Caesar, forever the tactician, was not about to lose ground so easily. "Thank you for letting me see him."

"How could I refuse you your own flesh and blood?"

Again he pretended not to have heard. "I am afraid my visit must be brief. It has been a pleasure to share your company again. Perhaps we might talk again soon. You are invited to a banquet at my house tomorrow evening."

You unspeakable bastard, she thought. "I shall have to speak to the court secretary. He can tell me if we have a prior engagement."

"Your husband, Antiochus, is invited also."

My husband. Does he deliberately intend to inflame me? "I'm afraid he cannot come."

"How is the young fellow, by the way?"

"He is unwell. The Roman air does not agree with him."

For just a moment Caesar dropped his guard. She looked into his face and thought she saw beyond the public face of Caesar. Was that longing she saw in his eyes or had she only imagined it?

"I have missed you," he murmured.

"Not as much as I would have wished."

"There is not a moment you were out of my thoughts," he said, a little too easily. Always the lover, saying whatever the woman wanted to hear. He took a step forward to kiss her cheek. She allowed the kiss but held him at arm's length. What am I going to do? I love him, but he will as easily destroy me.

He shrugged his shoulders. She sensed that he had been prepared for this rebuff, but he still contrived to look wounded. "Until tomorrow, then," he said.

She watched him leave, preceded by his lictors, surrounded by his bodyguard, an army decamping. So, Caesar had come. He was somehow different here, less his own man. As if Rome was a yoke around his neck.

For the first time she wondered if Mardian was right, if all her plans were not just a foolish young woman's daydreams. She felt a flaring of anger, dismissed her servants, and stamped back to the nursery and picked up Caesarion, held him fiercely to her breast. She felt bright, hot tears on her cheek and she immediately despised herself for her weakness. Crying like a girl.

"I will not let them deny you," she whispered to Caesarion. "You are mine and you are also his, and that is your birthright. I will not let him deny you!"

33

SHE CLUNG TO the sides of the swaying litter, the leather straps creaking as the porters made their way up the hill. She could hear the gulls screeching and fighting over the Tiber wharves, the hoarse cries of the beggars in the arcades. She peered several times through the curtains but glimpsed nothing of particular splendor in the narrow, twisting streets. The buildings were cramped and uniformly made of red-brown brick, so the streets were already dark by late afternoon. She was surprised by the array of faces: Africans with woolly locks, Arab hawkers in burnooses and flowing robes, flaxen-haired German slaves bearing some Palatine matron on her litter, even an Egyptian snake charmer. It was as if Rome had brought the entire empire back to its city walls.

As they passed the Circus Maximus some prostitutes cackled and made obscene gestures in their direction and she shut the curtains again.

There was no breeze and the afternoon was stifling hot. As they jolted up the Palatine she heard the strident voices of the porters calling warnings and instructions, competing with dozens of oxcarts on the cobblestones, the oaths of the draymen, senators chivvying their own trains of slaves to go faster. But the most overpowering sensation of Rome was the smell: the warm aromas of baking breads, the pungent stench of urine from the laundries, and over it all a heady potion of fermented fish sauce from the *tabernae,* smoke from the bathhouses, and bad sanitation.

❦ ❦

Caesar lived in the Reggia, in the heart of the city itself, near the Temple of the Virgins. An unsuitable place for Caesar, as Mardian remarked when he heard it. She had expected a palace, but instead Caesar's Roman residence was quite unimposing, a cramped little villa dwarfed by the public buildings around it. There was a stout iron grille outside and two centurions stood sentry.

A chamberlain led them through the marble portico into the atrium, which was extravagantly decorated with floral murals, the floor a mosaic of a mongoose doing battle with a cobra. The other guests had already arrived, and she felt herself immediately the subject of intense scrutiny, if not outright hostility. But then Caesar came forward, smiling, hands outstretched. He addressed her at once in Greek, a small kindness, for he knew her Latin was faulty and he did not want her at a disadvantage with his guests. They would now follow his lead and speak in Greek also.

She had brought with her just a small retinue: Mardian, some slaves, her personal bodyguard, all Nubians. She had not even told Antiochus of the invitation; she would not have wished to disappoint the little King of Egypt by telling him he could not go. To bring him here was out of the question. She did not want even the most obtuse Roman senator to think for a moment that she shared power in Egypt with anyone else.

Caesar introduced her to the inner circle of Rome. She knew many of the names already, through Mardian's spies, and had formed an image of them in her mind. She was surprised to find they were nothing as she had imagined.

Calpurnia, for instance. Cleopatra had expected a typical Roman matron of some grace and cool demeanor. But Caesar's wife was thin and awkward, with a face like a fisherwoman and the manners of a brothel keeper. Caesar deserved better, Cleopatra thought. But then, if legend was to be believed, he had bedded half the known world, so perhaps her sympathies were wasted. Calpurnia wore a robe of violet silk and so many jewels it was as if they were encrusted to her, like barnacles on a fishing boat. Caesar had married her, so Mardian said, for political reasons. It was also said, and she was not entirely sure this was a joke, that he had invaded Britain just to get away from her.

"I have heard so much about you," Calpurnia said with a cold smile.

Cleopatra returned her smile. "And I of you."

Caesar then introduced her to his great-nephew, Gaius Octavian, a quiet boy of sixteen with bad skin and what appeared to be a bad head cold. His best feature was his eyes, which were of the deepest blue she had ever seen on anyone, man or woman. He struck her as effeminate and not a little vain, if the thick soles on his sandals were indication—an obvious attempt to make himself appear taller than he was. These Romans. Bald, short, they treat each personal defect as an affront to the gods.

Then there was the redoubtable Marcus Brutus, a bull-faced young man whose legend had preceded him. Mardian's spies had described him as a mother's boy who thought the great god Ra rose and set from his nether orifice. He had sided with Pompey in the recent civil war, but Caesar pardoned him after the Battle of Pharsalus and had even made him governor of Cisalpine Gaul. He was with his mother, Servilia, who, Mardian had said, was also one of Caesar's paramours. But then, he had added, with a wicked grin, who wasn't, apart from the Vestal Virgins and Caesar's own mother? There were even rumors that Brutus was his son.

Brutus greeted her without even a smile.

There was Marcus Agrippa, a ruggedly handsome youth with dark close-cropped hair who was described to her as a friend of Octavian's. I can imagine. Finally there was Claudius Marcellus, in his purple, a balding clown with a vast sense of his own importance, with his wife, Tertullia, a graceful Roman decoration with impeccable manners and a voice like silk drawn across marble.

She had not expected much civility, not from Romans. Their opening gambits to conversation were conducted in tones more suited to the interrogation of a prisoner of war. It seemed they wanted her to immediately affirm their prejudices and provide more grist for the rumor mills of the Palatine bathhouses.

"What do you think of Rome?" Marcellus asked her at once.

"I have not seen enough of it to form an opinion," she answered carefully.

"It must seem grand after Egypt," he said, displaying both his ignorance of her country and his bad manners. She was tempted to rebuke him there and then but decided to wait until she had eaten and do it properly.

"They say that in your country you are worshiped as a goddess," Brutus said bluntly.

She was instantly wary of this young man. It was not a question derived of idle curiosity. "Some believe they see in me the incarnation of Isis."

"You encourage this belief?"

"I have always discouraged such childish thoughts—since the dawn of time." This aside brought laughter from Caesar and even the senator's wife, but Old Sobersides did not see the point of her wit. A worrying characteristic. In her experience a man who could not laugh at himself had no sense of perspective and became fanatical about any and every cause he felt himself disposed to. Dangerous.

"For myself I do not believe in divinity," Brutus said. "In our Republic everyone is equal."

"Of course they are. That is why we shall sit down tonight and have slaves serve us our dinner."

"I was referring to the knights and senators of Rome. Not the plebeians."

We have not even sat down to eat and already they are ready to tear me limb from limb, she thought. She looked to Caesar to rescue her.

"Let us go in to dinner," he said.

❦ ❦

They adjourned to the triclinium—the dining room—where the men gratefully cast off their heavy and cumbersome togas. There were three long couches—the triclinia—placed around a large table, the fourth side left free for service. Cushions divided the triclinia into three places, where each of the diners could recline, propped with pillows. There was a rigorous etiquette attached to the dining positions; the couch of honor was opposite the empty side of the table, and it was here that Caesar guided Cleopatra, to share the couch with himself and Brutus.

When they were comfortable, servants removed their sandals and washed their feet with rosewater while a maidservant placed garlands of roses around their necks. A *cellarius* brought two amphorae of Falernian wine and poured it into a large bowl called a krater, where it would be mixed with water and cooled with snow. Two slave girls played the lyre and flute in one of the alcoves.

The food was brought out and laid on a huge ivory and tortoise-shell table. The first course, the *gustum*, consisted of sliced quail eggs, mice cooked in honey, lobster dumplings with olives, a platter of oysters, and sea nettles. For the main course, the *mensa prima*, there was roasted boar's head in sweet nut sauce, its bristles gilt with liquid gold, baked gladiolus bulbs, boiled cucumber, baked teals, something Caesar called rose pie—made with calf's brains, eggs, and wine—and the centerpiece, a huge roasted mullet. She was told by the other guests that mullet was considered a delicacy in Rome and could only be purchased by the very wealthy in auctions at the fish markets. She also tasted pork, which was not eaten in Egypt.

They ate the food with their fingers, so their hands were washed frequently by slaves, who waited by the couches with ewers of water, pouring perfumed water over their greasy fingers and wiping them with a towel they carried over their arms.

As they ate, Cleopatra tried to avoid catching Caesar's eye. She did not want to appear the simpering mistress to any of these Romans, least of all to Caesar himself. She understood there would be no time for private talk tonight. This was a public ceremony.

During the *mensa prima* Caesar had skillfully steered the conversation away from politics to discussion of the Triumphs that were to take place in two days in the Forum.

"There will never again be anything in Rome to compare with this," Calpurnia was saying in her grating, high-pitched voice. "A single Triumph is the highest moment of even the most illustrious career. But four! Rome has never seen the like. When it is over his Triumphal chariot is to be placed beside Jupiter's on the Capitoline Hill."

Cleopatra found Calpurnia's adoration of her faithless husband sad and dispiriting.

Brutus was scowling. "Do you think that having a Triumph over a fellow Roman is a good idea?" he asked Calpurnia.

"What fellow Romans?" Caesar snapped.

"Cato and Scipio and the rest."

"Any Roman who fights under a foreign king ceases to be Roman."

Brutus shook his head. "Being Roman is a state of nobility that can be taken away from no man who is blessed with it."

"Like divinity?" Cleopatra asked him, and Caesar laughed, and the others laughed also, because Caesar had laughed. All except Brutus and his mother. It occurred to her then that Caesar was a great general but a poor judge of character. Look at these people he surrounds himself with, she thought, these people he calls his friends and his family. How could he bear it? She would rather be throttled slowly in a swamp than endure another dinner with Sobersides and his mother.

Then there was the boy Octavian with his suggestive walk and his pimples and his sniggering. And Caesar's wife was a shrew.

Perhaps he did invade Britain to get away from them.

🐏 🐏

For the last course, the *mensa secunda,* they were served honey custard, mulberries and sweet figs, and pomegranate juice, cooled with snow from Thrace.

"The trouble with Rome," Marcellus was saying, "is that we are losing sight of the moral codes that made Rome what it is today. These rites of Bacchus, as they are called, men and women disporting themselves and performing all kinds of lewd acts in the name of religion. Or this temple of Isis on the Aventine. It is known as a place not only for prostitutes but as a meeting place where men and women conduct their love trysts. It is no surprise to me that these are women's religions. All our troubles are caused by women."

He was addressing himself to Caesar and Octavian, but the lecture was plainly directed at her. Very well, then, if he wanted a debate. "All your troubles? Do I understand then, Claudius Marcellus, that you would blame your womenfolk for your military defeats in Parthia? For the recent civil wars?"

Marcellus seemed flustered at having a woman confront him on his opinions, even if she was a queen. But it did not blunt his rhetoric. "What I blame them for is our parlous deficit in trade with the rest of the world. They drain the empire with their endless fancies and endless demands for prettification, the Tyrian dyed robes and necklaces, brooches, rings, gold bracelets. Never a day goes by that I do not find myself accosted by my banker in the Forum over some bauble my wife has purchased and which I then have to find the money for." Really, she thought, he speaks about his wife as if she is not in the room. "And all of it must be bought from elsewhere in the empire. I could buy myself an estate in the Alban Hills with what my wife wears in her ears. And this silk she drapes over herself, pound for pound it is worth its weight in gold. No wonder Rome never has enough in the Treasury to pay the army!"

"Marcellus," she said, "does your wife have affairs?"

There was a stunned silence in the room. Marcellus looked at Tertullia, who studiously avoided his eyes. "Certainly not!"

"Then she is certainly unlike every other woman in all of Rome. It would seem to me that every intelligent, well-educated woman in this city is running wild, with her money and with herself, simply because she is bored to distraction by her husband. The men let them get away with it so they can be free to concentrate on politics and the particular pleasures of a brothel I believe is called the House of Venus, opposite the Circus Maximus."

From the corner of her eye Cleopatra saw Caesar watching her. He kept a straight face throughout this speech and she thought he might be angry over this outburst. But then she saw the corners of his mouth twitch, and he threw back his head and laughed out loud.

Marcellus's cheeks were burning with indignation. Caesar's laughter only wounded him more. "I believe what you are saying only proves the very point I am making. Woman is a headstrong creature and cannot be trusted with even the smallest amount of liberty or she will squander it on ostentation and license. How should a man do otherwise but keep her on the tightest rein?"

"How do you treat women in Egypt, then?" Octavian asked her.

Impudent little bum boy. How dare he. "Well, the really intelligent ones are made queen," she said, and Caesar applauded and Tertullia smiled. Even Calpurnia seemed to be taking vicarious delight in the conversation. But Brutus and Octavian exchanged a glance that told her she had won no friends there.

"You think a woman fares better in Alexandria than she does in Rome?" Calpurnia asked, suddenly an ally.

"She can borrow and lend money, she can buy and sell houses, all on her own account. She does not need a male guardian throughout her life, as she does in Rome."

"I believe women in Rome have too much liberty," Marcellus ranted on. "She may do much as she pleases as long as she does not meddle in matters that do not concern her."

"Such as?"

"Politics, for which she is ill-suited by nature."

"I think I understand. So you allow that she may spend as much time as she pleases at the baths or having her hair teased into curls with irons as long as she does nothing that might require her to use her mind and demonstrate that it is superior to yours."

"I have no fear on that account," Marcellus chortled.

"Let us test your hypothesis. Tell me, should you have a legion of 4,050 soldiers and 580 of them are killed in a battle with the Parthians and another 1,015 are wounded, how many soldiers would you have left to guard your standards?"

Marcellus puffed out his cheeks and thought about it.

"The answer is 2,455," she said.

"Why, you had the answer made up already!" Marcellus protested.

She turned to Caesar. "Give me another, then."

Three times Caesar proposed a similar mathematical problem, and each time Cleopatra came up with the correct answer while Marcellus was still frowning and staring at his hands.

"I think she has proved her point," Tertullia said finally, and her husband glowered at her furiously. That will be worth a slap when they get home, Cleopatra thought gloomily.

"I am sorry, Marcellus, but I think she is right," Caesar said, pressing the point. "I would certainly have the queen as my quartermaster before you." Then he spared the senator further humiliation by clapping his hands to call for the entertainments.

🌱 🌱

"I am told you have a son," Brutus said to her.

There was a stillness in the room. She caught Caesar's eye but could not divine what he was thinking. "Yes, I have a son," she said carefully.

"If I have a son I shall bring him up on strict philosophical and mathematical principles," Brutus said. "I am told you have some of the finest mathematicians in the world in Alexandria."

"We are fortunate in that way."

"Then you should understand the values of these sciences."

"Indeed. But I am interested in hearing how you would apply them to human life."

Brutus smiled triumphantly. All this man seeks from life, she thought, is a stage on which to parade his virtues. Such rigidity in such a young man. Really, a hundred gladiators pulling on a rope could not extract a pin from his backside.

"Each evening I account to myself for all I have done, the merits and demerits of my actions during that day. I believe in this way a man's worth can be calculated using such exact principles."

"It might appear to some a bloodless existence."

"The blood is a poor captain. Too many men are seduced by unrestrained passions. In truth, the correctness of the soul is worth more to us than this transient life. For instance, before the Battle of Pharsalus I spent the last evening copying excerpts from the works of Polybius while other officers were inspecting their cavalry." This pronouncement earned approving looks from Marcellus and his mother.

"What happened to your cavalry?"

"They were routed," Caesar murmured.

"Perhaps because their commander was reading Polybius," she said.

"You fail to understand my point."

"You fail to understand mine. But tell me, why were you on the side of Pompey?"

"I considered him the more virtuous man," Brutus said, helping himself to some of the less virtuous man's wine.

"I wonder if that more virtuous man would have shown you clemency had you fought on Caesar's side and lost," she said, and earned for the remark a look of utter loathing from Brutus and his mother. They left it at that.

〜〜 〜〜

The Romans, it seemed to her, were fond of their wine, the women as much as the men. Caesar drank sparingly, but by the time the entertainments had finished, Marcellus and Calpurnia were in their cups. For herself, Cleopatra always drank little, her wine heavily diluted. She had seen what wine had done to her father's reputation and how it had dulled his ability for statecraft, and she had vowed she would not make the same mistake.

The addition of fine Falernian wine did not add to Calpurnia's charms. She began to gossip viciously about certain Roman senators of her acquaintance. Finally the conversation turned inevitably to Caesar's former Captain of the Horse. "Your friend Marcus Antonius is about his tricks again," she said, her voice slurred.

Caesar looked annoyed at this remark but said nothing.

"He spends most of his time drinking and whoring with those actor friends of his," Calpurnia went on. "He even has a pet dwarf that goes about with him everywhere."

"I agree Marcus is a little too fond of wine," Caesar said stiffly.

"Fulvia is in an uproar about it, of course. They say at home she cuffs him about the ears like a tutor with a schoolboy. But then he goes right out and does it again." She seemed intent on baiting her husband. Perhaps it was the wine opening the doors to its warehouse of resentment.

"Nevertheless," Caesar objected, "Marcus is a fine soldier."

"He has no flair for the peace," Brutus observed, in his ruthless fashion.

"But one has to admit, he is a fine-looking man," Calpurnia observed. "Any woman should be happy to have him for a husband. They say he is descended from Hercules. In truth there are a number of Roman wives who should attest to the size of his club."

Caesar shot her a glance of disgust, but Calpurnia just cackled like a fishwife on the dock at Ostia. These Romans, Cleopatra thought. Barbarians.

It was later, when they had returned to the villa on the Via Campana, that she asked Mardian about this Marcus Antonius whom Calpurnia had been gossiping about.

"You would not remember him, Majesty," Mardian told her, "but he fought in the army of Galbinius, when they restored your father to the throne. He took Pelusium and spared the lives of many of the Egyptians there when your father would have had them killed. He is remembered fondly for it by certain Alexandrians."

"And what is his position in Rome?"

"He is considered something of a hothead, but his soldiers love him. He earned great merit with Caesar fighting the Gauls. He also made himself rich. When Caesar pursued Pompey to Africa, he made him Consul in his absence. Antony made a complete hash of it. The city was a shambles when Caesar returned, there were riots in the streets, and Marcus Antonius, it is said, was almost perpetually drunk. He also appropriated Pompey's house for himself without paying for it. Evidently Caesar dismissed him and they have not been on good terms since."

"Caesar seemed intent on defending him tonight."

"They say this Antony is a charming man, for all his faults. Perhaps even Caesar finds it hard to hate him. And he is still a man to be reckoned with. Before this quarrel he was Caesar's anointed heir."

Well, he has a new heir now, she thought. Which makes this Marcus Antonius my enemy.

She retired to her bedroom, tired but unable to sleep. So, tonight she had met Rome for herself. Its politics intrigued her. *Another nest of serpents,* she heard her father whisper. But she had survived in their company before. She was sure she would find a way to survive, perhaps even thrive, again. But so much depended on what lay in Caesar's mind, and that serpentine maze was almost impossible to negotiate.

She wished he were here lying with her tonight, to translate the politics of the evening for her, to draw her into his delicious conspiracies, make her a part of his heady ambition. To laugh at her profanities. And that she could feel the hard muscles of his arms encircling and protecting her.

But that is weakness, she thought, and I cannot allow myself that luxury. I have a duty to the Nile and its gods, and to my own son, to be resolute. I must beat these Romans at their own game. May Isis grant me the strength to do it.

34

THE TRIUMPHAL ROUTE began from the Field of Mars and proceeded around the great colonnades of the Circus Maximus, the great racetrack that lay between the hills of the Palatine and Aventine, and from there to the Forum Romanum, a crowded and ugly piazza of temples, statues, and law courts. The Forum exemplified Rome for her, its glories piled one upon another in haphazard fashion, its architecture borrowed from everywhere else. It was a barbarian's concept of beauty, without harmony or balance or scale.

They were seated in a special viewing stand looking out over the Forum, shaded from the sun by vast silk canopies. A place of honor had been reserved for her, in the same section of the gallery as Calpurnia, Caesar's nephew Octavian, and the rest of the dictator's inner circle. Antiochus sat beside her, quiet as always, intimidated by the occasion and the crowds.

She knew everyone was staring at her. Mardian had told her that all Rome was abuzz about her relationship with Caesar, gossiping endlessly about events at the villa on the Via Campana. If only they knew.

It was not only the commoners who stared. Several times she felt Calpurnia's eyes on her. And she caught Caesar's fop of a nephew staring at her, too. He was seated behind her, his close friend Agrippa on one side and another high-ranking fop, Maecenas, on the other.

There was a carnival atmosphere. The streets and balconies were crammed with people, the air pungent with the sweat of tens of thousands of bodies and the incense that was burning in every temple.

She could hear the Triumph's approach, far in the distance. The applause and cheering of the crowd grew to a deafening roar as the procession made its way down the Via Sacra, past the Temple of Castor and Pollux and the half-finished porticoes of the new Forum Julia. Heralds led the parade, blowing trumpets; behind them, sweating and stiff with age, came the magistrates and senators of the Republic, rank upon rank.

There were long lines of wooden wagons creaking under the weight of gold platters and silver goblets, the loot that had been plundered during the Gallic campaigns. It was endless. After a while she found herself growing bored with it. Even the mob became restless. There was only so much gold you could stare at before it started to make the eyes ache.

Then came the Caesar's legions, singing as they made their way into the Forum. The crowd began hooting with laughter when they caught the words:

> *"Home we bring our bald whoremonger*
> *Romans, lock your wives away*
> *All the bags of gold you lent him*
> *Went his Gallic tarts to pay."*

She heard Agrippa chuckling behind her. She wondered if Calpurnia was as amused.

At the rear of the column, weighed down with chains and surrounded by guards, came Caesar's prisoners, hair matted, beards grown long after years of imprisonment, ragged and filthy in their furs and leathers. They shuffled along, sad and pathetic figures, unaccustomed to the light, jeered by the crowds, who pelted them with rubbish.

Finally, walking alone, came Vercingetorix, the great chieftain who had resisted Caesar so stubbornly for so many years. Six years in the Tullianum prison had not bowed him. Head held high, he glared back at the mob that lined the street. His courage humbled them, and they fell silent as he passed.

The crowd erupted when Caesar finally appeared, riding on a golden chariot drawn by four white horses, an ivory scepter crested with the eagle of the Roman legions in his left hand, a laurel branch in his right. A slave stood behind him, holding the heavy gold crown of Jupiter over his head.

The purpose of the slave, she had been told, was twofold. First, to bear the weight of the crown, which was too heavy for any human head. The second was to remind the Triumphator of his mortality. He was to whisper in his ear, throughout the entire procession, while the feted man enjoyed the adulation of the crowds: "Remember, Caesar, you are mortal and one day you must die."

These Romans, she thought. An exquisite race.

She turned around in her seat. "The prisoners," she said to Octavian. "What will happen to them now?"

"They will be taken to the cellars below the Tullianum for their execution."

Cleopatra felt a sudden welling of revulsion. "Caesar kept this man Vercingetorix in prison six years so he could show him off for just one day and then kill him?"

The boy shrugged his shoulders carelessly. "Of course," he said, and grinned, showing off his bad teeth.

Our Julius, she thought. An enigma; a man of unpredictable clemency and unimaginable cruelty. He might turn on me as abruptly as make me his queen. Which will it be?

35

THE NEXT DAY was to be the Egyptian Triumph. As if there had not been feasting and drinking enough, Caesar held a party at his house to celebrate the event. He specified an Egyptian theme. She had been dreading the evening, and her fears proved justified.

What Caesar presented was a parody of Egypt, and it demonstrated for her exactly what Rome thought of her and her country. It was the Egypt of the priests and the *chora*; it was as if Alexandria, the most lovely city in the world, did not exist; as if the Museion that gave the world mathematics and astronomy and the largest library of books ever collected had never been heard of. How stubbornly these Romans clung to their prejudices.

~ ~

As she entered the house she saw, in the atrium, an alabaster statue of a hippopotamus and two alabaster crocodiles. Around the *peristylium* there were more statues in miniature: a sphinx, a pyramid, and several obelisks. All the slaves and servants had been dressed in what the Romans seemed to believe was the Egyptian style, with more material in their headdresses than their loincloths. Among the guests she saw Anubis, guardian of the underworld, wearing the mask of a dog and the dress of a pharaoh. There were slave women dancing half naked by an orchestra of flutes and drums, and many of the senators' wives wore four-tiered gold collars over sheath-tight gowns, golden cobras rearing on their foreheads in parody of the sacred Egyptian crown of the Lower Nile.

They had all conveniently ignored the fact that she and her entire court were Greek.

In defiance, Cleopatra wore for the evening what she would have worn to any state banquet: a loose-fitting Greek gown of the palest blue, a diadem of jewels, gold sandals. Now, looking around at the company, she wondered if any of the Romans here tonight would recognize her as the Queen of Egypt. Of all the women here, she was the only one who was not dressed like a pharaoh.

❧ ❧

He was smug and self-satisfied, soft and plump. His sycophants trailed after him, twittering in his wake. "Cicero," Mardian whispered in her ear. On his arm was a girl young enough to be his granddaughter. She disliked him immediately.

"Marcus Tullius Cicero," he said to her as Caesar brought him over. "Doubtless you have heard of me."

"No," she lied. "Were you with Caesar at Pharsalus?"

He glared at her. "I am no soldier."

"I can see that."

Cicero regarded her coldly and moved on.

Mardian leaned in to her shoulder. "You should not make enemies of such men," he whispered.

"You think friendship has any currency here? I could be closeted like a lover with any of these Romans, and the next day they would denounce me before the world without batting an eye. Who was that girl he had with him?"

"Her name is Publilia," Mardian said.

"How old is she?"

"Not very old. They say he married her for her money."

"Then he does not even have the defining virtue of human lechery?"

"When he divorced his first wife, they asked him if he would remarry. He said he could not cope with philosophy *and* a wife. But that was before he was forced to repay her dowry. So he married his second wife to enable him to divorce the first."

"Poor Cicero."

"Poor Publilia."

❧ ❧

All Rome wanted to meet her, it seemed, from curiosity perhaps, or merely to say that they had. Were they fascinated by her because of Egypt or because of Caesar? she wondered. It was hard to tell. Several times she looked up and found Caesar looking at her across the room, but he was as much in demand as she, and there was no time for private conversation. It must be exhausting being a public hero, she decided.

But finally he found a moment for her.

He looked tired, and she could see that it was an effort for him to keep his Triumphator's smile in place.

"A fine day for Caesar," she said.

"Thank you. You will be there tomorrow?" Tomorrow, the Egyptian Triumph. Of course. That was why he had invited her to Rome.

"I shall be there. I am curious to see how Alexandria was vanquished."

He looked almost abashed. "Remember it is just theater," he said. "Do not blanch at anything you see or hear. But you must be there to let everyone know it was not you I defeated, but your enemies."

How could she not blanch? Her own sister would be in the procession.

"Now we must perform the formalities," he said, and led her and Antiochus to a dais at the end of the room. As they ascended the steps the gathering fell quiet. Caesar made a long speech formally greeting Queen Cleopatra the Seventh and King Ptolemy Antiochus of Egypt to Rome, as honored guests of the Republic. "Today, we honor the King and Queen of Egypt," he finished, "and do hereby enroll them as Friends and Allies of the Roman People."

A toast was drunk and then the evening's entertainments continued.

And perhaps all I am to him now is an honored guest, she thought. She realized with a pang that in coming to Rome she had hoped that he would acknowledge not only Caesarion, but her too. I am lonely, she thought, and I miss his body next to mine while I sleep. I want him to touch me, to hold me, to make love to me.

But you must not let him know what a fool you are. You are just another conquest, like Eunoe, like Pompey's wife, like Gaul. Another triumph. Another one of his tarts. You must put away your gullible woman's heart and do what you must for Caesarion.

❦ ❦

She saw little of Caesar for the rest of the evening, and was forced to endure endless dull conversations and inane questions about herself and her city. Do Egyptians really worship crocodiles? Do they really embalm their dead? Do scorpions run along the city streets like ants?

In fact, the night would have been utterly forgettable if not for her first glimpse of the infamous Marcus Antonius.

He was perhaps one of the most striking men she had ever seen. He made a dramatic entrance wearing a lion skin, knotted around one shoulder, that revealed the taut muscles of his shoulder and chest. He had a wooden club casually thrown across a shoulder. He had the body of a gladiator, the face of a butcher, and a shock of dark, curly hair like a god. She watched every head turn toward him, the men in silent envy, the women in open admiration. She remembered what Calpurnia had said about him: *One has to admit, he is a fine-looking man.* Indeed, he did no disgrace to his gender. Cleopatra herself found it hard to take her eyes off him.

Defying the conventions of the evening, he had spurned the mandatory Egyptian costume and had come as Hercules, his alleged ancestor. Defying the conventions of any evening, he had come drunk.

He was barely inside the atrium when he tripped and almost fell on some invisible object. With the exaggerated care of the intoxicated he regained his balance, like a man fording a river on a fallen log.

Marcus Antonius did not arrive alone. He was accompanied by a train of musicians, actors, and whores. He held a woman, also drunk, under the crook of one arm. She was beautiful, in a tawdry way, and laughing too loud.

A woman with a shock of wheat-colored hair suddenly appeared in the atrium, pushing her way through the guests like a centurion breaking up a commotion in the Forum. She stood with her hands on her hips in front of the newcomer, who blinked at her in owlish surprise.

"What do you think you're doing?" she hissed at him.

Marcus Antonius turned to his coterie, some of whom looked shocked and abashed by the woman's presence. But Marcus grinned at them and shouted, "It's my wife!" as if he had discovered geometry.

"Get this cow out of here now," the woman said, pointing to Antony's companion. "And the rest of you stinking, talentless drunks can leave as well!"

Antony's companion gave her a haughty look, turned, and made her exit. The others filed away after her. Antony watched the departure of his friends with studied disappointment. He then held out his arms to Fulvia and said, in a theatrical whisper, "What about a quick fuck, darling?"

She hit him so hard it snapped his head back. Antony did not fall, but he staggered sideways into the fountain in the center of the effluvium. The woman called her slaves and left, a few minutes later, in a litter.

The man called Marcus Antonius vomited into the fountain. He then called for one of the attendants to fetch him a goblet of wine. And the party continued, as if nothing had happened.

Cleopatra was not sure if she was horrified or amused. In many ways he was the epitome of Rome—degenerate, irresistible, compelling, and with the manners and tastes of a complete barbarian.

〰 〰

"A disgusting display," Mardian said later that evening, when their party had returned home.

"Yes. They seem to think Egypt consists entirely of crocodiles and *hetaira*."

"I meant that Marcus Antonius."

She smiled. Her *tropheus* could be as prudish as a Roman senator when he chose.

"He was entertaining, at least."

"Majesty, the man is a degenerate, like most Romans, but much more so. It is said that when he was a youth, a certain Roman senator paid him half a million sesterces to stay away from his son. He said he was debauching him. He is a notorious drunkard and lecher and spendthrift."

"Caesar certainly cultivates some interesting relationships. What of the friends this Marcus Antonius brought with him tonight?"

"Mainly actors and musicians and other such hangers-on. From a Dionysiac guild. It is said Antony is much taken with the rites of Bacchus, and that some unspeakable things occur in the name of his god at his country estates."

"His wife seemed a formidable woman. Fulvia, am I correct?"

"Indeed, Majesty. There is talk of sending her to Parthia to regain the lost standards of Crassus. Alone." Crassus was the last Roman general to try and invade Parthia, suffering a catastrophic defeat.

Cleopatra smiled. "And I thought Roman women were mice."

"That one treats all Roman men as if they were cheese."

Rome. The more she learned of it, the more it astonished her. The old men pontificated endlessly in the Senate, while their sons debauched themselves in the brothels and the *tabernae*. It seemed to her that their much vaunted Republic was in decline.

The time was right for a strong man to take the rein of the city's affairs. It was time for a man like Caesar. It was time for a king.

And queen.

36

Rome was in a crush. People had poured in from all over the country for this spectacle of spectacles; four Triumphs for one man, and with it endless games and free feasting. The previous day at the Circus Maximus the crowd had stampeded and two senators were among those who had been killed. As Calpurnia said, Rome had never seen its like, perhaps never would again.

The Triumphs were spread over ten days of festival. It was yet high summer, and the overcrowded city baked. Unlike Alexandria, there were no cooling breezes off the sea. The sun hung over the brick apartments of the Aventine behind a nimbus of high cloud, the city suffocating in its own stink and sweat.

By the time of the Egyptian Triumph, expectation was at a fever pitch. The mobs' appetite had been whetted by the Gallic procession. Now they looked for another great spectacle. Afterward, Caesar had promised, instead of the normal chariot races or combats in the Circus Maximus, there would be a pitched naval battle on a specially constructed lake on the Field of Mars.

Nothing like free food and blood on the sand to stir the appetites of the Romans. The whole city was in uproar.

❦　❦

It was the same travesty she had witnessed at Caesar's house. He knew how to play to the crowd. Perhaps it was what had made him such a successful lover; give them what they want, and never mind the truth.

The crowd wanted the exotic, and that was what he gave them. It began with a procession of naked men beating drums and blowing trumpets, their oiled bodies gleaming in the sun, and women in gauzelike gowns that concealed nothing, swaying to the sinuous rhythms of the drums and systrums. In fact they were not Egyptians, but Syrians, for all that the crowd cared. Behind them came a knot of priests, from one of the city's own temples of Isis, incense trailing from their thuribles.

The crowds were going wild.

"They are mocking us," Antiochus whispered in the seat beside her.

"Just watch," she whispered, irritated.

This was the East that Rome held dear in its fantasies, she thought: a land of cheap, oiled women and barbarian music. Not Egypt as it was: a well-administered state with a vast bureaucracy, the greatest collection of scholars and mathematicians on earth, and a civilization that predated Rome by thousands of years. No, to these people, we are exotic curiosities. Mud wallowers.

A wagon lumbered by, a model of the lighthouse of Pharos suspended atop it, smoke actually billowing from its beacon. The crowd gasped at some crocodiles, snapping in their cages, and women shrieked at the growling, padding panthers on their long chains and the startled-looking ostriches. Then a ripple went through the crowd, a collective gasp. She thought it must be Caesar making his entrance, but it was a giraffe, the first ever seen in Rome, apparently. Neither panthers nor giraffes were found in Egypt, but why let that disturb the spectacle?

The mob was enjoying this as much as any of the previous Triumphs, but there were some in the viewing stand around her who already felt a sense of surfeit. She heard someone say behind her: "This is too much, too much for any one man. It is even too much for a god."

She turned around to see who had spoken. It was Marcus Brutus.

The legions marched into the piazza, singing one of their bawdy songs. Eyes turned in her direction, and she felt her cheeks blush hot.

"Caesar came to Alexandria
Venus met by Mars
When he saw his Cleopatra
His lighthouse pointed to the stars."

Remember it is just theater, he had said. Do not blanch at anything you see or hear.

Just theater? No, to her it was much more than that. How could she not blanch? But she would endure it. She would endure it to prove that Caesar's victory had been won not over her, but over her enemies.

Huge wax statues of Pothinus and Achillas went swaying past on great palanquins. The crowds responded by pelting them with dung off the streets and ripe fruit. Then came the prisoners; Antiochus gasped as he recognized the eunuch Ganimedes, no longer fat, his oiled ringlets hanging in matted clumps down his back. He, too, was jeered and pelted with refuse.

Then, walking straight-backed behind him, was Arsinoë. She looked painfully thin after her sojourn in the Tullianum, but she won the respect of the mob with her beauty and her poise, as Vercingetorix had done. Cleopatra felt eyes again turned toward her in the crowd, some curious to see her reaction, others overtly hostile. Perhaps they thought she should have spared her sister this.

Cleopatra felt her stomach churn. Though we are enemies, she thought, she is still my sister. Must I watch this? Mardian looked away, and young Antiochus covered his face with his hands. She took hold of his wrists and wrenched them away. She would not let him shame her further.

As Arsinoë passed the podium, Cleopatra made herself a promise: *Whatever happens, I will never let them do this to me. I will die by my own hand before any Roman leads me through the Forum in chains.*

∿∿

She saw Caesar briefly after the parade. He was surrounded by his functionaries and young army captains, all of them basking in his glory. He looked utterly drained. She remembered how he once swam across the harbor at Alexandria in full armor, and how invincible he seemed that day. Perhaps the endless campaigns were finally taking their toll. There were lines on his face she did not remember, and the skin under his neck hung in folds.

"I have to ask you," he said formally, "what you wish me to do with Arsinoë."

She looked away. "She is your prisoner."

"She is your sister. It is tradition that prisoners are executed after the Triumph."

"Why did you have to ask me this? Could you not act without my involvement?" She felt everyone's eyes on her, Antiochus gaping like a simpleton, Mardian's face unreadable.

Caesar just stared at her. "I have to know," he repeated. "What is your decision?"

❦ ❦

She was carried in a litter to the Campus Martius—the Field of Mars. A lake, four stadia in length, had been constructed there and wooden galleries erected on one side of this vast body of water for the guests of honor. On the other side of the lake the mob crowded the banks and strained for a view as best they could, using their shoulders and elbows.

Two navies faced each other across the water: biremes, triremes, and quadriremes arrayed in battle formation, the banners of Egypt and Tyre flying from their masts.

Again she was guided to a place of honor directly in front of Caesar. "I hope you enjoy the afternoon's entertainment," he said to her. "I have arranged a reenactment of a great naval battle that took place between the Egyptian navy and that of Tyre many years ago."

"It is just theater?" she asked him.

"Where would be the amusement in that? The men on the ships are prisoners of war or condemned criminals. They will be literally fighting for their lives."

Cleopatra felt a heaviness in her limbs. More needless slaughter. How much blood was enough for these people?

Caesar gave the signal to the heralds. There was a blast of trumpets and the two navies cast off and began to row toward each other across the lake. Six thousand men, their lives forfeit, for the pleasure of Rome.

The ships closed up, charging at each other with their great bronze rams, and grapnels were hurled across the water. Brands spiraled into the rigging of one of the quadriremes, setting it ablaze.

The mob on the far side of the lake were in uproar, and certainly the Romans around her seemed to find the spectacle engaging. Even the senators in their purple were on their feet. Behind her, she heard Octavian's friend Agrippa arguing loudly over tactics with Maecenas. Then she turned and looked around at Caesar. He alone seemed sanguine, watching with a familiar expression of detached amusement.

The noise was deafening, the clash of steel swords, the splintering of wood as a bronze ram tore open a hull, the screams of the spectators, many of whom had laid bets on the outcome. Already, one of the ships had started to sink. There were bodies floating on the surface of the water.

She experienced a sensation she had not felt before, as if someone had poured cold water along her spine. She felt sick in her stomach, a feeling that had nothing to do with the bloodletting taking place for her amusement less than a stadia away from where she was sitting.

She could watch no more. She got to her feet.

"You are leaving us?" Caesar said, his face betraying both anger and disappointment.

"I do not feel well," she said, then hurried from the stands, her retinue trailing behind her. Even as her litter left the Field of Mars, she could still hear the sounds of the battle from almost a mile distant, the screams of dying men and the smell of burning timber and pitch, and it chilled her to the very bone. Later on she would remember that day and recall that Isis had tried to warn her, even then.

꒰ꔛ꒱ ꒰ꔛ꒱

They were deep below the streets. Arsinoë could hear the cold dripping of water from the stone. The floor under her feet was slick with blood. The executioner straightened, resting his back muscles. He was a huge man with bad teeth and dead eyes. He looked exhausted. There were gobs of dark blood on his sword.

It was her turn.

She felt herself finally lose control, the wetness running down the inside of her thighs. Her legs collapsed under her, and one of the guards had to hold her upright. They had just finished with Ganimedes. A centurion pushed the headless body down the well with his foot. It landed with a splash in the sewers.

The Captain of the Guard stepped forward. "Not this one," he said.

"I am . . . to live?" she asked him, even yet not daring to hope.

"You are to be exiled to Ephesus."

"My sister . . . spared me?"

He gave her a savage grin. "No, they say she wanted your pretty little head pickled in vinegar. These are Caesar's orders. Just as well. Would have been a waste to throw such delectable goods as these to the Cloaca Maxima!"

And he and the executioner laughed.

On the final evening, Caesar was borne on a litter between two elephants, along an avenue of flaming torches to the Capitol. There, he made his sacrifices to Jupiter for the final time and thanked the Roman Pantheon for his victories. Afterward Rome feasted at Caesar's expense. In the Forum thousands of tables were set out for the mob, dancers and acrobats performing to entertain the crowds as they ate and drank their fill. As the hot summer night wore on, the Via Sacra became a shouting, singing hubbub, drunken revelers sprawling down the steps of the Curia, wine spilling over the cobblestones among the shattered amphorae.

Rome had truly never seen such a time. One of her sons had become one with the gods, and not a few of those looking down from the Palatine Hill that night wondered if, like all gods, he must die so he could be resurrected and claim his due.

37

THE TABLE, laid with a carmine cloth, supported trays of apples, pomegranates, breads, and a pitcher of the best Falernian wine. Servants moved around the room lighting the wicks on the standing holders of the oil lamps. Their soft yellow light threw a muted glow across the couches and tables.

He came at the second hour of the night, but not as a lover stealing secretly to his mistress, as she had expected. With him were at least a century of his bodyguard, who immediately surrounded the villa, standing sentry at all the doors. If Caesar was a god, he was one in fear for his mortal life as much as, if not more than, any ordinary man.

Charmion and Iras had finished attending her hair and toilet. She was dressed simply in green chiton, a matched set of gold scrolls at her ears. She stood up and went to stand at the window, watching the leaves of a horse chestnut tree shiver in the wind.

"You look as a queen, fit for a king," Charmion told her.

"Thank you, Charmion," she said, and the hairdresser slipped from the room, leaving her alone. But Cleopatra thought: Here in Rome I am no queen, I am just Caesar's plaything. In the Brucheion I have reports to read, matters of justice to decide, every day there are endless meetings and councils. Sometimes I tire of it all. But it is infinitely preferable to being just another Roman's mistress.

And this terrible ache, this loneliness. It made her wonder what it would be like to choose a man for his company and to raise a child with no other expectation than happiness. Impossible to know. Why contemplate what you can never have?

When she turned around again, he was standing there, a pale figure in the light of the oil lamps, almost ordinary-looking in the simple, white tunic. She waited for him to say something, to explain the meaning of the Triumph, but he pulled her roughly toward him and said nothing. She thought to push him away but then was overtaken by her own need. She would possess Caesar for at least a little while and the rest could wait.

*~   *~

Later, after their lovemaking, she lay on the bed in the darkness, listening to the slow, even sound of his breathing, and thought he was asleep. But then he said, "Do you remember how once you compared me to a eunuch?"

She thought he needed her woman's assurances of his virility, so she said: "No one could ever compare you to a eunuch. Not if they saw you tonight."

"Yet you did, once."

"It was not your knowledge of the arts of love that I criticized."

"It was not my mastery of love that I wished to speak of. I believe in calling me a eunuch you meant that no matter how many victories I won on the battlefield and in the Senate, in the end I would be remembered no longer than any of those plump little bitches you call your councillors."

She felt herself growing angry at this characterization of Mardian. And so she said, to needle him: "Yes, I think that is what I meant."

"Well then, you were right."

This startling admission took her off balance. "Julius?"

He sat up in the bed, suddenly agitated. "I am fifty-four years old. I have given Rome true greatness, an empire not seen since the days of Alexander, and what do I have to show for it? Shall I spend the last years of my life arranging who will be Consul, who will be praetor? Passing out offices to whoever pleases me most or bows lowest? Is this a fitting way for Caesar to end his days?"

Precisely. She felt a lifting of her spirits. She had been right all along. *He does want this as much as I do.* "Then change your history, Julius! Take what is rightfully yours."

He turned away from her. "If it were only as simple. You do not understand Rome."

This man! How to make sense of him or her own complex vortex of emotion for him? "No, I do not understand Rome. But I think I understand you."

"This will not be easily achieved."

"Greatness never is. But think of what is at stake. Is it not time to make Rome pay you your proper due?"

"Yes," he whispered. "I think it is time. After all, if Egypt can have a queen, why should Rome not have its own king?"

Cleopatra lowered her hand to his groin, felt him growing hard in her hand. "If they made you king, should you not then be free to choose your own queen?" She cupped the future of Rome in the palm of her hand. Egypt's king would be Rome's king. East would marry West, and everything she had done would be vindicated.

"This thing must not even be whispered of to your closest advisers," he said, his voice hoarse. "It is five hundred years since Rome had a prince, and some Romans fear kingship like they fear poison."

She lay back on the bed, pulling him toward her. "Make me another king," she whispered.

She had never wanted him so much. He was the only man in the entire world who she felt in her heart to be her equal in ambition and intelligence. They were alone at the pantheon of souls. She felt a fierce elation, beyond mere physical pleasure, as she welcomed him inside her. Her Julius. She closed her eyes and saw a line of princes stretching away into the future, new kings of a new world.

38

AMID THE CLOUDS of steam, Antony sitting naked on a marble slab. I'm sweating like a Nubian porter on market day in summer, he thought. He heard the steady slap of a masseur's hand, working on some senator's flabby body, the shouts of the sausage sellers hawking their wares in the *caldarium*. There was a splash as some bucket of fat jumped into the pool, while elsewhere some young fancy was yelling as he had the hairs plucked out of his legs.

He looked up and saw Cicero coming toward him, naked, pink, and shining with sweat. They exchanged greetings. Cicero, the great orator, Antony thought, with a cock the size and shape of an acorn. Life is odd.

I wonder what he wants? I'm sure we shall get to it eventually.

Just idle banter at first. He wanted to talk about Caesar's new calendar. The Roman one was based on the moon, so the current year was only 355 days long. Despite constant fiddling with it, the calendar now bore no consistent relation to the seasons. The previous November they had sweltered in a heat wave; this year's harvest festival was celebrated long before the grapes and corn were ripe. Now Caesar had consulted with one of Cleopatra's famed mathematicians and astronomers from the Gymnasium in Alexandria, one Sosigenes, and had instituted a new calendar based on the sun, to last 365 days. In order to adjust to the timing of the new calendar, Caesar had just declared that this year there would be three Novembers.

"Did you hear about Marcellus?" Cicero was saying. "He was seen coming out of a brothel near the Circus Maximus. His wife was furious with him, but he countered her by saying he could do as he liked as the first two Novembers of the year didn't count." Cicero chuckled. He loved relating the misfortunes of others.

"I heard Lepidus is thrown in a panic," Antony said. "He is writing everything down that he does each day, so that he can do exactly the same thing on the corresponding days in the two Novembers to follow. I asked him why he was doing it and he could not answer me."

"A strange man."

"A pansy with a voice like a laundry girl."

The talk turned to the revolt in Spain. Sextus, Pompey's son, had fled there and raised another army, with thirteen legions. There were two legions of veterans, though considerably depleted after the ravages of Pharsalus and Numidia; the eleven others were mainly levies. He had made his headquarters in Corduba.

"I fear these civil wars will never end," Cicero said. "There are too many proud and ambitious men in Rome."

"There are proud and ambitious men everywhere," Antony said. In fact, I'm sitting next to one right now.

"I fear for the Republic if one man becomes too powerful. Do you not agree?"

"I fear for Rome if Caesar should not come back from Spain."

Cicero looked disappointed. When a man goes to fish, Antony thought, he always hopes for a bite. "You do not think he will lose?"

"He will have fewer legions to take to the field, but they will be better trained than those of Sextus. And he has the cavalry that the Mauretanians gave him. Against that, Sextus has Caesar's old lieutenants, who knows the old boy's ways as he knows them himself. And they will spend the winter under dry roofs, while Caesar's army must live in tents. The conclusion is not foregone."

"Do you know when Caesar will leave Rome?"

"Soon. But it is already too late to sail, so they say he will have to travel overland to Spain."

"You will go with him?"

"I think not," Antony answered.

"You are not reconciled?"

He knows too well that we are not, Antony thought. He is searching for some calumny that I will throw against him. "I think the old boy wants me to keep an eye on Rome."

"And an eye on this certain lady of Egypt?"

Ah, so that is why you wanted to talk to me. "She is certainly a flighty little piece. No doubt Caesar passed some pleasant nights with her in Alexandria. I doubt he spent all his time there discussing the new calendar. Unless it was to work out ways of adding a few extra nights."

"She will be the ruin of him."

"I should like to be ruined by her myself."

"Really? I have met her but a few times and I found her arrogant and careless of civilized forms. I agree she has her charms, but you can get the same fare for much less trouble under the colonnades at the Circus Maximus."

"Well, I am sure you would know," Antony said, unable to resist the gibe. "But they say she is well-versed in the secrets of the bed-chamber."

"Indeed?" Cicero said, and raised an eyebrow, eager to hear more.

Antony leaned closer. "They say she can control the muscles of her orifices so that they ripple like the back of a snake, taking a man to the highest pleasures while yet lying perfectly still. They also say she thinks of nothing of adding to her own pleasures. I have heard from one of Caesar's spies inside her villa on the Via Campana that he once found her in abandonment with a python she had brought especially from Egypt for that purpose."

"No!" Cicero gasped.

Well, no, Antony thought, you're right. I just made it all up on the spur of the moment. But isn't it a good story?

At that moment a boy, no more than sixteen or seventeen, his pale body appearing almost translucent in the netherworld of the baths, shucked off his towel and stood at the water's edge, about to dive in. He was thin, his body hairless, his golden hair curled carefully around his ears.

"Octavian," Cicero muttered.

Antony examined him critically. "Look at him. Bottom as hard as a camp bed. Talking of beds, they say his friend Maecenas has camped there overnight once or twice."

The boy jumped into the hot water and disappeared from sight.

"They say he is Julius's favorite," Cicero murmured. "One day he might be named as his heir."

"That little bitch? He would make a Consul a nice wife, certainly. But I doubt he shall ever amount to anything. The first rain and he sickens like a wet cat."

"So if anything should happen to Caesar, who will be master of Rome?"

"You think something will happen to the old boy?"

"The great Caesar is constantly on campaign. I believe he pushes his luck a little far. They say it was a miracle he survived Alexandria." Cicero shrugged. "Perhaps we will go back to the Republic. Some have said that I might lead us there. Do you long for the Republic, Antony?"

Well, you know, some have said that *I* might take over after Caesar. In which case, I should not find myself too nostalgic for your democracy. "I think the old boy will be around for a while yet."

"Well, of course, we all hope so. As long as he treads carefully." He gave Antony a curious smile. "In Spain, I mean."

Of course, Antony thought. What else would you mean?

39

THE VILLA AT Campania had become an arcadia even for her enemies. It was even said that old Asinius Pollio, one of Rome's greatest orators, was bringing his speeches to her for her criticism. One Atticus was considered an expert on antiquities; him she charmed with delicately illuminated Persian scrolls, then further astonished him by producing some ivory sculptures from the lands of the Seres, works of art that were unknown in Rome.

Even Cicero came to call on her. For him, she produced an antique manuscript depicting the history of the pharaohs. She translated the hieroglyphics on the ancient scroll, and afterward let him take it home to his villa at Tusculum for inclusion in his library.

While the mob in the Forum whispered salacious details of the black slaves with their gold earrings, and the *castrati* with their high-pitched voices and thick wigs, and of the innumerable orgies that were said to take place within the walls, the upper circles of Rome were being charmed, against their will.

If she had chosen to go home just then, they might even have loved her.

🐏 🐏

Cleopatra and Caesar were never completely alone. Even when they walked in the gardens of the villa at the Via Campania, his bodyguards were everywhere, picketed around the gardens or lounging in small groups by the statues and fountains. But at least here they were away from the prying eyes and ears of the servants.

Late one afternoon they strolled along the path that led away from a statue of Jupiter; the trees were turning to the russets and golds of autumn, and leaves had piled in drifts under the hedgerows.

"I must leave for Spain within the week," he said.

She said nothing. She had been expecting this, but was frightened for him, and for herself. "Who will rule Rome while you are gone?"

"I have nominated a council of eight urban prefects with the powers to override the Senate. They will have the authority to act in my name."

"What of this Marcus Antonius?"

A grim smile. "I do not think Rome could survive another term with Marcus as Consul."

"Really? People talk about him as if he is the next Caesar."

"Marcus Antonius follows orders, he does not make them. Look at his wives, for instance."

"His wives."

"You can always tell a fellow by his wife. Antony's wives have all been shrews with loud voices, bad manners, and a dominating nature. That is why Antony will never rule Rome. He does not even rule his own house."

"He's the size of a mountain and he dallies with every actress in Rome."

"He's an overgrown child. Sooner or later he always runs home to his mother."

"I thought you were friends."

"A man does not have friends in Rome, he has associates." He stopped, frowning. "Why so many questions?"

"He intrigues me. They say he is devoted to Dionysus, for instance."

"Dionysus was a god. Antony is just devoted to the wine his followers drink."

"My father was known in my country as the New Dionysus."

"Your father? Another drunk. You should stay away from them."

She gaped at him. It was not only a callous thing to say, it was blasphemous. Caesar loved to topple other men's statues while raising his own. "That is a vicious thing to say."

"I did not say it to hurt you. But it is the truth. Your father was a weakling. You are worth a hundred men like him."

Well, her father was a weakling, though it hurt her to hear him say it. He doubtless meant it as praise, and it was no easy thing for a Roman to compliment a woman on anything except her beauty. She should feel flattered.

And then, in the next breath: "You have outplayed us all, I think." He said it with both regret and admiration, as if she somehow had the advantage of him.

"What do you mean?"

What was his expression? He was so hard to read. "You always wanted to conquer Rome, didn't you?"

What could she say to him? To protest would sound hollow. Yes, she had always wanted this. What she had never expected was to feel this admiration and . . . yes, longing . . . for Rome's master.

"It is within your grasp, kitten. A formidable achievement."

"It is what we *both* want."

"Indeed. That is part of your cleverness."

"Anyway, it is not won yet. How much longer must we wait?"

"The Senate is still the legal ruler of Rome. If it is to be done, it must be done with slow haste. I would not hand our son a poisoned cup."

"Then I wish you did not have to go to Spain."

"I have no choice. This thing must be finished. When I return, there will be no one to contest with me. Pothinus and his ministers may have cut off Pompey's head, but if I leave his sons unchallenged in Spain he will continue to grow more."

They stopped by a fountain. Water bubbled around a statue of Venus, the Roman imagination of Isis. *Goddess of all women, help me take this one final step.* So much within her grasp. So much that she wondered if she dared hope, even now. "I do not understand this delay."

"That is because you do not understand Rome. Besides, I am not the only one with impediments."

"Antiochus," she said.

"Exactly."

The gall of the man. "That marriage was not my idea," she hissed.

He shrugged, conceding his mistake. "That is true. But even if you had not married him, the boy would still present a problem for us. He has a claim to the throne of Egypt—"

He stopped suddenly. His face had turned ashen, and he looked as if someone had plunged a knife in his back. He gave a small cry and then fell twitching onto the path.

This time she did not panic. She recognized the symptoms of his malaise, knew that the gods had come to him again, as they had that day in Alexandria. She shouted for his guards. Decimus came at the run, with a handful of soldiers.

"It seems the gods visit him more often these days," Decimus muttered, bending over Caesar.

There was a bloody froth at his mouth and nose, and his eyes had rolled back into his head. It was a fearful thing to see, but after some moments the spasm passed and Caesar lay unconscious on the ground. The soldiers carried him back to the villa. Cleopatra hurried after them. Dread had settled like cold fat in her stomach. A world without Julius was too terrible to contemplate now.

❦ ❦

It was a simple, square building hidden among the squalor of the Aventine, one of its walls shared with a theater of a Dionysian company. Isis had been relegated to the poorer quarters of the city, because the Conscript Fathers disapproved of her. There was a stunted facade with four colonnades, the walls brightly painted in greens and ochers, Isis herself with Horus, as hawk, or suckling the child at her breast. Two temple prostitutes waited in the shadows of the porticoes for custom, shivering in their wraps, looking tired and gray in the twilight.

Two other litters waited outside in the street, their porters lounging on the steps. Cleopatra brought with her an escort of soldiers, as she did every day. She stepped out of her litter and went inside, escorted by Charmion. After the squalor and stink of the street, the sweet smell of incense was reviving.

There were few worshipers this late in the afternoon; a Nubian woman, perhaps a slave, making offerings at the altar, two highborn Roman ladies in their fine cotton *stolas* returning to the litters she had seen outside in the street. She heard the priests chanting their hymns from somewhere in the sanctuary.

She brought her offerings, the best Attica honey and rare and expensive Falernian wine, and laid them at the feet of the goddess statue, whispering her prayers to the Great Mother. As she stood up to leave she heard a soft moan, saw something move in the shadows behind the pillars. She knew the temple prostitutes serviced their clients inside the precincts, so it was not unusual to see the goddess of love honored here in other ways.

But she dared a curious glance in the direction of the sounds and was afforded, for just a moment, a view of a man's bare buttocks, and two long and delicate ankles squeezed around the base of his spine.

The man—no, he was no more than a boy—looked around for a moment, and she realized she knew him. The woman's face was hidden by a veil, but Cleopatra recognized the litter she had seen waiting in the street outside, the same she had seen that night at dinner at Caesar's, the one that had brought Marcellus and his wife Tertullia.

It did not surprise her that the wife of Marcellus might choose to have affairs. But she had misjudged young Octavian. She had thought him incapable of such high deceit and assumed his tastes ran more to other young boys like himself.

Perhaps the young nephew was more like Caesar than she had first imagined.

The next day Caesar left for Spain. He presented himself at the villa on the Via Campania in his purple general's cloak and military armor to take his leave. His bodyguard waited and watched from their horses.

"May the gods grant you a safe journey and bring you safely home," she said.

His manner was stiff and formal. He bowed to her and returned to his horse. They did not touch.

She watched him leave, the breath from the horses leaving white vapor on the still morning air. The horses' hooves clattered on the cobblestones. The leaves had piled in drifts at the side of the road, touched by the first morning frost. Her future, the future of her son, the future of all Egypt, went with him to Spain today. He was her husband now, in all but name, and she wondered what would happen to her if he did not return.

Hard to imagine any sort of life without him now.

40

She passed her first winter in Rome. It was bitterly cold, a cold such as she had never known or imagined. One morning, soon after Caesar left for Spain, she woke and found the garden and the tall pines blanketed in white. It was the first time she had ever seen snow.

Little Caesarion was entranced by it and spent hours playing outside. Antiochus shivered and cried and developed a congestion of the lungs. Her doctors feared he might die.

There were regular letters from Caesar, couched in the formal language of the court in case they were intercepted. A new longing insinuated itself into her life. She discovered that she actually missed his company. Who else was there in the world that she could talk to as an equal?

In January, Caesar's nephew, Octavian, left to follow Caesar to Spain. He had been sick all that winter with a fever, and his departure was as surprising as it was foolhardy. She heard later that his boat was shipwrecked. He had been given up for dead.

And so the season passed, wet, lonely, cold, and depressing. Few ships dared navigate the Mediterranean in winter, in case they shared the same fate as Octavian. She was cut off from Alexandria, unable to send or receive messages, kept from the everyday business of government that had become as essential as lifeblood to her since she won the throne.

Mardian urged her to leave Rome as soon as practical after the winter storms, fearing another plot if they were away from Alexandria too long. But Cleopatra was confident in the ability of Caesar's legions in Egypt to maintain order, and besides, her future lay in Rome now. Caesar held the key to all their destinies. If she returned to Alexandria now, she would not be in Rome when vital decisions were made, those that would affect Egypt and the whole world for years to come. If Caesar were made king, she would be the mother of his heir, mother to the whole world.

But for now there was nothing to do but wait.

❧   ❧

Spring came and with it a blossoming of yellow wildflowers along the banks of the Tiber, squeezing through the packed frosts. The spring festivals of Lupercalia, Anna Perenna, and Liberalia were celebrated, but the festivities were restrained. The city was held in the grip of its waiting; the future of Rome was being decided in Spain.

One day Mardian announced that she had a visitor. It was Marcus Antonius.

A cold rain was falling outside, the *tramontana* blowing across the city from the mountains to the north. Cleopatra received him wrapped in thick furs. The heat from the braziers was quickly dissipated in these Roman villas of cold marble. It was impossible to get warm.

Antony entered, wearing the uniform of a cavalry officer. He was an imposing sight in his red tunic and leathers, the heavy cloak around his shoulders. She took a moment to compose herself, feeling strangely nervous around Caesar's Consul.

Marcus Antonius bowed. "I have good news for Your Majesty."

She felt a jolt inside her chest. *Caesar!* "He is safe?" she murmured.

"Not just safe, Majesty. Victorious. Thirty thousand of his ene-mies are dead on the field at Munda, including the renegade general Labienus and Pompey's son, Gnaeus. Only Sextus escaped."

She wanted to dance around the room. He had won, again. Now only Rome stood in their way. But she did not dance. She allowed herself just a small smile.

"He lost just a thousand of his own," Antony said.

"It is indeed good news," she said. "I thank you for bringing me word so quickly."

"I thought it would please you."

She studied him. Sober, he was an imposing man, the strength of his character evident in the authority in his voice, but he was also blessed with a boyish smile that could melt snow off a branch. She remembered how she had first seen him, at the Egyptian party at Caesar's villa. *How about a fuck, darling?* Caesar indeed chose the strangest lieutenants.

"You have seen him?" she asked. "You are sure he is in good health?"

"Marcus Brutus and I have just returned from Gaul," he said. "We saw him with our own eyes. He sent us ahead so that all Rome might hear the news."

She turned to the window. Ice was melting off the roof and drip-ping from the eaves. "I think it will soon be spring," she said.

⚮ ⚮

After Antony had left, she found Caesarion on a bearskin rug in front of a raging fire of pine logs. Charmion and Iras were with him. He was playing with a model chariot, and there was a throne and a doll with a crown on its head. She watched him play.

You will have it all, my son, she thought. You will be the future for Rome and Alexandria, for the whole world. You will not have to strug-gle in fear of your life, as I have had to do. I promise you that.

⚮ ⚮

After the Battle of Munda, the Conscript Fathers of Rome in the Senate fell over each other in their rush to throw titles at him; he was named Imperator for Life, a title they further stipulated would be made hereditary; he was to be Consul for the next ten years; all the anniversaries of his previous victories were to be celebrated with annual holidays; and a statue was to be erected in the Temple of Quirinus, beside the statues of all former kings of Rome, bearing the inscription *To the invincible god*.

They did everything but confer on him the title he so desired, the last and irrevocable step they still shrank from, thanks to the rumblings of the small band of dissenters like Cicero.

They still would not make him Caesar Rex, King of Rome.

The baths in the new Forum Julian had been only recently completed, and were part of Caesar's benediction to Rome. The floor tiles were heated from beneath, and there was even hot and cold running water in the faucets. They were considered a marvel.

Marcus Brutus undressed in the changing rooms and walked through to the *tepidarium,* the warm room that prepared the bathers for the hot water in the *caldarium.* He carried with him a flask of oil, a towel, and a strigil for removing the sweat. He lay down naked on a marble slab and had a slave rub the oil into his back and his shoulders.

Afterward he strolled through the *caldarium,* where he found Cicero and Gaius Cassius Longinus waiting for him. What a pair they made, Cassius with his squat, hairy body, Cicero as pink and hairless as a sow.

The two younger men flicked the sweat from their faces and fidgeted on the marble. Brutus was conscious of the fact that he was sitting with one of Rome's foremost lawyers and statesmen; conscious, too, of his youth and the difference in their age and experience. Why, then, did he feel so superior to the big bag of wind beside him?

"Poor Marcellus," Cicero was saying, gossiping shamelessly as usual, "Livia is growing impossible to manage. I hear he was banished from her bed for ten nights because she was keeping vigil in the Temple of Isis and wanted to remain pure."

"We all know what that means," Cassius said.

"She's the wife of a senator. It's disgraceful."

"These foreign religions are undermining the foundations of our Republic," Cassius said.

"I blame Caesar," Cicero said. "But Caesar does nothing. He lets that Egyptian woman have her sway and fosters this foulness."

Brutus nodded. "Some people say she is his prisoner."

"Others say he is hers," Cicero countered.

Cassius shuddered. "They are a foul and unnatural people, these gypos. Have you seen these *castrati* she keeps as her minions? It is one thing to own slaves, another to rob them of their maleness and have them as your chief ministers."

"They say she bathes in milk and drinks wine from goblets of pure gold. And Caesar flaunts this foreign queen in our faces!"

Brutus kept his silence, and Cicero construed it as agreement.

"They also say," Cicero went on softly, "that the great Julius is planning a union with her."

Brutus felt as if the blood had drained out through his feet. "What, marriage? Had the old boy gone completely off his head?"

"He wants to establish a royal lineage."

"He would not dare!" Cassius hissed.

"He dared to challenge the great Pompey and he won. He dared to invade Britannia and he dared to hold a Triumph in the Forum for a victory over fellow Romans. Who can know what the great Julius will not dare?"

Brutus could not accept that Caesar would ever think of going that far. But the more he thought about it, the more the pieces fell into place. "They say he plans a campaign to Parthia in the spring."

Cassius whistled softly between his teeth. "If he succeeds, he will take his place in history alongside Alexander."

Cicero showed a flicker of irritation. "If he succeeds, Rome will lick his feet and he will take the crown he has been coveting for himself. And our Republic will die."

"You are sure of this?" Brutus asked him.

"See for yourself. Rome is becoming infected with all this talk of kings and queens. Cleopatra has infected us with her perfumes and her ointments and her pretty boys. All evil comes from Alexandria. She must be stopped."

"Or Caesar must be," Cassius said.

And they all fell silent at the enormity of that particular thought.

41

CLEOPATRA PEERED OUT from between the curtains of the litter. The temple was gone, or rather, what remained of it lay on the ground, a rubble of stones on the marble floor. The goddess herself lay on her side beside her pedestal. The features had been shattered with a blow from a hammer.

A woman appeared through the fog and, seeing the litter and Cleopatra's guards, took fright and started to hurry away again. Mardian sent the guards to catch her and bring her back. Cleopatra heard the brief interrogation clearly from behind the curtains of the litter.

"Madam, we mean you no harm," Mardian said to the woman in his faultless Latin. "Can you tell me what happened here?"

"Who are you?"

"My mistress came here to pay her devotions to the Great Mother. She is most distressed to find the temple wrecked."

"It was done by order of Senator Claudius Marcellus. He came here with workmen and the order, signed by himself, for the temple's destruction. I saw it with my own eyes. The workmen would not obey the order so he removed his toga and battered the statue down with his own hands."

"But why?"

"Who knows why those bastards in the Senate do anything? There must be profit in it somehow."

"My mistress will be most distressed," Mardian said.

"So are we all who love the Great Mother. Why would they do this?"

Cleopatra thought she knew the answer to that.

❦   ❦

Forgive me, My Lady, Cleopatra thought as her porters carried her back through the teeming streets of the barbarian city. They did not do this to you. This was to show their fear and hatred of me, the Great Foreigner, your incarnation here on earth. Rome is afraid of me.

And in time I will give them just cause.

☙ ☙

Caesar regarded Marcus Antonius with his piercing black eyes. He had not hurried to return to Rome after his victories, as expected, and the anniversary of his Triumphs had come and gone without him. Antony was relieved to find that the long separation had apparently cooled the feud between them.

Before Caesar left for Spain, they had a bitter argument. Antony's house had once belonged to Pompey. It was a sprawling stone palace in the Carinae, a short walk from Cicero's house. It had been forfeit after Pompey's defeat at Pharsalus, and, without consulting Caesar, Antony had simply moved in. Caesar had expected payment for the house, and when Antony did not meet his demands, he had left him behind in Rome. Personally, Antony would never have jeopardized a friendship over something as inconsequential as money. But there is always a stick up the old boy's backside over something.

"So how were things in Rome in my absence?" Caesar asked him.

"Much the same. In the Senate they still fuss and squabble with each other over points of law. Some of them are hoping that since now the civil wars have ended, you will restore the Republic."

"And they demonstrate their commitment to this democracy by giving me the title of Imperator for Life! What a bunch of old women!"

"Still, you should tread carefully. There are some dangerous men among them."

"No, Marcus, I am a dangerous man. They are a noisome crowd of geese who could not raise an erection between the lot of them, let alone an army. I have vanquished their enemies for them and won a vast empire for Rome, so now they wish me to hand them back their old autocratic powers without them having to lift a finger. They wish to enjoy the fruits without having to climb the tree."

"All I say is that you should not misjudge the tide of opinion. Some of these old geese have a great deal of power."

"Power lies in the sword."

"Not everyone yet believes it."

"Not everyone has yet felt the sharp edge of my blade."

In the name of Jupiter, Antony thought. Munda has gone quite to his head. I have not heard him talk this way before. Is he not going to be satisfied until he has killed the lot of us? "I just urge caution," he persisted. "There are many who are still in love with the idea of a Republic."

"The Republic is a bathhouse full of flabby landowners who have never been outside of Italy. The Republic is dead."

Hot words. He was right, of course, but Antony was unsettled by this forthright and unabashed arrogance. Something had happened to him while he was in Spain. The old boy was always so careful, so . . . well, cold-blooded, really. But there was a recklessness about him now. Perhaps he had begun to believe what the mob said about him on the Aventine. That he was divine.

"Caesar, I came to ask you to reconsider your plans for the Triumph."

Caesar's lips curled into a smile, but there was no warmth in it. "You do not think my victory at Munda warrants a Triumph, Marcus?"

"It was a war against fellow Romans."

"It was a Spanish rebellion aided by a few rebellious Romans."

Oh, really? With Pompey's sons at the head of this Spanish rebellion? "The people will not see it that way," he said.

"The people will see it any way I wish them to see it."

Antony stared at him. Had he really said that? The old boy was getting a little crazy. Perhaps what Cicero and the others were saying was true; it was the witch in his villa at Campania making him think this way.

"I do not stand against you," Antony said. "I just urge you to proceed with caution."

"The gods have their own ways of doing things."

"But we are not gods," Antony said, even then unsure if Caesar might contradict him. "We are still subject to Rome."

Caesar glared at him. "I know who I am subject to."

"Since you have returned from Spain you have spent a lot of time at the villa on the Via Campania. There are those who say—"

"What do I care for gossipmongers?"

"When it is said in the Senate chamber it is no longer gossip, it is politics. Some of that crowd are afraid of that woman. They think she rules you."

"And what do you think, Marcus Antonius?"

Antony shrugged. "You know me. I'm not one to lecture other men over their dealings with women. I always make a hash of my own."

Caesar smiled at this frank admission. "Look, Marcus, this woman is different. I can relax with her, talk with her as an equal. I can even discuss politics with her and have an intelligent discussion. It is not sex that keeps me going back there, boy."

"I just urge you to caution."

"Oh, you know me," he said. "I am always cautious." And he smiled. The smile could have meant anything. I wish I knew what was going on, Antony thought. He's not really serious about making himself king. Is he?

42

When Caesar comes.

When Caesar comes, he comes with his lictors and his bodyguards, not as a lover in the night but as a man who cannot sleep without fearing the assassin's footfall. When Caesar comes, he comes as a man who can have no secrets of his personal life, who cannot spend a night with his mistress without a century of soldiers standing sentry at her door.

Tonight she held him entwined, her arm over his chest, her thigh draped over his, her lips against his cheek. Tonight Caesar had been unable to conquer, his power was dissipated by worry and intrigue. In striving to be one with the gods, he had lost the power of an ordinary man.

A plump harvest moon hung fat over the seven hills, rippling in the dark waters of the Tiber. It left a splash of silver on the marble floor. After a while he got up and went to stand by the window, staring in brooding silence at the night. She watched him from the bed, a dull and empty ache inside her.

Tonight Caesar had become a eunuch, like Mardian.

"You are tired," she whispered. "It does not matter. Come back to bed."

He said nothing. His anger was a towering presence in the room.

"Julius," she said.

"This has never happened to Caesar before."

Then perhaps it is me, she thought. She had no experience of this and did not know what to do, or say. If a man desired a woman, did he not show it in the normal way?

This is just your pride, Julius. If you cannot leave your seed inside a woman, you can hardly bear to look at her. He wanted her comfort, but he was too proud, too much the man of Mars, to say so.

"Rome is crowding in on me," he said. "On the battlefield things are always clear. I have an enemy and I know how to outmaneuver him. Here in Rome I never know my enemies. Everything is shadows."

"You have left too many of your enemies alive."

"But clemency is a virtue," he said.

It was true. Caesar had become as renowned for clemency as he had been for ruthlessness. The same man who had mutilated prisoners of war in Gaul had pardoned hundreds of his enemies at Pharsalus. He was an enigma, impossible to understand.

She heard a trumpet in the remote distance. They were changing the watch in the camp on the Field of Mars. "I heard a story today," she said. "There was a combat in the Circus Maximus. A gladiator, Hirtius Grattus, was killed. He asked for clemency, but you put down your thumb."

"His opponent would not spare him. I only confirm the wishes of the mob in the galleries. They wished him dead also."

"The man who killed him. His name was Didius. Grattus had spared him in a combat just two months ago."

"What are you telling me?"

"That perhaps there is a lesson there. Grant a man a mercy and you perhaps make your own death." She thought of the ruthlessness with which Caesar had gotten rid of her brother, Ptolemy, and how she had admired his cold pragmatism then. Now here she was, lecturing her own mentor.

"By enemies, you are referring to Pompey's followers."

"There are many in the Senate who owe you their lives. Do not suppose that it makes them all your friends."

"The Senate," he said, his voice thick with contempt.

"Because you have shown them a mercy, do not think they will not stand against you."

"They do not stand against me, they stand against an idea. Some of them still talk of this Republic as if it will solve all of Rome's ills. Our empire is too great now to be ruled by a few old men who have never traveled farther than Brundisium."

"Then do as you must. Stop tormenting yourself with laws and forms. You are Caesar. Take what is yours, as you always have."

"Not yet, kitten."

"When?"

"You remember Alexandria? I let them throw themselves at the gates of the palace day and night because I could not be certain of victory at that moment. I waited until everything was ready before striking. You are too impatient."

"It is just that sometimes I fear for my son. I fear for myself. You would not abandon us, Julius?"

He turned around. "Do you doubt me?"

"You forget that I am yet a queen. Would you have me wait another winter here in Rome and have them say of me in Alexandria that I am just some rich man's mistress? I would rather go back to Egypt now, empty-handed, than have you humiliate me further."

"I do not humiliate you. We want the same thing, kitten."

"How can I be sure of that?"

A deep breath. "I will prove it to you. Tomorrow."

⬝ ⬝ ⬝

The Forum Romanus, one Roman glory piled upon another until even the Romans regarded it as excessive. The statues and temples and palaces now crowded upon one another so that the broad piazzas of the original plan had been swallowed up by marble colonnades and porticoes.

It had moved Caesar to dedicate another Forum to the city, to be named the Forum Julian, which he would pay for from his private funds, as a gift to the city, a vast extravagance. It was said that it would cost Caesar more than a million sesterces, but it would also mean that Caesar would never be forgotten.

❦   ❦

Cleopatra stepped from her litter in front of the great portico of the Temple of Venus Genetrix. The Forum Julian, as yet unfinished, rising around them in travertine stone faced with porphyry in marbled gray or pure white. The new stone seemed almost to shimmer like pearl. A mounted statue of Caesar on a white horse looked out over the new piazza that bore his name.

Caesar was waiting for her when she arrived. Together they ascended the steps. She looked up; above her the huge marble pillars seemed almost to touch the cold blue autumn sky. The laborers were still at work; she heard the chip of mason's hammers, the rumble of carts bringing in still more stone.

As they stepped inside the temple, Cleopatra was aware of the dust smell of new masonry. It was cold in here, and dark, a vast, echoing, stone chamber. As her eyes grew accustomed to the gloom, she was able to pick out the murals that soared up the walls. The paint was vivid and fresh, in deep blues and greens; Venus with a child at her breast, Caesar on a white horse, victorious, some battlefield in Greece or Gaul in the background.

As she moved through to the inner sanctum, Caesar watched her expectantly. There were three statues on the high altar. In the center was Venus herself, with her calm and enigmatic smile, the mother of Rome. The Caesars claimed her as ancestor and protector of the House of Julian. The statue was breathtaking, a work of high art; it was carved by Arcesilaus of Greece, Caesar told her. Arcesilaus! He was considered the greatest of all living sculptors. It was clear from this that his reputation was not undeserved.

On the right of Venus the second statue was of Caesar himself, dressed as Triumphator, the distinctive laurel wreath on his head, taking his place among the gods.

She turned to the third statue and caught her breath.

She found herself looking up at her own face, high on the pedestal. She was dressed in the robes of Venus, the Roman Isis, and holding Caesarion on her knee. The message to Rome was clear, and a brave one: Caesar was descended from Venus, which made him divine; his consort was Cleopatra in the incarnation of Venus; Caesarion was his son, and because of the divine union, was himself divine.

She thought of the coin she'd had minted after Caesarion's birth. This was a matching declaration from Caesar.

"Now do you doubt me?" he said.

What was there to say? There never was a man like this one, she thought. She smiled with relief, triumph, desire. If only the Piper were here to see this. He put his faith in me. I have vindicated him.

43

Roman month of the Februa,
forty-four years before the birth of Jesus Christ

A CARRIAGE ARRIVED at the villa late that night, the iron shoes of the horses ringing on the cobbles. It was a heavy, four-wheeled transport known as a *carpentum,* with gleaming coachwork and silver finials. There were four white horses in the traces, with millefiori enamels on their headbands. Dark curtains were drawn across the carriage window.

A servant opened the door and Caesar stepped out.

Cleopatra received him in the room that led off from the atrium. It was a pleasant chamber, extravagantly decorated with murals of arbors and bright-painted flower garlands, with an imposing floor mosaic of cupids frolicking around two lovers. The whisper of the water in the indoor fountains meant that their conversation might not be easily overheard by curious servants.

Caesar threw himself down beside her on one of the long couches, and servants hurried off to bring food and wine.

She stared at him in astonishment. "You have come alone? Where are your bodyguards?"

"I have dismissed them."

"Dismissed them? But why?"

"The Senate has declared my person sacrosanct."

She laughed and was about to compliment him on his dry wit. But instead he gave her an angry look and she realized that it was not a joke.

What had he done? "Have you gone mad?" she asked him.

"My destiny is with the gods."

She was shaking with fury. She could not believe he could be so reckless. It was not only his life at stake here, it was all their futures, her own, her son's. "We make our own destinies. And now you have surely made yours. You have signed your own death warrant!"

"I am tired of this constant fear," he snapped. "It is worse than death itself."

"A man has the right to fear death, but he should not invite it into his house!"

He turned away. "It does not matter to me now."

"Let this matter to you," she said, and she took his hand and led him down the passageway to one of the cubicula. Caesarion lay asleep in his rosewood bed.

"Look, Julius."

So like his father. The same shape to his mouth, the same strong jaw. "He is your son," she whispered. "The future king of the world, if you wish it."

"He must make his own way, as we all must."

"You know that is not true! His future depends entirely on what you choose to do next!"

"It is with the gods," Caesar hissed, tore his hand free from hers, and walked out of the room.

The gods! He was the least devout man she had ever met, and here he was talking about the will of the gods. It was not religion, it was arrogance, arrogance and recklessness. He had always liked to flirt with disaster, and because Fortune always smiled on her favorite son, he had won a reputation for courage and genius when it was merely luck. She thought back to those dangerous days at Alexandria, when he was pitted against Pothinus and Achillas, and the Alexandrian mob were beating at the gates of the Lochias palace. That had been characteristically reckless, for he had allowed himself to become embroiled in a fight when he did not have the soldiers or supplies to back his own arrogance. But the Fates had been kind to him, as always.

His recent victories in Africa and Spain would only have fed the monster inside him. Perhaps now he really did believe the legend of his own invincibility, she thought.

And she felt suddenly afraid.

44

IT WAS CLEOPATRA'S first visit to Antony's house, and Caesar's captain kept her waiting long enough in the atrium to feel insulted. But when he appeared, she immediately understood that no slight had been intended. It was evident that he had spent the previous night in the company of Bacchus, and although it was the fourth hour of the day, he must have been in his bed when she arrived. His toga looked to have been thrown on hurriedly and his thick, curly hair was untended. He looked bleary from lack of sleep and smelled like a wine vat.

"Majesty," he said. "My apologies. I did not expect you."

"That much is obvious."

"Please. Sit down."

"Such a fine house. So little furniture."

"I live simply."

"That is not what I have been told." In fact, Mardian told her that the villa had once had a peerless collection of statuary and furniture, fashioned by some of the empire's greatest craftsmen, but most of it had now been lost in dice games or given away to Antony's friends.

She arranged herself on the only other couch in the room and Antony sent an attendant scurrying away to find them refreshments. Through the windows she could see down the densely wooden Palatine Hill to the dilapidated *insulae* of Rome's poor, the teeming cook shops and *tabernae* and bathhouses around the Circus Maximus.

The servant returned. Antony, she was astonished to find, poured himself a goblet of undiluted wine from the great pitcher that was set before him. Breakfast! She contented herself with a little scented rosewater.

"To what do I owe this great pleasure?" Antony asked her, having drained the goblet, droplets of the red wine gleaming in his dark beard like tiny rubies.

"It is about Caesar."

He rubbed his face in an effort to stir himself awake. "Caesar?"

"I am concerned for him."

Poor Marcus Antonius. Blinking like an owl, his brain still muddled from wine and sleep and, probably, fornication. Even simple conversation seemed a Herculean effort. "The old boy knows what he's doing," he said.

"You know he has dismissed his bodyguards?"

"Yes. I know about that."

"It is madness. Can't you talk sense to him?"

He stared at her. Roman women never meddled in their husband's affairs. Well, Fulvia perhaps. But Fulvia was not a woman, she was the spawn of a devil.

"You have talked to him about this?" he asked.

"Of course."

"And?"

"He still travels Rome without his lictors, so it is evident that he paid no attention to me."

"Why would Caesar listen to me if he will not listen to his . . ."

"Mistress?"

"Advisers. His secretary, Balbus, has also tried to persuade him against this."

"Balbus is his secretary. You are his closest friend. You are also a man. He might listen to you, while he will not listen to me."

"You know Caesar's person has been declared inviolable by the Senate."

"And no doubt he will remain inviolable until the first dagger slides between his ribs."

"All Rome loves Caesar, Majesty."

She gave him a withering look, and he could have bitten his tongue. "If you are going to insult my intelligence, I shall leave."

He stared at her. Her eyes had been darkened with malachite, and they seemed to bore into him. An exotic creature, a heady mix of Levantine and Macedonian blood. He had heard her mother was Syrian. When he looked at the long curve of her neck, he wanted to bite it. This was why women were forbidden from participating in politics. They made it so damned hard to concentrate on the business at hand.

"The old boy has made up his mind," he said. "Who am I to argue with a god?"

"Would you wish him dead, Marcus Antonius?"

He thought: This is not a conversation to be having when your head throbs from the wine from the night before, when your stomach wishes to revolt, and your mouth is as dry and furry as a camel driver's ass. "I would guard his life with my own, Majesty."

"But then, if someone else did the job for you? Who would become Rome's most powerful man should he die?" She gave him a bitter smile. They both knew the answer to that question.

"You misjudge me," he said. "I may not have the intellect of Marcus Brutus, or Cicero's oratory, but when I give my word, it is my master. And I have sworn that I will protect Caesar's life with my own, and I would never break that oath."

She gave him a dark smile. I think she believes me, he thought. She should, because I mean it. "Not all men are as honest," she said.

"I have many flaws, as you doubtless know. But they are small faults. I drink too much, I fall in love with every woman I meet, I gamble, I owe a small fortune to half of Rome. But I would never play any man false."

She looked at him for a long time, as if he were some extraordinary beast she had never seen before. "Marcus Antonius, how did you come to rise so high in Rome?"

He grinned. "Charm."

⚜   ⚜

As the litter bore her back across the Tiber, Cleopatra thought about what he had said. Marcus Antonius was not as simple a character as she had first thought. She supposed you did not become Caesar's henchman by your fondness for drink and actresses. Her own father had been a lover of wine and a devotee of its god, Dionysus, as many Greeks were in Alexandria. Indeed, in Egypt the Ptolemies had made their ancient Greek god palatable by fusing him with Osiris and calling him Serapis.

Here in Rome the Rites were notorious for their excesses. Drunkenness was supposed to help them gain a personal experience of the divine. For men like her father, wine had not been a pathway to his god as much as an escape from the demands of state. But then, her father was weak.

Beneath all the bluster and the well-oiled muscles, did Antony have a reserve of purpose? Or was he just another wastrel, like her father?

≈ ≈

Even in winter they spent much of their time together walking in the gardens. It was a simple pleasure they both enjoyed, but it also meant they were free to talk of whatever they pleased without fearing that their conversations would be overheard.

The cold was intense. The branches along the dark avenue of cypress trees were bent with snow, the fountains frozen. A marble athlete bent to throw a discuss among the bare, brown hedges, the cold white body layered with frost. The statue of a winged Mercury looked as if he had been frozen in mid-stride by some malignant god of ice.

Even Caesar had submitted to the winter, wrapped this day in a thick fur cloak. The gray skies and the white winter garden lent an extra pallor to his skin.

"You look tired," she said to him.

"I suppose I am. Rome is not an easy city to govern."

"Perhaps because it is ungovernable the way it is."

"You are probably right."

"I would have a new Rome."

That idea seemed to amuse him. "And how would you rule this new Rome, kitten?" His tone was playful.

"You might not like my ideas."

"Even if I do not agree with them, they are always entertaining."

"Well, first of all, I would have you as king."

"Of course. And you as consort."

"Queen of Rome. Yes. When that was done, my first act would be to send those ridiculous old men in the Senate back to their farms in the country to dribble into their wine and grow forgetful."

"Ah."

"I would instead have our edicts enforced by a hierarchy of secretaries and governors, as we have in Alexandria."

"You would have some hook-nosed Greek pansies run the empire for us."

She ignored his mocking tone. "The king and queen, as divine beings, would rule the empire. Their court would simply do their bidding. Anyway, better my hook-nosed pansies, as you call them, than this gaggle of callous landlords whose only thought is for themselves and their own enrichment. What have they ever done that serves Rome?"

He gave her a rueful smile. "Cicero would have apoplexy if he heard us talk this way." He looked down at his feet. A single courageous crocus pushed a green shoot through the frost.

"You have not heard my second edict," she said.

"I am listening, kitten."

"I would not rule Rome from Rome."

He raised an eyebrow, intrigued, appalled, and amused.

"It is too far from the sea for commerce. The streets are narrow and filthy and prone to flood, the city itself is cramped and filthy and prone to disease. And the river stinks."

"Where would you have the capital of Rome, then, if not in Rome?"

"Alexandria."

He threw back his head and roared with laughter at her effrontery.

"It looks like a capital. It has marble buildings and wide thoroughfares. And in case it has escaped your notice, it is in the heart of the Roman Empire, while Rome itself is on the edge. It is closer to Tarsus, to Ephesus, to Antioch, and to your main trading routes in India and Arabia. Your Rome could only be mistaken for capital of the world by some turnip from the country."

He stared at her, as if seeing her for the first time. "Are you not afraid of the gods?" he whispered.

The question astounded her. Was Caesar prey to superstition like some peasant working in his cornfield?

"I fear that if we try to outstrip the gods, they will bring us down," he went on. "Perhaps we ask too much of them."

"We act in concert with the gods."

"Perhaps you are right. We shall see." But his voice was gloomy. He was not convinced.

❦   ❦

Caesar was in his private study in the Reggia when Antony found him. It was the fifth hour and Antony had only recently risen. He knew that Caesar would have been at work since dawn.

A porter peered at him through a sturdy iron grille before finally unlocking the gate and leading him through the house to Caesar's study. Antony noticed that unlike on previous visits, there were no soldiers posted guard on all the doors. Caesar's new faith in his own inviolability was unnerving.

Caesar did not look up from his reports. "You wanted to see me?" he snapped.

"I thought you ought to know," Antony said. "The city is abuzz with rumors again."

"What is it this time?"

"They are saying in the markets that the priests have consulted the Sibylline prophecies about this invasion of Parthia."

The oracles of Sibyll. They had been brought to Rome centuries before by an early king and were invested in the Temple of Jupiter. Like all prophecies, they were dense, ambiguous, and open to interpretation and manipulation by those in power. But the mob took them seriously.

"And what do the rumors say they have divined?"

"That no Roman may invade Parthia but a king, else he will be annihilated and Rome humbled. So the priests have concluded that if Rome sends Caesar, it will have to be as Caesar Rex. It has caused much comment."

"I, too, have heard this rumor." He smiled and laid aside his brass stylus. "In fact, I started it."

Antony nodded.

"But you suspected this, of course. That is why you wanted to see me."

"Well, you are chief priest," he said dryly. Caesar had been elected Pontifex Maximus, the highest sacred office in Rome, for a period of twenty years. It had been a fair election in that Caesar had paid a fair price for the votes. "If anyone can interpret an oracle, it is you."

And Antony thought: So, it's true. Cicero was right. The old boy wanted everything. Well, why not? He had never been short of ambition. When he crossed the River Rubicon to go against Pompey, he had cast off all limitations on his behavior. Antony certainly would not stand in Caesar's way, if that's what he decided to do. After all, what was good for Caesar was good for Antony.

"Do I have your confidence, Marcus?"

"You know you do."

"Then I wish you to help me. I have heard you are to lead the Feast of Lupercalia."

Antony shrugged. "I offered my services. You get to whip a few naked young girls. Why should the priests have all the fun?"

"I would not keep you from having your sport." He leaned forward and instinctively lowered his voice. "But at the end of the procession, there is something I want you to do for me."

45

THE FEAST OF the Luperci.

It was a bloody and messy business, Cleopatra decided, one of those pieces of savagery the austere Romans loved so much, like the chariot races and having condemned prisoners torn to pieces by wild animals in the Circus Maximus. For all their laws and courts and Senate houses, their theaters and poetry, at heart they were savages. The rest was a sham.

The Lupercalia was supposed to celebrate the return of spring and fecundity, although the change of seasons had not yet made itself apparent in Rome. In fact, it was a chill day, the sky ice blue, and there was still snow on the mountains. Caesar presided over the festival, seated on a golden throne on the rostra, dressed in the purple robes of the Triumphator, a gilt laurel wreath on his head. The Forum was packed, and there was a riotous atmosphere, the pie sellers doing a good trade from the stalls scattered around the piazza and on the steps of the temples.

Cleopatra and Caesarion were carried into the Forum on a litter and took their places along with the other dignitaries in gilt chairs that had been readied for them on the steps of the Temple of Saturn. Marcus Brutus was there also, sitting with Decimus and Cassius. She greeted them curtly and they acknowledged her in the manner of well-bred and courteous men who hated her heartily.

They all look so pale, she thought. Like men under great strain. But this is a festival. Can they not forget their politics for a day?

🐏 🐏

The feast day started with the sacrifice of a goat and a dog, the symbols of Pan and Lupercus, the ancient nature gods. Two young men from Rome's noble families had been chosen to act as priests. They stripped naked, and their torsos were smeared with blood from the dead animals. The hides of the corpses were then flayed and torn into thin strips called *februa*. It was from these that the Romans gave the name to the month in which the festival was celebrated.

Wild-eyed, half naked, and bloody, the two men then ran through the streets of Rome with their whips, slashing at anyone who got in their way. The festival was primarily a fertility rite, and the Romans believed that any woman who was touched by the whip would conceive shortly after. So the progress of the two young priests through the city was slow, as young married women ran in front of the Luperci for the painful blessing of the primitive whips. The procession skirted the base of the Palatine Hill and traditionally ended in the Forum, later that morning.

🐏 🐏

The crowd parted suddenly and Cleopatra heard the excited squeals of the women as they ran across the cobblestones and the cracking of the bloody leather strips. Several women ran through the crowd, the tops of their garments stripped off, their bare backs striped with weals. Behind them two men pranced into the Forum, wielding the bloody *februa*.

She recognized one of them. He was almost naked, wearing only a loincloth made from the flayed skin of the dead goat. The muscles in his thighs and chest and shoulders glistened with sweat and spatters of blood, a male indeed in all his primitive magnificence. There was a gasp from the crowd around her.

Marcus Antonius.

She recognized Decimus's voice behind her. "But he's a Consul! Has the man no dignity?"

"It's a disgrace," Calpurnia said. But Cleopatra noticed that her face betrayed something other than embarrassment.

She had to force herself to look away. For all his excesses, Marcus Antonius indeed retained a disturbing physical presence, sleek and exciting and dangerous. The crowd gasped at the sight of him, as they did when the lions were released from their cages in the Circus Maximus. She might have gasped herself, but it would have been indelicate. No wonder women threw themselves at him.

The mob followed the two faun men into the Forum. A young girl, her arms clutched across her bare breasts, shrieked with the shock of pain as Antony slapped the *februa* across her bare shoulders. The crowd parted for her and she ran like a panicked deer to try and get away.

Cleopatra shifted uncomfortably in her seat. Something beyond the wish for fecundity here, she thought. The whip cracked again and again, the young girl trapped by the crowd. She could feel the excitement of the men around her, was suddenly aware of the same supercharged atmosphere here that she had experienced in the Circus Maximus. There was a violence to these Romans, never far below the surface, sex and blood lust inextricably mixed into a disturbing, intoxicating brew.

Finally, just as it seemed the girl might collapse, Antony turned away, allowing her to escape. The men shouted their disappointment, but the girl quickly vanished into the mob, and the crowd looked for a new victim.

But then something happened that the mob was not expecting, something beyond these ancient rites and the Romans' dark desires.

She did not know if Antony had the crown in his hand when he entered the Forum or if it had been passed to him on a prearranged signal by someone in the crowd. But suddenly he leaped onto the rostra, clutching a white royal diadem. The spectators gasped again.

He moved toward Caesar. A hush fell across the square.

"Jupiter," she heard Brutus murmur behind her, "what is the fool going to do?"

Antony fell on one knee in front of Caesar and held out the diadem. "Caesar," he said, loud enough that she could hear even from her position on the temple steps, "I offer you this diadem on behalf of the people of Rome. They wish you to take it and be their king!"

There was a hiss of astonishment and outrage from the senators around her. The crowd itself was utterly still, waiting to see what Caesar would do. Then, from around the Forum, voices shouted for him to take it. But perhaps they had been planted there by Caesar or by Antony, for their cries were not taken up by the rest of the mob.

Instead there was a long, icy silence.

Caesar's lip curled in a frown of irritation and disappointment. She knew what he was waiting for. He wanted the acclamation to be taken up by the crowd. He wanted to be able to say he was forced to take the crown at the urging of the mob.

Instead he reached out a hand toward the diadem . . . and pushed it away.

Antony appeared surprised at this reaction. "Caesar, this is your crown!" he said again. "The people wish you to be their king!"

Caesar looked around, but again the offer from Antony was greeted with utter silence. There was no mistaking the mood of the crowd.

Take it anyway, Cleopatra thought. Take it anyway and end this! It is your crown by right! Who will stop you?

But she knew Caesar's instincts were right. He could act without the support of the Senate and he could move without the mandate of the ordinary people, but he could not defy them both.

Or was this just another maneuver? Did he intend by this to convince the Conscript Fathers of the Senate that he did not covet the kingship so he could take them by surprise? She had no way of knowing Caesar's real mind on this.

For a third time Antony held out the diadem to him. But Caesar seemed now to make up his mind. He stood up and pushed the crown away. "Jupiter is the king of Rome," he said. "Take this crown and place it on the head of his statue in the Capitoline."

At this there was a wild roar of approval from the crowd. As Antony loped away with the diadem, she felt as if her heart had been scooped out with a dull spoon. The opportunity was gone and Caesar had judged the time was not right. For one moment the future of Egypt had hung in the balance. The scales had tipped against her again.

When she stood up to leave the Forum, she discovered she was shaking. Caesar did not speak to her afterward, and she had her porters take her directly back to the villa in Esquiline. She tried to tell herself that she was too impetuous and that she must trust Caesar's judgment. He had been right in Alexandria against Pothinus. Surely he would outwit their enemies again this time.

46

SUCH A FINE *house,* Antony thought. *So little furniture.*

The Egyptian minx was right. It does look bare. I must stop gambling.

A cold draught rattled the doors and made the lamps sway on their ornate stands. The braziers had been lit in the corners of the rooms, but they did no more than make the cold bearable. Brutus and Cassius lay on couches, sipping mulled wine.

"It seems that Caesar is serious about his great exploit to Parthia," Brutus said.

"He is talking of it as the crowning achievement of his career," Cassius said.

Brutus looked at Antony. "Of course, it causes some concern about Rome."

Antony looked surprised, as if he was unaware of the talk in the private bathhouses of the Palatine. "In what way?"

"Caesar has absolute authority here. Rome will be helpless without him. Does he intend to give up his authority before he leaves on his campaigns?"

"He has not spoken to me of it."

"Perhaps he will pass his authority on to you?"

"Perhaps. Though I must confess that if Caesar goes to Parthia, I shall be eager to go with him."

"But he will be gone two years, perhaps three. What is to happen to Rome?"

I wonder what they want, these two, Antony thought. They have the look of plotters. But Cassius owes Caesar his life, and if you can believe the talk, Brutus is his son. It was Caesar himself who appointed these two former enemies to their present exalted positions. Antony could not believe they would betray him.

Yet, for all that, he himself distrusted intellectuals like these men. Men who spent their whole lives thinking could persuade themselves of anything.

A servant came in to refill the lamps with oil. Cassius and Brutus stopped talking. Rome was full of spies. You could not trust the servants. After the man had gone, Antony said: "You know what the old boy's like. He does what he wants."

"And we love him for it," Cassius said.

"But we would love him better if he did not disport himself as King of Rome," Brutus said. "If he builds himself any more statues, we will not be able to move the carts down the streets. And someone should tell him he should take off his Triumphator's robes occasionally to have them washed."

"All the honors he has, he richly deserves."

"So this talk of kings does not worry you, Marcus Antonius?"

"No, it does not worry me," Antony said. "Dictator or king, what is the difference? Caesar is Caesar. I would rather have him in charge of Rome than some of the old women in the Senate."

Cassius gave him a chill smile. Brutus said nothing at all. Antony helped himself to some more wine, and the conversation turned to other things.

⟜ ⟜

They lay together in her bed, staring through the window at the fog drifting through the pines, the moon rising over the Janiculum Hill.

"You have made up your mind? You are going to Parthia, then?"

"Parthia is my destiny."

"And what if you die there? Is that your destiny also?"

"If I fail, then I cannot count myself as great as Alexander, for he conquered there and he did not die."

Was that what all this was about? Had he still more to prove to himself? "I do not understand this."

"Parthia is the kingdom we can rule equally," he said, his eyes burning with his private vision. "We will be far from Rome's interference there. It will be my legacy to our son. By law he can inherit nothing I possess here in Rome. But I can give him an empire of his own—"

He stopped abruptly, clutching at his head.

"Are you all right?" she whispered, fearing that the gods might be about to possess him once more.

"These headaches," he said. He had turned very pale. His face was gaunt, haggard. She realized with a lurch how old he was looking.

"Caesarion *can* inherit everything," she whispered, "*without* Caesar going to Parthia."

"You saw how the people reacted at Lupercalia. I fear it may not be possible. But if . . . if I win Parthia, then perhaps Rome will accept this."

He was impossible. Why did he choose not to see? "You ask me to spend my men and my money to chase your dreams. What of *my* dreams?"

"Without Rome, without me, you can dream of nothing more than slavery."

She stared at him. At last the truth, bluntly spoken.

"I have to have Parthia. I will not have the shadow of Alexander over me the rest of my life! I will be as great as he!"

And there is the kernel of the problem, she thought. It torments him, this constant comparison he makes. Perhaps in his heart he does not truly believe he has the right to be king until he is in Babylon.

She took a breath. "If you must go, then make me your queen before you leave. Let me rule here while you are in Parthia."

He stared at her in the candlelight. It was a breathtaking idea. "A *pelegrina*, sole Queen of Rome? Your life would be forfeit as soon as I set foot out of the city, even should I be mad enough to do such a thing."

"Marry me anyway."

He sat up in bed, gripped his temples, his knuckles white. "I cannot."

She felt the energy drain out of her. She had begged him constantly to seize his moment, but it seemed there was always some excuse. The great Caesar, so renowned for the swiftness and decisiveness of his action, paralyzed with uncertainty.

"When I return from Parthia," he said, "the whole of Rome will hail me as god. Then we may do as we wish and there will be no one to gainsay us."

"Let them gainsay you all they wish. They cannot stop you now!"

"You do not understand. Rome has not had a king for four hundred years!"

He was right, she did not understand. The alliance of one throne with another made perfect sense to her. Why should Rome resist what was right and natural in the rest of the world? If men were to be led, they needed a leader. In every henhouse there was only one rooster, in every pasture there could be only one bull.

"What about Calpurnia? Why will you not divorce her? Must that wait until you return from Parthia, too?"

He grew irritated, as he always did when his judgment was questioned, when he was asked to explain himself. "What difference would it make? I cannot marry you until my position here in Rome changes."

"And when it does?"

"When it does, I shall have to put her aside, though it will not please me to do so. She is barren, and no one else will have her."

"Because she is barren you have cause to divorce her whenever you wish."

"She is a Roman lady, and you have no right to tell me what to do!"

Of course. Calpurnia, for all her faults, was a matron of Rome, and she, despite the son she had given him, was still a *pelegrina*, a foreigner.

"Besides," he said, "I am not the only one with an impediment."

"My little brother."

"I cannot marry you while you are yet married."

"It was your idea!"

"I had my reasons for acting as I did. What is done is done. But when the time comes, you must give some thought to your own situation."

"He is only twelve years old."

"Every twelve-year-old boy must grow into a man. And this twelve-year-old boy has a claim to your throne. Think on it, kitten. Think on it."

She remembered how she had admired his ruthlessness when he sent Ptolemy out of the palace. Easier, of course, when your victim wasn't your own family. But then her own family had never been to her as brothers and sisters are to common people. They were rivals, snakes from the same nest.

So, with so much at stake, could she be Caesar?

47

THERE WAS FROST on the vines and ice still floated on the still waters of the fountains, but there were buds on the peach and cherry trees. The Kalends of March had come and gone and the army that was to accompany Caesar to Parthia was mustering on the Field of Mars.

⚜ ⚜

Caesar, freshly shaved, in cloak and ceremonial armor, arrived, as he did that first day, on a white horse, his generals with him, Antony, Decimus, and Marcus Lepidus. They had just come from inspecting the troops on the Campus Martius. Caesar looked tired and pale.

He dismounted his horse. She waited for him under the portico with Mardian and her secretaries, wearing thick furs against the cold.

"I have come to say good-bye," he said.

"When will you leave?"

"In three days."

So soon. No turning back from it now.

Relations between them were strained. These last weeks she had hardly seen him at all. His late-night visits had become increasingly rare. He had been consumed with his preparations for

Parthia. As for herself, she was resigned to whatever bitter disappointment was in wait for her in the future. Unable to dissuade him from his course, she was bracing herself for another betrayal. After all, you never knew which game Caesar played. If he could not be persuaded to act in the name of his only son, who knew what he would do after Parthia?

If he returned.

"What will you do?" he asked her.

"I shall return to Egypt as soon as the weather allows."

He nodded, seemed relieved. "That would be as well. You have enemies here."

"I am not running away from men like Cicero. I have work to do in Alexandria." Such arrogance. As if Rome was the whole world. "I will pray to Isis for your safe return."

He did not respond. Instead he murmured: "We may yet see our dream fulfilled before I leave."

She stared at him, hardly daring to breathe. He had crushed her hopes so many times before. "What are you telling me?"

He gave her a tired smile. "Tomorrow the Senate will debate the Sybilline Oracles. At the end of the debate I believe they will make me Caesar Rex."

Was this another of his games? Why had he not whispered to her of these plans before? "This is certain?"

He shrugged his shoulders. "Nothing is certain. But I have assurances from Marcus Antonius that he has the numbers among the Conscript Fathers to ensure the vote is in my favor. He has made a few judicious bribes on my behalf, threatened some of those that will not be bought. It is our Roman democracy in action."

"You will be King of Rome?"

He looked away. "There may be a compromise."

Ah, of course. Her Julius. There was always a deal to be cut. "A compromise?"

"I will be king, but not of Rome. Instead I will take the throne of all the empire outside of Italy, entitled to a crown. I shall be free to marry a queen of my choosing, establish my royal capital in Alexandria, and make Caesarion my heir."

She could not believe her ears. "But without Rome your son will never be safe. Nothing will have changed!"

"It will have changed for me," he said, his eyes cold and bleak.

"And you will divorce Calpurnia?"

"It will not be necessary. She will remain the childless wife of the dictator of Rome. *You* will be my queen."

She understood what he was doing. As always, he had found the perfect accommodation for himself. If the Senate allowed him this, his marriage to her could be explained as a policy move, a clever tactical maneuver by their Imperator. The mob in the Forum would not mind; a marriage would bind Egypt with its royal line and overflowing treasury even tighter to Rome. He wanted everything and he wanted Rome's love as well. He had not quite betrayed her, he had merely rearranged the pieces on the board.

He kissed her lightly. "We shall be gods," he whispered.

She did not respond to the kiss.

You bastard.

He shrugged. He had undoubtedly anticipated this. Well, he could afford her to be cool. He would be away for at least two years, time enough for her to forgive him. And there would be other men's wives to entertain him on the way to Parthia. They said Herod had a new wife, for example.

"May all the gods go with you and grant you a safe journey," she said with stiff formality.

There was a look in his eyes. Regret perhaps, though she would not have gambled on it. *"Vale,* kitten."

She said nothing, watched him leave. One way or another, she thought, these Romans are going to cheat me again.

∿ ∿

She could not sleep.

March had broken upon the city, the winter unabated. Snow muted the rumble of the wagons at night, cloaking the statues and summer houses in white. Then the gales came from the north, bringing driving rain and fierce winds that uprooted several of the cypress pines in the garden.

Cleopatra lay awake, listening to the winds crashing in the pines, the creaking of branches, the howling of the draught under the doors. Somewhere a gust brought a lamp stand crashing onto a marble floor.

The last few days the whole city had been on edge. Everyone in the city knew that tomorrow, on the Ides of March, the Senate would debate the Sibylline prophecies when they met in Pompey's Theater. Meanwhile, Mardian reported that he had heard rumors of plots against Caesar's life. But there were always rumors.

In the Aventine markets and down at the Tiber wharves the gossip-mongers and soothsayers were feted like oracles. There was endless talk of portents, babies born with two heads, statues weeping blood, lights in the heavens. A story circulated of a wolf that had pulled a sword from a sentry's scabbard at one of the gates and run off with it into the woods.

She lay awake, debating with herself whether Caesar's compromise was really so bad. After all, it was more than she could ever have hoped for when she took the throne. Caesar, King of the Roman Empire, and husband of the Queen of Egypt. It would mean peace for her country, a throne secured for Caesarion.

Or would it? Caesarion was still just a child, and Caesar might not live to see him enthroned. There would be other Consuls, other dictators. The next Imperator would surely want to take back everything that Caesar had given away.

Unless I have Rome, she thought, I have nothing.

She could not sleep. The great treasure was still beyond her reach. Tonight it seemed that until she finally had it in her grasp, she would never sleep again.

48

THE BRANCHES OF the pines dipped and swayed in the blustering wind. The sky was overcast, a flash of lightning illuminating for a moment the statuary in the garden, making them appear to move, like ghosts.

She watched the storm, a profound sense of unease sitting like rotten food in her stomach. The storm threw an odd, greenish light over the city. Even the cats she had brought with her from Egypt darted about the rooms, snarling and unhappy. The servants started at every flash of lightning, touching the amulets at their necks to ward off the evil eye.

Later that morning one of the servants heard the sounds of a commotion from the city, but by the time it was reported to her, the shouting had ceased. She supposed that the legionaries had imposed their peace on the population. She wondered if it had anything to do with the events at the Senate. Was it popular acclamation for Caesar's assumption of Rex? Or had the debate among the Conscript Fathers spilled over into a riot in the Forum? Where were Mardian's spies when they were needed?

It was just after midday when a carriage appeared at the gates, the Consul Marcus Antonius with a heavy bodyguard. The soldiers immediately fanned out across the gardens of the villa, tense and alert, their weapons drawn.

Something had gone wrong.

She received him in the room overlooking the garden. She hardly recognized this Marcus Antonius, so gray-faced, so sober. Outside, a spatter of rain burst on the house, like small stones heaved at the villa from a siege machine. Thunder rumbled over the seven hills.

As soon as he walked in, as soon as she saw his face, she knew.

"He's dead, isn't he?"

He nodded.

The world yawed off its axis. It was impossible. Yet it was the moment she had been dreading ever since her arrival in Rome. The invincible god—dead? She thought of the morning when he had thrown himself into the harbor at Alexandria, had swum in full armor with spears splashing into the water all around him. Had he survived that only to be ambushed in his own Senate chamber? She remembered her father's prophetic words from so long ago: *Every palace is filled with snakes twice as deadly as these.*

So much, too much, had depended on one fragile heartbeat.

"He was murdered, in the Senate, at the foot of Pompey's statue, in front of everyone. More than a score of them crowded around him and stabbed him to death."

She closed her eyes. This was like a dream, a bad dream. My Julius. Gone. For a moment the loss of dynasties and empires figured as nothing for her, subsumed by her own sense of loss. What am I going to do without him? "Who did this?"

"Dolabella. Cassius. Decimus. Even Marcus Brutus. Afterward, they ran into the Forum shouting about liberty and the Republic. All the other senators lifted their togas and scurried away like old women. There's a riot going on there now, a whole cohort of gladiators looting everything they can find."

She felt numb. Why couldn't she feel? "I warned him."

"We all warned him, Majesty. I'm sure the old boy knew the risks he was taking."

Caesar was dead. And if Caesar could die, no one was safe. "Are you in danger, Marcus Antonius?"

For the first time he smiled. "They will have to outwit me first. Unlike Caesar, I rely on a bodyguard before I rely on the good graces of others."

It occurred to her there was a little boy playing in a room down the corridor who might be next on the assassin's list. If they would kill Caesar, they would wish to kill *all* of Caesar. "And me? And my son?"

The smile vanished. "It may be well for you not to linger in Rome now. The days are uncertain. With the old boy gone, who knows what will happen here?"

True. It could even be that this man will be my next adversary, she thought. Antony was Caesar's protégé, his fellow Consul. They had spoken of him as Caesar's successor, though no one had really believed that day would come so soon. This news cast him in a new light.

"I take it you have made plans for your own protection," she asked him.

"Indeed."

"Are Brutus and Cassius masters of Rome now?"

"Brutus and Cassius are addressing the crowd in the Forum. While they are waving their traitor's daggers and shouting about liberty and the Republic, I have taken the precaution of asking Lepidus to mobilize his legions on the Field of Mars. Give me two days and I will take back all they think they have won."

She could see now why Caesar had loved him. Some men were born for the great action. They might be mediocre in peace, but when there was blood in the street they put aside the wine jug and made the time their own.

"Are you all right, Majesty?" he said.

She sat down heavily on a couch, her knees giving way beneath her.

She could not yet believe that Caesar was dead. She had thought him indestructible, despite the lines that creased his face a little deeper with every passing month, despite the falling sickness that had left him pale and gaunt. She expected him to march through that door any moment, a scroll clutched in one hand, barking orders as he came; she could imagine that familiar worn and angry expression he assumed in times of crisis, as if his patience was too sorely tried by having to deal with mere mortals every day.

Well, he would no longer have to concern himself with that particular problem. In a moment the world had turned, had changed irrevocably.

"Thank you for bringing me this sad news, Marcus Antonius. I shall never forget that on this day you were a friend."

He bowed. "Majesty."

He left and she sat there, for a long time, staring into the garden, watching the wind bend the trees, the lightning crackling over the hills of Rome. A hot tear began to course its way down her cheek. It surprised her. She had never thought to cry for a Roman.

~ ~

By the time he arrived at Caesar's house, Calpurnia had already heard the news. A servant had run all the way from the Forum. She looked drawn and red-eyed.

Marc Antony stood there, fidgeting in his armor, wanting to get on with this. Time to weep for the old boy later. Right now, there were things to be done.

"I told him," she was saying, over and over, "I told him to be careful. It serves him right."

"They betrayed him, Calpurnia."

"Of course they did. What did he expect?" She had not attended to her toilet yet that morning. It was the first time he had seen her without her jewelry and face ointments, and her hair hung in untidy bunches around her shoulders. She looked like an old woman. "I suppose you went to see his gypo tart first?"

"Cleopatra has been informed."

"I imagine she wept a bucket."

Antony took a deep breath. He had never liked Calpurnia and had not imagined she would accept this news with any grace. She seemed determined not to disappoint him.

"Were you there?" Calpurnia asked him.

"Do you think I would be alive now if I had been able to put my body between him and them?"

She gave him a look of sudden and unexpected compassion. "No. I don't think you would be. I know you loved him, too, in your own way."

"We must mourn Caesar tomorrow," he said, determined to avoid maudlin conversation with this harridan. "Today there are things that must be done to keep Rome safe from his assassins."

She gave him a wolfish smile. "Straight down to business, then, Marcus?"

"The best way we can avenge him is by making sure Brutus and his friends do not profit by what they have done."

She gave a small nod of assent. Suddenly she looked so small and lost. This grief, he realized, was real. He was frankly surprised. He had not believed she had loved Caesar so much.

"You have his will?" he asked her.

She seemed uncertain. "My father ordered the Vestals to release it as soon as he heard the news."

"You have opened it?"

She nodded.

"I must see it."

She left the room, returned a few minutes later with two scrolls, which she threw on the table in front of him. "See for yourself what he has done."

Two wills. He sat down at the table, opened the first scroll and held it in his left hand while he unrolled it in his right. It named his nephew, Octavian, as principal heir to his fortune. The will also allowed the boy to assume Caesar's own name, as his adopted son.

"I should have given him a real son," Calpurnia murmured. "Now his little bitch of a nephew gets everything."

"What is in this, then?" he asked her, holding up the other will.

Calpurnia's face was pale. "Read it," she said.

It was dated two years after the other. It was a truly extraordinary document. In it, Caesar bequeathed a part of his fortune to his nephew but left the bulk of it to his son by Cleopatra. It also allowed the boy

Caesarion his name, acknowledging paternity to a boy who might one day be the King of Egypt. The implications were unthinkable.

"This document is illegal," he said.

"Immoral was the first word I thought of, but then, how can we attribute morals to someone like Caesar?"

"The old boy must have been mad to write this."

"He acknowledges his bastard to the whole world. Not content with having screwed every well-bred lady in Rome, he now trumpets his bastard gypo as if it were a matter for pride!"

Antony stared at the parchment in astonishment. Caesar, of all people, well knew that it was against the law to pass on Roman possessions and Roman capital to any but a Roman citizen. It could not stand. But should the contents of this document become common knowledge, it would make it impossible for anyone following in Caesar's footsteps to rule with real authority. Caesarion would be a shadow looming over their legitimacy forever. The only recourse for the next Imperator would be to murder the boy, and probably his mother, too.

"We have to decide which of these wills we take before the Senate," he said, knowing the answer before he even spoke the words.

Calpurnia stared at him. He could not believe the thought had not occurred to her.

"You mean—destroy one?"

"Peace of mind is no further than the nearest candle, my lady. Besides, by law, this earlier one is the only one that can stand. The other is illegal. It is political propaganda."

He was tempted to destroy both wills, but one of them had to stand. Besides, Octavian was of no account, he would take the money and squander it on his pretty boys. He could be easily managed. Perhaps that was what Caesar had intended all along. Devious bastard.

He picked up the candle. Within minutes Caesarion's inheritance was ashes on the table. Antony brushed the blackened pieces onto the floor. "Well, now Octavian is Caesar's heir. He shall take the news well, I am sure."

"He will take it up the bottom, as always."

Antony winced at Calpurnia's gross observation. She had long been famous for her crudities, and he was at a loss to explain why

Caesar had tolerated her for so many years. She had long ago worn out her usefulness, politically.

"I must take this will with me. I shall also need all his papers."

"His papers?"

"It is my right and my duty as the sole remaining Consul." He had no idea if this was true, but he was sure Calpurnia would not know enough about Roman law to contradict him.

While she went to fetch Caesar's papers, Antony stared at the ashes of the will on the floor at his feet. What could have been going through the old boy's mind when he wrote that?

He looked again at the earlier will and studied the list of secondary heirs. It evinced a grim smile from him. One of them was Decimus Brutus, who was also one of those who stuck him with his dagger. The old boy was a great soldier, but by the sacred tits of the she-wolf, he was a rotten judge of character.

※ ※

Cleopatra ran from the villa, feeling cold darts of rain on her face. She ran blindly, tottering through muddy puddles, her chest heaving with racking sobs, and finally threw herself down on a cold and rain-soaked marble bench.

She had warned him. When he had dismissed his bodyguard, it was almost as if he was taunting them all to unsheathe their knives and come at him.

Why hadn't he listened to her? Why?

She wanted to rant, to scream. Everything gone, just thrown away, not only his life, but hers, and her son's. "You fool," she shouted into the wind and the stinging arrows of rain. Her body was rigid with fury. *You fool!*

And then it struck her what must have happened. There was something about this race, this city. They believed in the greatness of being Roman more than in anything else, and in the end that was what had killed him.

He must have doubted in his own heart the rightness of what he was about to do. He wanted the approbation of those hard-faced Roman gods he claimed he did not believe in, and so he had thrown himself on their protection, testing his ambition against his fate. His stiff-backed Roman conscience at war with his own ambition. Perhaps, deep in his Roman soul, even he thought that his Rome should not countenance a king married to a foreign queen.

The anger seemed to drain out of her as quickly as it had come, and she started to weep. She wept for Egypt; she wept for Caesarion; and finally she wept for herself. She wept because she had let him leave yesterday while she was still angry with him, without even having the chance to say good-bye.

49

THEY HAD MURDERED Caesar, in itself a monumental act, Antony thought, but in all other respects they were schoolboys. They had made the mistake of letting Brutus address a mob in the Forum in an attempt to rally them to their side. His oratory was as dense and impenetrable as always, littered with references to the Republic and to liberty, when all that mob ever wanted to hear was that you were going to invade Gaul and lower taxes. Brutus forgot that the common people had loved Caesar, in their own way, and growing tired of the sound of Brutus's voice, they had turned on him and chased him and his friends out of the Forum.

The next mistake the conspirators made was to name Cicero as new leader of Rome. That old fart. A great talker but without a clue as to how to manage a rebellion. While he and Cassius and Brutus were planning their perfect new Rome, Antony had secured the backing of the Captain of the Horse, Marcus Lepidus, second in command to the dictator and fiercely loyal to Caesar. He also fancied himself as the new Pontifex Maximus, an ambition Antony promised to help him with.

Antony had him put three cohorts of his legionaries in the Forum and had the rest of his soldiers reinforce the city gates. Then, after he had taken possession of the will and the rest of Caesar's papers from Calpurnia, he met with Caesar's banker, his secretary, and his Consuls designate. Within days he was in control of Rome, having secured the blessed triumvirate of money, respectability, and an army.

All the conspirators had were their principles. All the good it would do them now.

❦ ❦

Two days after Caesar's murder, the Senate reconvened in Pompey's Theater. Cicero immediately suggested an Act of Oblivion. Others wanted to go further. Certain friends of Brutus and Cassius proposed a resolution that the conspirators—or the liberators, as they called themselves—be granted special honors and hailed as public bene-factors. One senator even wanted Caesar to be declared a tyrant and all his acts illegal.

Antony bided his time and let them all have their say before finally rising to his feet, and, playing the voice of reason, reminded the Conscript Fathers that such an act might not be wise. "If every-thing Caesar did was declared illegal," he said, turning to Brutus and Cassius, "then you will both have to resign your positions as praetors. And you, Decimus Brutus, cannot assume the governorship of Cisalpine Gaul. Tillius Cimber here will not be going to Bithynia," he said, wagging his finger at another senator as if rescinding sweet treats for a naughty child, "and no Asia for you, Trebonius."

His reproaches were greeted with gales of laughter.

Unable to gain majority support for their proposals, Cassius and Brutus then tried to force through an agreement that Caesar be buried privately and without honors. Antony sighed and reminded them that their proposal could not be considered, as every Consul who died during his time of public office had the absolute right to a public funeral. It was the law.

Smiling and reasonable, and for once sober, he carried the day, as he knew he would. But, unknown to the Senate, he also had Lep-idus's legions standing ready in the Field of Mars.

Just in case.

50

THEY BURIED CAESAR on a gray evening, clouds the color of lead scudding over the rooftops, the north wind bitter cold, moaning through the narrow streets. Some said it was the ancient kings of Rome mourning their beloved Julius.

He is gone, Cleopatra thought. And with him my dreams.

At that moment she hated Caesar more than she had ever hated anyone. So typical of him to think of nothing or no one but himself. His death was as he would have chosen it, quick and theatrical. He had been taken at the height of his powers, without ever having to test his greatness in Parthia. Rome had already given him the mantle of Alexander in expectation of his victory, but what if he had been defeated?

Caesar would never have to know. Greatness had been lent to him by default.

And what had he left behind? A son without a throne; and a mistress, a queen in waiting, to whom he had promised so much, holding bitter ashes. In the end he had fallen in love with his own death, and had consummated that passion with no thought for any other woman to whom he had promised himself, just as he had done his whole life.

But I must not allow myself this maudlin reflection, she thought, this bitter pitying of my own situation. I knew it was a gamble. And I did not lose everything. Caesar won me back my throne, and for that I must be grateful. From now it all begins again. I must find another way to save Egypt and secure my son a life without the shadow of a Roman boot over his head.

But it will take me many years to count the cost, for besides politics, I have lost something that cannot be regained in this life; my lover and my companion, the only man I could talk openly with, the man who taught me everything I know about power and all its refinements. She had resigned herself to the loneliness that comes with being royal, and had even come to accept it. But Julius had given her a glimpse into another world, a place where those burdens could be shared with another like-minded heart. I had never bargained for this; I had thought in terms of politics, and never counted that his passing might leave a hole in my soul that I could not refill.

Indeed, he led me into the trap I always promised myself I would avoid. He left me knowing that I loved that faithless, conniving bastard more than he ever loved me.

~~ ~~

The bier had been placed in the Forum, the logs in the funeral pyre arranged with something approaching artistry. The bier had been constructed after the Temple of Venus; there were great columns of plaster on all sides, and beneath it a couch of pure ivory, covered with rich cloths of gold and purple.

The guests of honor were led to the curving steps of the Temple of Vesta, where a gallery had been hastily assembled for the dignitaries to watch the ceremony. The atmosphere in Rome was volatile now, and there were soldiers everywhere.

Cleopatra took her seat. She glanced to her right and saw Calpurnia staring at her. I do not know why you look at me like that, she thought. You have lost a husband who did not love you. I have lost the chance to be queen of the world.

~~ ~~

It began with the mournful dirge of trumpets, the dolorous beat of drums.

Torches had been lit all around the Forum and they set grotesque shadows dancing around the walls of the temples and Pompey's Theater. The cold wind freshened and Cleopatra shivered in her cloak.

The litter bearing Caesar's body was borne through the crowd by ten magistrates and placed reverently on the bed of ivory that was waiting to receive it. Marcus Antonius followed the body into the Forum and mounted the rostra behind the bier.

He waited, his head bowed in respect, as a herald recited one by one all the decrees that had been passed in Caesar's name by the Senate. There was a low sigh from the crowd when he read the oath of inviolability that had supposedly given Caesar protection from his fellow lawmakers. Then the young captain recited the list of Caesar's military campaigns and the victories he had won, in Gaul, in Britannia, in Alexandria and Spain and Africa, the value of the treasures he had sent home, the number of territories he had added to the empire, the list of honors voted to him by a grateful Senate.

The recitation appeared endless.

By the time Antony stood up to give the oration, it seemed to everyone that they were there not to bury a man, but a god.

The crowd was hushed. Antony's gaze took in the packed and silent square as if looking into every eye. The only sound was the crackling of the torches in the wind that whispered across the piazza. From that moment he held them all in the palm of his hand.

Even Cleopatra studied him with a dawning respect. You have managed this piece of theater to perfection, she thought. Rome has underestimated you.

"Caesar," he said softly, so that they all strained to hear him, "my Caesar!"

He waited, his lamentation hanging on the wind.

"Tell me, my brothers, was there ever in our history a Roman such as this? Was there any one man who loved Rome as much as he?" He waited, as if expecting them to answer. "Our city has seen many great generals and statesmen, but never, never, has there been another to match Gaius Julius Caesar. And now he is gone."

He appeared too choked with emotion to go on. The crowd seemed to hold their breath. Finally, he seemed to compose himself.

"To the gods, Caesar was high priest; to us, he was Consul; to the soldiers, he was Imperator; to our enemies, he was dictator. He brought us more glory in his short time than any other man in our long history. Caesar *was* Rome.

"But now he is dead and we are here tonight to mourn him. If it were old age that had borne him away, then perhaps we could bear it. If it was some sickness that had lain its vile hand on him, then perhaps we could say: the gods had wished it so. If he was wounded in some foreign war, then we would know that it was Fortune's command. But no. His fate was crueler than this, too cruel to bear. Caesar, our Caesar, our great general who led the armies of Rome to glory in Britain and Africa and Spain, died right here within these walls, at the hands of his fellow Romans.

"Caesar, *our* Caesar, the man who risked his life at the furthest corners of the world for Rome, was ambushed and slain inside the city he loved. Our Caesar, the man who built Rome a new Senate house, was murdered by his fellow senators. Our Caesar, the man who survived countless battles, was struck down while he went unarmed in his own city, our foremost judge and magistrate, executed in the house of judgment, without trial. This Caesar, whom our enemies could not kill, even when he fell in the sea at Alexandria, who should have disappeared under the waves with the weight of his armor, who should have died a thousand times fighting for our cause, was finally murdered by his fellow Romans. Our clement Caesar, who showed mercy even to his enemies, was finally betrayed by those whose lives he had pardoned."

Antony paused, and she heard a soft moan pass through the crowd, like a ripple on the surface of a lake. His deep orator's voice held them all in its thrall. Cleopatra watched him now with unstinted admiration.

"Caesar, as you all know, was a humane and merciful man. How did it benefit him? He pardoned Brutus and Cassius at Pharsalus. To what end? What gratitude they showed him!

"And what of the inviolability granted him by his fellow senators? It was these men who thrust their knives in his back! What good are the laws these same senators pass when they themselves can treat them with such violence?"

Antony hung his head, apparently exhausted by his own rage.

Then a voice called from somewhere in the darkness: "Is this the way these men repay my mercy? Did I save them just so they might murder me?"

The voice appeared to come from the bier, from the corpse itself. There was a murmur among the crowd, fear working together with their anger now. Another clever piece of theater, Cleopatra thought.

Antony produced a toga, stained dark brown with blood. He held it up to the crowd, who recognized it immediately as the robe Caesar had worn when he was murdered. There was a howl of outrage.

"Look at what they did to him!" he shouted, and now his voice had risen to an angry roar that echoed around the Forum, and was taken up by the crowd. "Count the rents, each one made by a separate dagger thrust. Look what they did to our Caesar! He who loved you so much!" With a flourish he produced a document from his toga and held the scroll aloft so they all could see it. "I hold here Caesar's will! Let me show you how much he loved you, Rome!"

A wonderful sense of timing. Little wonder his best friends are actors, she thought.

"To the people of Rome . . ." He paused as the hubbub around the square fell to an absolute hush. "To the people of Rome, I leave in their entirety the gardens of my villa at Transtiberina, to be vested as a public gardens for the enjoyment of all. Further, to every Roman citizen I leave the sum . . . of thirty sesterces."

Bedlam.

"He left his gardens to you! He left his money to you! And look what they did to him! Was this his reward for loving you, for loving *Rome*?"

It was enough.

The soldiers were clashing their shields together, an unbearable cacophony of noise. Then someone threw a firebrand onto the pyre and those nearest the bier siezed the benches and chairs they had been seated on and tossed them into the flames as well. Women joined the frenzy, throwing on their jewelry, other men their clothes, soldiers their breastplates. Sparks and smoke spiraled up to the sky.

One man was recognized as one of the conspirators, and in an instant the mob turned on him and started to beat him. He disappeared beneath a sea of trampling boots and waving fists. Then the mob set off toward the home of Marcus Brutus, torches held aloft, shouting that they would burn it down. Smoke hid the moon. Madness ruled the night.

51

OFF THE COAST OF EGYPT

THE GREAT SHIP pitched and rolled as another swell passed underneath the hull. Cleopatra was assaulted by the stench from below, a nauseating mix of bilge and the sweat of the galley slaves. She staggered along the corridor, fighting the revolt of her own stomach and the taste of bile in her throat. The ship lurched sickeningly again, and she clung to the cedar paneling, felt one of her carefully manicured nails splinter on the wood.

All this luxury no use to me now. Perhaps better to be lying in my tomb right now. Like Julius.

Up on the deck, Mardian had told her, the sun shone in a pale blue sky; the captain had told her it was a perfect day for sailing. The purple-dyed sails billowed and stretched in a favorable wind. But she would not go up there, would not let the crew and the rest of her servants see her like this. *Isis Pelagia,* Queen of the Sea, sick as a child! This was her secret, to be shared only with her doctor and her own trusted circle: Mardian, Charmion, Iras.

Along with that other, more terrible secret.

She struggled to the next cabin, where Antiochus lay on his bunk, looking as shrunken as an old man. His complexion was gray. His slaves hovered around him helplessly in the airless little room. The stench of stale vomit was choking, forcing a cold sheen of sweat to erupt again on her skin. The room seemed to lurch alarmingly, and Mardian threw out a hand to support her.

Her physician, Olympos, looked up at her from the bunk, his face solemn.

"Out," she said to the others, and the slaves melted away.

"How is he?" she said to Olympos.

He shook his head and said nothing.

Antiochus muttered in his sleep. He smelled foul. She could make out the bones of his skull through the skin.

"I have been feeding him myself," Olympos said. "He keeps nothing down. He has started vomiting blood. I fear it is the lung rot. He stayed too long in Rome."

"I do not want him to suffer this way," she said. "How far are we from Alexandria?"

"Another two days' sail."

She put a hand to her belly. The constant retching had broken something inside her. This morning there had been blood.

"Are you all right, Majesty?" Olympos said.

The child. Please don't let me lose another part of Julius. Let me at least keep his child.

Or perhaps this was the goddess's judgment. A life for a life.

The room began to spin. She clutched again at the paneling, but another yaw of the great ship sent it lurching out of her reach. She felt a jarring blow as she hit the floor. Then blessed, spiraling darkness, drawing her down into a whirlpool of silent oblivion.

PALATINE HILL, ROME

Fulvia was awake at the second hour of the day, had roused out the slaves with their buckets and cloths and ladders, their brooms of green palm and myrtle, and set them to work cleaning the house. It was a pigsty after last night's drunken debauch; there were lobster shells and pork rinds on the tiles in the dining room, and smashed *amphorae* lay around the *peristylium*. There were even pottery shards at the bottom of the fishpond, which even the slaves jokingly referred to as the "vomitorium."

The Master of Rome lay on one of the couches, snoring his head off, oblivious to the racket. Fulvia's nostrils twitched at the rank odors of wine, stale sweat, and cheap women. She assumed her husband had procured the latter exclusively for the use of last night's guests; if she ever discovered that he had fucked any of them in her own villa, she'd pull his balls out by the roots.

The vase her father had brought her back from Palmyra was missing. And the marble bust of Pompey. No doubt the Master of Rome had given them away to his guests or had lost them at dice.

"Wake up!" she screeched at him, grabbing him by the shoulders and using all her strength to pull him off the couch. He rolled onto the floor. She grabbed a jug of water and emptied it over his head. He roared like a bull and sat up.

"Have a good time last night?"

He ran a hand across his face. His eyes were still swollen with sleep, like raw red Damascene plums.

"Is this how you conduct yourself while Octavian makes himself Lord of Rome?"

"Fulvia." He spoke her name as if it were a curse.

"You're a pig."

"The night . . . is never long enough."

"Did you give away my father's vase?"

He blinked at her, as if she had spoken to him in Aramaic or Persian. "What?"

"The vase my father bought in Palmyra. It was worth a fortune." He stared back at her, uncomprehendingly. What was the use? He wouldn't remember what he did at one of his legendary *commissatia*. "You stink. You should be on your way to the Senate."

"And listen to Cicero drone on about public morals?" He abandoned the effort of sitting up and collapsed onto his back on the marble tiles, his arms outspread.

"Octavian will be there."

"That little bitch."

"That little bitch has Caesar's legions behind him now."

"You make my head ache."

Fulvia swung back her foot and kicked him twice in the ribs. Antony groaned and tried to roll away from her. "Get up! Don't you see what you're doing! Caesar is dead! You must be the new Caesar!"

"Leave me alone."

"You have to get up!"

She kicked the Master of Rome until he staggered to his feet, and then she sent him off to his *tonsore* and sent the slaves to fetch a new toga. She would have put on the purple herself if she could and make her own entrance to the Senate. He didn't understand, the lumbering ox, that Octavian was a threat. He might be a bitch, but he was a calculating little bitch, and Antony didn't see it. Now that the immediate danger was past, all he wanted to do was enjoy himself again.

Well, she would not let him slide back to his old ways. She would make him Master of Rome, and Master of Italy, too, even if she had to stand behind him and whip him all the way there.

52

ALEXANDRIA-BY-EGYPT

THE OIL LAMPS in Cleopatra's private apartments flickered into the night, long after the moon had set over Pharos. She labored on into the seventh hour, surrounded by brass-bound boxes and pigeonholes with their copies of decrees, formal correspondence to heads of state, census rolls, ledgers of tax records for each of the forty *nomes* of Egypt. All the people see of their queen is the pomp and ceremony, she thought. They do not see the endless drudgery, the administration of detail that must be attended to. I will not trust it to others, like my father did. To be a queen is not to just make a show of governing, but to do the thing yourself.

And there was so much to do. While she had been away, her *strategioi* had allowed many of the canals to fall into neglect. Many had almost completely silted up. There would almost certainly be another famine this year.

Finally, she laid down her stylus and looked around the room, stretching her aching back muscles. But in a way she was glad there was so much to be done. It meant there was less time to think, to reflect, to feel. The memory of Caesar was like a toothache, a constant, drumming pain that wouldn't leave her.

In the mornings she would wake to the sounds of the harbor, the chanting of the priests from the royal temple on Lochias, the beat of the waves on the rocks of the peninsula, the murmur of the sea breeze, and, drowsy, she would stretch and luxuriate in the feeling of being home again, away from the brooding cypress pines and the suffocating hills of Rome.

But then she would reach out a hand to the empty expanses of the great ebony-wood bed and remember what they had done to him. She would recall that there would be no more loving and planning and talking, not today, not ever. Then an image would come to her, unbidden, of the bloody mess on the deck of her cabin in the royal galley, all that remained of Caesar's second son. And she would remind herself again that she was not safe, even here; and it was not safe for little Caesarion.

The only relief was to throw herself into work to escape from the torment of memories.

She had lain in her bed for almost a week when she arrived back in Alexandria, weak from the loss of blood, in mourning for Caesar and Caesar's son. She would not eat, so Olympos had prescribed warmed wine and infusions of herbs. His medicines had revived her, and she surprised them all by going back to work. She was, after all, the Queen of Egypt. Politics had no time for sentiment.

Olympos had warned her against working this diligently so soon after her return from Rome, but she found it as beneficent as the physician's potions. Sleep was impossible unless she was beyond exhaustion. And there were always matters to occupy her attention. The whole world could be convulsed with crisis, but in Alexandria the mountains of papyrus created by her bureaucracy continued to grow.

She stood up and went to the window, breathed in the fresh, salt air. The flames from the beacon on Pharos rippled on the waters of the harbor, throwing red shadows over the fishing fleet moored at the lee of the island.

Somewhere out there, beyond that black ocean, her enemies were still plotting.

Brutus had fled Rome for his own safety. He had made his headquarters in Macedonia. The other "liberator," Cassius, had raised armies in Asia and plundered Xanthus and Tarsus in Asia Minor. Now he had turned his armies toward Syria and Syria's governor, Dolabella, one of Caesar's men.

One piece of good news at least. Trebonius, one of the conspirators, had the gall to take up the governorship of Bithynia, a post Caesar himself had given him. Dolabella pursued him there, routed his soldiers, and made an accounting. Evidently he had thrown Trebonius's head to some little boys, who amused themselves by kicking it through the streets of Smyrna like a ball.

The legions Caesar left behind, she had sent to Dolabella. Her *dioiketes* and the other bureaucrats didn't like it, they said Dolabella did not have enough legions to hold off Cassius when he attacked, that she was aligning herself with the losing side. But what else could she have done? Would they have her send soldiers to the men who killed her son's father?

Where was Antony in all this? Still involved with the internecine politics of Rome, it seemed, quarreling with everyone from Octavian to Cicero. Well, she would not wait for another Roman to come to her rescue. She would do what she could to keep Egypt safe. She had decided she must have a new navy. The Roman legions were unmatched on land, but they had won few great victories at sea. That was the key to Egypt's future, she was sure of it.

She had commissioned the building of two hundred ships. Such a navy would drain most of her Treasury, but then what was the point of having the coffers overflowing if the Romans could march in and take it all? She had ordered the felling of cedars from the forests of Syria and had set up dockyards throughout Alexandria and the Delta. Half the fleet would be made up of the biggest warships ever built, quadriremes with four banks of oars, as well as lighter Liburnians, a fleet of which even Isis, Queen of the Sea, might be proud.

She turned away from the window, but knew she could not sleep. Too much on her mind tonight. Instead she found her feet taking her down the corridor toward the apartments set aside for her little brother, her husband, her consort and king.

〜 〜

They had moved his bed out onto the terrace these hot nights. He looked adrift in the vast bed, a frame of black ebony inlaid with tortoiseshell. The flesh had wasted off him, and his eyes seemed huge in the shrunken skull. Olympos had expressed the hope to the court that he would mend quickly now that he was away from Rome and its frosts and gales, but it seemed the seasickness had weakened him terribly and still he languished.

Tonight his eyes were fixed on the heavens. The stars seemed brighter here than in Rome, but it was not the stars that had drawn the boy's attention. A comet had appeared without warning soon after their return, and now it hung in the night sky with its brilliant tail reaching almost to the roof of the Pharos. It had been there night after night, and learned magi had come from as far away as Parthia to study the phenomenon, and to gaze at it from the roof of the Museion.

Some believed it was a portent from the gods, saw it as omen or herald as their disposition allowed. Others believed it was the spirit of Caesar himself, his soul farewelling the earth before taking his place in the pantheon of the gods.

ᵛ   ᵛ

And so, here was Julius, streaking across the heavens, leaving his burdens behind him. In death he had forgotten her. Never mind that Octavian was just a schoolboy, with no military skills, that he was even too young to take his seat in the Senate; it was he that Caesar had chosen. He has inherited a fortune in Caesar's will, and most of all he has a name, Caesar's name. The name of a god.

It was the name that was important, for there was a magic in names worth more than gold, than armies.

She had not expected a legacy in Caesar's will for her son, because by Roman law a foreigner could not inherit Roman property. But if Caesar had only bequeathed his name to his son, it would have given Caesarion legitimacy, a place in the world. Instead he had given his name to Octavian.

Why had he done it? Another of his games? Even in death he remained an enigma to her. Grief was made worse by her anger. Even beyond the grave he had remained faithless.

"I hate you, Julius," she whispered to the night sky.

After a time the comet trailed down the sky and out of sight. Caesar has found time to rest, has lain aside the burdens of his office. Hers were still waiting.

She leaned forward and put her lips close to her brother's ear. "Antiochus," she whispered.

But the boy did not turn his head or show any sign that he had heard. His eyes were open, as clear and blue as the waters at the foot of the palace steps, but there was no sign of the soul within. She held out a hand to feel for breath, to convince herself that he yet lived. Why did these things take so long?

"Antiochus, I am sorry," she said.

Mardian was waiting for her when she left the chamber. What was that look in his eyes? Was it reproach?

"How is he?" he asked her.

"I fear he is dead."

He nodded slowly, as if this was what he had anticipated. "Poison," he murmured.

"Don't be absurd. You heard what Olympos said. It was the lung rot. That last winter in Rome was too much for him."

It was as if he had not heard. "Was it on your orders, Majesty?"

She stiffened, felt the blood rush to her face. "How dare you speak to me that way."

"I have known you from a child, Majesty. I always knew it would come to this one day." He shook his head. "Poor Antiochus. If he had been born to any other family in Egypt he would have posed no threat to anyone."

She swallowed hard. Did he think it had been easy to do this? This was for Egypt, and it was for Caesarion. "I had no choice," she said.

"I know that, Majesty," he said, but his eyes were mournful. He turned and waddled away down the corridor.

53

HE WAS LED inside the palace, past ebony doors the height of three men, across floors of onyx and alabaster that shone like polished glass. There were countless treasures in each room, handworked metal tables from Damascus, candleholders of Nubian silver, statues of Egyptian gods in basalt and porphyry, woven carpets from India, Greek vases as tall as a man, tables of citrus wood supported on elephant tusks. A long way from the circumstances of their first meeting, he thought, in the gritty tent on the edge of the Sinai, the camels barking outside.

She had not changed her style, he was pleased to see. Still as haughty as ever, though she dispensed with the pomp for their informal meetings. Today she was lying on a couch looking at a papyrus scroll. When the chamberlain led him into the room, she looked up as if she had been interrupted in her reading by an importunate beggar.

She was surrounded by her advisers; her prime minister was there, of course, Mardian and Charmion, as always, and her secretary, Diomedes. The *dioiketes* regarded him with a hostile glance. Probably because he was Sicilian. These Greeks were born with their thumbs up their asses.

Still, he was pleased to serve the queen. Mardian had recruited him through family ties, and the royal patronage had assisted his businesses. His trade also proved the perfect disguise for the ring of spies he cultivated in Rome and elsewhere for the royal house. And he was handsomely paid.

"Apollodorus," she said.

He met her eyes. Very few saw her like this, without the lavish costumes and jewelry and intricate hairstyling and cosmetics. She wore a simple chiton, a flowing gown belted at the waist, gold anklets and arm bracelets, her dark hair held in a chignon at the back of her head. An alluring creature, dark and olive-skinned and sinuous as a snake. She was wearing a perfume of lotus oils; all sweet-scented arrogance, her black eyes looked right through you.

Don't try and intimidate me, he thought. I have had you across my shoulder, my girl, and you owe me, so don't ever forget it.

The last time he saw her had been the night he smuggled her inside the Lochias palace. Mardian saw to it that he was richly rewarded for what he had done, and it had been Mardian's idea to use him again, the one man he could trust for such a delicate task.

"Well," she said. "My faithful Apollodorus. What is the news from Rome?"

"I have dispatches here for your eyes, arrived just today."

"Tell me what they say."

"It is much as you prophesied, Majesty. The city is falling to pieces, there are riots every day, the rabble doing just what they will because the army itself is in uproar. Everyone thought Octavian would take Caesar's money and go back to Greece, but instead he has decided to stay and make a play for power. Marcus Antonius rebuffed him, so he enlisted Cicero's support. He and Antony are open enemies now. Cicero is whipping up feelings in the Senate against Antony, talking of reestablishing this Republic they speak of, with Octavian as Imperator of the army."

"But he's too young, surely," the *dioiketes* said.

"With respect," Mardian interrupted, "that is what Pothinus said of our queen when her father died."

"And look what happened to him," Apollodorus said.

Cleopatra stared at him in stony silence, and he thought he had offended her. He stared right back. "You should never lose your head in a crisis, isn't that right, Apollodorus?"

Was there a ghost of a smile on her lips? Impossible to say. "Yes, Majesty."

"But we interrupt you."

"Cicero has accused Marcus Antonius of stealing funds from the state and of using Caesar's seal to forge documents for the advantage of himself and his friends. Fulvia is furious."

"Is it true?"

"Well, yes, it's true, he makes no secret of the fact. But that's not the point. Not as far as Fulvia or Marcus Antonius are concerned. It is the fact that Cicero has come out and said it."

"How is Marcus Antonius?"

A curious question to ask. And spoken in such a dismissive way. There had to be more to it. By all accounts she had bewitched Caesar when she was in Rome; perhaps she had bewitched his captain too. She could bewitch any man.

"His attention has been somewhat divided, Majesty. His appetites still run to the grape and the tart."

Cleopatra smiled.

"Is it going to come to war?" Mardian asked, interrupting the flow of Apollodorus's thoughts.

Apollodorus turned to his brother-in-law. "There is no doubt about it. Antony has finally marched against one of Caesar's assassins, Decimus Brutus, presently governor of Cisalpine Gaul. In response, the Senate has recruited Octavian to take command of Caesar's legions and help this Decimus."

"Octavian is going to help one of the men who murdered Caesar?" Cleopatra said, her voice suddenly hoarse with anger.

He shrugged. "He has no choice. It is just politics."

"And the legions?" Diomedes asked.

"Octavian is Caesar's chosen successor, so the soldiers remain loyal, no matter how they feel about Antony. He has the Mars, and the Fourth, and a number of other crack legions behind him now."

"You are not saying Marcus Antonius could lose this war?" the *dioiketes* asked.

Apollodorus shrugged his shoulders. He was no military expert.

Diomedes shook his head. "But why are these people supporting this Octavian? My information is that he is barely out of school."

Poor man, Apollodorus thought, he could not understand. He had no grounding in the curious world of Roman politics.

"Octavian needs Cicero's support against Antony," Cleopatra explained, "and Cicero needs Octavian's legions. Doubtless he thinks to use him and then get rid of him when Antony is defeated. Then they will have their Republic again."

Apollodorus smiled at the queen's acumen. She had been worth his efforts that night. "Indeed, Majesty," he said. "Cicero is privately telling all his friends that 'the boy' is easily controlled, and his to command."

"Then he has made a mistake," Cleopatra said. "Octavian will not play Cicero's bum boy for long."

The *dioiketes* looked shocked at his queen's language. Apollodorus bit his lip.

"Cicero and his friends are too puffed with their own importance to see what is plain to everyone else," she went on. "He's an old man, his time's past. For their part, the army hate Brutus and his lot, and Antony's soldiers won't attack Octavian because of the Caesar name. It seems to me that if Octavian is clever, he can play one half of Rome against the other, and when the dust has settled he'll be cock of the dunghill."

There was silence in the chamber at this ominous summation of events. If the queen was right, it did not bode well for the future of Alexandria. A victory for Octavian would spell disaster for Egypt. Caesar could have only one heir, so while Caesarion was alive, there could never be peace between the queen and Octavian.

"What are we to do, Majesty?" the *dioiketes* asked her.

"Do?"

"I understand there is a delegation on its way to us from Cassius asking for ships and supplies to help him in his war in Syria."

"Yes, and it speaks loudly for the gall of the man. He murdered my son's father. Now he wants my assistance."

"It may be politic to comply."

She turned her chilling black eyes on him, and the poor man found something of intense interest on the floor. "No, it is neither conscionable nor is it politic."

"But if we refuse and Cassius is victorious . . ." he mumbled, showing more courage than Apollodorus gave him credit for.

"If he is victorious, Brother, do you think he will look with any more favor on us, whether we send him soldiers or not? The only difference will be that we helped him secure our own bondage. I would have thought that was plain. The next time you come into this chamber I expect you to bring your brains with you."

A sudden, shuffling silence. No wonder the queen makes enemies, Apollodorus thought. She says the things that others only think. Perhaps because she is a queen she has never been taught the little kindnesses that others give to their friends and their associates in the form of lies. But she has no need to be so blunt. The *dioiketes* is a court professional and a time server. He cannot help being cynical and shortsighted. It's in his training.

"Is there more?" she asked.

"Only the details of the matter. They are in my missive."

"Thank you, yet again, for your service," she said. The dark eyes lingered on him for a moment, and he speculated, as all the courtiers did, on how Cleopatra the woman might be different from Cleopatra the queen. But before that moment's fantasy could take flight he was ushered out of the chamber by a guard.

It is as well that I am not a prime minister or a court secretary, he thought as he left. I would give her a clip around the ear, as a good man should when a woman gets too haughty.

But then, I would have my queen no other way.

54

AT THE EDGE of the white desert, over the flat marshes of the Nile, a chanting rises above the sound of the night insects as a rust dawn stains the sky.

Down a cobbled alley in the great capital of Rome, below the hill of the Aventine, the ancient rattle of a systrum can be heard from the gloom of a marble temple.

In a white and trackless forest in the wilderness of Gaul, a Roman general watches the sun rise over the cold mountains and wonders if he will ever again see the Forum Romanus. . . .

In the Brucheion in Alexandria a woman is bent over her papyrus scrolls, as she has been all night, the smoke from her oil lamp smudging the early-morning air. . . .

In a gloom-dark shrine on the Lochias peninsula, the sounds of the sea whispering along the worn marble of the temple walls, a shaven-headed priest whispers his dawn litany. . . .

Isis. *Isis.*

Oh, these arrogant Romans, she thought. He walks in here as if he is reviewing his troops. Well, you do not own Alexandria yet.

She regarded him from her throne in the Audience Hall. The leather lappets made a slapping noise as he strode into the hall. He held his helmet beneath his right arm. His breastplate was enameled with a scene from some heroic Roman victory. He had a nose like a hawk's beak and eyes as black and shifty as a crow's.

She stared at him for longer than was comfortable for him, knowing court etiquette forbade him to speak before she had acknowledged him. She was happy to make him wait.

Finally she signaled the court chamberlain to give him leave to speak.

"I bring greetings from General Gaius Cassius Longinus, Majesty. He sends greetings to the Queen of Egypt and requests the presence of your fleet in Antioch immediately."

Immediately. Was that the word he had chosen to use in her presence?

"So you can invade Rhodes," she said. A convenient base for an assault on Egypt.

"For whatever purpose he desires."

She smiled, imagining this pompous son of a jute salesman being publicly flogged. She waited until she had her voice and her temper under control. "We would like to assist you, but there are circumstances that make your request impossible."

He stared at her down the length of his not inconsiderable nose. "Majesty?"

"I wonder if you smelled the peculiar stink of the city when you arrived? It is the smell of the corpse fires. Alexandria has the plague. Have you witnessed it for yourself? The victim's skin turns black and bursts open like a fig ripening in the sun. Many of my shipwrights have died this way, many more have fled the city. A ship cannot sail without keels or masts, so this fleet you speak of rots in the shipyards at Rhakotis. The remainder of my fleet has sailed to Cyprus, where I believe your general has appropriated them already without my permission."

In fact, the governor of Cyprus, Serapion, had surrendered them to Cassius without a fight. Another treachery. She had appointed Serapion to his post herself. Not that she blamed herself overmuch. Choosing allies in Alexandria was a matter of deciding which snake to turn your back on.

"The general was hoping you would show your love for him."

"I showed my love for him by sending him the Roman legions that Caesar had left here in Alexandria for my protection."

The man had the effrontery to smile. "It was my understanding that they were intended for Dolabella. Fortunately, when they reached Syria, they chose instead to lend their services to Imperator Cassius."

"They were Roman soldiers, and not mine to command."

The man did not attempt to hide his displeasure at this reponse. No doubt he cut his teeth as an ambassador ordering around the court at Pontus or Bithynia. "Can my lord Cassius count on your support, then, for supplies for his army? We badly need grain, and they say Egypt has enough for the entire world."

"Again, you must tell your lord that I would gladly assist him if it were within my power. But this year the Nile has once again failed to rise, and there is no grain in our storehouses. My people have a choice between dying of pestilence or leaving the city to starve. With her country ravaged by famine and plague, it is Cleopatra who needs assistance."

"The general will not be pleased to hear this," the upstart said.

"Then you must tell him the facts of the matter. We would aid him if we could, but as you will see, if you care to wander through the streets and sniff the air for corpses, it is quite impossible."

〜 〜

After he had gone, she turned to Mardian. "Do you think he believes us?" she whispered.

"Perhaps we should arrange to have him tossed in one of the plague pits outside the city so he may get a better view of the dead," he said.

The *dioiketes* leaned forward. "Majesty," he murmured.

Oh, you gloomy old Greek, she thought. You are about to tell me I am wrong. "Yes, Brother?"

"This is a mistake," he said.

Perhaps it might seem so, to you. Cassius had fourteen legions now; eight more had gone over to him in Syria and Bithynia. Dolabella, Marc Antony's ally, was under siege in Laodicea. Her spies told her the city was about to fall.

But what choice was there but to feign neutrality? The only way to save Egypt was out of their hands. Of the three powers vying for Rome, only Antony offered them any hope from being swallowed up by the Romans and their voracious appetites. And she did not see how Antony could win.

This was what Caesar had led her to. She had no way to avenge herself on his enemies, no clear way to save herself or her son from them, or even from his opportunist little nephew. Antony had been noble and brave for just a week before the wine jug called him back like a siren.

Fear, anger, and grief had drained her resources, but she would not give in. She would yet find a way to save herself and her son from these Romans. She would bring offerings to Isis, champion of women everywhere. As Goddess of Fate, perhaps she could yet order the stars to change hers.

She lay in the deep marble bath feeling the silky touch of the water against her skin. Iras had added perfumed oil to the water, and the rainbow sheen on the surface left tiny droplets on her breasts. She touched one dark nipple with her fingertips, gently, as Julius used to do. How she missed him. This need for physical comfort had left a cold ache inside her. Sometimes she wondered if it would ever go away.

She might go days now without brooding like this. But then grief would come up on her, without warning, lying in wait like a thief in the street, and it would start again, this longing for his touch, for his company, for his casual certainty, his always knowing what to do.

She heard Mardian fretting and pacing anxiously on the other side of the ivory screen. Urgent business to attend to. Always there was urgent business, more burdens to bear alone.

And they could have had it all. She could have been free of this constant toadying to Romans, the constant fear. If only he had kept his bodyguards. If only he taken that crown on the Feast of Lupercalia. If only he had listened, for once, to her. Regret, she thought. A useless emotion. All we have is today and tomorrow, she reminded herself, and tried to focus on that.

"What is it, Mardian?" she said at last.

"News from Syria, Majesty," he said, and she could hear the agitation in his voice. "Cassius has announced he will invade Egypt to punish us for supporting Dolabella. He now recognizes Arsinoë as true Queen of Egypt. I have learned it was she who persuaded Serapion to hand over the fleet to Cassius."

She gripped the edges of the bath, her knuckles white. Suddenly the water was too cold and no longer the pleasure it had been a few moments before. She closed her eyes and laid her head back on the marble. Brutus, Cassius, Arsinoë, they had all profited from Caesar's clemency. This was how they repaid it. It affirmed for her that she should not feel such guilt over what had happened to little Antiochus.

"There is worse."

"Oh, do continue, Mardian."

From behind the screen she heard him shuffle his soft boots on the marble tiles. "It is Marcus Antonius, Majesty. He has been defeated by the armies of Octavian and Decimus Brutus at Mutina in the north of Italy. He has been forced to flee into the mountains. They say he and his army are living on snow and roots."

She stood up suddenly, her body's fearful and instinctive reaction to this piece of news. Iras immediately rushed up to her with warmed and scented towels and started to dry her.

Poor Marcus. A decent man, for all his faults. He deserved a better fate. He alone had stayed faithful to Caesar. Now Rome repaid him for his loyalty.

What else does Tycho, Queen of Fortune, have in store for me? she wondered. She knew what the *dioiketes* and the rest of her ministers would be thinking: that she had miscalculated, that she had become a liability. They would already be wondering if they could save their own skins by offering up their queen as trade. If Antiochus were alive now, they might already be whispering to the Captain of the Guard about rebellion.

Which Caesar would save her then?

She lay facedown on a couch while Iras massaged her back and shoulders with almond oil. Her shoulder muscles were tight and she winced as the Nubian's strong knuckles set to work.

"So much good news," she said.

She could feel Mardian's hesitation even from the other side of the screen. So, there was more. She tried to relax, surrender to Iras's expert fingers.

"What else, Mardian?" she said.

"Majesty, they say Octavian is now calling himself the Young Caesar."

The Young Caesar. There could only be one young Caesar in the world, and the real one was at that moment asleep in the nursery, watched over night and day by armed guards.

What was she to do? Octavian wanted to destroy her son, and he had command of Caesar's legions; Cassius and Brutus wanted Egypt for themselves, and they were masters of Asia. Her one possible hope, Marc Antony, was wandering around the mountains with ice in his beard and his legions starving by inches.

She had come so close to claiming the whole world for Egypt. Now she was going to lose everything. I might as well have died with Caesar.

"What are we going to do, Mardian?"

"Perhaps . . ." He hesitated.

"Yes?" she snapped.

"We might protect ourselves with a judicious alliance. You cannot rule alone. Bithynia perhaps, or Pontus . . ."

"You mean, you wish me to marry again? You do not think I can handle this situation?"

"Around the court they are saying—"

"Get out of here!"

"Majesty, I only—"

"Get out!"

She heard him shuffle from the room. She looked over her shoulder. Iras was standing back from the couch, her eyes wide as plates. "What are you staring at?"

She lay back on the table, but her muscles were taut as bowstrings and Iras's probing fingers were a torture. She groaned against the pain. The whole world was in conspiracy against her. But she would not give in. There must be a way to save Egypt, and to preserve her throne for her son. Isis had given her a destiny, and she would not betray it.

55

THERE WERE TIMES when she was like any mother, and times when she was like no other woman in the world, ordering the affairs of millions. But today, at least, she could be ordinary again; she sat on the wide, stone steps of the palace, watching little Caesarion collecting shells in the sandy shallows. He was naked, his bare bottom bent over to retrieve some object of great delight. She felt a surge of pain and love. All a mother's loves and hopes and dreams invested in the small, brown body, hopes not only for her son but for her country, her dynasty, her own destiny.

The summer had come and gone, long months of waiting for news of a world once more torn apart by blood and violence. Once, in Rome, she had seized control of their destinies for a brief moment, but Caesar died before he could pass her the reins. Now there was just the waiting.

The Nile had failed for the second year. The irony of it was not lost on her. She was Isis, Goddess of Plenty, but each time she returned to Egypt from some exile, the river betrayed her. This year in the domed Nilometers at Memphis and Babylon, its waters lapped at the cubits of death.

But at least it had solved the crocodile problem in the Upper Nile. Her *strategioi* reported that Sobek's ancestors had retreated to the swamps and the villagers could once again send their children down to the riverbanks, knowing they would return.

She had done all she could to ease the famine. She had posted soldiers around all the granaries, and imposed a rationing of wheat and barley, enough to prevent riots breaking out, at least. But people in the *chora* would die, those who hadn't already been infected with plague.

"At least there are fewer mouths to feed," she had said.

Mardian had frowned and said her heart was made of iron. She answered that she was just being practical. How else could one govern a country like Egypt if one was not practical?

Caesarion giggled and splashed in the water. Enjoy these days of carefree innocence, she thought. They will end soon enough. The world is not all blue water and seashells. Did you know your father nearly died here in these same shallows?

This life. So much of it was waiting. But there was nothing else she could do. She could not save Marcus Antonius, and she did not have an army to defeat Cassius. All she could do was wait and see who prevailed in Rome. Then, somehow, she knew she must make an accommodation with the new lord of the world and try to save her Egypt, and herself.

The irony was that it was Cicero who gave her hope.

He and the other *boni* in the Senate had used Octavian to gain a victory over Antony and had then rewarded him by voting the Triumph to Decimus Brutus. They had handed the navy to Pompey's son, Sextus, and confirmed Cassius and Brutus in their provinces in the East. And what had they given Gaius Julius Caesar Octavianus, the Young Caesar? Nothing. Not even a vote of thanks, just a demand that he hand over the crack Mars and Fourth legions to the Senate's control.

Cicero's doing.

Meanwhile, Marc Antony, tired of living on tree bark, had emerged from the Alps to form a new alliance with Marcus Lepidus, Caesar's Captain of the Horse.

She heard footfalls on the steps above her and caught her breath. Mardian.

"If this is bad news," she told him, "I shall pitch you bodily into the harbor."

"You were right. Cicero indeed has a lion by the tail."

"Our Young Caesar has bitten back?"

He handed her a scroll. She recognized the seal; it was from Apollodorus in Rome. She read it through quickly.

Octavian, the boy Cicero thought he could push around, had responded to Cicero's treatment of him by forming a new triumvirate with Lepidus and Marcus Antonius. Now they were marching on Rome with seventeen legions and ten thousand cavalry.

She started to laugh. It excited Caesarion, who stood up in the shallows and started splashing at the water.

So, Octavian, Caesar's little bitch—as Antony would call him— had shown the Senate his teeth. She would have admired his gall and his dexterity if she did not know that he would as easily slit Caesarion's throat as he played there in the shallows.

"Do you think this news will save us, Majesty?" Mardian asked her.

"What do your spies think?" she asked, tossing the scroll back to him.

"They say I shall not be tossed into the harbor just yet."

She smiled. "No, with luck you may remain dry for a little while longer." And she sent a stone skimming across the surface of the harbor, a girl again.

ON ANY NORMAL day the Forum Romanus would have been packed with butchers and bankers, merchants and men of affairs, fishwives and hot bread sellers; there would be strings of slaves snaking between the sweating, jostling crowds and the porticoes of Pompey's Theater, and the steps of the temple crammed with hucksters and money changers, lawyers and cutpurses. The square would have been a bedlam, reeking of sweat and garlic and cheap pomade.

Today it was empty, except for two corpses, blood draining into the sewer from the severed neck of one of them. There was a riot in progress somewhere down the Palatine Hill, toward the Circus Maximus. The sound of hobnailed boots echoed on the cobblestones of a nearby alley, a cohort of the Fourth Legion at the run.

It would be over soon. Order, which Romans loved more than life itself, would soon be restored. When the killing was finished.

The proscriptions, Antony told himself, had been necessary. The senators who opposed them had to die. They could not afford Caesar's clemency. Look where it had gotten him.

Besides, they needed their money.

Cicero had been the first name on the list. Octavian wanted revenge, Antony just wanted him out of the way, and Lepidus had just agreed to everything. It was said that when the soldiers came for Cicero, he had been too proud to run, and when his servants finally persuaded him to climb into his litter it was too late. Octavian's men stopped him less than a mile from his country villa, on the road to Brundisium. When Cicero put his head out of the curtains, a centurion simply lopped it off without further ceremony. Cicero would have hated that, the old windbag. Doubtless he had prepared a speech to read to his executioners.

Perhaps that was why they killed him quickly. A mercy to Cicero, a kindness to themselves also.

Indeed, the *boni* had paid a heavy price for their intransigence. Nearly two hundred of Rome's richest men, who had made the mistake of declaring for Brutus and ordering Octavian against Antony before betraying him, too, now watched the proceedings from the rostra, their heads exhibited there for all Rome to gawk at. The plebeians wouldn't care. They loved to see blood spilled, as long as it wasn't theirs.

Antony made his way toward the Palatine Hill, and on the road he came across another mob, trying to set fire to some senator's house. A cohort from the Mars Legion was trying to stop them. They saw Antony and his escort and interrupted the mayhem to cheer him wildly. Antony accepted the plaudits with a grim salute, trying to push from his mind exactly what he had done to secure this peace.

꙳ ꙳

There was the usual crowd waiting for him at his house, all the well-wishers and the toadies and the freeloaders. Fulvia had prepared a feast to celebrate his return to the city. It had been a miraculous reversal in his fortunes, after all. It was late autumn now; the spring had seen him still camped in the Alps, an outcast drinking melted snow.

He pushed his way through the crowd in the atrium, ignoring the hail fellows and the slaps on the shoulder. He heard shrill laughter and saw Fulvia—his wife, by all the gods—there in the middle of the dining hall. The tables were loaded down with pheasant and duck, roast oxen and suckling pigs. Fulvia herself was holding something in her hands and the guests were laughing, though it seemed forced.

As he got closer he could see that it was a human head, Cicero's—the old boy looked better than he had in years—and she was sticking pins through his tongue. His right hand was in the center of the table, there among the sweetbreads and the sturgeon, like some pale and rancid crab left over from the *prima mensa*.

"Husband," she said. She was glowing.

The hall fell silent. "What are you doing?" he said to her.

"Let him revile you now," she said. She addressed herself to the slightly blackened head she held in her right hand. "Come, Cicero, make us one of your famous speeches. Bore us all to death!"

"What is that doing here?"

Fulvia was delighted with herself. She held her trophy toward him. "The tongue that reviled you in the Senate has paid its price," she said. There were more than a dozen hairpins through the swollen and blackened tongue. "And the hand that wrote the Philippics attacking you in the Senate will stir against you no more."

He turned to two of the bodyguards who had followed him into the *triclineum*. "Take that away and have it displayed on the rostra with the rest. The hand, too."

Fulvia stared at him. "Don't tell me you've gone soft? Like Caesar?"

The gall of the woman. In front of everyone! She was truly a witch. He just wanted to get away from her. She terrified him.

"Killing is one thing. But bathing in the blood is another." He turned and left the room without another word. By all the gods, he hated Rome sometimes.

"What is wrong with you?" she demanded.

The feast was over, the guests gone. The slaves were already at work, sweeping up the crab shells and meat bones that were scattered around the tiles. Antony looked on, sober for once. Perhaps my sojourn in the mountains has changed me, he thought.

"I can see you don't have the stomach for this," Fulvia was saying. "You have to show these people what you do to your enemies."

"Stick pins in them when they're dead?"

"You are too soft."

Too soft. Was that it? In the horse trading that had followed the alliance, he and Lepidus and Octavian had bartered over their death lists like small boys trading horse chestnuts in the winter: that uncle of yours who reviled me in the Senate for this cousin of mine who supported that faction against you; that *equine,* your close friend, for this banker, my brother-in-law. Lepidus had traded the life of his own brother for the life of Antony's uncle, an old man as blameless as he was wealthy. In the end their proscriptions had included as many supporters as enemies, dead now not because they had supported Cicero but because they had once slighted one of the new triumvirate.

Or because of their money.

I am sick of this business, Antony thought. I am sick of that trilling pretty boy Lepidus and I am sick of that clammy stick insect, Octavian. They both give me the squirts. I will do what I have to do to secure power, then I must get out of Rome. Without Caesar there is no one to take the blame for the ills and murders anymore.

I underestimated the old boy. He carried a heavier load than I thought.

"You have to get rid of Octavian," Fulvia was saying.

"Octavian?"

"In the name of Jupiter, man, you don't think it's over, do you? Have you forgotten what he did to you at Mutina? You said when he first came to Rome that he would take his inheritance and run back to Greece. Instead he mobilized the whole of the Senate against you and left you two years later wandering around the Alps with your ass dragging in the snow."

By all the gods, she can be crude. Although he had to admit, she also had a point. But he'd had enough of bloodshed for now. Yes, he had underestimated the little bitch. But then the boy had only done what any man would do in the same circumstances. And he had given his word on the peace. You had to give the kid a chance. "When the time comes, I will settle with Octavian," he said. "But do not think I could raise the legions to fight against him now. He still has Caesar's name, and the soldiers will not bring themselves to fight against Caesar's heir. Besides, they are heartily tired of fighting against fellow Romans. As we all are."

"There are other ways."

"By Jupiter, you're a bloodthirsty bitch."

"He's dangerous."

"He barely has a beard on his chin. What happened at Mutina was Cicero's doing."

"You have to get rid of him, Marcus."

"I shall not break my word," he said, and fled the room before she could get crazy again and start breaking ornaments. He wished he had never married her. But that was the trouble with having so many debts.

The old man had the right idea. Cleopatra. Now there was a woman. Refined, witty, and energetic enough to make a man think about giving up actresses and bathhouses for a while.

Once they had dealt with Marcus Brutus and the rest of that rabble, he might think about getting out of Rome for a while. He'd had enough of politics to last him a lifetime.

And enough of Fulvia as well.

57

OFF THE AFRICAN COAST, TWO DAYS OUT OF ALEXANDRIA

A TORRENT OF water poured through the open window. Cleopatra heard Iras scream. She gripped the rails of the bed, her hands greasy with sweat. The lamps had been smashed in the storm, and it was pitch-dark in the cabin, the howling of the gale and the creaking of the new timbers deafeningly loud. She felt her gorge rise again but barely had the strength to move. She no longer cared that the Queen of Egypt, Mother Isis, Goddess of the Sea and reincarnation of Venus Genetrix, had vomited all over herself.

So easy to face death in the mind, but when it comes with the crashing of waves or the sounds of battering rams and screaming men, courage can so quickly desert us, she thought. She tried to close her ears to the shrieking of the storm and begged Isis to keep her safe, moaning and babbling like a child for respite from the misery of this seasickness and the terror of the night.

PHILIPPI, GREECE

*Roman month of Octobris,
forty-two years before the birth of Jesus Christ*

Cold in Greece with winter drawing on. A haze of camp smoke hung over the tents sprawled along the blue mountainside, and lost itself in the mist rising from the valleys. A chill and lonely plateau, but as good a place as any, he supposed, to settle the argument over whether it was just to have killed Caesar.

Octavian lay on a cot in a goatherd's hut, damp and stinking with fever, spitting into a brass bowl held by one of his pretty Syrian boys. Maecenas and Agrippa were with him. Maecenas had his hair freshly curled, as if he were on his way to the Circus

Maximus to watch the chariot races. He gave Antony a soft and mocking smile as he walked into the tent. By Jupiter, Antony thought, that boy would be bent over a couch with his tunic pulled up in a second if I gave him any encouragement at all.

And there was Agrippa, all manliness and woolly beard, glowering at him from the shadows, over by the brazier. How he fits in with this shower, I don't know.

Fulvia is wrong, he thought, looking at the sickly creature peering up at him from the cot. I have nothing to worry about on Octavian's account. This diseased little faggot won't last the winter. I heard he was like this right through the Spanish campaign with Caesar, and they say it was a miracle he survived that. He won't be lucky a second time. He has the stink of death on him already.

"You're looking better, son," Antony said, sitting beside the cot and slapping him cheerfully on the thigh. This was how he was with the soldiers. You could lose both legs and an arm, the centurions said, and Antony would be around the hospital tent that night telling you you'd be as good as new in the morning.

"The doctors say it is a chill. They have bled me."

Drained you, more like, Antony thought.

He had to admit that for a while he thought Fulvia had a point. After the proscriptions, they had formed a triumvirate to rule the empire, to last for five years, he and Marcus Lepidus and the Young Caesar, as he liked to call himself. Octavian had sealed the deal by marrying Fulvia's daughter, Claudia. Fulvia had nearly choked on that raw bone, but she had no choice.

Antony had tried to mollify her. "Look, we're doing this for Rome, old girl. Don't worry about it. When he's dead, you'll have her back in the same pristine condition in which we hand her over. He fights for the other side, does our Young Caesar. Likes to attack from the rear."

Fulvia had given him a withering look. "He has been conducting an affair with the wife of Claudius Marcellus for the last year and a half."

He had stared at her in astonishment. "Tertullia?"

"That was why he named Marcellus in your proscriptions. He wanted the chariot race all to himself."

"Really? I thought he was a pansy."

"That's the trouble. None of you heroes really understands that boy."

Perhaps she was right. Shortly afterward Octavian had the Senate—who was going to argue with the young pup now?—formally declare Caesar a god. Lucky Julius. Lucky Octavian. For now the Young Caesar had added *divi filius*—son of a god—to his adoptive title. Nothing like a little name-dropping. The Senate also ratified the Triumvirate's declaration that the assassins, Cassius, Brutus, and the rest, were traitors to the state and had to be hunted down. The battle lines had been drawn.

Which had brought them here to Philippi, to face Old Sobersides and his friends in the field and settle the matter once and for all.

Yes, I was worried about you for a while, Antony thought, watching Octavian's eyes rolling in his head. But not anymore. Whatever is wrong with you, it's going to kill you. It's as plain as that spotty nose on your lily-white face.

"You'll have to take the field without me," Octavian said.

Oh, I'll manage, he wanted to say. "It's a pity you'll miss the day your uncle's finally avenged."

"My father," Octavian managed to correct him.

A moot point. You were adopted by Caesar's brother, fact, and none of the Senate's toadying to you, or that little piece of paper in Caesar's will, is ever going to change that. Not in my book. "You must get yourself well for the victory parade."

Octavian was about to reply but instead subsided into another fit of coughing. The little Syrian boy hurried over with the bowl for Octavian to hack up some more green mess. I think I shall leave now, Antony thought. It's quite put me off my dinner.

⟁ ⟁

He stood outside in the twilight and looked down the valley. Time was on his side now. He would win his victory here at Philippi and fate would take care of the rest. When Octavian succumbed to the lung rot, as he surely must, he would share power only with Lepidus, and Lepidus was a fool. Let fate decide the justness of Caesar's will.

58

Morning, and a greasy light crept into the cabin. The wind had eased but the galley still wallowed in a wild sea. Cleopatra woke, realized she must have slept, no more than an hour, exhaustion taking over from fear. Charmion lay across her legs on the bed. Iras was propped in a corner on the floor among the lapping seawater and indescribable mess. Her eyes were open, but she seemed beyond caring for anything, for her queen, even for herself.

Cleopatra staggered to her feet, her spirit screaming against the effort, dragging herself past her own misery to assume once again the burdens of Egypt. She put on a waterlogged cloak and staggered along the passageway, bruising her shoulders against the ornate cedar paneling with each lurch of the ship.

One of the crew helped her up the companionway onto the deck. A huge, gray swell running, seas higher than the mast, no sign of the fleet of almost one hundred ships that had set off with her from Alexandria bound for Brundisium. Another roiling swell passed under the ship, and the oars lifted high out of the water. Cleopatra gasped, felt a cold, oily sweat erupt all over her body. Isis Pelagia, save me.

The captain stood alone at the helm, his beard and hair encrusted with salt, a wild look in his eyes, accentuated by the storm light. She guessed he had been there right through the night.

"Majesty," he said, alarmed to see her on the deck, shocked to see his queen without her fine clothes and her jewelry, her hair hanging in limp strands around her face, just another frightened and filthy passenger on a beleaguered ship.

"What is happening, Captain?"

"The fleet scattered during the night. We have lost sight of all but two quinqueremes, off our stern."

She saw a great wave frothing toward them, part of a mast and several smashed oars bobbing on the crest, witness to the violence of the storm. She wondered how much of her fleet had survived the tempest.

She could not help Marcus Antonius now.

"Turn back," she said, "it is pointless to continue. We must return to Alexandria."

PHILIPPI, GREECE

They were a ragged bunch, shivering in their cloaks, their beards ragged and unkempt, the empty look of the defeated in their eyes. Octavian studied them from the saddle of his horse, his fingers clamped tight around the reins. He felt weak and light-headed. For the last three days he had lain in a fever in his cot while Philippi was decided.

"Who are these men?" he asked a centurion.

"They belong to Brutus, my lord. His manservant, his equerry, and two of his officers. What do you want us to do with them?"

"Well, I think you can kill them, centurion," Octavian said.

He looked around. The battlefield was littered with the red cloaks of fellow Romans. The stench of death was carried on the cold wind. The legionaries would not be singing their bawdy songs tonight.

"Where is friend Brutus?"

The centurion pointed to a white horse standing almost motionless by a gnarled tree a hundred paces from where they stood. A small group of officers were gathered around the horse, talking among themselves. A man lay across the horse's poll and there was blood streaked along its flanks. "They have just brought him in. He fell on his sword. He died honorably."

"He did not live honorably," Octavian said.

He got down from his horse. His legs felt weak from the fever, but he was determined not to falter in front of these men. He pushed his way through the knot of officers. Marcus Brutus was gray as a dead fish. His eyes had a film of death on them, like cold aspic. It took all Octavian's strength, but he pulled the body from the horse, trailing guts behind it. Then he took out his sword and hacked off the head. A messy business and not as easy as he had thought it would be. He kicked it across the ground to his equerry.

The effort made him stagger. "Wrap that in your cloak and bring it with you," he said. "We will take it back to Rome and lay it at the foot of my father's statue."

As he made his way back to his horse, one of the prisoners pushed his way out of the rank. Perhaps what he had just witnessed unnerved him. "You will at least grant us a decent burial," he said.

Octavian stared at him. Why did men expect mercy when they had just lost a battle? Caesar's *clementia* had been Caesar's weakness. He would not be making the same mistake. If you won, you took everything; if you lost, you were meat for the butcher.

"A decent burial? You can take up that matter with the carrion crows," he said to the man, got on his horse, and rode away.

~ ~

It was late evening when Antony arrived. He stared at the knot of bodies on the frost-hard ground. They had been executed, apparently. A short distance away a white horse was picking at tufts of tough grass. A body in the purple cloak of a general lay beside it, the corpse mutilated.

Brutus.

Antony climbed off the horse, took off his cloak, and laid it over the body. Bad enough for a common soldier to lie on the ground with his guts half out and his head gone; for a general and a Roman senator it was unthinkable.

He saw a centurion watching him. "Make sure this man has a proper burial," he said.

"But Caesar said that—"

"He is not Caesar!" Antony roared at him. "Caesar is dead! The man you speak of is just a vicious little boy! Now do as I say! *I* won this battle while your Young Caesar was in bed with the sniffles!"

He stalked away.

~ ~

And so it went.

Antony's vicious little boy returned to Italy, to deal with the burdens of the state his birthright had brought him, settling the veterans from his legions with the traditional rewards of money and land. It was a thankless task, for despite the proscriptions and the confiscations of estates that had followed the civil war, there was still not enough land to make the men happy, and the little they appropriated had to be stolen from someone else. And there was little money to be had, either. Caesar's inheritance had been spent on the wars.

Meanwhile, Pompey's son Sextus, to whom the Senate had promised the navy, made use of his preeminence on the ocean to turn pirate and strangle the sea routes into Rome. Italy starved and blamed Octavian.

The Young Caesar, Antony laughed to his friends, was not as clever as he thought he was. Let him stew on greatness for a while.

And so, to the victor the spoils. Octavian, having lain in his bed while the final battles were won, could not now dictate terms to the soldier hero. Antony let him have Spain and Sardinia. And welcome to them. Antony himself, adrift in the Alpine snows just two years before, now inherited all of Gaul as well as the entire eastern empire. And while he took care of more lucrative and enjoyable business, he would let Octavian deal with Italy and all the problems that went with it.

Oh, and Lepidus got Africa. Hot place. Too much sand.

🌱 🌱

Antony made his triumphant way through his new domains, putting his stamp on Greece and Asia, collecting taxes to pay for his wars, celebrating his triumph. Everywhere he was hailed as the New Dionysus, God of Wine and Salvation, of Celebration and Peace.

In Ephesus they put him in a grape-laden chariot, and scantily dressed girls leaped ahead of the procession, tumbling and dancing, the young men following, dressed as satyrs and pans. The dancers were wreathed in ivy, musicians from the Dionysian guilds joined in with zithers and flutes and reed pipes, the crowds crying out the city's welcome for Dionysus, Bringer of Joy.

It was what Antony had always dreamed of. And no less, he decided, than what he deserved.

59

THE WINTER BELONGED to Antony, Bringer of Joy.

He assembled around him the best dancers and actors, tumblers and whores, from the whole of the East. He held court in Ephesus, no longer warrior but reveler. The wine and women and adulation were balm to his soul after the long night of the proscriptions, the venomous world of the Senate, and the butchery of Philippi.

A watery sun filtered through the green leaves in the great arbor of the god. A lattice of ivy and grapevine wrapped itself sinuously around the beams, entwined like thighs, supported by columns shaped like Dionysus's sacred thyrsus wand. Antony had ordered it built, his cave, cave of the god Dionysus.

The aim, through wine, was ecstasy. *Ecstasos*, the Greeks called it; the release of the soul from the body, transcending the restraints of the mind, the search for the gods through wine and sex.

Here under nature's boughs, Antony could celebrate to the full the rites of drunkenness and ecstasy, perform the whispered Bacchanalia, banned in dignity-conscious Rome. Surrounded by actors and musicians, with his pet dwarf Sisyphus, he laughed and caroused, the sacred ivy chaplet tilted on his head, wine goblet in his hand. The half-naked maenads danced to the sound of the flutes and pipes and then joined the wine-soaked satyrs in their pursuit through the forests.

Under the dappled leaves then, see the sinuous writhing of bodies, limbs entwined, bodies without faces or names sliding across each other like reptiles in some dark nest. A brown hand weighed the plumpness of a white breast, an olive hand slid along a pale thigh, mouths and fingers busy like bees at a flower, myriad busy pleasures for pleasure's sake.

Mellow wine blurred the faces, lending each body its own anonymity. Antony busied himself in the lap of a girl whose body was hidden by the thrusting buttocks of a man. Tiring of his plea-sures here, he moved his attention elsewhere, losing himself further to the effects of the wine and the attentions of so many fingers and tongues and lips, taking his own turn at women and men alike, aban-doned among the pink moist places and the swollen flesh.

He saw a young Syrian girl with skin the color of molasses and a bottom like a peach, on her knees, working feverishly with her tongue at the penis of an older man, his body matted with short silver hair. As he watched, the man lifted the girl effortlessly by the hips, turned her around, and mounted her from behind. While in Greece.

Antony, no longer bound by earth or body or mind, his whole world expanded into pure sensation, pursuing the god long after he had spent his seed in the tight, sweet cave of some forest nymph. He allowed himself to be tossed on a tide of bodies, moving from one to another, until the moment that pleasure became pain, and then going beyond even that until he felt his soul leave his body and merge with the stars and the sky above the green bough of Dionysus.

Until he was one with the gods.

ALEXANDRIA-BY-EGYPT

"Quintus Dellius, Majesty. I am sent at the express pleasure of my lord Antony."

She remembered this unctuous Roman when he was running errands for Caesar. A dandy, and with eyes you would not trust on a snake. She had kept him waiting as long as diplomatically possible without openly insulting him.

He looked around, his attention drawn to the marble statue of Dionysus on one side of the chamber, dressed in panther skin, hold-ing a kithara, a kind of lyre, in his left hand. Did he realize that his lord was not the only disciple of the nature gods?

She wore a chiton of pale gold, had deliberately chosen a golden diadem, fashioned into twisted ribbons with a Heracles knot. Another subtle message for Antony's ambassador: Hercules's descendants would find a sympathetic ear at the court of Queen Cleopatra.

Mardian leaned forward and whispered to her, in Egyptian. "I know this one, Majesty. He was Dolabella's man, then he changed sides to Cassius just before Laodicea, and then jumped ship to Antony at Philippi."

"As loyal as the wind."

"Which is all he needs to blow his tongue about, if he is like every other Roman we have had before the court."

Cleopatra returned her attention to the embassy. "So, Dellius," she said in Greek.

"Greetings, Most Exalted Queen of Egypt, from my lord Antony. I bear a letter from my lord which he wishes you to read."

He held out a scroll, which was accepted by one of the chamberlains and handed to her. She read it quickly. To the most Divine and Mighty Queen of Egypt, and so on, and so on . . . Lord Antony requested the pleasure of her company at his court in Tarsus.

"Tarsus," she said.

"My lord Antony is most eager to see you and resume your former friendship. Of course, he would also like to know why you handed your fleet to Cassius and sent him four legions in his war against Dolabella."

The impudence. She thought about the lord Antony, drunken and staggering at Caesar's villa, half naked: holding the bloody *februa* at the Feast of Lupercalia. This same Roman barbarian now wished to summon her to his presence as if she were one of his centurions. Or one of his women. "A Roman magistrate seeks to question the Queen of Egypt?"

"He feels that you were formerly friends and he seeks some explanation for such bewildering actions."

In truth, she wanted to see Marcus Antonius as much as he wished to see her. He was, she thought, her only friend in Rome. But she would not go to him as supplicant, begging his forbearance for imagined crimes. Neither would she go before another Roman wrapped in a carpet. "You may tell my lord Antony," she said, "that I shall consider his request."

Quintus Dellius smiled. It was not a request, of course, but a demand, but he was too much the diplomat to say so. "I shall bear your message," he said.

"Thank you, Quintus Dellius. May the gods grant you a safe journey."

"But you must go," Diomedes said to her.

"When he stops demanding my presence in Tarsus, I will go. Not before."

"But he is lord of all Asia now."

"And I am the Queen of Egypt, not his chamberlain!"

She knew what they were all thinking. First the famine, then pestilence, and now half the Egyptian fleet lost in the storm on the way to Brundisium. They were in no position to stand up to the Romans, indeed if they ever were. The country was almost bankrupt. And after the miraculous reversals that had seen the demise of Cassius and Brutus, Antony must appear to them some beneficent god, a savior.

Even more reason, in her opinion, to hold her head high and go to him on equal terms.

The *dioiketes* was shaking his stupid old head mournfully. "Do you know this Marcus Antonius? In Ephesus they are calling him the New Dionysus."

The New Dionysus. They had called her father by that name. "The Ephesians call any Roman with a sword and a taste for wine the New Dionysus."

"This one lives up to the name," Mardian said. "The talk from there is of unspeakable orgies every day. He takes the sacred rites of his religion to extremes, I believe."

"Marcus Antonius was never one for restraint," she said.

"You know him, Majesty?" the *dioiketes* asked her.

"We were on cordial terms in Rome."

"Then perhaps a visit now will ease the strain on Egypt."

"When I am ready."

"But should you offend him—"

"What is it you are all frightened of? That he will attack us, as Cassius planned to do? Well, do not fear on that account. Octavian and Lepidus would never let him have Egypt. Such an act would shatter their truce, and he does not want that."

"It is a dangerous game, Majesty."

"Politics is always dangerous, Diomedes."

"We need his friendship."

"Romans do not make friends, they make alliances." How the tide had turned. Alexandria had tried for years to keep a distance from Rome, but it was impossible. Rome was a fact of life, like the crocodiles in the Nile and the cobras in the desert. All that was possible was a wary accommodation.

The change was irrevocable, her affair with Caesar had made sure of that. But now that the dream of putting Caesarion on the throne of both empires was gone, she knew she would have to get the best bargain she could from Antony.

She saw Mardian smile.

"Mardian?"

"I was thinking that if you do go to him, Majesty, it will indeed be a great occasion. The meeting of Aphrodite and Dionysus. It should make for a great spectacle."

The thought had also occurred to her. In Egypt she was Isis, Aphrodite to the Greeks, Venus Genetrix to the Romans, the goddess of love and compassion. Now he had been acclaimed Dionysus, the god of Redemption and Joy, the Egyptian Osiris. Between them they represented the two great gods of the East, the two deities Rome had frowned upon and tried to suppress.

What had Mardian said to her? *You cannot rule alone.* He wanted her to marry a prince. What better prince, then, than a godly prince, the perfect consort to a goddess. If she could not have Caesar, perhaps she could have Caesar's heir?

It would be the sort of marriage she had always imagined for herself, a loveless political alliance, and no more. Not that Marcus Antonius did not possess certain charms, but he was hardly Caesar's equal in intellect or accomplishment. But still. It might not be an unpleasant duty to perform for her country.

She smiled. Mardian was right. It should make for a great spectacle indeed when she went to Tarsus.

A greater spectacle than any might ever expect.

60

CITY OF TARSUS, ASIA MINOR

THE SLOPES OF Mount Tarsus, richly green and dark with forest, rose behind the temples and amphitheaters of the city. Tarsus, on the flat, rich plain of Cilicia, was one of the great cities of the East, its name spoken in the same breath as Ephesus and Antioch. Once the Ptolemies had owned it, along with Cyprus and much of the Syrian coast. And perhaps, Cleopatra thought, one day the Ptolemies would own it again.

To dream of survival alone seemed such a mean, desperate thing. Even in her darkest hours, when her sentries fearfully scanned the horizon for Cassius's warships from the pinnacle of the Pharos beacon, she had not abandoned her dreams. She could never be just an appeaser, like her father. She had Alexander's blood in her veins, and it was time that a Ptolemy, even if it was a woman, finally do him credit.

❦   ❦

She felt like death. The long voyage across the Mediterranean had been an unremitting torture. She was violently ill for the duration, and had not eaten for days. There is nothing in the world more miserable than seasickness, she thought. Even death would be a mercy. For now, I wish only to get off this hulk of creaking timber and stale bilge and stand once again on dry land. But I have set my course and I shall not abandon it; this is no time for weakness.

Charmion and Iras helped her walk from her cabin up onto the deck. They had dressed her in a gown of shimmering gold. Even that small effort left her light-headed with fatigue, and she lowered herself gratefully onto the couch that had been readied for her on the cedarwood deck. It was draped with leopard skins, shaded with a canopy of gold silk. Young slave boys, costumed as Cupids, hurried into position with their fans of ostrich plumes.

"Anchor in the harbor," Cleopatra told the ship's captain, "we will not be going ashore."

As they navigated the lily-choked river, the oars of plain cypress pine used in the passage across the Mediterranean were replaced with others, black ebony, the blades coated with silver, flashing in the sun as they dipped through the water.

Sails had been prepared especially for their arrival, dyed with royal Tyrian purple and steeped in an essence of cypress tree oil so that when the wind blew, they carried with them the fragrance of the forest. They were quickly unfurled, and then the dark-skinned sailors shinned down from the yards, their job done, to be replaced in the rigging by young girls, dressed as sea nymphs. Other slaves lit great censers of frankincense and myrrh.

Cleopatra saw waves of people rushing toward the docks. Even at a stadion distant from the quay she could hear shouts and gasps from the gathering crowds, as astonishment took hold among the spectators.

Despite her wretched condition, she managed a smile. It was precisely the effect she had hoped for. No matter that you felt like death inside, she thought. The truth is what people see. If they see the goddess of the sea, Isis Pelagia reborn, in golden robes, then that for them is the truth. They cannot imagine this frightened woman, without allies or friends, trying desperately to save herself, her son, and her dreams.

〜 〜

Antony held court each day in the city square, seated on a gilded chair set on a raised dais. It was here that he heard petitions and administered justice to his dominions. Over the preceding months, he had received the kings of Armenia, Thrace, Judaea; the tetrarchs of Pontus, Sidonia, Galatia; the principals of every nation of Rome's vast Eastern empire, who had all made their way along the dusty Asian roads with their trains of servants and soldiers and courtiers, camels and gilded litters, to pay their respects to their new patron. Many of them brought their wives and their daughters with them also, to aid their diplomatic efforts, for they knew Antony's tastes well enough. One Glaphyra, famous for her beauty, used her favors to secure the satrap of Phrygia for her son; Mariamne spent several nights closeted in Antony's quarters, confirming the throne of Judaea for her husband, Herod.

The months had passed, and now Antony waited only for the great Egypt, impatient, irritated, and eager.

Life had been like a dream for Antony since Philippi. He was welcomed everywhere as Dionysus, Benefactor and Bringer of Joy. His senses had been sated in every way; wherever he went he had been welcomed with wild revels, with enough wine and young girls to satisfy an entire legion, let alone one man. Asia had indeed been a revelation. Out here he was not treated as just another Roman magistrate, Imperator of the Roman legions, but as a god.

It was the kind of thing a man could grow accustomed to.

Now he was master of the woman Caesar had called his mistress. The old boy would be impressed if he could see him now. With any luck at all, he would not only lay claim to her money, but lay claim to her as well.

Only, where was she?

With increasing irritation he watched the crowds melting away from under the colonnades and the cobblestoned square until there remained just his staff of Roman officers and his own bodyguard in attendance, and a handful of city burghers.

He turned to Quintus Dellius. "What is happening?"

"I do not know, Imperator."

"Find out."

There was a terrace on the palace overlooking the harbor, and it was from here that Dellius saw the great flotilla enter the harbor, Cleopatra's flagship with its purple sails at the van. He gaped. It was like no vessel he had seen before. Silver-tipped oars beat time to the music of a drum, and he made out the thinner, reedier sounds of pipes and flutes. There were sea nymphs working the ropes and the rudder, and at the heart of it all, dressed like Venus in a painting, was Queen Cleopatra herself, Cupids fanning her with colored ostrich plumes. Her two hand servants stood at the helm, dropping rose petals into the sea. He sniffed the air at the waft of perfume that accompanied the Egyptian fleet, carried to him on the prevailing breeze.

Small boats were streaming away from the quay as the local people set off for a better view of this amazing spectacle. He saw one rowboat rock and capsize in the middle of the harbor as her occupants all rushed to one side of the tiny craft at once to gawp.

Despite himself, Quintus Dellius could not suppress a smile of admiration.

He saw a slave hurrying past him on the terrace and grabbed the man by the arm, swinging him around. "What is going on here?" he barked.

"It is Aphrodite," the man gasped. "They say she is come herself to revel with the Lord Dionysus!"

Dellius released the man, watched him stumble away toward the docks. Aphrodite come to sport with Dionysus! This Queen Cleopatra not only dresses for great theater but knows how to stage it. The spies must have been in the city days ago ready to spread that little tale at the right moment.

He wondered how the lord Antony would take this news.

❦ ❦

Cleopatra watched a Liburnian make its way through the milling craft on the harbor, saw the flash of red cloaks, unmistakably Roman. She waited, Venus reclining, as the sun moved down the sky. All around her, on the shorefront and the docks, huge crowds were watching the great spectacle being played out before them. They would tell their grandchildren about this day. When Venus came to Tarsus.

The Liburnian hove to alongside and the delegation was helped aboard. It was a small party headed by a familiar face, Quintus Dellius.

He stood there, the great Roman nose twitching at the scent of rich perfumes, ogling the slave girls in the yards and the fine trappings of gold silks. Perhaps even the somber Dellius was a little impressed by her show.

"Your Majesty," he said.

She acknowledged him with a glance.

"The most noble Antony bids the Queen of Egypt welcome to his court, and invites you to come ashore and dine tonight at a banquet that is to be held in your honor."

She said nothing. It was Charmion, dressed as a sea nymph, who answered for her. "The queen does not wish to come ashore, my lord. She instead invites the noble Marcus Antonius to dine tonight as her guest on board the royal galley. His officers and all the leading officials of Tarsus are invited to the feasting."

Dellius looked around, wondered what sort of banquet the queen might prepare in such surroundings. He should like to see it. "I shall give my lord Antony your message," he said. "I am sure he would be most pleased to attend."

He bowed and returned with his party to the Liburnian. Well, I hope he presents himself here halfway sober, she thought. This is my moment. I can yet win everything as I had once planned with Julius. If he was watching her from the Pantheon, she wondered what he would think of the little girl in the carpet now.

61

HE HAD BEEN feted by kings all over Asia, had dined with Caesar and with Pompey and Cicero, had attended orgies in dark woods and country villas, and elegant dinner parties and riotous symposia in the best of Roman houses. But he had never seen anything like this.

Cleopatra's flagship was a massive craft with six banks of oars, uniquely refurbished to resemble a floating palace more than a royal galley. It was now moored at the quayside, and vast crowds of gawpers had gathered there and had to be kept at bay by a cohort of Roman legionaries.

The first guests arrived as the sun was sinking down the sky; tendrils of mist clung to the harbor, and torches had been lit on the deck. Antony mounted a gangplank draped with Tyrian purple, staring in frank astonishment at the costumed attendants, the mermaids, nymphs, and Cupids waiting to welcome them.

His attention was drawn first to the stern of the ship, which had been painted entirely with gold leaf, so when he boarded he did not notice at first that there was a springy cushion beneath his feet instead of a hard wood-planked deck. He looked down and found a thick carpet of rose petals strewn across the planking, held down by a net. Wherever the Romans trod, the crushing of the flowers under their heavy boots released a powerful scent.

He caught his breath. There, waiting to greet him, was Cleopatra, reclining under a great carved canopy sheeted in gold silk and carved in the shape of an elephant's head, its trunk raised aloft. In the rose twilight she seemed to shimmer with pearls; there were rich clusters at her throat and at her ears. Her hair had been artfully curled, and long tendrils trailed over her shoulders and down her back or coiled at her cheek. She was dressed in a gown of rippling golden silk, and on her feet were golden sandals, studded with emeralds. Serpents of rare lapis lazuli entwined around her bare arms. She lay on a couch, leaning on one elbow.

Deathless Aphrodite, Venus Genetrix, Isis, Queen of the Sea and of Egypt.

Antony gaped, the great collector of women, lusting for the one piece he did not yet own. Finally he stepped forward and bowed. "Majesty," he murmured.

He saw her eyes glitter in the half-light. She beckoned for him to come closer. He leaned toward her, breathing in the rich scents, perfumes of incomparable price mingled with the essential fragrance of a beautiful woman. *Ah, Antony, you have truly died and are consorting with the gods in their heavens!*

Her lips brushed against his ear. "I want you inside me," she whispered, and drew away.

❦ ❦

Everything around them shone red or gold. The banquet chamber in the stateroom was a dazzle of gilt goblets and plates, and the triclinia were covered with ruby silk; there were marble tables with legs of pure gold and studded with carnelian, and hangings of rose silk on the walls. Perfumed doves were released to fly about the chamber. Slaves anointed their heads with cinnamon oil and washed their hands and feet with wine.

Mountains of food were brought by flaxen-hair Cupids and olive-skinned nymphs; there was smoked desert hare from Libya, purple shellfish, oysters dressed in seaweed, roasted peacocks, white cakes made from Egypt's finest flour, toasted papyrus stems, jellies flavored with pomegranate juice and honey. Amphorae of the best Chian wines were brought and mixed in the kraters. Beautiful slave girls played silver lutes while they ate.

All this magnificence was reflected from the mirrors on the walls, abundance upon abundance, luxury multiplied on luxury.

But Antony found he had no appetite for the food or even, by the sacred balls of Jupiter, the wine.

I want you inside me.

He could not take his eyes off her, could think of nothing else but what she had proposed. Yet she now treated him as if he were no more than another of her three dozen honored guests, as if the startling intimacy had been imagined.

But there was neither time nor opportunity to talk privately with her. She ignored him, instead swapping easy banter with his officers and the city burghers, who fawned around her; except for Quintus Dellius, who leered at her from his couch as if she were a prostitute in a city temple.

After they had all finished eating and drinking, she led them back onto the deck. Night had fallen and the guests gasped as they looked up at the yards. Lanterns had been suspended above their heads with silk lines, and now the masts and rigging appeared in the perfect dark like an enchanted forest.

"Each of you will take with you tonight the gold couches you lay on," Cleopatra announced, "as well as the gold plates you have dined from and the gold cups from which you drank. I will have servants accompany you home with torches to light the way and others to bear the gifts."

There were murmurs of astonishment and gratitude.

As the others were taking their leave, Antony took her to one side. "My lady," he said, "I hoped we might have some private moments together. There is much we need to discuss."

There was a look of amusement in those dark eyes. Why, you little vixen, Antony thought. "There will be plenty of time for talk, Lord Antony," she answered. "Tonight we have feasted the occasion of your great triumph over Brutus here in Asia. Let us not spoil the celebration with talk of politics and state."

Politics and state are the last things on my mind, he thought, and you know it. He could still hear the husky words close to his ear: *I want you inside me*.

"I would still desire a moment of your company alone," he insisted.

"It has been a long journey and I am tired," she said. "Perhaps tomorrow," and with that she gave him a slow and deliberate smile that left him tossing restlessly in his bed almost till dawn. When he finally slept, his dreams were of Egypt.

I want you inside me.

62

FOR ANTONY'S BANQUET the next night, she went as Cleopatra, not as Venus. She wore an emerald chiton, made of Sidonian silk and fastened at the shoulders with pearl clasps. She arrived in a curtained litter, her Nubian escort running ahead with flaming torches through the falling dusk.

One of the reasons Antony was so adored by his troops was that he often took his meals with them, standing up at the common mess table. It seemed that he would make no exceptions to his eating arrangements, even for her. Before his arrival in Tarsus, the building he appropriated for his dining hall had been used as an emporium, and it still reeked of the market, of spices and offal and fish. It was built of gray stone, its vaulted ceilings supported by three rows of high arched pillars. Antony had tried to pretty it up, she thought, looking at the Syrian embroidered hangings and the ornate bronze lamp stands. But it still looked like what it was: an empty bazaar.

Musicians played on a dais near the entrance, but the sound of the flutes and lyres was lost in the cavernous hall, which was alive with the chatter of a thousand voices. But as she stepped through the huge barred oak doors, two heralds announced her arrival with trumpets and an abrupt silence fell over the vast assembly.

She looked around. The majority of the guests were soldiers, rank upon rank of them, sitting at long wooden trestles. There were a dozen triclinia arranged at the center of the hall for the elegant repose of Antony, his senior officers, and their guests. Several of the city burghers were in attendance, and their wives had been pressed into service, as decoration, no doubt.

Every head was craned in her direction, eager for a glimpse of the great queen, this goddess that had set the whole of the city alive with speculation and gossip. She took a deep breath. *This is my moment. I must not waste it.*

Her Nubian bodyguard escorted her into the hall, Mardian and Diomedes in her train.

⚜   ⚜

Antony came forward to greet her. He was dressed as a Roman tonight, in bronze armor and scarlet cloak, an imposing presence. *Look at how his men look at him. Any soldier here would follow him into Hades.*

He was also unbearably attractive. *Hard not to twitter like a girl when she was around him.* She had forgotten the effect he could have, with those dark curls and his muscles oiled up. *I must remember who I am.*

He smiled, and she felt a silky sensation in her stomach, like a nest of warm puppies. The most lovable thing about this rogue was that he was so transparent. She knew with one glance what was on his mind. He was hoping for another easy conquest, like Herod's wife. *Follow in Caesar's footsteps.*

One day soon, Hercules, you shall have your wish. I am warming a place for you in my bed. But beware. Once you have Cleopatra's thighs around your hips and her nails in your back, you may not wish to leave. You cannot imagine the heady plans I have for you and me.

After they exchanged formal greetings, he turned to the entire gathering and welcomed her, according to protocol, his voice echoing through the vaulted hall.

"We are here to honor Queen Cleopatra of Egypt, who has traveled across the ocean from Alexandria to see us. We wish her welcome to our humble quarters, which we have tried to make royal for her."

The racket began again as soon as they sat. Cleopatra reclined on a triclinium, in the place of honor beside Marc Antony. He was gawking again, but she pretended not to notice, treating him with the elaborate courtesies diplomacy demanded, but avoiding any suggestion of intimacy.

The food arrived.

"Swill," she heard Mardian mutter, but not loud enough that any but she could hear. It seemed that Antony felt he could not compete with her banquet, and had decided instead to impress her with his spartan lifestyle: roasted kid and some tunny fish, served on wooden plates.

But, she noticed, there was plenty of the best Falernian wine.

☙ ☙

Antony had his dwarf with him tonight, Sisyphus. An ugly little fellow, with a hooked nose too big for his face and an unpleasant laugh. Antony seemed to find him amusing.

"The queen must be impressed with our arrangements," he said, grinning at Antony. "You have outshone the poor banquet of last evening. Will you also make the queen a present of the goblets and plate?"

Antony turned to Cleopatra, grinning sheepishly. "She can take them tonight or she can have her servants buy a gross in the marketplace tomorrow. There would not be much difference in cost."

"Where are those damned rose petals?" Sisyphus said, feigning anger. "They must have blown away from the draught under the doors. I shall chide the servants later."

Cleopatra decided to come to Antony's rescue. "If you had outdone me tonight, it was I who would have been ashamed, for I had six months to prepare for our meeting."

"Still, our Imperator might have done better," one Canidius, a general, said. "But as a god he has many requests to fulfill."

Antony shrugged good-naturedly. He seemed not to mind his men chucking him in this way. "And why not? Octavian is only the *son* of a god. I had to go one better to put the boy in his place."

They all laughed at that.

"They are calling you the New Dionysus," she said.

"That is because of his wand," Dellius said. "As a thousand maenads will testify."

"It is a wand of some magificence," Sisyphus joined in. "It is not only the length of it, but the shape of the pinecone at the top."

Antony stopped smiling, perhaps unsure how the queen would react in the face of such bawdy talk. Perhaps it is a test, she thought. I can behave as if I am affronted and it will serve me nothing but the enmity of the Romans. Or I can show them that I can jest as well as Antony, and perhaps win their affection as he does.

"I am told that when the lord Antony rides in procession through the streets, he waves his wand at all the people," she said, "so it must surely be worthy of remark."

Even Dellius applauded at that.

It seemed Antony's exploits in the bedchamber were also the talk of the soldiers' tables, where the wine flowed as freely as it had around their own. A group of Gallic recruits began a chorus of one of their marching songs, which was soon taken up by a hundred voices.

> *"We come to serve the god of wine,*
> *He serves it to the queen.*
> *When Glaphyra's drunk her fill,*
> *He'll give her back again."*

"Glaphyra," Cleopatra said. "She is the mother of our new prince of Phrygia, am I correct?"

"Indeed she is," Dellius said, eyes glittering. "She came to Antony on her knees."

Oh Antony, she thought. This Dellius does not love you. His jests are in earnest. Can you not see that? "It seems you have been very busy with affairs of state, my lord," she said.

He had the good grace to appear embarrassed. Meanwhile, the soldiers had started on another verse.

> *"The Jews believe in just one god,*
> *Their lord parted the skies.*
> *Herod sent his wife along*
> *And our lord parted her thighs."*

"I apologize for my men," Antony said. "Sometimes they forget themselves."

"Oh, it's just the high spirits of soldiers," she said. "I remember I heard a similar song they sang about my lord Caesar."

"Home we bring our bald whoremonger,
Romans lock your wives away.
All the silver coin you lent him
went his Gallic tarts to pay."

A silence fell across the room. For a moment no one spoke. Then Antony threw back his head and roared with laughter and a thousand Romans joined him, beating on the table with their fists and banging their goblets in applause.

She realized in that moment how she sorely had offended them the evening before. Perhaps she had impressed the people of Tarsus with her wealth, but Antony and his soldiers had felt belittled by her display. Now she had won them over, not with opulence but with a little vulgarity, innocently expressed. She could see in the eyes of the men around her that if Antony loved her, they were prepared to love her, too.

Except perhaps Quintus Dellius. She would put a sword in her own side before she trusted that little snake.

63

THE TERRACE OF the palace overlooked the harbor, today a deep indigo blue. A canopy had been erected for shade, and this was where Antony and the Egyptian queen now sat as his servants served them refreshments—wine cooled with snow for Antony, scented water and fruits for Cleopatra. Below them on the harbor her flagship rode at anchor, the gilt-painted stern glittering in the morning sun.

I want you inside me.

Had she really said those words or had he imagined it? He was impatient to taste a little of Egypt. Glaphyra, Miriamne; he had sampled most of the East already. The mother of a satrap here, the wife of a king there; it was like taking fruit from another man's orchard: a stolen plum always tasted better than one you had paid for. And this Cleopatra would be Caesar's fruit. This particular orchard of delights had belonged to a god.

"A happier occasion than the last time we met," she said to him.

"Indeed. The old boy left us with a lot of problems to sort out."

"And have they been resolved, Marcus Antonius?"

"I do not need to answer that," he said, enjoying this fencing. "Doubtless your spies keep you informed of everything that happens in Rome."

"I heard that Caesar's nephew was not as easily led as many supposed."

"Yes, him and his pretty boys," Antony grunted. "We had a few differences in the early days, I admit."

"Differences that had you keeping the shepherds company in Cisalpine Gaul."

She was baiting him, the little minx. "That's all over now. And that is not what I wished to discuss with you."

"And what is it you wished to discuss, my lord Antony?"

"Let us start with Cassius. He was your enemy, and mine. I would like to know why you sent your legions to his aid against Dolabella." His wine steward poured him another goblet of good Falernian wine from the krater.

He was pleased to see that Cleopatra's perfumed, mocking smile had vanished. "If something appears too absurd to be true, then there is a good chance that it is not true," she said.

"You deny it?"

"They were *Roman* legions. Dolabella sent for them, they departed Alexandria to go to him. On the way their commander decided that Cassius was more likely to triumph, so when he arrived in Syria he changed his allegiance. His guilt, not mine. Do you really think I would have helped Cassius under any circumstance? As you have pointed out, he was my enemy. If it wasn't for him and his friends I would be Caesar's wife by now."

Antony believed her. Yet Cleopatra's duplicity had sounded plausible enough when it had been first suggested, by Octavian. "What about your fleet?"

"If you wish to know who persuaded the governor of Cyprus to send his fleet to Cassius, you should perhaps start your search in Ephesus, in the Temple of Diana."

"You mean Arsinoë?" But Cleopatra's exiled sister had spoken so sweetly when he had interrogated her. Whom did one believe these days?

Cleopatra shrugged her shoulders with bitter resignation. "I told Julius that she would be the cause of endless troubles if he let her live. He seemed to think clemency was a virtue, though I think Brutus proved him wrong. Now my sister also proves the point."

"I see."

"If Cassius had won, he would have installed her as queen in my place. Come, my lord, you have lived in Rome all your life. You should know the way of these intrigues as well as I. Someone has tried to poison you against me. It is not hard to imagine who, or why."

"I thought it was merely expediency on your part."

"I have no argument with expediency, but to help Cassius would have been suicidal. Because of my son."

"But you also promised me in a letter that you would send your fleet to Brundisium, to support me in my war against Brutus. . . ."

"Which I tried to do, even though it was winter. As a consequence I lost half my remaining fleet in a storm. The wreckage is still washing up on the shores of Greece. I led the fleet out of Alexandria myself, even though I detest the sea and cannot take a bath without feeling nauseous. I did it because I wanted to ensure your complete victory." She leaned toward him, her black eyes glittering. "You think I did not want revenge against the men who killed my Julius?"

She was trembling with rage. Remarkable. Perhaps she had really felt something for the old boy. Women never failed to mystify him.

Well, he believed her. It would be the last time he listened to Octavian. Poisonous little bitch. He should have known better.

He was in many ways relieved. He needed Cleopatra right now as much as she needed him, and he did not want any inconvenient betrayals to stand in the way of an alliance between them.

Her eyes, enhanced with her cosmetic, burned into him.

"You said something to me, when you arrived here in Tarsus, when I stepped aboard your royal barge."

"Did I?" All wide-eyed innocence now.

He lowered his voice to a murmur and held her eyes. "You said you wanted me inside you."

"Perhaps after I heard about Glaphyra and Miriamne I thought again. Perhaps I felt I should not be valued any more than a slave girl. Or a maenad."

"You know there is never a woman in the world quite like Cleopatra."

She smiled. "Unlike you, I have had only one lover in my life, but I have seen enough of the world to know that a man will say anything to get his way with a woman."

He grinned. "I am afraid that is true."

She sipped her rose-scented water and watched him over the rim of her cup. "But I did not come here to talk of such things. We are here for politics. You wish Egypt to help you in your campaign against Parthia."

She made a face at him, mocking the look of surprise on his face. She was like a sweet-tempered, witty Fulvia in many ways, enamoured of intrigue, always a step ahead of him. "I would want to know what you would wish from me in return for your grain ships," he said.

"My demands are prepared. And the first of them is one that cannot be negotiated."

"I see. And what is that?"

And she told him.

CITY OF EPHESUS, IN ASIA MINOR

The Temple of Diana was famous around the world, its white marble columns as high and as dense as the cedar forests of Lebanon. There were gold statues of the virgin huntress all around the colonnades with nymphs and fawns, and huge murals on the wall, depicting her with Alexander. Like Isis and Aphrodite, she was the goddess of women and fertility, but unlike them, she had a dark side, demanding her priests be castrated before they could serve her.

The temple and the surrounding woods had offered asylum to every kind of exile in the past, from runaway slaves to thieves and beggars, who flocked around the temple precincts hawking fake silver statues of the goddess and picking purses. Prostitutes plied their trade among the pilgrims who had come from all over Asia to bring offerings to the goddess.

Arsinoë had lived four years at the great temple, after escaping the executioner in Rome. As a priestess of the temple, her body was held to be inviolable. She had attracted a court of her own, a government in exile of disaffected courtiers from Alexandria, those with a grudge against Cleopatra or simply those whose ambition had outstripped opportunity. She had received them all in her sparse quarters in the temple and frequently played host to emissaries from the governor of Cyprus—Serapis, who saw himself as one day *dioiketes* to Arsinoë, Queen of Egypt.

This hot spring afternoon, she had left the bright Aegean sunshine of the courtyard and entered the gloomy recesses of the shrine to make her devotions to the goddess. The sanctuary was dark, lit by winking oil lamps. The goddess herself had none of the softness of Isis or the eroticism of Aphrodite. She stood stiffly on her pedestal, like a sentry at his post, her torso covered with dugs, a bow held in her right hand.

Arsinoë was on her knees, before the altar, when the soldiers arrived. They crashed through the courtyard, pushing aside the protests of the castrati priests and the virgin priestesses. Two of them grabbed her by the hair and dragged her screaming from the high altar, their hobnailed boots echoing on the marble.

She was forced to kneel under the great portico of the temple, her hands pressed behind her back. Without warning, a centurion took off her head with one practiced stroke of his sword. Blood spurted down the temple steps, where it formed in dark and rapidly congealing pools.

It was not hate, not even war. Just politics and good sense.

Nobody's body was inviolable. Caesar could have told her that.

04

CITY OF TARSUS

THIS TIME THERE were no Cupids, no nymphs, no beds of roses. A crescent moon hung over the yards, in place of the myriad oil lamps of that first night. There were no flutes nor harps, just the lapping of the sea against the hull of the royal barge.

Charmion led Antony silently belowdecks to Cleopatra's stateroom. The door closed softly behind him.

In the dull glow of the oil lamps, he made out a bed covered with leopard skins, and curtained with silk of the sheerest kind to keep out the night insects. The walls were paneled in rich cypress, and there was another curtain of silk across the square window. The air was sweet with frankincense.

"I want you inside me," a woman's voice murmured.

Five days since she had spoken those words to him for the first time, five days he had waited for this moment. No, he had waited longer than that. He had waited for this moment since he first saw this dangerous woman at Caesar's house in Rome.

She lay under a single sheet, no more than a shadow, a promise in the darkness, darkness that allowed his imagination to create the perfect woman of his dreams. He slipped out of his cloak and tunic and shifted aside the curtain.

She gave a throaty laugh. "I see you have brought your famous wand."

Her vulgarity shocked him. Perhaps I, too, have been confounded by her illusions, he thought. But now I shall see the woman behind the queen. And you shall see the man behind the god, the sweat and semen of an ordinary mortal. Here, at least, I can be myself.

He threw back the sheet. Lately there had been so many women, so many bodies. But this was a woman he would remember forever. This was not just a woman he bedded now, this was Egypt, this was Caesar's wife. This was glorious conquest, but with sweet clemency in its wake.

His breath was strange; he had a masculine smell, leather, sweat, wine. She parted her lips to kiss him. She expected him to be rough, to take her with all the subtlety of a soldier, but his gentleness surprised her. He slipped his mouth away, and his lips moved to the lobes of her ear, his teeth biting very gently, teasing. She knew it was only artifice, one of a thousand tricks no doubt picked up from his endless encounters. He was trying to impress her.

She offered him her throat, her breasts. He found her nipples, already risen for him, hard and brown as the pits of small fruit. He sucked each one in turn. "You are so beautiful, kitten," he whispered.

"Don't call me that," she hissed.

Her tone of voice must have surprised him, for he stopped what he was doing. But she grabbed his hair and brought his head back to her breast. Despite herself, he had woken something in her, a physical need that had lain there, dormant like a seed, since Julius had died. He still wanted to tease her, but instead she drew him to her, wrapped her ankles around the base of his spine, suddenly wild with need. He slid easily inside her.

Do not be gentle with me, she thought. Be the gladiator tonight. She pushed her hips into him, trying to satisfy her need, impelling herself to the finish. But it was no good; like trying to recapture a dream on waking, to re-create an old memory. The craving would not peak, the desire would not dissolve. Antony sweated and grunted on top of her as she arched her back to receive him, the muscles in her toes and calves and thighs cramping with strain. Antony, thinking he was pleasuring her, moved even more violently astride her.

But something was wrong. The intense craving remained, without the attendant pleasure. She pretended to reach the blissful moment and then lay beneath him, exhausted, frustrated, and bewildered.

Antony gasped and cried aloud. Not like Julius, Julius who had to always be in control, who reached his ecstasy without a sound. And as he finished, a great welling of grief seemed to bubble up from inside her, like lava, and she wept.

Antony gentled her, holding her in his arms and stroking her hair, astonished by this sudden outpouring of emotion, comprehending the reason for it as little as she.

❦ ❦

They stood together on the deck watching the light stain the eastern sky. The lamps had been left in the rigging from that first night. They had seemed like stars that night; now he could see they were just simple clay pots. An illusion and nothing more, he thought. Life was an illusion. You conjured dreams and fears from the raw stuff of life and made mortals believe it to be real. Like Dionysus, like Aphrodite.

"Come to Alexandria," she said.

He had expected her to ask him. He was tempted. "It is impossible," he told her. "There is trouble in Judaea between Herod and the Maccabees. And there are rumors that the Parthians are preparing to attack Syria. I am needed here."

"Parthia can wait for the summer. And there will always be trouble in Judaea while you leave the Jews to govern themselves. Winter is cold in Tarsus. In Alexandria it is mild and I will find a thousand amusements to entertain you."

He did not answer her right away, wavering.

"You have just ended one campaign and now you wish to go off and fight another? Is there no rest for Dionysus, the Bringer of Joy?"

She heard him sigh. "You are right. I am tired."

"You and your staff will be my guests at the palace. You can sleep in the bed where Caesar slept."

An overgrown child, Caesar had once called him, to his face. I suppose the old boy was right. Like a child, he enjoyed a holiday and did not want to go back to school, as he now did not want to resume the responsibilities of Imperator.

"Come to Egypt," she persisted, "and I will wed you to Alexandria."

"No," he said. "It is impossible. Do not ask me again. I cannot come. For the final time. No."

65

ALEXANDRIA-BY-EGYPT

HE ARRIVED ON a cold, blue day at the beginning of winter. In his honor, the Gate of the Sun was hung with garlands, the Canopic Way swept clean. Trumpets blew from the palace walls as he approached, guards sent ahead to escort him into the palace.

Crowds lined the street in curiosity, and when they saw he had not come in the toga of a Roman magistrate, but in the simple chlamys of a Greek gentleman, they cheered and applauded.

So already he is popular with the mob, Cleopatra thought, watching from the palace windows. Wait until they see how much he can drink. Then they will cheer him even louder.

❧ ❧

Antony threw himself at Alexandria with abandon, as if he had finally found his ancestral home. Alexandria was just as enthusiastic about Antony. Finally there was a man who had taken on the mantle of the New Dionysus who actually looked and acted the part.

He had folded up the cumbersome toga, emblem of Roman rule, and gave his equerry, Eros, his armor to winter in its barred oaken chest. He took to wearing Greek robes and white Attic shoes. He dismissed his bodyguards and ate Greek and Egyptian food, as his hosts did.

Perhaps to impress Cleopatra, he went to the Museion every day to listen to the scholars in their lecture halls as they explained their new discoveries in mathematics. He let them guide him through the endless corridors and rooms of the famous Library, to take him onto the terrace roof at night to explain the principles of astronomy. He watched them dissect the corpse of a criminal for their studies of medicine, and even endured a three-hour lecture on modern philosophy.

But the boy in him soon grew bored and he spent more and more of his time at the endless rounds of *commissatia*—the great drinking parties that followed an evening banquet. Life soon became an eternal round of parties and pleasure, Dionysian mystique fashioned into a way of life. He formed a club, the *Amimeto-bioi*, the Company of Life.

The society was composed of the leading members of Alexandrian society, Friends and Kinsmen from the court, as well as rich merchants and bankers from the Brucheion, and every evening one of them hosted a *commissatio* at his home, each trying to outdo the other with the richness of the food, the celebrity of the wines, and the variety of the entertainments.

PALATINE HILL, ROME

Munatius Plancus, fresh from the barber, was admiring himself in a wall mirror as Fulvia laid out the map on the table. He was Antony's general, not hers, an ass-kisser who knew more about the latest gossip on the Aventine than he did about the army. But then, she didn't want someone who knew what they were doing, after all. She was giving the orders here.

Lucius sat in the corner, glowering. He wanted a share of Antony's greatness, which accounted for his ambition. But he wanted people to love him as well, and that was his trouble. You couldn't have both, not in her opinion.

"The Young Caesar has gone too far," Lucius was saying to Plancus. "He is in flagrant disregard of the treaty he signed at Brundisium. He has settled all his veterans from the wars, while Antony's men are still penniless and waiting for what is rightfully theirs."

"Justify it how you will," Fulvia said to Lucius. "When you bring down this little bitch, my husband's gratitude will know no bounds."

"Now is the time to do it," Plancus said, reluctantly turning away from the mirror. "The blockade that pirate Sextus is running is starting to bite. There were riots this morning, at Ostia and on the Aventine. They even set fire to a granary! Starving, so they burn down the storehouses! That's Romans for you."

"Can you raise enough men to stand against Octavian?" Fulvia asked.

"The army will follow me anywhere," Plancus said.

Fulvia glanced at Lucius. More correctly, they would march to Antony's drum, while you scurry along behind, she thought. But I don't care how it's done as long as we get them in the field against Octavian. This is the time to strike. His own troops are on the verge of mutiny, the country's agriculture has been ruined by the endless civil wars, the whole country is in turmoil.

My husband will soon be the new Master of Rome, if I have to lead him by the nose to do it.

66

ALEXANDRIA-BY-EGYPT

"THEY SAY," ANTONY murmured, as one of the servants washed the grease from the roast goose off his fingers with rosewater, "there is a woman in the marketplace who is two hundred years old. She reads fortunes."

Cleopatra helped herself to some Jericho dates. "If you listen to every story you hear around the docks, you will lose both your money and your virginity."

Antony laughed. "Well, one is already gone and the other I never really cared for."

They were dining alone in Cleopatra's private salon, off a table of carved ivory. Even the couches were inlaid with ivory. The walls were inlaid with tortoiseshell, and the windows offered a view of the entire royal harbor, the colonnades of the Temple of Isis on Antirrhodos white as bone through the swaying palms. Servants hovered. It seemed that since coming to Alexandria, Antony had lost his taste for eating with the men.

"I believe we make our own fortunes," Cleopatra said to him.

"Yet it would be an entertainment to go there."

"To Rhakotis?"

"You have never been there? Never visited your own city?"

"It stinks. Why should I wish to?"

"We could go there in disguise. It would be fun."

She laughed, the adventuress in her excited by the prospect. She would not have balked at such an idea once. It had been a long time since she hid in a carpet.

Antony constantly surprised her. He could be diverting in his way, always intent on finding some new game. Being with him was like reliving her own childhood.

"Whatever you wish, then, Lord Antony," she said. "Alexandria is yours."

He grinned. "You never know," he said. "Perhaps we'll find you a sailor."

She tossed a red apple at him, and he tossed it straight back. She laughed, and pelted him with oranges. The servants watched with astonishment as their queen and the Roman lord played like children. They had never seen anything like this. When the god and goddess had finished their food fight, the tortoiseshell walls and alabaster floors were littered with lobster shells, pie crusts, and squashed fruit.

〜 〜

Rhakotis was the poor quarter of the city, to the west side of the city, near the docks. At night it was the haunt of drunken sailors and prostitutes. Sisyphus showed them the famous wall known as the Keramik, faced with colored tiles, where clients chalked messages for their favorite courtesans.

Cleopatra had never seen the poor quarter at night and she was overcome by the smell as much as by what she saw. There was, as she had expected, the stink of the sewer and the fish markets, the sharp wafts of camel and donkey dung, but also a thousand other fragrances to the air, the heady scent of a quarter of the city whose warehouses were stacked with perfume oils, spices, and henna.

There were four of them embarked on this adventure, Antony, Sisyphus, and Dellius disguised as itinerant traders, Cleopatra as Antony's woman. They roamed along dark narrow streets where rats stared brazenly back at them, orange-eyed, from piles of refuse. They headed for the quay, and the dark *tabernae* where Phoenician and Sicilian sailors came to get drunk and find themselves a whore for a few copper coins.

She had not imagined that people would live like this. She had seen poverty among the fellahin in the *chora,* but not this smoky hell. The taverns were dark and choking with the poor oil they used in the lamps and the perfumes of the harlots. Oyster shells crunched under her feet. Antony bought her one of the hot gravy pies, and she spat it out on the floor. She had never tasted anything so disgusting in her life.

And the people who inhabited this netherworld: fat sailors spilling a few copper coins onto the tables to paw some half-dressed hag with hardly a tooth left in her head. Antony and his friends seemed to find the whole thing vastly entertaining and ordered cup after cup of wine.

Afterward, Antony, reeling drunk, decided to have a little fun. He stopped outside a modest house and banged with a fist on the door. "Open up in there!" he bawled. "I am looking for a runaway slave called Cicero!"

After a while they saw a glimmer of light, as the house's owner descended the passage with an oil lamp. Guffawing, Antony grabbed Cleopatra by the arm and dragged her away down the street, Dellius and Sisyphus scampering behind him.

"Who are you?" they heard a voice shout at them as they ran. "Who is that? I was asleep! You donkey dung! You camel farts!"

They turned a corner and Antony fell against a wall, his shoulders heaving with laughter.

"Enough," Dellius gasped, out of breath from running. "Let us go back to the palace. It is almost dawn."

Cleopatra found, to her surprise, that she was reluctant to return. The adventure appealed to the girl in her, the five-year-old who used to throw rocks at the sentries from the palace walls and once held a candle to her tutor's robe and set him alight, laughing hysterically as he jumped into the lily ponds to quench the flames. A long time had passed since she did anything that was not calculated to help the state.

Antony was about to let Dellius drag him back to the Brucheion, but then he heard groans from an upstairs window. "Listen!" he said.

"Enough, my lord," Dellius repeated. "Let us go."

"Hear that?" Antony said. "Some men can never leave their wives alone." He fumbled in the darkness for a stone. He found one and hurled it at a wooden shutter above their heads.

Moments later the window was thrown open with a clatter.

"Who's out there?"

"Is the lady of the house open for business?" Antony called up.

"Who is that?"

"I admit she's fat and ugly," Antony shouted, "but last time I was here she only charged me half a watermelon and I think it was worth it."

An oil lamp was hurriedly lit and they heard the man crashing downstairs.

"Oh, come away," Sisyphus said.

But Antony was laughing so hard he could not move.

The front door of the house burst open and a shadow charged at them through the darkness. By the light of the lamp Cleopatra could see that the man's head reached barely to Antony's shoulder. But in his fury he flailed blindly at the bigger man with his fists. Antony, offering no resistance, sat down hard on the cobblestones.

"Drunks and whores!" the man shouted.

Antony just sat there on his haunches, still laughing. The man went back inside and came out holding a piece of firewood and started to flail at Antony's head. Dellius had to drag the outraged householder away before he did Antony serious injury.

I wonder what this man would say if I told him who I was, Cleopatra thought. *That he has been woken up in the middle of the night and insulted by his own queen? I suspect he would not believe me. Without my gowns and my bodyguards and my thrones, I am no longer Cleopatra, or Isis. Life is all illusion.*

"All right," Antony was shouting as the man broke free from Dellius and started flailing away again with the club, "a whole watermelon, but that's my final offer!"

It was a wonder, she thought later, that he wasn't killed.

⚜ ⚜

"Enough for one night, my lord," Dellius said, dragging Antony along the alleyway as a man would pull at a large and recalcitrant mule.

"Did you see that dwarf? He had a punch like Hercules. Am I bleeding?"

Foolishness, she thought. *And yet there was something liberating here, away from the strictures of the guards, the ceremony that had to be attended to at all times of the day. Here she was just another whore abroad in the city, a slave girl in rags, free to laugh and breathe*

in the foul stench like everyone else. Like a god visiting the underworld, she supposed.

With Antony she could be a girl again, remind herself of the
adventuress who had led a mercenary army in the desert, the brazen
young girl who had insinuated herself into the presence of the great
Caesar wrapped up in a smuggled carpet. Sometimes she lost sight of
that spirit, sometimes she was too much the queen.

In the darkness a hand reached out for them, clawing at their
clothes. An old woman, a beggar. "Spare a coin?" a voice crowed.

"Let go of me, you filthy old crow!" Dellius shouted, and shoved
past her, but Antony stopped, plunged a hand into his cloak, and produced his purse. There was the rattle of coins as he tossed it to the
old woman. "Here," he said, "take it."

"Are you mad?" Dellius hissed at him.

"Am I mad, Quintus Dellius? No, I am only drunk. But in the
morning I shall be sober and I shall be living in the palace. This
wretch will still be poor and waking up on this stinking street."

"She will spend it all on drink," Dellius said.

"What do you think I was going to do with it?" Antony said, and
roared with laughter. He staggered away. Cleopatra smiled, too, in the
darkness. She'd had fun tonight. A long time since the Queen of Egypt,
for all her wealth, had been allowed that small luxury. It made it hard
not to love this Antony, just a little, for his roguery and his high spirits.

It also made it impossible to guess what he might do next.

❦   ❦

Antony lay sprawled on his back, dawn staining the dark sky outside
the window. She threw herself on the bed beside him, stroked his
tangled curls, touched her lips to his forehead. In the morning he
would have several bruises on his head to show for his escapades.

"I love Alexandria," he murmured.

"Alexandria loves you."

"Except for that dwarf."

"He was no dwarf. He was a man of ordinary size. It is you who
are a giant."

"A giant," he murmured happily.

"Or a king," she said. "That is what my Alexandrians want. They
want a king. It could be you, my Hercules. It could be you."

He blinked slowly, his eyes watching the sudden, yellow splash of sunlight that had appeared on the ceiling. The sun was rising over the desert.

"Egypt is yours, if you would take it. And any man who has Egypt has Rome for the asking."

He did not answer her. He continued to stare at the shadows creeping across the room, stealing to the corners like frightened slaves. She kissed him, and when she looked again, his face was composed in sleep. When he finally woke, at the eighth hour of the day, he did not raise the subject of their conversation with her and gave no sign that he remembered it at all.

67

MARDIAN WATCHED THE queen as she conducted that morning's Council and wondered again at her powers of recovery. She had been carousing with Antony all night at a *commissatio* with their so-called Club of Life, but here she was at the third hour of the day, attending the affairs of state, while Antony and his fellow Romans snored like pigs in the staterooms. He knew that she heavily diluted her own wine so her consumption did not even begin to match Antony's own prodigious efforts, but he still could not imagine how a person might survive on so little sleep.

"I shall sleep when I am in my tomb," she had said to him once when he remarked on it.

It was not as if she gave herself relief during the daylight hours. She would work in the mornings while Antony slept, and then in the afternoons she would go off with him to watch him practice his swordsmanship and his wrestling in the Gymnasium, like a twittering young girl, or else she would take him on camel rides through the deserts to the east of the city, or go fishing with him or take him for picnics on Lake Mareotis.

Like she was trying to live a lifetime in the space of one year.

At that moment she was stretched out on a couch, looking as alert as if she had spent the previous evening asleep in her own bed instead of dicing and drinking through the night with Antony and his friends. She had conducted a thorough interrogation of her head customs official, had Diomedes take down a letter to her overseer of tax collections, reviewed an audit by the guardian of the state treasury, listened to a long report on the reconstruction of several important dikes and canals with her inspector of irrigations, and then had a private audience with the chief priest of Serapis.

Remarkable.

When the business was concluded and they were finally left alone, she looked up at him sharply. "What is it, Mardian?" she snapped.

"Majesty?"

"That look on your face. It's been there all morning. What is wrong?"

Was he really so transparent? "I was wondering at your powers of recovery, Majesty."

"It is more than that."

He stared at the floor. Well, better to get it over with, he supposed. "The head of the palace guard sought me out this morning. He is a troubled man."

She did not look up from the ledgers. "Go on."

"He seems to think you have been leaving the palace buildings without informing him and without proper escort."

"He thinks I am so unloved that if I am seen outside the palace without him I will be immediately struck down, is that it?"

"It is unwise for any head of state to leave themselves unprotected at these times. At any time."

She gave him a look. Amusement or annoyance? He could not tell.

He took a deep breath. "There is also talk that you have been accompanying Antony on his jaunts into Rhakotis disguised as a slave girl."

She did not answer him.

"Majesty?"

"How long have you known me, Mardian?"

"Since you were an infant, Majesty."

"Does this sound like something that I might do?"

"Yes. It does."

She grinned. And there it was, on her face, the look of a willful fourteen-year-old child. He remembered that expression only too well. So, it was true.

"I wish you would be more circumspect," he scolded her.

"My companion on these 'jaunts,' as you call them, once held two gladiators above his head, a feat of strength I have never seen repeated anywhere. I have nothing to fear when I am with Marcus Antonius. It is like having the Macedonian Guard with me."

"It is undignified for a Queen of Egypt, the reincarnation of Isis, to behave in such a way."

"Not if I am in disguise."

"Word gets around."

"Talking is not the same as seeing. Talk adds to the mystery, only seeing destroys it. You have a lot to learn still, Mardian."

He persisted. "I do not know what you hope to achieve."

She laid aside the scrolls and turned to look at him. "The crown of Rome and Egypt for my son. That is all."

"How?"

"There will be another Caesar," she said, and returned to the ledgers.

Mardian was about to say more but kept his peace. What was her game here? Did she secretly thirst for pleasure, had she finally found a soul mate in this blundering Roman boy? Unlikely. Perhaps she thought to enslave this Antony by allowing the full rein of his pleasures here in Alexandria? Or was she merely humoring him, trying to portray herself as the counterpoint to a matronly Roman wife?

Whatever the reason, he hoped she had not miscalculated. She said there must be another Caesar, but he doubted if Antony was that man. His queen was trying to fashion a silk cape from a dog's hide. What Antony had here in Alexandria was the sum total of his ambition, ease and pleasure. Mardian suspected he did not possess the guile and ruthlessness that went hand in hand with maintaining such a way of life.

Antony was a child. He wanted his toys, but he did not want to pay for them.

"No . . . no . . . look out, it is Caesarion! It is Caesarion's flagship!"

The trireme crashed into the starboard of the smaller Liburnian, swamping it and setting it on its side in the water.

Caesarion giggled and smashed his fist down on the model boat.

"You should not treat them so," Cleopatra chided him gently. "Apollodorus spent hours making these models for you."

"I don't care!" he shouted. "I'm a famous admiral!"

"Then you should be on your guard," she said. "Even a famous admiral has to watch for storms." She flicked the scented water with her fingertips and it splashed into his face. The little boy stared at her, surprised, and then he laughed and splashed her back, with both hands.

She dismissed Charmion and dried the little boy off herself. As she rubbed his face with the towel she realized with a pang how like his father he was. The same bone structure to his face, the same deep and penetrating eyes. Yet she also had to fight down a flicker of irritation. In other ways he was not his son at all. She watched him every day for traits of his father, and saw only a boisterous, selfish little boy.

He looked up at her earnestly. "Who's that man you are with all the time?" he said.

"You mean Marcus Antonius?"

"You like him, don't you?"

She stared into his face. Such a serious expression for such a little boy.

"Are you going to go away with him?" he asked her.

"Of course not. I'm never going to leave you."

"You never spend time with me anymore. You're always with him."

He was jealous. She sighed. No matter what she did, little Caesarion always wanted more. Perhaps he was so greedy for her because he did not have a father to instruct him. It was exhausting. There was never enough hours in her day, between affairs of state and entertaining Lord Antony and spending time instructing her son—she could not entrust it entirely to his tutors, for he was no ordinary boy—it was a wonder that she slept at all.

She put her arms around him and held him to her. He was stiff and unyielding. More like his father than she realized, perhaps.

"I'll never leave you," she whispered. "You are everything to me. I live my whole life for you."

And perhaps, in the end, that was the trouble.

⟋⟍ ⟋⟍

Alexandria was so different from Rome, in its proliferation of colors and languages, the colonnaded streets along Canopis and the Street of the Soma so different to the twisting alleys of the Aventine, the villas and palaces white with marble and alabaster instead of Rome's dismal brick. This city makes you feel alive, Antony thought. Which is why these people's preoccupation with death puzzled him.

Cleopatra's masons were busy on the mausoleum she had ordered built next to the Temple of Isis on the promontory of Lochias, next to the palace. Great slabs of red porphyry were being hauled into place at the entrance, to be flanked by the sphinxes that even now were being shaped out of the marble. When the work was done, a second story would be added.

Antony stared at the hundreds of slaves scurrying around the site, naked or in loincloths, the whole area alive with the chipping of hammers, the crack of the overseer's whips. He shook his head. "I do not understand this Egyptian obsession with death," he said to her.

"It is not an obsession, Marcus, to be wise in the face of the inevitable. Because we do not wish for a thing does not mean it will not happen."

"But you are yet young."

"I am a queen. My three sisters and two brothers are already dead. When you are of the noble house of Egypt, youth is no defense against death. Have you never thought of it?"

He shrugged his shoulders. "No," he answered her. These Egyptians. Despite what she said, it seemed to him they were preoccupied with death; the whole land had the whiff of the tomb about it with their mummified bodies and their embalmer's shops. When it came to it, he would know the time and fall on his sword, if need be, without a second's thought, give his own death no more concern than he did the setting of the sun at the end of the day.

He was sure of that.

68

To the south of Alexandria was the great lake of Mareotis, rich with fish and game birds, and surrounded by the papyrus marshes that kept the whole world supplied with writing paper. Cleopatra kept a summer house here, as did many of her wealthy ministers and Greek and Jewish merchants. It had its own landing for the royal barge and was surrounded by acres of gardens, vineyards, and orchards.

Cleopatra brought Antony here, when she could escape the demands of the state, and the servants would set up their couches on the lawns, under a yellow winter sun, to talk and drink wine and pass the hours.

One afternoon on Mareotis, Cleopatra decided the time was right to raise the topic they had both studiously avoided since he had arrived in Alexandria. Politics. "Do you think much about Rome?" she asked him.

"Hardly at all."

"Do you not miss it? Do you not sometimes wonder if Octavian is making mischief for you there?"

"We have an agreement."

"The only thing I know about agreements is that one day all agreements are broken."

Antony shrugged his shoulders. He did not want to talk about this now.

"You know, you have only to lift your finger and the whole world can be yours," she said.

"The whole world *is* mine," he answered. There was a note of irritation in his voice.

"No, not yet. Just one part of it."

Perhaps he knew what she was about to say. He could not look at her.

"You have the legions and the power. I have the money. Think of it! Rome with Syria is still just Rome. Rome with Judaea, you are still Rome. But Rome with Egypt, you are the whole world! I am the East. You are the West. If we join, we are everything."

She could see his uncertainty. These Romans were so afraid of themselves. Even Caesar was afraid of taking that one final step without sanction from Rome. And what was Rome? An idea, a shadowy sense of duty and guilt that dogged every Roman she had ever known.

She could see from the expression on his face that this idea had never crossed the mind of the great and noble Antony. While Caesar was alive, he was happy to be his lieutenant, let Caesar make the hard decisions. Caesar had judged him well. Antony takes orders, he does not give them, he had said. Perhaps he was afraid of power and the responsibilities that went with it; not just the decisions over taxes and government, but deciding who was to live and who was to die, the leaving of blood on the hands. After Caesar's death he had allowed Octavian his toehold in Rome because he could not conceive how power could be gained and held.

Perhaps deep down he was too kind.

She ran her fingers through his hair. "Ally with me and you can have everything. You will indeed be a god then. Even in Rome."

"You mean marriage?"

"Of course."

"There is Fulvia."

"When has a wife ever stopped a Roman from doing what he wished? Divorce her. You will do it one day anyway."

"I cannot marry a foreigner by Roman law."

"When you are married to me you will *be* Roman law."

She could see that she had scared him. This great hulking man who generaled armies, this veteran of a hundred battles, was scared.

"I will think on it," he said.

Very well, she thought. Think on it, but think on it soon. The winter is nearly over. It is almost time to go back to the world.

PERUSIA, ITALY

Octavian shivered in his cloak and watched the city burn. It gave grim satisfaction, this evidence of the increasing turmoil inside the town. He had never thought seriously of storming the fortress itself, perched up there in the mountains, a natural stronghold. He knew he could not get in, so they would have to come out.

By all the gods, it was cold. The ground was frost hard under his boots and covered with two inches of snow. The siege had gone on all winter, and he had spent most of it shivering with fever in his tent while his men hurled stones at the walls and blocked up the wells so the springs would run dry. Fulvia and her crowd would have to give it up eventually.

It was already the Ides of March, and the north wind still cut through the northern mountains with ice on its breath and fanned the flames on the other side of the walls. Earlier that day his spies had informed him that some of Fulvia's soldiers had gotten drunk and started looting the town. They were presently trying to fight their way out past their former companions to join him. It looked as if they had fired some of the buildings as part of their efforts. His generals had urged an attack, but he had told them to wait. They did not have to force the situation. It had been his experience that most enemies defeat themselves. He would wager that Fulvia and Lucius were at each other's throats at this very moment.

Fulvia. She had taken to hanging any town burgher who spoke of surrender and suspending the corpse from the palisades. Blood-thirsty witch.

The wind buffeted him in his cloak, nearly rocking him off his feet. It carried with it the acrid stench of ash and smoke, the metallic odor of blood and the foul odor of death. Oh, things must be at a fine pass inside there. Any day now it would all be over.

The Ides of March. Almost four years since Caesar had died, to the day, and still no peace in Italy. Julius had left too many people alive to stir up trouble. That was his trouble. He would not be making the same mistake.

ALEXANDRIA-BY-EGYPT

Night on the lake, the oil lamps casting a perfect reflection on the still black surface of the water. The Club of Life were being entertained tonight on the royal barge, while the music of flutes and lyres drifted across the still and perfect night. A round of toasts was in progress in the banqueting salon. Antony was in his cups and all the world was his friend.

Mardian watched aggrieved as he caressed the queen in improper ways, a hand cupped beneath her breast as he drank, then nuzzling her neck with wine-glossed lips. While Alexandria's elite drank and laughed and sang, the two of them slipped away alone. They returned perhaps an hour later, the queen with her coiffure disarrayed, her cheeks aglow with that special fire that made it obvious to all what had happened.

To Mardian, a man with no lust for sex, it was incomprehensible. How could men and women make such fools of themselves?

Most of all, he could not understand how Cleopatra could humiliate herself with this man in this way. He was not worthy of her. He never would be.

69

TOWN OF CANOPUS

ALL AROUND HIM the unimaginable, the unspeakable, dancing in the flame shadows of the torches, the stone and marble assuming a life of its own. There were stallions raping centaurs, goats mounted by panting satyrs, maenads penetrated by snarling lions, bacchantes at the mercy of horses. Above them, on every frieze, presiding over this carnival of debauch, was Aphrodite, smiling her approval.

Ahenobarbus was shocked to his soul. He came from a republican family of ancient tradition and good name. Antony was more than a friend to him; he was a comrade-in-arms, they had fought side by side in the storming of Pelusium in the Egyptian campaign over fifteen years before. He had always loved and admired Marcus Antonius for his courage, his powers of oratory, his leadership of men. For him, Antony symbolized the vitality of Rome.

Which was why he had been mortified to arrive in this stinking gypo city to find his Imperator dressed in silk gowns and soft slippers, wearing jewels like an Oriental and perfumed like a pansy nigger boy.

He had come here to warn Antony of the problems brewing in Syria and Italy, but it seemed that in the year since he had last seen him, the noblest Roman had gone Greek.

Tonight Antony had brought them to the Temple of Aphrodite at Canopus, fifteen Roman miles from Alexandria; the inner court, some wealthy Greeks and Jews, Antony's own inner circle of officers and sycophants, and, of course, the high and mighty queen herself. They had been ferried across the lake, along a canal and down the Canopic branch of the Nile by a fleet of pleasure boats.

The temple was one of the largest in Egypt, half a stadion in length, its doors made of solid gold. It was surrounded by gardens, inside a circular terrace the height of six men and eighty stadia around. Dotted among the gardens were hundreds of little houses where prostitutes of every race and color practiced their trade, dedicating the proceeds to the service of the goddess; dark-skinned girls with golden rings through their noses from faraway Ganga in India, Nubians with skins glistening like jet, Germans with white hair and pink flesh, dark-eyed Syrians, Spaniards with hair as black as midnight, Armenians and Persians, Asians and Gauls.

Each of the houses where they lived and . . . worshiped . . . had a door of red copper, and on the door a carved phallus as door hammer.

"Each of the girls is trained for seven years in that building over there," the disgusting little man, Sisyphus, was telling him. "They call it the College of Aphrodite. I am told it is there they learn all the secrets of erotic refinement and embrace."

That is all very well, Ahenobarbus thought. But while Antony is immersing himself in this debauchery, the world is turning, and if he does not act soon it will leave him behind.

The noble Imperator had studiously avoided him since his arrival the previous day. Tonight, too, he had offered him little opportunity

for conversation. He had promised all of his party some special entertainment, though what manner of sport it was to be, Ahenobarbus
shuddered to think.

He leaned forward and tapped Antony on the shoulder. "Marcus,
when may we talk?"

Antony looked irritated at this interruption. "Later."

"It cannot wait! I have news that one of Cassius's old generals,
Quintus Labienus, has defected to the Parthians and is busy helping
them organize an army to invade Syria. War is inevitable."

Antony waved a dismissive hand. "If it is inevitable, then what am
I to do about it?"

"You must go to Syria and reinforce Saxa!"

"The governor is capable of organizing his own defense. He is a
competent soldier."

Ahenobarbus found Antony's complacency galling. Was he so
immersed in his own pleasure that he cared for nothing else? "That is
not all. I have heard also that your wife has raised a rebellion against
your fellow Triumvir, Octavian."

Antony knew about this, of course. He just didn't want to do anything about it.

"I do not care what they do in Rome," Antony said. "I am happier
here than I have ever been. Let them tear at each other's throats, if
that is what they want."

Ahenobarbus could not believe his ears. How could a Triumvir
not care what they did in Rome?

Meanwhile, a hush had fallen over the crowd and, despite himself, Ahenobarbus's eyes were drawn to the spectacle about to take
place in the tiny arena below them. A full moon had risen over the
temple, throwing the palm trees into silhouette and making the white
marble of the pillars glisten like bone. The lower half of the colonnades were made of porphyry the color of purple, which did not
reflect the moonlight, so the temple appeared to hover suspended
above the ground.

Ahenobarbus was aware of the press of people, the combined
sweat of thousands of bodies, the air thick with clouds of smoke from
the burning torches and the smell of resin.

As he watched, perhaps twoscore of the *hetairas* had emerged
from a strange triangular monument that Sisyphus told him was

called the Cotytteion. They all wore ritual wooden phalli at their waists. Disgusting.

"These are the best of the best," Dellius whispered. Ahenobarbus was not surprised to find that this quintessential ass-licker had already surrendered himself to these barbarities. "They are the high priestesses of the temple. If you wish to buy one of these women, it would cost you at the least one mina of gold for a single night."

One mina of gold! You could keep a cohort of legionaries in the field for a whole year on that!

They were indeed beautiful women, although the wooden phalli at their waists rendered them grotesque. They were all naked, their bodies slick and gleaming with oil and sweat. They began to dance, clearly in the grip of some trance or potion.

Ahenobarbus found himself starting to sweat.

The music of flutes and drums rose a pitch, and one of the women was brought a copper vessel. She removed the stopper from the bottle and swallowed down the contents.

"What is happening?" he whispered to Dellius.

"This ritual takes place once a month," Dellius answered, his voice thickening with lust and horror. "I have witnessed this on two occasions. That woman there has been in the Cotytteion now for three years, so it is her turn. After three years every high priestess must be sacrificed to the goddess."

"She has drunk down an amorous philter, a lethal dose," Sisyphus added, his eyes gleaming with excitement. "Knowing she is going to die, nothing matters to her now. She will do anything."

"What do you mean by anything?"

"Watch."

Ahenobarbus had attended the circus many times for the combats, had seen men and women torn apart by wild beasts, mutilated in combats, dragged screaming from the arena after being trampled by horses in the chariot races. He thought he had witnessed every kind of violence. But what now took place before his eyes left him utterly shaken.

The woman who had been chosen as sacrifice was dragged by the other women to a kind of stone altar at the center of the arena. She spread-eagled herself upon it, and now the other priestesses took their turns at her, penetrating her from the front and behind with the massive phalli at their waists, a ritual orgy of blood and violence, dance and pain. The howls of deranged ecstasy and shrieks of agony reverberated around the temple enclosure, must surely have penetrated into the darkened shrine of Aphrodite herself. Pressed on all sides by her fellow priestesses, the victim twisted and writhed in a paroxysm of love, and whether it was the philter that finally and mercifully killed her or the violations of the painted wooden phalli, it was impossible to know.

After it was over, he found he had almost forgotten to breathe. His clothes were rank with perspiration. He looked across at Marcus Antonius. The noble Imperator's face was glistening with sweat, his eyes inner lit with some dark and ecstatic fever.

"Oh, noble Antonius, what have you done?" Ahenobarbus groaned. He knew of Antony's dalliance with Dionysus, of course. It was a secret spoken of darkly in Rome, an aberration common to greatness perhaps, no more. But it seemed to him now that Antony had ventured too far into his shadowy places and that these Egyptians and their iniquitous queen were driving him to madness.

70

PERUSIA, IN ITALY

OCTAVIAN WRINKLED HIS nose in disgust. The creature sitting opposite him was Marc Antony's brother, they said. He looked like a knot in a piece of rope, quite frankly, with neither his brother's strength nor size. He smelled of wine and fire smoke, and there were unidentifiable stains on his cloak and his enameled armor.

Octavian tried to look sympathetic as he listened to his story; how he had been led into the rebellion by Fulvia, against his will, recounting one by one the unimaginable horrors she had subjected him to.

"The men will not fight for her anymore," he said. "They are on the point of mutiny."

"This is the trouble with allowing women to meddle in politics," Octavian said. "It is a salutory lesson to us all."

"If you will accept our surrender, do I have your guarantee of clemency?"

You're not in any position to bargain with me, Octavian thought. You have virtually told me the garrison is about to fall anyway. But he spread his hands and forced himself to smile. "But I am Caesar's son," he said.

❦ ❦

A few days later Lucius left Perusia, to take up his posting as governor of Further Spain. As far away from Rome as one could go without actually falling off the edge of the world.

As he rode away from Perusia, escorted by a troop of Octavian's cavalry, he saw his staff officers hanging in chains from the trees at the side of the road. Riding past the long line of bodies, rotting in the chill morning, he heard the ugly caw of a crow. He looked up and saw it set to work on the eyes of a fresh corpse. Breakfast.

He remembered Octavian's promise to him: *But I am Caesar's son.* So this was the extent of Octavian's clemency, he thought. I am well away from Rome.

71

ALEXANDRIA-BY-EGYPT

Kalends of March, on the Roman calendar, the Egyptian month of Tybi

WHITE FLOWERS HAD burst open on the bean plants along the shores of Lake Mareotis, the almond trees in the Lochias palace had budded to flower, insects murmured among the shrubs and flowers of Olympos's gardens.

Spring had come to Alexandria, and with it the harbor returned to bustling activity. Caravans had trailed in from the desert with their great bundles of spices and silks, to be stored with the grain and olive oil and amphorae of wine in the warehouses at Rhakotis, waiting for the end of winter, the end of the storms. Now the big merchantmen set out again past the Pharos, bound for Rome, Ephesus, and Athens. Soon, sails were seen on the horizon, heading toward Alexandria and the great beacon for the first time since the end of autumn.

And with the ships came news of the rest of the world.

〰 〰

Antony woke, naked, on a couch in one of the staterooms. Quintus Dellius was standing over him, shaking him by the shoulder. Antony rubbed his face and rolled over onto his back. Dellius raised an eyebrow. The Master of Rome might be asleep, but there was one part of his body that was very much awake.

"Quintus Dellius. What time is it?"

"It is the fifth hour, my lord."

"So early," he grunted. His hand moved to his groin and he started to rub himself. He toyed with himself idly, his face concentrated into a frown. "What a night it was."

"Indeed, my lord. I shall be glad to go back to the wars. My body can stand it better." He was nervous. He had to get this over with. "My lord, urgent matters of state have arisen."

Antony grinned. "Indeed. As you can see."

One of the Syrian slave girls had entered the room, and when she saw Antony, in all his glorious tumescence, she gasped and was about to back out again.

"Come here," Antony called to her. "Don't run away. I shan't bite. Unless you want me to," he added, with a grin at Dellius. She came, but haltingly.

"My lord, there is news from Syria. . . ."

Antony ignored him. "Come here, my kitten. That's it. Don't be afraid."

"My lord . . ."

"Dellius, avert your eyes if you must."

Antony took the girl's hand and pulled her down beside him. Her eyes were huge, like dinner plates. Antony laughed and rolled her over quickly, lifting her tunic. The girl shrieked, mostly in surprise, for she was accustomed to serving eunuchs in the queen's apartments. But she knew better than to resist a Roman and a god.

Dellius watched as Antony wet himself with his fingers and eased himself inside the trembling girl. A nice-looking little piece, Dellius had to admit, a bottom like a peach and skin the color of cinnamon.

"Ah, now the sun has risen," Antony groaned.

"There is news from Syria," Dellius persisted.

Antony held the girl by the hips, his eyes closed. "I have news of Syria also," Antony said, grinning at the girl. "And it is all good."

"Lord Antony, the Parthians have invaded and overrun our legions there."

Antony's eyes blinked open. "Our governor? Saxa?"

"Decimus Saxa is dead."

Antony did not appear to have heard. He shut his eyes again and resumed his pleasures. Dellius felt himself growing agitated now, and not just with matters of state. The girl did not seem comfortable, bent over the couch in such an unnatural position, but otherwise she did not seem to mind the experience. Not every slave girl had the opportunity to consort with a living god, he supposed.

"The Parthians have moved south and taken Jerusalem," Dellius went on. "Everything is gone but Tyre. Two legions in Syria, along with their eagles' standards, are lost."

Still Antony did not react. The muscles of his body went taut as cord and he finished, quickly. He gave a small gasp.

"Only Herod holds out at Masada."

Antony collapsed over the back of the couch. He lay like that for long moments, catching his breath, then released himself. He pulled at one of the huge emerald rings on his finger and handed it to the girl. "Here," he said. "For your sweetness."

The girl took the ring with alacrity and then picked up her loincloth, which lay on the marble at her feet. With a quick glance at Dellius, she rushed from the room.

"My lord, you must return to the real world. We have enjoyed the entertainments here long enough. Now there is work to be done."

"If only . . ." Antony began, but he did not finish. He seemed to make up his mind. "Get Eros," he snapped. "I need my clothes. Where in the name of all the gods are my clothes?"

❦ ❦

She was in her private dining room, on a couch, taking her breakfast as she worked; there was flat bread, a paste made from figs, cheese from goats, and black olives, arranged on a silver salver. Her ministers, along with Mardian, Diomedes, and several of her *strategioi*, were standing around the room; another man, his face burned by the sun, his beard full and glossy, was standing in the center of the room.

Antony burst in, followed by Dellius and several of his staff officers. He has been drinking again, she thought. And he has been sleeping with my slave girls, if what Mardian tells me is right. Does he never grow tired of all this? Does he never wish to do something useful with his time? Surely there is only so much play an intelligent person could indulge himself in before he becomes bored?

It should not bother me so much. I am just using him, after all, as he is using me. A pity, then, that I find him so much in my heart these days. I should be more robust with my emotions. This bastard has made me love him a little, despite myself.

"Ah, my lord Antony," she said. "We were just about to send for you. This man has news which may interest you."

Antony studied the other man. The arrogance of his stance, the haughty eyes. A Greek perhaps, or a Sicilian.

"His name is Apollodorus," Cleopatra went on. "He is a merchant. He left Rome at the first break in the winter storms and is the first to reach us from Italy."

"Octavian?" Antony said hopefully. "He has fevers? He has boils? He is dead?"

Cleopatra did not smile. So, he thought. More bad news.

"My lord," this Apollodorus began, "as you must know, your brother Lucius and your wife Fulvia raised an army late last year and caused a rebellion against the Young Caesar. It did not go well for them. The last news is that they are besieged in the mountain fortress of Perusia."

Antony closed his eyes. It was a beautiful spring day; outside the windows the harbor glittered in the sun, and there was spring warmth in the air. I have been away from the world for just a season, and in that time I have lost the East and I have lost Italy. Am I not to take a moment's ease without torment?

"What about my legions?" he asked the man. His own voice sounded hollow.

"They are still in their camps. Without your orders they would not join the rebellion."

Antony nodded. His head beat like a drum. Someone had split it in half with a sword. It was too early in the day for such news.

"Sextus rules the sea around Sicily and Sardinia," Apollodorus went on. "No Roman ship can pass by him. Scores of high-bred Romans have fled to his protection now."

Antony looked at the queen. Oh, look at those eyes. This is exactly what she wanted. She does not even try to look disappointed for me. She wants me to go against my people and my country. Women betray me at every turn.

"It pains me to bring you this news," Apollodorus said.

What a liar. "It pains me to hear it," he said. "I should consult with my staff and pass them this news." He quickly took his leave. By all the gods, he needed something to drink.

Antony paced the apartments, drinking again, then sent his goblet bouncing across the room in a fit of temper and leaving dark wine on the alabaster floor like spilled blood.

Cleopatra watched him, experienced a perverse sense of satisfaction at his discomfort, which she battled to conceal. You should have listened to me instead of interfering with my slave girls. Finally the world has forced you to move. You cannot prevaricate any longer. If you will be guided by me, I can show you a glimpse of Caesar's dream. You can be all those things your master would have been, if he had not been betrayed. Let us see now if you are Hercules or just another posturer in a lionskin.

"I cannot lay the blame for this at the feet of Octavian," Antony was saying. "Fulvia raised legions against him and even issued her own coins. I have no legal basis to refute him."

Legal basis? she thought. Did Julius have any legal basis to take his legions against Pompey? When you are a simple farmer in the fields, you look to the law. When you are a king or queen you make your own. "This is what Octavian wanted all along," she said.

"No, this is what Fulvia wanted! She did this because I came to Alexandria instead of returning to Rome!"

"Then divorce her. She is of no help to you. All she has done is create trouble. I can buy you fifty legions, a fleet of ships. Soar with me! Marry me and I can deliver the world!"

There, it was said. A chance to rule the world, plainly spoken. But he hesitated. "I have a pact with Octavian and Lepidus. I have given my word. What will Rome think of me if I break it now? We have had enough of civil wars."

"No empire can be ruled by two men, and three is impossible. Power can only reside in one person. You know that. This pact was just a way of buying time while you rid yourselves of Cassius and Brutus."

He bit his lip.

She felt the child move inside her. Her breasts were larger, swollen, preparing for the child's arrival. Antony still had not noticed. And she would not tell him, not yet. Let him prove himself to her first.

"If you do not destroy him," she said, "he will destroy you."

His eyes were hard. He knew she might be right. But he did not want to hear it.

Oh, what is wrong with you? You cannot spend your whole life on a couch with a woman on your lap and a goblet in your hand. There comes a time when you have to rouse yourself and go out into the world and pay the ferryman.

The look on his face. She could not believe that he could refuse such a chance. "I cannot break my word," he said.

72

TORCHES CRACKLED ON the terrace. She stood with her arms crossed looking out toward the sea. Her face was half lit by the flames, the flambeaux throwing long shadows dancing along the walls of the palace.

Antony emerged onto the terrace. He was dressed this morning once again in the uniform of a Roman Imperator, purple cloak, enameled armor. A tunic instead of Greek robe, sandaled boots strapped halfway up his shins instead of soft Attic shoes. "Dove," he murmured.

She did not trust her voice to speak to him. She was too angry.

"I am leaving with the first light," he said.

"Yes."

"I shall go to Syria and deal with the Parthians. Then I shall confront the problems of Italy."

"I have told you how to confront the problems of Italy."

"I will be back when I have sorted out this mess."

"That is what you say."

"I mean it." He hesitated. Look at him standing there. Like little Caesarion after he has been scolded. I have shown him the keys to the whole world, and it is still not enough for him, still I count less to him than his duty to Rome. I have indulged him, I have shown him every delight of this city, every delight of my own body as well. Does he think a queen gives herself so easily? How could I not be mortally insulted?

"Not one kiss before I go?" he said.

"I will save my kisses for your return." She could not even bear to look at him. I am going to miss him, she realized. For a while I played the whore for you. I spent the winter laughing instead of poring over ledgers and listening to the drone of clerks and tax gatherers. I want you to stay. We could have pleasure *and* power. We could be gods.

He fidgeted, looking stiff and awkward in his armor. He turned to leave.

Her frustration boiled over. "You can have everything, Marcus Antonius! Together we can be more than Rome!"

"I will come back" was all he said.

She was so angry she could not even stand to watch him walk away.

PART III

*Cupid and Dionysus are two of the most violent of the gods,
they can grasp the soul and drive it so far towards madness
that it loses all restraint.*

ACHILLES TATIUS

73

CITY OF ATHENS, IN GREECE

THIS FUCKING WIFE of mine.

Antony could hardly bare to look at her. Perusia had aged her ten years. She had dyed her hair with henna, after the Germanic fashion, but it could not hide the fact that there were more lines around that cruel little mouth since last he had seen her, and her eyes looked as dull as lead. Her complexion was more suited to a soldier with a festering spear wound.

But it was not her physical appearance that pained him as much as the memory of what she had done. This beast, this virago, had interfered in his life. Not with one of his mistresses, which he could understand if not forgive, but with his *political* life.

Munatius Plancus, that ass-licker, was standing behind her, looking pained and sorry. Unlike Fulvia, who glared at him as if it were all his fault.

The villa—palace, really—overlooked the bay. In the middle of the room there was, unfortunately, a floor mosaic of a scene from the Nile, a crocodile and a hippopotamus. They took their positions on each side of it, divided by Egypt and his sins in Alexandria.

Perhaps she had commissioned the floor especially for the occasion.

"Well," she said, "the warrior returns. And how have you spent the winter?"

Her audacity took his breath away. "I might well ask you the same question."

"You've passed a whole season boozing and banging that gypo of yours."

"It hardly compares," he said to her. "I leave you for a few months and you bring the whole of Italy to the brink of civil war."

"I did it for you. It's not as if you could say the same thing."

Plancus was still standing there, a greasy look on his face. Antony wanted to throw him out of the window. "Did you support my wife in her crazed schemes?"

Plancus's Adam's apple bobbed in his throat like a cork on a wild sea. "My lord . . ." he managed, and then ran out of conversation.

Antony returned his attention to his wife. "Do you realize what you've done?"

"Perhaps it would have turned out differently if you had been in Rome, instead of hawking your pork in the Orient."

Speechless. Where had she learned such language? Too long in the company of soldiers, obviously.

The last few months had been a testing time for him after the wild abandon of Alexandria, a harsh return to the realities of a Roman magistrate's life. From Alexandria he had sailed to Ephesus, only to discover that the Parthians now occupied almost all of Syria and had even captured Tarsus. But there was nothing to be done about that problem until he had regathered an army.

A task that would have been easier if his eleven legions in Gaul had not been assumed by Octavian after the farce at Perusia.

He had arrived in Athens to find both his wife and his mother, Julia, in residence, having been forced to flee from Octavian. Pompey's pirate son, Sextus, had sheltered Julia for many months. So now, on top of his other problems, he found himself indebted to the Triumvirate's bitterest enemy.

One winter away from the hurly-burly, and the world had fallen apart.

"Clodia is here," Fulvia said. Clodia was Fulvia's daughter. She belonged to Fulvia's previous husband so was not of his loins, strictly speaking, but still his responsibility. It was Clodia who had sweetened the deal with Octavian when they had formed the Triumvirate. "Octavian sent her back with this letter," Fulvia said. She threw a scroll at him. "He claims she is still intact. He had her three years. What was he doing with her?"

"Not much, apparently."

"It's your own fault. You've let yourself be outfoxed by that little ballet boy!"

"This war was not my doing. It's not me that he outfoxed!"

"You can't see it, can you? Octavian was behaving as if he was master of all Rome. He just wanted an excuse to take your legions away from you in Gaul. And you let him!"

"No! You did that!"

"You were needed in Rome. What were you doing while I was fighting your battles?"

"While you were *losing* them."

"That little pansy is out to get you. He wants to end the Triumvirate!"

Antony took a step back. By Jupiter, she was a terrible woman. Truly terrifying. Fulvia stepped up to him so they were almost touching and leaned into his face. "One day you'll see. He wants your blood. He'll destroy you, Antony, if you don't kill him first."

"I had an agreement with him. You broke my word."

"Do it now. Crush him and you can be undisputed Master of Rome!"

"You're a monster," he said, and walked out.

ALEXANDRIA-BY-EGYPT

The city was so white in the summer sun that it hurt the eyes. A salty breeze came off the harbor, carrying with it the tang of seaweed and burning charcoal from the Pharos. Gulls screeched and wheeled over the wharves. There were dolphins out there in the deeper water, playing and arrowing by the breakwater.

Antony had already been gone three months. The palace was quiet again without his uproars, the Company of Life disbanded. She was getting enough sleep again. But still, in a strange way, she missed him.

"You are on everyone's lips in Rome," Mardian was saying.

She turned away from the window. "Still?"

"I have a report from Apollodorus. He says all the talk is of Antony's stay here. Of his excesses. And yours."

"Mine?"

"They say in the Forum that his appetites are matched only by your own. That you torture prisoners for amusement and that you sleep with a different slave every night."

"That is disgusting. I would not touch a slave, let alone sleep with one!"

"It is what they are saying. The rabble in Rome are much like they are here. They love to spread ugly gossip."

"And so in accompanying Antony in his excesses, I am reckoned to be his equal?"

"Apparently so."

"And what of the Inimitable's reconciliation with his wife?"

"It did not go well."

Cleopatra smiled. She could imagine.

"He is under sail for Italy. There is talk of another civil war."

"And Fulvia?"

"She remains in Athens. Unwell, I believe. Some say the siege at Perusia wasted her health."

"Thank you, Mardian. Keep me informed of further news."

"Yes, Majesty."

After he left, she turned back to the window. So, they were still talking about her in the Republic. It did not disturb her, unduly, what they said. She could not stop Octavian's rumor mills from turning over, even if it did.

I wonder what they will say when they learn I am carrying Antony's child, she thought, resting her hands on her swollen belly. Doubtless they will say it belongs to one of the slaves I have tortured, or one of the innumerable serving boys I am supposed to have bedded and beheaded.

She eased herself onto a couch. Too hot to be carrying a baby in your belly.

So, the noble Antony was not reconciled to his Fulvia. She did not think for a moment that he would ever be, not now. Fulvia had proved an impediment; even he must see that he had to be rid of her. But Antony was not to be relied on. He was just as likely to run away from his problems as face up to them. He might need a little help.

She called for her chamberlain. "Find me Olympos," she said.

74

To the most gracious and wise Queen of Egypt, Lady of the Two Lands, Father-Loving Goddess,

Sad news from Egypt. I regret to inform Your Majesty that the wife of the noble Imperator Antony, Triumvir of Rome, has this day passed away here in Athens, from a malady brought on by the tribulations to which she was subjected during the wars in Italy. She is much mourned by all here in Greece who knew her.

I count myself fortunate to have met this great lady before she died, and I passed on to her your felicitations, as you asked me to do, along with your gifts, including the figs in honey, a delicacy which I am told she found particularly to her liking.

A messenger has been sent to Antony, informing him of his wife's tragic passing.

Your devoted servant and friend, Olympos

Cleopatra stole into the nursery, leaning her weight onto the walls for support. She felt light-headed; the midwives said she had lost a lot of blood. The physicians had prescribed her strong doses of pennyroyal and made her drink their foul-smelling potions to revive her. She had told them all she needed to make her feel better was the letter from Olympos.

Antony was doubly blessed, with not just one child but two. Alexander and Cleopatra lay asleep in their cots, his inlaid with an ivory frieze of tigers, hers with elephants. So, she thought, now I have the children of Rome's two greatest sons in my care. Let them deny me now.

Alexander was like his father, a plump healthy boy with a mop of luxuriant hair. Little Cleopatra Selene was smaller, darker, with olive skin. She knelt down beside her bed, watched the almost imperceptible rise and fall of her breathing, studied the heart-shaped mouth in the moonlit room. A daughter, a woman like me. The next Isis.

How will you deal with this world of men? she wondered. All they have ever given me is pain. They are faithless, reckless, consumed only with themselves. They drink too much and love too little.

One of your brothers is Caesar, your twin is Antony. I have to protect you, each from the other. I will not have you at each other's throats, as I was with my brothers and sisters. I will find a way that you each have your own birthright.

Sleep well, for now. And I will bring your father home.

75

ALEXANDRIA-BY-EGYPT

SHE HAD RETURNED to her work long before her doctors considered it advisable. "The fellahin women drop their babies in the field," she had told them. "Besides, there is too much to do to just lie here in bed drinking your foul elixirs."

It was the dawn of the Egyptian new year, what the Romans called the Kalends of Septembris, the season when the Nile would start to rise. Or so they all hoped. For the last two years in succession there had been droughts, and they could not afford another without the country sinking into anarchy and mass starvation.

Cleopatra was closeted with her ministers, studying the reports from her *oeconomi* and the district governors. She was questioning Diomedes more closely on the exact state of their warehouses and the reserves of grain when Mardian burst into the chamber unannounced. She could tell from his expression that the news was bad, the worst.

"Leave us," she said to the others.

The officials looked at each other and at Mardian. This would go around the palace like wildfire, she thought. Speculation, then rumors. But if it was bad news, she wanted to hear it first, give herself time to prepare.

She took a deep breath and tried to settle herself. What could it be? Perhaps another rebellion in Upper Egypt. Or perhaps it was Antony! Had his ship been lost in a storm? Had he been defeated in battle with Octavian?

Mardian stood there quivering like a slave caught pilfering from the kitchen. Out of breath, terrified. This must be disaster.

She drew a breath. "Is Antony dead?" she asked.

The eunuch shook his head, jowls flapping. "No, Majesty. He lives."

"What is it, then? Have we been invaded?"

"Apollodorus is here, Your Majesty."

She fidgeted. Apollodorus! If he came in person, then it must be the worst. Well, let us be done with this. Bad news is better behind us. "Show him in, then."

And there he was, with his customary swagger and the hint of a smile about his lips. As if the matters of nations were an amusement for him. She felt a familiar breathlessness at the sight of him. She remembered how she had watched him that night in her tent, with the Jewish *hetaira,* Rachel. Perhaps one day I shall tell him. That will take the smile off his face.

"Majesty," he said, and made a halfhearted attempt to prostrate himself before the throne.

"Apollodorus. You have news."

"Indeed. Of Antony, Your Majesty."

She held her breath. "Tell us."

"He has made peace with Octavian."

She felt the blood drain from her face. "Again?"

"They have met at Brundisium. They have agreed to renew the Triumvirate and the war between them has been averted."

Well, it was disappointing, but it did not explain the greasy pallor of Mardian's face or the tremor in his hands. She returned her attention to Apollodorus. He enjoys this. Has he no fear? Impudent man. "That is not all the news. What is it you're not telling me?"

"The peace comes at a price."

She knew then, even before he said the words. The dread settled in her stomach like a piece of cold fat.

"He is to marry Octavian's sister, Octavia." As Apollodorus said the words, Mardian flinched beside him, waiting for the tirade. But she just stared at them. She felt only numb. Besides, what was the point of raging? It detracted from her dignity as a queen and served no useful purpose.

But something inside her died.

It was not just that he had betrayed her. What was new in that? Rome betrayed Alexandria constantly. But how squalid! At the very moment he was negotiating this ignoble treaty, she thought, I was bearing Antony a son and a daughter. I offered him the world, and he has settled instead for the easy way; I offered him greatness, and he has bargained instead for mediocrity.

I knew what he was like; the whole world knows what Antony is like. I even told myself I could stand it when he amused himself with the slave girls here in the palace. But did everything that happened here in Alexandria mean so little to him that he could betray me so casually? I opened my city and my soul to him.

"So," she said. "The Inimitable has done the unspeakable."

"I am sorry to bring you this grave news."

"We should have expected it. Like all men, he is faithless, selfish, and vile."

Apollodorus seemed not to appreciate this calumny against his gender. "It is said that he was forced to it, Majesty. Octavian closed the port at Brundisium to his ships and he was forced to land to the north of the town. Their legions faced each other on the battlefield, but the soldiers refused to fight each other. Many of them had fought side by side at Philippi and are now heartily sick of war. They forced this concord on the two men."

"And I suppose they then dragged Antony kicking and screaming to some other woman's bed?" This Antony, he was like a bear bumbling from here to there, sticking his paw in hives and tasting all the honey in the wood. "Is she beautiful, this Octavia?"

"Not as beautiful as you, Majesty."

"If you treat me as if I was some empty-headed girl, I shall have your head off."

That wiped the smile from his face. For the first time. But he still had the temerity to raise his head and look her in the eyes. "They say she has a neck like a swan and the face of Aphrodite herself."

"Poor Antony. He must be desolate."

"One can imagine his despair."

She was silent for a long time. Then she seemed to rouse herself, as if from a long sleep. "What did he get for this concord?"

"Octavian kept the legions he had confiscated in Gaul. They have agreed that Octavian will clear Sextus from Sicily and Antony should take on the Parthians."

"In other words, Antony has given up the West without a fight."

"He seems to think the East more important."

The numbness in her limbs was wearing off. Now she did want to rage. She must restrain herself. "Well, there is nothing to be done," she said. "We have thrown the dice and we have lost."

Mardian spoke up. He looked utterly miserable. "Do you wish to be alone, Majesty? Shall I send your ministers away?"

Yes. Send them away. I do not want to speak to another living soul ever again. The petty affairs of harvests and taxes are nothing to me now. But instead she found herself shaking her head. "No, Mardian. If they stand outside the door hearing me throw vases around the room they will construe that I am upset. I would not make more of this than it is. It is but a minor setback. Send them back in. I have work to do."

A minor setback.

There was a tight, crushing pain in her chest. In the end these Romans are all the same. They will give me their seed, but they will not give me their word.

I am just a *pelegrina* to them, a gypo.

But the game is not over. I must struggle on. As I have said to Mardian, I have work to do.

76

PALATINE HILL, ROME

ANTONY HATED WEARING the toga. Cicero, of course, used to make a show of it, but Antony couldn't walk in one of the wretched things without it falling down in a heap around his ankles. They were hot and they were heavy and the wool made his skin itch. He wondered what demented Roman worthy had devised such an exquisite torture for his fellows to endure.

He and Octavia were reclining on couches in the courtyard of his villa on the Palatine. A pale sun warmed the urns and statuary, a lizard sunned itself on the lichen-covered wall, a peacock screeched and fanned its great tail in the garden.

He was wondering what Octavia looked like without her clothes. Hard to tell with these shapeless and voluminous gowns Roman women wore. Not like the Egyptians.

A pretty little filly, Octavian's sister. Her hair was braided on top of her head, in what the women called a melon coiffure, exposing the long, cool curve of her neck, the sun bringing out the highlights of gold in her fair hair. She had brought a parasol to shade her from the sun, and was accompanied by the aromas of expensive cinnamon perfume.

The conversation until now had been stilted and formal. It made him long for the caustic humor of Cleopatra, the vulgarities of Fulvia. He wondered what would happen when he blew the candles out on their wedding night. Well-bred women fell into three categories, in his experience: those who slept with gladiators, those who slept with anyone, and those who stayed home. Octavia, by all accounts, preferred to stay home. She had never been one for the gladiator circuit, preferring her embroidery to well-oiled pectorals and a little bit of rough. There had been no temple assignations either, and no affairs with other senators. She hadn't even fucked Caesar, which made her an object of curiosity on the Palatine.

"How did you find the East?" she asked him.

The question startled him. Was she making polite conversation or was there a barb there? A veiled reference to the Company of Life perhaps? Such a cold fish. Hard to read, like her brother. "Alexandria has a wonderful library," he heard himself saying. "The finest in the world." How he hated himself sober.

"You spent much time reading, then?"

Was she mocking him? "Alexandria has many pursuits. The gymnasiums are without peer. There is fishing and hunting. I rode a camel." By all the gods, listen to me. I sound like Plancus. I would rather be exchanging abuse with Fulvia. One pleasure now denied me forever.

When he heard she was dead, he had gotten drunk with Sisyphus and Dellius to celebrate. He reached for the wine pitcher. "Wine?"

She shook her head.

No, of course not. He took a gulp from the jewel-encrusted goblet on the table in front of him, felt a little better.

"I was sorry to hear of Fulvia's death."

"Had you ever met her?"

"Only on a few occasions. I did not know her well."

"If you had known her well, you would not be sorry to see her dead. You know they brought her back to Rome for burial? They would not plant her in Greece for fear she would blight the crops."

That brought a lull to the conversation. Perhaps that was a little forthright for her, he thought. Such a pale creature. I should like to bite her neck, see if she bleeds.

"It is my brother who wishes us married," she said.

"He does me great honor."

"It serves his purpose. And yours."

Well, at least that was said. "Nevertheless," Antony answered her, truthfully, "your beauty is renowned in Rome. I should consider myself a fortunate man to have you as my wife."

"You will find my loyalty is worth far more to you than my beauty, Marcus."

The peacock screeched again. The sun disappeared behind a cloud. That I should need the loyalty of a woman! I would rather taste the down between your thighs.

"Let us be clear," he said. "When we are married, I would not have you harping on my freedoms. You should do well to remember that I am a hot-blooded creature."

"I should like to think that I shall make you happy."

He didn't like the sound of that. When women promised to make you happy, they always wanted something in return. Even Cleopatra. But she only wanted military and political control of the Mediterranean. He had understood her motivations far better than Fulvia's.

"Ours will be a wedding all Rome shall talk of," he said, to mollify her. He had a servitor pour some more wine into the krater.

"You should take care not to drink so much," she said.

By all the gods, it has started already. "I shall do whatever I have a mind to do," he answered. The things we do for concord. I can see the future now, even without my astrologer. This woman detests me. She is going to carp at me like Fulvia, dilute my wine bottles, rage at me for my mistresses, and in bed she is just going to lie there.

If it saves us all another war, perhaps it will be worth it. For himself, he was not at all sure he would rather not be in Alexandria, with his Cleopatra. Now there was a woman.

He hoped he was doing the right thing. It was what his advisers would have him do. He only wished he could stop thinking of his Egyptian and that his sleep was less troubled by doubt.

77

CLEOPATRA, ALONE IN her bed, watching the moon float over the harbor, the sound of the gentle waves against the rocks below the palace windows. It was a rare, baking night in Alexandria. Her body felt heavy, soft, compliant. She closed her eyes, but sleep would not come. She had been closeted with her ministers all day, discussing the state of the canals, and she was too tired to sleep.

And tonight she could not stop thinking about him. His betrayal.

She had received a letter from Antony today.

To her dread Majesty, Queen Cleopatra of Egypt,

Salutations from Rome. We would like you to know of the joyous occasion of our wedding to Octavia, an event which has all Rome rejoicing. We would like also to pass on our felicity at the birth of your royal children, an event which has only now been made known to us.

We extend our thanks for your hospitality during our visit to your great city, and we shall carry with us always memories of your warm friendship. We are happy to have received your assurances of friendship to ourself and to Rome.

The noble Imperator Marcus Antonius, Triumvir

Her fingers slid down her body and she rubbed softly between her legs. She wet her fingers with her tongue and slipped them inside the silky lips. She began to pleasure herself, arching her back, her fingers moving faster and faster, accelerated by anger. The release came suddenly and unexpectedly, her gasps catching in her throat. Afterward she lay in the darkness, yet awake and still unsatisfied.

The pleasure was worth nothing, she thought, if you could not have a man hold you in his arms as you slept. But such an emotion was weakness, and she had promised herself that she would not be so weak again.

PALATINE HILL, ROME

Moonlight dappled through the dark cypress outside the windows, flooding the room with shadows and light. Antony watched Octavia remove her *stola*. Beneath it she wore a loincloth and simple breast band. She appeared as slender as a nymph, her skin as pale as marble in the darkened room. Like one of the statues in the garden.

She would not allow him to see her naked, but slipped beneath the sheets like a good Roman matron to remove her underclothes.

He rolled toward her. Having compared her in his mind to a marble Aphrodite, he somehow imagined that her body would be cold to the touch, and the sudden heat of her surprised him. But he'd had hundreds of women, and he was prepared to be disappointed by her. Indeed, as he embraced her, she wrapped herself around him like a vine around the trunk of an oak. More wrestling hold than embrace, he thought sourly.

He kissed her. The taste of her mouth was as cool as patchouli. She returned the kiss, responding to him with unexpected fervor.

He threw back the sheets to look at her in the muted silver light from the window. "By all the gods, you really are beautiful," he murmured. Somehow her perfection was daunting. It was a little too—well, precise.

He bent to kiss her breasts. Her skin smelled as clean and sweet as mountain water and pine. He sucked each nipple in turn, nipping her gently with his teeth so that he made her gasp and pull away. A reaction, at least.

He pulled her hips toward him.

He entered her suddenly, pushing too hard and too fast. He had not meant to hurt her, but her pliant beauty somehow made him angry. He knelt on the bed, holding her hips to him, lifting her off the bed, excited now. Her fair hair and white skin reminded him of milk and water.

But when he closed his eyes it was not Octavia with him in the bed. He found himself thinking of olive skin, dark hair framing a painted mouth, black, wicked eyes. Instantly he returned to those exotic dreams he had surrendered when he left Alexandria, his taste of Egypt.

He had drunk too much wine at the wedding feast, and it had robbed him of physical sensation while increasing his need. His moment of pleasure came as no creeping wave but with a sudden and unexpected violence that left him panting and exhausted on top of his fair goddess.

Shall I never again be able to reach my sublime moment without conjuring an image of Cleopatra? he wondered. *I have left Alexandria behind. But Alexandria will not leave me.*

78

ALEXANDRIA-BY-EGYPT

CLEOPATRA TOOK CAESARION'S hand and led him through the cold and echoing vaults of the Soma, the royal mausoleum. The smell of decay hung sweet and heavy in the air. All around them, the ancient tombs of the Ptolemies, crumbling with age. The avenue of their ancestry, from the plain and unornamented granite sarcophagus of Ptolemy I to the riotous tomb of her own father with its Dionysian frieze of grapes and ivy. Here, punished by anonymity even in death, undecorated and marked only with his name, the tomb of her brother, Ptolemy XIII; next to him, young Antiochus, the pink granite polished to a sheen and carved with the horses and chariot races he had loved as a child.

Crackling torches lit the way along the dank catacombs. Spiders and beetles scurried into the shadows at their approach.

"This is the mausoleum of Ptolemy the Fourth," Cleopatra was saying, her voice echoing along the cold passageway. "He murdered his own father to take the throne. This one here is the one they called Ptolemy the Fat. And this one here, under the stone carved with boats and elephants, during his lifetime murdered his nephew and then married his own mother, Cleopatra the Second. They had a child together, but then he fell in love with his niece, Berenice. He married her, murdered the infant he had had with his mother, and sent the body back to her chopped into a dozen pieces. After Ptolemy died, Berenice murdered Cleopatra as well. This Berenice we are speaking of was your grandfather's mother. When he grew up, she tried to poison him as well, so he had her executed."

Caesarion stared up at her wide-eyed. He held her hand in a death grip. He looked as if he were going to be sick. "Why are you telling me all this?"

"I am telling you so that you will know the truth about your family and your heritage. One day you will be King of Egypt, Caesar Ptolemy the Fifteenth. Before that day comes, you need to understand that to rule Egypt is as much burden as it is a gift. You must learn to respect these ancestors of yours even if many of them have done terrible things." She hesitated. "I myself have done terrible things."

"What terrible things?"

How can I tell him? she thought. How can I tell him about Arsinoë and Antiochus and Fulvia? How could he begin to understand? "I will tell you when you are older. Enough that you should understand it is the right of rulers to fulfill the plans they have, even though others might suffer for it. Soldiers will die in your battles, rivals be executed at your command. If you cannot assume that burden, then you cannot be king."

He took a deep breath. "I understand," he said, but his voice sounded very faint. Such a frail and serious child, she thought. Every day he looks more and more like his father, even down to his walk. I pray that he has inherited his guile, his strength.

"No, you do not understand, not yet. You will not truly understand until you have used your power for the first time. But you must know that kings and queens do the will of the gods. That is where we obtain our authority and pardon for what we do here on earth."

A rustling, from the shadows, a scorpion scuttling away from the light.

"I don't like this place," the boy whimpered.

"You must understand your heritage, Caesarion."

His small, pale face stared up at her.

"You are descended from Isis herself, through me and through Caesar your father, whom the gods chose to join Rome with Egypt."

"Why isn't he buried here?"

"He was Roman and they have different customs there."

"What was he like?"

"Your father . . ." She wondered how she could describe him. Would she tell him everything, about his arrogance, his ruthlessness, his ambition? Or would she just tell him about his genius for war, his gentleness at love, his brilliant mind? How could she really explain everything about Julius, when she still did not understand the reasons for everything he had done? "Your father was the greatest warrior who ever lived. As great as Alexander. He ruled Rome, and he intended for the empires of Rome and Egypt to be yours."

"I wish . . ." he began, but whatever it was he hoped for would not translate itself to mere words.

She knelt down in front of him and took him by the shoulders. "You have a destiny, Caesarion. When you grow up, you will unite Rome and Egypt and rule an empire greater than Alexander. You will save the East from the Romans. That is what you were born to do."

He nodded, overcome by the chill smell of death in this dark place, by the intensity in his mother's eyes. He believed everything she said. He was only seven years old, too young to sense her doubt or divine her fears. Too young for the snake pit yet.

79

ALEXANDRIA-BY-EGYPT
*Egyptian month of Phaophi,
thirty-nine years before the birth of Jesus Christ*

THE PALMS SWAYED in the breeze from the sea, ruffling the waters on the harbor. A plume of spray leaped at the foot of the Pharos lighthouse. A fine day, one of the last of summer.

The whole morning, as usual, had been given over to the details of government; she inquired after the health of the Divine Bull from the new High Priest—Pshereniptah had died in the spring—listened to Mardian's chief informer report on what was being said about her in the markets, then she had held an audience with her chief administrator of the Nile, who spread his maps over the polished cedarwood table to show her which canals had silted over the previous season, which others needed widening.

After a light lunch, it was her habit to spend an hour closeted alone with one of her advisers, Mardian or her *dioiketes*, before spending time with her children. Then she would commence work again in the late afternoon, sometimes working long into the evening. But she would always be awake again just before dawn, at her toilet, preparing herself for the audience chamber that morning.

Mardian was continually surprised by her capacity for work. Unlike her father, who had been devoted to the wine bottle, this woman thought of nothing but duty. Her luxuries, even her pleasures, were all to further her one goal, that of Egypt and her son.

Cleopatra read carefully through the scroll, holding the dowel in her right hand, holding it open with her left. Every now and then she would look up and question her *dioiketes* sharply on one of the figures, looking for hesitation, a lowering of the eyes. A careful reading of all the reports was one way to keep her ministers honest. They were rich enough, but you could never go wrong overestimating a man's greed.

The other way to maintain their integrity was to have the ministers check on each other. They could all be relied on for diligence in exposing one another's shortcomings.

When she had finished the interrogation, she dismissed the man, who scurried gratefully from the room. She allowed a servant to pour a glass of scented rosewater and sat herself at her table by the window, piled with letters and reports from the various *nomes*. She turned to Mardian. "Well?"

"You were harsh with him," he said.

"He is my *dioiketes*. What does he expect?" She began to read through a report from the royal shipyards on the progress of her new fleet. There was a metal cylinder on her work desk. She picked it up and tossed it to him.

Inside was a scroll, bound in leather. It was a message from Apollodorus, in Athens. He read it through quickly.

Things went well for Marcus Antonius. His general, Ventidius, had defeated the Parthians in Syria, and his wife had presented him with a daughter, Antonia. Meanwhile there had been riots in Rome and Octavian had been attacked by a mob. Antony had intervened to save him. *The fool.* Octavian had escaped with a few bruises.

Antony was now cheerfully esconced in Greece, where the locals had greeted him like a long-lost son. They had championed him as the

New Dionysus, patron of culture and the arts, and redeemer of men's souls through *ecstasis,* the frenzy brought on by wine and dancing. An inspired choice. In this new role, Antony had thrown himself back into the degenerate lifestyle he had so reluctantly abandoned in Alexandria. His life, it seemed, was now an endless round of festivals and banquets, and there had been orgies of drinking and depravity that had left even the Greeks astonished, which by all accounts was no easy task.

"They are making him statues," Cleopatra hissed, "and raising inscriptions to Antony, the Great and Inimitable."

"The Great and Inimitable what?" Mardian said, and immediately wondered if he had spoken too freely. But it seemed the queen was of a mind with him.

"For the moment Fortune smiles on him," she said. "But it cannot last. And then he will be sending messages to Alexandria professing his undying love. I know it."

"It does seem he is blessed," Mardian agreed. Blessed with an excellent general in Ventidius Bassus, who had driven the Parthians out of Syria, while Antony drank himself senseless in Athens.

"I should not be angry," she said. "But his blindness leaves me speechless. Perhaps the Greeks are right, perhaps he *is* Dionysus. Like a god, his virtues and his faults are given to him in giant measure."

"They say he is jolly enough to be Dionysus."

"The gods can afford to be jolly. They are immortal." She shook her head. "He *saved* Octavian from the mob in Rome. Apollodorus says that if he had not intervened with his soldiers, the crowd would have torn Octavian apart, limb from limb." She took a deep breath and let it out very slowly. "What could he have been thinking of?"

"I admit, I do not understand why he would do this. Some perverted sense of honor, perhaps?"

"Oh, Mardian, what am I going to do?"

He understood her frustration. What *can* she do? She is Egypt; she must marry Rome or defeat it. They could not win at arms. Yet there were only two men she might make her consort; one of them was her implacable enemy and the other was Marcus Antonius.

He had never seen her this way before. He remembered taking her out to the Hippodrome when she was a small child, for her horse-riding lessons. Her younger brother Ptolemy fell off once and would not get back on. She had fallen many times, until her body was covered in bruises, but each time she remounted immediately. By the time she was ten she was an accomplished rider.

He had decided then that nothing could bend this woman's spirit. Yet now, although she still tended her duties diligently, it seemed to him as if there was something broken inside her. He wondered if it would mend in time to save her—and save Egypt.

CITY OF ATHENS

Kalends of Mars, thirty-seven years before the birth of Jesus Christ

Octavia followed the sound of laughter along the marble-clad halls, past the porphyry vases, as tall as a man, the purple wisteria spreading up the fluted columns of the outdoor court, the topiary hedges, the music of the water fountains; past great marble statues of Dionysus and Hercules, of Antony himself. She made her way through the colonnades around the *peristylium,* where the gardeners tended the beds of violets and white roses. She found him finally in one of the rooms that led off the *peristylium,* with Antonia, throwing the child up in the air and catching her again in those tree-trunk arms. The little girl was giggling uncontrollably.

She watched for a while, unseen, smiling at this huge man and this tiny child together. The toddler obviously adored him, and there was no doubt that he adored her in turn. If only it was always like this.

Then something made him turn around and he caught her staring at him. He grinned.

"I did not think to find you here," she said.

"She has grown," he said. "One day she will look just like you."

"As long as she does not look like *you.*"

He laughed at that. "Big muscles and a butcher's nose? I hope not. Don't we, little princess?" He tossed her up in the air again and she laughed, chewing frantically on a tiny, pink fist.

She felt her heart go out to him. Sometimes he was such a good man.

"Our cook wishes to know what you would like prepared for your dinner," she said.

"Tell her nothing. We shall not be here. We shall be attending a symposium at the house of Quintus Dellius."

Her smile faded. "I thought tonight we should spend alone together."

He looked appalled at such a suggestion.

"Perhaps you should go alone, then," she said. "I feel unwell."

"You look well enough to me."

She avoided his eyes. "It is the new baby. You know how it is. I cannot keep my food down when I am carrying."

He laughed. "I cannot keep my food down either. It doesn't keep me from enjoying myself."

"Nothing keeps you from enjoying yourself," she snapped, and immediately regretted it.

The smile vanished abruptly. "I am just a man with red blood in his veins—"

"Red blood? Some say it is red wine," she heard herself say.

That look on his face. He was really getting angry now. "Come with me tonight," he said. "Enjoy yourself. It will do you good."

"I would rather stay here. You know I do not like wild talk and drinking." She had not meant to nag him like this. Like a real Roman matron.

Antonia was squirming in his arms like a newborn calf. He sat her down on the floor and she started to cry.

Octavia picked up the child and tried to soothe her. "This came for you," she snapped, and dropped the papyrus scroll she had been holding onto the tiles. It had been rolled, tied with cord, and sealed with wax.

Antony picked it up and read it quickly. His lips curled into a sneer. "It is from Octavian. Your brother asks for my help once more." He tossed it back at her.

Octavia read the letter, Antonia still squirming in her arms. The war against Sextus was going badly, and there had been food riots along the wharves and in the Forum itself. Now he wanted his fellow Triumvir to bring ships to help him.

Antony's light mood had evaporated. "I went to his aid last year, at Brundisium. On that occasion he did not even deign to make an appearance. I wasted a whole summer at his bidding. What game is he playing now?"

"You cannot ignore this. Rome is still your country."

"If I go, I waste another summer there instead of preparing for Parthia."

"My brother would not dare spurn you again. This must be genuine. You know he is no strategist. He is selfish and conceited, but he needs your help."

"And why should I give it to him?"

"Would you rather have Sextus Pompey master in Rome?"

He thought about that. Finally he relented. "Well, all right," he said. "But this is the last time. I have my own problems."

"You cannot desert him."

"I do this for you," he said.

Well, in a way. A man always likes to keep his wife content, if he can. But Antony knew if he wanted to recruit an army in Italy, he could not afford to offend her brother. She suspected Octavian knew that, too.

80

TARENTUM, IN ITALY

An April dawn, the sun touching the mountains of the Basilicata with pink, the streets around the fish market already thronged with crowds. A gray swell pushed against the rocks of the breakwater, the harbor itself choked with ships, the masts of more than three hundred warships like a forest. Population of the small town was swelled to bursting by the sailors and soldiers of Antony's fleet.

Out in the harbor Antony paced the deck of his flagship, wrapped in a scarlet cloak, surrounded by his staff officers. "He's not coming," Antony said. He shook the letter in Octavia's face.

She looks pale, he thought. The child had swollen her belly and the sea voyage was a misery for her. She had not kept any food down for days. "He knows what you are saying about him. He has his pride."

"And I have my pride, Octavia." He had wasted more precious time, only to be treated with disdain yet again. But he knew it was wrong to be angry with her. It was not her fault.

Little Antonia had started crying. He picked the child up and tossed her in the air until she was laughing again.

"I shall write to him," Octavia said. "Let me make this right between you."

"Make it right between us," he muttered. As if she could. He stared at her. Poor Octavia. Her position was as unwelcome as his own. In his own way he supposed he was quite fond of her. He should let her have this chance. After all, he did not want the treaty to break down any more than she did. He wanted just to be free of these problems so he could go to Parthia unhindered. The East was his future. He didn't care about Italy anymore. If Octavian wanted it, he could have it, as long as he could have his army.

"Write to him, then. I'll wait. Let's see if we can fix this mess."

⤙ ⤙

They waited almost two months in Tarentum, while the couriers hurried back and forth to Rome with letters. Spring turned to summer, the days grew hotter, the ocean was blue and flat. I should be warring in Parthia, Antony told himself, instead of drinking wine and cursing here in this stinking port town. The kid is pushing me too far. . . .

81

A WARM BREEZE stirred the tent flap. Antony stared across the table, biting down his rage. There he sat, morose and sniffling, the vicious little dandy, with his pansy friend Maecenas and that big oaf, Agrippa. Octavian had given the clod control of his navy now. He had won a few land skirmishes on the Rhine and now he thought he was an admiral.

But what really galled Antony was how Octavian had spread those stories about him and Cleopatra in Alexandria. Hypocrite. From what he had heard, Octavian and his pansy friends didn't mind a spot of dicing and whoring themselves. Young Caesar had a liking for virgins, apparently, procured for him at no little expense by Maecenas.

You'd never think it to look at him. High summer, and Octavian still wore two tunics, his nose was running, he was sneezing all the time. Incredible that he had lived this long. You felt sick just looking at him: skin like parchment, teeth covered in weed like rocks in a stagnant ditch.

"You're looking well," Antony said. In fact, Octavian looked as if he was dying. Shivering in the heat of the day. This time next year you'll have Italy by default, Antony told himself.

"I have a trifling cold," Octavian said. "It will not leave me. And my feet ache. I should not have left Rome. Octavia implored me to come."

You little weasel. "I should not have left Athens," Antony said, slamming the scroll on the table between them, "but you sent me this letter."

Octavian stared at it as if it were something he had coughed up onto the table. He made no move to pick it up. "It was a mistake."

"One that has cost me most of the summer."

"I have decided now to deal with Sextus in my own way."

Antony wanted to pitch him out of the chair and kick his ribs. The insolent little puppy. "Then why," he thundered, "did you send me this?"

~~~ ~~~

And so it went, Maecenas and Agrippa whispering their advice in Octavian's ear, while Young Caesar sat there, the foremost man of Rome, in a badly fitting tunic made for him at home by his wife.

But finally they thrashed it out, yet another agreement; Antony would leave behind 120 of the ships he had brought with him—he didn't need them anymore anyway, but no need for Octavian to know that—in exchange for twenty thousand legionaries from Gaul to help him with his campaign in Parthia. The Triumvirate was renewed for another five years, and as a mark of good faith Octavian betrothed his daughter, Julia, who was two years old, to Antyllus, Antony's son by Fulvia, now nine.

It was an agreement not lightly entered into. During the negotiations, Antony's general, Canidius, had privately counseled him to consider an alliance with Sextus instead. "After all," he insisted, "the man gave shelter to your mother when she asked for it, and even now could give you mastery of the seas around Italy." But finally Antony, for the troops and for the peace, settled instead for the Triumvirate and the status quo. His concentration focused on the East; he wanted nothing to do with Rome and its problems right now.

Besides, he reasoned, once he had Parthia, the rest would follow.

PART IV

*Later we will have a long time to lie dead, yet the few years
we have now we live badly.*

Sappho

82

ANTONY WAITED THE summer at Tarentum. Octavia had her baby, another girl. The season passed quickly, but still the four legions Antony had been promised by Octavian did not arrive.

It was another year wasted, another summer when he should have been in Syria, fighting the Parthians, following the footsteps of Alexander. Or perhaps that was what all this was really about. Octavian knew that if he returned from Babylon loaded with spoils, Rome would have him as god and the little bitch would be finished.

Antony finally gave orders for the fleet to sail for Greece. They crossed the Adriatic and a week later he put in at Corcyra.

Antony stood on the deck of his flagship, watching the mare's tails chase each other across the sky. Across the bay Corcyra slept in the afternoon sun. He breathed in the boat smells, wet canvas and pitch, watched the whitecaps drift across the harbor, the westerly wind on his face, blowing him away from Rome.

His knuckles were white on the gilded rail. That *boy*. That *boy* had done it to him again. He had been more than forbearing, kept his word when others would have turned their backs. What thanks did he get from the little bastard? He had been continually insulted and tricked. Just last summer Octavian had pulled this same stunt, summoning him to Brundisium for a crisis council meeting. On that occasion he had not showed up at all.

He had continually hindered Antony in his efforts to mount a campaign against Parthia. He had stolen his Gallic command, and now broke his word by not sending him the twenty thousand soldiers as he had promised at Tarentum.

He had made a decision on the voyage from Italy. He would no longer be his dupe, toyed with by this brat who thought he was Caesar. Octavian had used his sister to ensnare him in marriage.

It now occurred to him that Octavia might be spying for him, for all he knew. Well, he had had enough.

❦ ❦

Octavia emerged from belowdecks, a wet nurse clutching the infant, the other children trailing behind her, like lost ducklings. She looked pale and weak.

A Liburnian had been sent from the shore, and was now pulled alongside. She stared at it in consternation.

"I have decided you should spend a few days ashore," Antony said to her. "You should rest before the journey back to Italy."

Octavia looked at him in bewilderment.

"We are going back to Italy?" she said.

"Just you and the children."

"You are not coming with us?"

"I have arranged an escort. You will come to no harm."

She swayed on her feet and had to support herself against the ship's rail. The childbirth and the voyage had sapped her strength. *This must come as a shock to her,* he knew. *But it had to be done. I just hope she does not weep. I hate weeping women.* "What about you?" she said. She sounded as if she was choking.

"I shall go on to Athens."

"But my place is with you."

"You are not up to the rest of the voyage. You're still weak from the childbirth and I do not want you to suffer anymore. Besides, as soon as we are back in Greece, I have to travel to Parthia for the war. In my judgment, it is best if you return to Rome with the children."

"I do not want to leave you!"

He turned his back. "I have made up my mind," he said.

"But, my lord—"

"That is my decision," he snapped.

Although his back was to her, he could imagine the look on her face. She imitated hurt and betrayal very well. Or perhaps the hurt was real; the trouble was, he had no way of telling. Was she Octavian's creature, or was she his?

But there was one person he could trust. Well, if not trust exactly, at least he knew what she really wanted. It was as he had always believed; in the end a man did what his nature allowed. His nature drew him back to *her*.

He would tell Canidius and the others that it was for her money and her ships. But from the first he had recognized her as a creature like himself. Let them say what they liked in Rome.

The die was cast. With this action he would send a clear message to that little bitch in Rome: "Here, have your sister back, I don't want her or her children. Or you."

The children made a scene when they realized what was happening. Antyllus, and little Antonia of course, most of all. He would miss them, especially Antonia. They were just too young to understand.

Sometimes a man had to harden his heart and do what he must.

He avoided Octavia's eyes, which were bright with grief and accusation. She was helped down into the Liburnian, the children after her, then the sailors unhitched the lines and the small craft slipped away and went crashing through the swell, back toward the wharf at Corcyra.

He knew that from that moment a part of his life was ended. It was time to take control once more. He knew where his destiny lay.

In the East, with Cleopatra.

83

ALEXANDRIA-BY-EGYPT

SHE RECEIVED GAIUS Fonteius Capito on the terrace of the palace, rather than in formal audience. She had known him from Antony's sojourn in Alexandria almost—was it so long?—four years ago. Which was perhaps why Antony had chosen him to lead the delegation.

Sitting here with Antony's envoy, she felt unexpectedly calm. Where is the anger? she wondered. She searched her emotions with something close to panic, looking for the bitterness she had nurtured there, like a woman searching a jewel chest for some missing gem of incomparable worth. She found only an eagerness to see him once more. No, she promised herself, he will not be pardoned so easily. I will not let him charm and smile his way out from under. Cleopatra is going to harden her heart and make him pay for the pain he has caused.

But for now it was enough that he at last understood; his future lay with her, and Alexandria.

The sun was hot under the silk canopy, the Syrian slave boys working hard with their great peacock fans to cool them and keep away the insects that hummed in the late-summer air. Capito was served a goblet of wine, cooled with snow, while Cleopatra sipped scented water from a jade cup. There was no wind, and the water in the harbor was flat and blue. From up here she could see anemones swaying on the sandy bottom.

"Revered Majesty, I bring greetings from my lord Antony, Imperator of Rome."

"Who?"

Capito had the grace to smile. "He has never forgotten *you*."

She was in no mood to be patronized. "There is a difference between remembering and keeping in reserve. One relates to the heart, the other to the battlefield."

"Be assured, Majesty, I am speaking of Antony's heart. He bade me expressly to tell you that he regrets the time that has passed since he has had the pleasure of gazing on your lovely countenance, as I am privileged to do now, and invites you to be his guest in Antioch."

"A pretty speech, Capito, and well-rehearsed. But I am not so easily flattered. Not a kind word from the noble Antony these four years, and now he sends you to me, asking for my presence in Antioch. Am I to run to him like a heartsick girl?"

"The past is done. He did what he must."

"He did what he *chose*. And he chose to betray me. When he left here four years ago, it was not his avowed intention to marry another woman."

Capito did not wilt in the face of her anger. She admired him for that. "That was just politics, Majesty."

"Just politics? I have heard this Octavia is a beautiful woman."

"If you like that sort of thing."

Despite herself, she smiled. "What sort of thing?"

"A statue is lovely, Majesty. But I'm told they are not easily warmed."

"Octavia cannot be too cool to him. They have two children."

"As I said, Majesty, a man does what he must."

"Or as he pleases. It's the same thing."

He gave her a shrug that could have meant anything. "You have been constantly in his thoughts. You have his word on that."

"I know the value of Antony's word." She looked away, toward the harbor, giving herself some time to think, and giving Fonteius Capito some time to sweat. A trireme was setting off through the harbor breakwaters. More grain for Rome—if it found its way past Sextus's pirates. Poor Octavian. Son of a god, yet the Young Caesar could not even feed his own city. He was ripe for the plucking if Antony had the steel and the stomach.

"Majesty, may I venture to say that I know his heart. Many is the time I have sat with him at dinner at the end of a long day and his talk has been only of you."

"Ribaldry, I imagine."

Capito feigned outrage. "No, indeed. If he was free to choose, it would not have been Octavia he made his wife. Politics demanded he did what he did."

"You have a silver tongue, Fonteius Capito. You lie like a carpet salesman."

"He longs to see his children."

"From what I hear, he can step off a ship anywhere in the Mediterranean and see his offspring." Antony had never seen little Alexander and Cleopatra. Even for a man with so many children and such an entangled private life, the curiosity must be vexing.

"His marriage with Octavia is over," Capito said. "He asks to see you."

"The look on your face, Fonteius Capito. You should have been an actor."

"I only speak what I know to be the truth."

The gall. After all he has done Antony thinks he can appeal to my heart in this. But the truth was, she needed him as much as he needed her. She had Caesar's son, and one day Octavian would come looking for him. There was only one man who might be able to stop him.

"Why should I help him?" she asked Capito.

"It is not your help he asks for."

"So if I go to Antioch he will not ask for my soldiers or my money or my grain to feed his army?"

Capito decided to change course. "He has made up his mind to go to Parthia. If you do not support him in this, he will go anyway. If he wins, he will remember you when he returns. If he loses, there is nothing that stands between you and Octavian."

She smiled, but the smile was utterly without warmth. *Now we come to the heart of the matter.* "Did my lord Antony send you here to threaten me?"

"I think you are as much aware of the realities of your position as he is."

She nodded slowly. "All right," she said. "I will come. But not because of his threats, as he will see. You will tell my lord Antony that this time I do not come as the Queen of Love and Compassion. This time I shall be Cleopatra."

He smiled and bowed his head, satisfied, his job done. He must have known that she had made up her mind to go anyway, before he even arrived with the delegation in Alexandria. In fact, she knew she would go to Antony someday, long before he had even thought of sending for her. As Fonteius Capito said, there really was no choice, for her, for her sons, or for Egypt. Although she might appear reluctant, she knew that finally the dream was again within her grasp.

84

ANTIOCH SEEMED TO hang suspended from the mountains; forts had been erected on the rocky slopes, and were joined by a wall that followed the line of hills that surrounded the ancient town. It was perched on the rim of the Gulf of Alexandretta, inland from the fertile plain that bordered the coast, a short sail along the mouth of the Orontes River. Pilgrims came here to worship in the famous Temple of Apollo, the marble pillars stark as bone among the dark cypress groves of Daphne.

This morning Mount Silpius threw its ragged shadow across the city streets, while the gleaming white villas of the wealthy, surrounded by groves of deep green cypress, bathed in yellow sun. The river sparkled like a ribbon of liquid mercury.

It was to be a private audience, he had decided. He would not risk her perfumed condescension in front of the whole court. No doubt she would pretend to be angry with him for a while.

He supposed she had cause to be upset with him. He had never intended things to turn out this way. He could not choose his consorts as easily as the Queen of Egypt. The woman did not understand how difficult it was to be a *Roman*. In truth, he had missed her more than he had ever thought to mourn for any woman. He ached to see her again yet dreaded how she might receive him.

She was the only woman who really understood him. That was why he was sure she would forgive him, given a little talk and sweetness. Then she would lend him the money and the ships he needed, and he would come back from Parthia like Caesar, weighed down with gold, and everything would be all right. Octavian would be put in his place and he would be undisputed master of Rome, with Cleopatra and their children in his thrall and under his protection.

Like Dionysus, he would be Bringer of Joy, and make everyone happy.

Except that little bitch of a brother-in-law, perhaps.

🌱 🌱

When she entered, Antony was standing by the window in his headquarters. He had commandeered the old palace of the Seleucids, built on an island in the middle of the fast-running river. The window behind him looked out over the river and the wide flat fertile plain that led through the mountains to the distant shore.

It was a huge chamber, the high ceiling almost lost in the gloom. The vault was supported by massive beams, gleaming dully with gilt paint and huge decorative studs. Rich but dark, somber, and cool. Hardly Antony's style at all. How he must hate it here, she thought.

Four years since she had seen him. Had he changed? she asked herself. A little, perhaps. He had the same dazzling smile, like a naughty boy who knew he would not be scolded if he smiled broadly enough. A god's curly hair, although there was a little gray in it now, and there was a little more flesh on his bones. He had dressed for the occasion, a breastplate of pure gold, decorated with artwork, purple cloak. Still regal, still Antony.

"My lovely, beloved queen." He did not try to embrace her. Just as well. She would not have tolerated that.

How different from the first time she had come to the East to greet him. Instead of the golden robes of Isis, today she was merely a mortal Hellenic queen, an emerald gown with gold border, sandals of white, soft kidskin on her feet. There were emeralds at her throat, her wrists, and her ears, and on her arm was a bracelet in the shape of the royal cobra of Egypt.

"Marcus."

"Please. Make your ease." He indicated a couch.

Servants brought sweet grapes, silver salvers of aromatic roasted nuts, and a white wine from Laodicea, which they laid on a carved sandalwood table. Cleopatra dismissed Mardian and her royal bodyguard. They were left alone.

"Where are our children?" Antony said.

"They are in Alexandria."

"You did not bring them with you?" He looked wounded.

"It is a long sea voyage. If you would like to see them, you know where they are."

"They are well?"

"They grow sturdy and strong."

There was a pause. He seemed to be waiting for some word of apology from her. But then, she knew he always was an arch-manipulator in matters of the heart. One area where Caesar had nothing at all to teach him. "What did you name them?"

"The girl is Cleopatra, the boy, Alexander."

"Alexander," he repeated. He approved of her choice, as she knew he would. "What does he look like?"

"He has your curly hair and the body of a bull. He is also honest, clear-eyed, and utterly lacking in deceit. If it wasn't for the hair and his build, people would have begun to suspect that you were not the father."

He let that barb go unremarked. "Why didn't you tell me . . . before I left Alexandria?"

"Would you have stayed if I had?"

He did not answer that directly. "But some word, at least. I did not know about the children until it was announced in the Senate."

"You were busy with your wedding preparations. I did not wish to worry you with something of such little consequence to you."

A long silence. What could he say? "You look wonderful," he said.

"*You* look guilty."

"What was I to do?"

"What you should have done is clear to everyone except you."

"I know what you think of me. But you do not know my heart, though you think you do. I have missed you these last four years. I cannot count the nights I lay in Octavia's arms and thought of you."

"Marcus, I have noticed something about you. Whenever you kissed me, you never closed your eyes. Now I know why."

He remained silent, sullen in the face of her attack.

"Because you were wondering if something better might be walking past."

He reached for one of the silver wine goblets, drained it in one swallow.

"I knew this day would come," she said.

"I have prayed that it would."

She laughed. "Please, Marcus, you have spent too long with your actors and actresses! That long face does not become you. You left Alexandria and did not give me a second thought."

"That is not true!"

"It's close enough to the truth."

He looked angry, his cheeks flushed the color of copper. "Laugh at me all you want. You don't understand the predicament I was in. I could not marry you, by Roman law. I could marry *her*."

"Ah, so it was a legal problem. Stupid of me. I thought it was the fact you loved me that gave you pause."

"You are not even trying to understand my position."

"I do understand. She was good for you then, she is not good for you now."

"Well, she never was, really."

"I despise you."

He was staring at the floor, this big, hulking man, like a pupil chastised by his tutor. Suddenly he looked up at her and grinned, with that impossible little-boy smile that so infuriated and melted her. "I do love you," he said.

She felt her resolve slipping away. He was her fatal weakness; hard to look at him and still remember to be angry. The look of sincere penitence on his face made her smile, even though she knew it was feigned, and she found herself wondering how it would feel to have his arms around her again.

He took a step toward her, but she backed away. There was a steel band around her chest. She ached to have his arms around her again, and she hated herself for it. She decided she would make him wait, make herself wait, as punishment.

"You need me at your side again, don't you?" she said.

"It is the dearest wish of my heart."

"It is Egypt you wish for."

His demeanor shifted from misunderstood lover to the casual arrogance that was fed to Romans with their mother's milk. "I can take Egypt away from you whenever I wish. You forget I am lord of the East and you have your throne by my patronage. Egypt is a Roman province."

A Roman province! She looked him in the eye. "There will be no annexation of Egypt by you while Octavian lives. It would be his excuse for war. You can have Egypt through me, but no other way."

Antony regretted his outburst. She was right and they both knew it.

"You can have us both, if that is what you want," she said. "But first, we have our demands. You will repay Egypt and you will repay me for the four years of torment and humiliation we have suffered at your hands."

He took a deep breath. He had been afraid this would happen. "What are these demands?" he asked her.

TREATY SIGNED THIS DAY BETWEEN THE TRIUMVIR MARCUS ANTONIUS, AND QUEEN CLEOPATRA THE SEVENTH OF EGYPT, PHILOPATOR, PHILOPATRIS, QUEEN OF THE TWO LANDS.

ITEM ONE. *Queen Cleopatra shall place all the resources of Egypt, financial and military, at the disposal of Triumvir Marcus Antonius, who may use them for his needs as he sees fit.*

ITEM TWO. *In return the contracting parties shall celebrate a legal marriage according to Egyptian ritual.*

ITEM THREE. *Consequent to this marriage Marcus Antonius will not assume the title King of Egypt but that of Autocrator of the East.*

ITEM FOUR. *Marcus Antonius shall recognize Ptolemy Caesar, son of Cleopatra and Julius Caesar, as the legitimate heir to the Egyptian throne, his own two children, Alexander and Cleopatra, receiving from the Queen some minor kingdoms.*

ITEM FIVE. *The Treaty shall place under the sovereignty of Egypt and the domain of Queen Cleopatra and her descendants the following outer territories: Sinai, Arabia (including the citadel of Petra), the Oriental coast of the Dead Sea, the valley of Jordan including the city of Jericho, the Judaean districts of Samaria and Galilee, the Phoenician coast excepting the free cities of Tyre and Sidon, the Lebanon and the northern coast of Syria, Cilicia including the city of Tarsus, and the island of Cyprus.*

> *In witness to this agreement:*
> *Marcus Canidius Crassus*
> *Gaius Fonteius Capito*
> *Marcus Quintus Dellius*

85

THEY WERE MARRIED in the Great Hall, according to the Eastern rite, watched by Marc Antony's staff officers in their leather cuirasses and scarlet cloaks, and the ministers of Cleopatra's court, luscious and despised by the Romans for their silks and brocades. Cleopatra reclined on a throne of ivory and ebony wood, wearing the double diadem of Egypt and the sacred Uraeus of the Lower Nile. Marc Antony sat beside her on a gilt throne, in the golden breastplate of Imperator of the East.

After the ceremony, while her clerks created the hieroglyphics that would record the marriage and declare little Alexander and his sister as its legitimate fruit, Cleopatra's ministers and her High Priest prostrated themselves at the foot of the thrones. It was done. Cleopatra had in a few short years restored an Empire that twelve previous Ptolemies had taken centuries to fritter away, and had at last found a place of safety among the vipers' nest of Rome.

🐏 🐏

She watched him from the bed, her bare skin sensitive to the touch of the silk coverlet, anticipating a man's touch. I have sacrificed too much for Egypt, she thought. Tonight is for Cleopatra.

Antony closed the door behind him and began to unwind his toga. I was right, she thought. He has been too long in Greece, wasted too many nights at his revels. The flesh hung looser on his bones than it once had. Four years of debauch have taken their toll. But she should have expected that. It is only Dionysus himself who never grows older.

She pulled back the sheet and held out a hand toward him. "It's been four years," she said. "Don't keep me waiting any longer."

He stepped naked toward the bed. "You are still as beautiful as you ever were," he said.

She smiled. "I can see that. You have built me my own obelisk."

He looked down at himself and laughed. "I erected it in your honor."

For all you could say of him, he knew how to please a woman. She had the appetite of one who has starved, and threw herself at him with an unqueenly abandon. As the candles guttered and died, one by one, her limbs drew him in and for a few dark hours his sins were forgotten, pardoned by her eagerness to have him once more in her arms and in her bed.

86

SPRING RETURNED TO the Mediterranean, promising warm winds from the ocean, sails flowering on the horizon, whispers of war.

Mount Silpius emerged from its wreath of cloud. Violets and marigolds, wild orchids and poppies, made splashes of color in the meadows and plains along the Orontes, goat bells made their music on the mountains. It was a time of renewal, a time also for death.

Cleopatra and Antony set out from Antioch on the Kalends of April, heading east toward Armenia. The army formed a great snaking column along the river that took two hours to pass, hundreds of lumbering wagons carrying supplies for this vast host. There was a huge battering ram eighty feet long with an iron head that needed a train of several flat wagons, each articulated from the others so it could negotiate the winding roads into the Medean Mountains, and a clumsy wheeled machine like a giant grasshopper that could hurl a boulder a quarter of a mile and crumble away the stoutest city walls.

Then came the infantry, the Romans in their uniforms like an army of beetles, with bronze cuirasses and purple cloaks and sturdy nailed sandals. Each soldier carried with him three days' worth of food in a bronze box, as well as a kettle and hand mill, spade, pickaxe, saw, and palisade stakes. This on top of his weapons, a javelin, sword, dagger and shield, and heavy bronze helmet. Even fully laden, a ten-year veteran could cover fifteen miles in a day.

There was the Fifth Legion, recruited by Caesar himself from native Gauls, huge blond giants who had withstood charging elephants at the battle of Thapsus; and the Ironclad, leathery veterans who had served Caesar in the Alexandrian War and had avenged him at Philippi.

There were sixteen Roman legions in all, a formidable army, supported by thousands of native auxiliaries and levies. Even Caesar had never commanded a host like this. It was impossible to imagine that they could be defeated. Perhaps Antony was right to take this opportunity, she thought. He might yet emulate the feats of Alexander. After all, he had never been on a losing side. He might be suspect in the peace, but when it came to war, he was hard, sober, and brave.

And this was his time.

〰 〰

In May they reached the city of Artaxata on the Araxes River, far to the northeast. The city was more Parthian in influence than Greek, Cleopatra thought, gazing at the many-domed roofs of the citadel, and at the Armenians in their baggy trousers, fringed tunics, and oiled ringlets. As they rode through the gates they were greeted by the king, Artavasdes, in a spectacular ceremony, and feted and feasted for three days. The Armenian formally pledged himself as Antony's immutable ally.

When they marched out of the city, the army was augmented by a further thirty thousand Armenian troops, half of which were cavalry, some of the finest in the East. It was a colorful and impressive brigade. Long afterward Cleopatra would remember the sight as they marched toward the eastern mountains, the bright costumes of the Armenian cavalrymen, their hands glittering with the chunky rings they wore on their fingers and thumbs, the jangle of the bronze caparisons on their horses. How they cheered Antony as he rode past them on his bay, at inspection.

In later years when she thought of it, she could appreciate the irony.

〰 〰

Nothing grand tonight for Dionysus, warrior, redeemer, Bringer of Joy, just a goatskin tent stretched over an oaken frame, a simple camp bed, some stools, a folding table with maps spread over it and held in position at their corners with rocks, some water pitchers, and basins. A feeble yellow light seeped from the lantern that hung from the cross beam. Around them the sounds of an army at camp, the bellow of a donkey, the oaths of the soldiers, the air heavy with the grease smoke of the cooking fires.

A long time since she had lived in a tent, not since her days as renegade at Mount Kasios. Such hardships meant nothing to her then, meant little again in return for a few more stolen days with Antony.

He had waited until now to show her this, his treasure of treasures. He placed the palm of his right hand reverently on his charts. "These plans are Caesar's," he said to her. "They are the reason we will succeed, why I have wanted Parthia so badly. They are the blueprints of the greatest military planner of all time, framed at the peak of his career and his experience. He might have given that ballet boy his name, but to me he gave the greatest bequest of all. The way to conquer Parthia."

His eyes glittered in the gloom, his face alight with enthusiasm. Of course, she thought. The day Caesar was murdered, Antony had gone to fetch all of Caesar's papers from Calpurnia. These must have been among them. He had harbored them secretly ever since.

"We shall attack from the north, not the west as Crassus did. And we have come prepared, we have siege engines with us, just as the old boy planned."

It was Antony's dream, as it was Julius's. It was where he believed his destiny lay. He wanted glory, he wanted a Triumph. Veni, vidi, vici; as Caesar had.

"I shall pray to Isis for your victory," she whispered.

"I will not need Isis," he said. "I have Caesar watching over my shoulder."

Perhaps he does, she thought. And if he comes back from Parthia loaded with treasure, my own future is assured. I will finally have the great prize, Caesar's true legacy, that has been kept from me for so long. Perhaps this had been his plan, when he died. So like him to have left this final test for Antony, knowing that victory in Parthia was worth more than any bequest he made in his will.

It was their last night together, but Antony was already far away from her. They made love in his tent, but he seemed distracted. His eyes were set on the mountains of Persia, not the small consolations she could offer him. And in a way, she understood that about him. She herself owned a heart divided between glory and love.

He was convinced he would win, that he would return to her. It was left to her to contemplate life once more without her Caesar, dread and cold.

The next day she watched the army cross the river, toward the mountains, and the barely mapped lands of Alexander's time. She would like to have gone with him, but it was impossible. She had, as always, affairs of state to attend to in Egypt. That was her duty now. And there was a further, and very good, reason why she could not go.

The long winter in Antioch had yielded much. Most important, she had secured her empire once again; by the treaty, she had wrung back from Antony almost all the territories her ancestors had lost. In doing so, she proved herself perhaps the greatest of the Ptolemies. In fifteen years she had raised Egypt from subservience to greatness again. But she now had one other possession of Antony's that had not been named in the charter.

She was pregnant again.

87

ALEXANDRIA-BY-EGYPT

THE FIRST GALE of winter lashed the Pharos, now only occasionally visible through gray sheets of rain, the huge seas throwing great plumes of spray over the marble colonnades. She held a hand to her belly, felt her child move there, little fluttering kicks of eager life.

Harder these days to concentrate on the work of the Council chamber, the turgid customs inventories, the long reports from the shipwrights and the canal inspectors. It was not just the child sapping her energy. In Parthia, battles had already been fought and won. Their destinies had been decided. But which way?

The wind hurled itself at the colonnades, tore up young trees in the gardens, bent the palms in its rage. Her child stirred again.

Alexandria, as indeed much of the world, was alive with expectation, rumor, and unease. The Potter's Oracle had been revived and was spoken of in hushed tones everywhere, from the fish markets to the bazaars to the corridors of the palace itself. The ancient prophecy had been translated from demotic Egyptian into Greek three hundred years before, and foretold an Egyptian queen who would conquer Rome, reconcile Asia, and usher in a new golden age, the Age of the Sun.

> . . . and while Rome will be hesitating over
> the conquest of Egypt, then the mighty queen
> of the Immortal King will appear among men.
> Three will subdue Rome with a pitiful fate,
> all men will perish in their private homes
> when a cataract of fire pours down from heaven . . .

Fanciful nonsense, of course, but nonsense she might yet use to her own ends. Everywhere people were looking for a champion and liberator who would break the yoke of Rome. Could not that be Cleopatra and Antony and Caesarion, saving the world in a blaze of Dionysiac glory?

The oracle also spoke of a golden child that would be born on the birthday of the sun, the twenty-fifth day of the Roman month of Decembris. She doubted if Antony's baby would wait that long to see the world. But there were other ways of shaping prophecies to fit the facts.

Everyone loved her now. In the *chora* she was Isis, Queen of the World; in Alexandria, even the poisonous Greek court had been silenced by her diplomatic maneuvers. She held the Mediterranean in the palm of her hand.

But her future, for once, was not to be decided in Rome, but on the other side of the Persian mountains.

❧ ❧

News arrived from Apollodorus in Rome, all of it bad. Against all odds, Octavian had won Sicily. Sextus had been utterly defeated at sea; the untried Agrippa had confounded his critics and won the day from him. His newly constructed fleet of big ships had proved too much for the Son of Neptune, god of the sea. Sextus had risked all on one great sea battle and he had lost. He had fled to the East, with the remains of his fleet, just seventeen ships remaining from three hundred.

There had been a further twist. Sextus's land army had surrendered to Marcus Lepidus, the forgotten member of the Triumvirate. Bitter at past slights, Lepidus had used these appropriated legions as a basis for claiming Sicily as his own, in direct challenge to Octavian. But he had misread the mood of his soldiers. They were sick of fighting. The Young Caesar rode into Lepidus's camp with a handful of officers and bought them off. Lepidus had been forced to grovel for his life, throwing himself at Octavian's feet and kissing his sandals. Octavian had been generous for once, and sent him into exile, instead of giving his neck an airing.

Octavian now had his own army as well as that of Marcus Lepidus's, a total of forty-five legions, 120,000 soldiers. Like the Hydra, Cleopatra thought. One day you thought him finished, but he just reared up again, growing heads in other places. It was dispiriting how this spotty young man could make such a fist of things.

※ ※

In the second month of the Egyptian new year, at the height of the Nile, she gave birth to a son, Ptolemy Philadelphus. Soon after, she received more news from Rome. Octavian had erected a notice in the Forum declaring the civil wars at an end. A frightened Senate had granted him the right to wear the laurel wreath at all times, like Caesar before him.

This changes things, she thought. Unless Antony comes back from the East with the King of Parthia's head on a plate, we are all in serious trouble.

88

AN EERIE SENSE of premonition, Quintus Dellius marching across the marbled hall, all leather and bronze, the helmet with its red crest under his right arm. But something jarred with the image as she had seen it countless times in her imagination. This was not the joyous messenger she had supposed. Instead his face was set in a grim line, his cheeks hollowed with exhaustion and suffering.

"Majesty," he said, and bowed. "Greetings from Imperator Marcus Antonius."

"Tell me what has happened," she said, steeling herself, for she had already guessed. You only had to look at the man's face.

"He needs your help," Dellius said. He sounded as if he was about to choke on the words.

"Where is he?"

"In Syria, Majesty, at Leuce Kome, a place called the White Village, north of Sidon. He asks that you come. He needs money, food, clothes for his soldiers."

She stared at him. All she could think of was: *I warned him not to go.* So much for Caesar's legacy.

"How bad?" she asked him.

Dellius swallowed, hard. "Twenty thousand of us, back from the mountains."

A murmur around the court. Twenty thousand. Forty thousand Romans lost, then. More than even Crassus had lost. What could have gone so wrong?

"I will come," she said. "Tell him I will come."

89

LEUCE KOME, IN SYRIA

ALL THAT WAS left of a dream.

Row upon row of the sick and injured were stretched out on the bare earth or lay on wooden cots covered by threadbare blankets. Awnings had been erected in places, sparse shelter for the weakest and the sickest. A haze of dreary camp smoke drifted across the town and the fields beyond, men crying out, delirious with pain or with fever.

His unconquerable army. Caesar's legions.

As Antony walked among them they recognized the purple cloak and some shouted out his name. He stopped to all who called to him, whispered a few words of comfort, was shamed rather than flattered by the gratitude with which they were received. These men had deserved better. He had let them down.

He wondered how many more men he would lose. Some would return to their homes, useless, without limbs or eyes. Still others, weakened from loss of blood, would die here in these bare hills from the cold or from sickness. His army had looked so fine when it marched out of Antioch. The finest ever gathered in the East, he had boasted to Cleopatra. What was left? A ragged band of skeletons.

He shivered inside his cloak. So cold. He had on three tunics and had wrapped woolen strips around his legs, under his boots, but still the wind bit into him like steel.

He wandered for an hour among the stench of death and putrefaction, the men calling his name like a benefaction. "Antony . . . Imperator!" They still loved him, even after what he had led them to.

Finally he found the man he was looking for, the body of a child and the face of a hag, lying under a stinking and bloodied blanket. He knelt down beside him, put a hand on his shoulder. The man opened his eyes.

"Sisyphus," Antony said.

The dwarf opened his eyes, attempted a smile. "These Parthians are real marksmen," he murmured, "to hit so small a target."

A freezing drizzle had begun to fall from the sky, rain dripping slowly off the flimsy awning that protected the wounded here from the worst of the weather. The gentle rhythm of rain, the particular cadence of defeat.

Antony lifted the blanket. The surgeon had removed the dwarf's arm below the left elbow. Just a stump left, wrapped in a rank, bloodied bandage.

"How are you, old friend?"

"A one-armed dwarf. You can truly say you possess the oddest of all oddities now."

"You're going to be all right. We'll get you out of here."

The little man's eyes were bright with fever. "It's not been an easy life up until now. If it's over, I shan't miss it."

"Don't talk this way. There are many more *commissata* to enjoy yet."

Sisyphus closed his eyes, resigned to whatever future the goddess of Fate had prepared for him. "What did we do it for, my lord?"

"We did it for Rome."

"No, I think we did it for you. Tell me, was it worth it?"

❦ ❦

Quintus Dellius found him standing alone on the long seawall, staring out at the gray ocean, the whitecaps hastening before the wind. The long purple cloak billowed and flapped around his legs.

"Imperator?"

"Where is she, Dellius?"

"She said she would come, my lord."

"We have no food, little water. My army is dying here by degrees, but they are too sick too march. If she does not come—"

"You can at least save yourself," Dellius murmured.

By that, of course, Dellius meant he wanted Antony to save him. If he were to ride on to Alexandria, he would have to take his general staff with him. While he remained here, they suffered, too.

Antony shook his head. "I will not abandon my army. If she does not come, they will die here. I will die here with them."

Dellius looked disappointed with that decision, as Antony knew he would. Antony turned away from him, returned his gaze to the ocean, searching the gray horizon for sails, for sign of a savior.

🜨 🜨

Desolate and gray, a harbor of sorts fashioned from rock, the hinterland flat and featureless. It was known as Leuce Kome, the White Village, although the jumble of houses she could see on the beach were a chalky gray. Still, even this squalid fishing village was a welcome sight after the miserable crossing from Alexandria, welcome landfall after the wretchedness of seasickness and storms. She shivered inside the thick, fur-lined cloak, though her cheeks burned from nausea. The cold wind felt good on her face.

Her flagship led the small fleet into harbor. Crammed below the deck of the *Antonia* were blankets, tunics, cloaks, enough for twenty thousand men. Her support ships were loaded with grain. She had also brought money, three hundred talents, gold the weight of a hundred men.

I have proved more faithful than you, Marcus Antonius, she thought.

As they came closer to the shore she could see the smoke of a hundred campfires, the ragged remains of the army she had watched across the Euphrates now camped along the shore. *Oh, Marcus. Is this all that remains of your grand designs?*

🜨 🜨

Canidius and Dellius escorted her to his tent. Antony was still too proud, or perhaps too ashamed, to meet her at the wharf himself. As she walked through the camp she could see the ravages the Parthians had visited on the army for herself, at close hand. *Oh, Antony, what have you done? These men are just bleeding, stinking skeletons. Where is that proud army that marched out of Antioch?*

His tent was comfortable enough. There were thick carpets on the ground, and Antony himself was collapsed in a chair and wrapped in a thick purple cloak. He stood up to greet her but could not meet her eyes. He had never experienced failure before, not like this. At Mutina his defeat had been due to overwhelming numbers;

he had been hemmed in on two sides, tricked and betrayed by the Senate. But this was his campaign, at his time, at his choosing. His whole life was supposed to have led to this moment.

Caesar, thanks to Brutus and Cassius, had been spared the ultimate test of Parthia. Had he been denied glory or spared defeat? No one would ever know.

"Antony," she said.

He had aged ten years. His eyes were haunted, his cheeks chiseled down to hollows by hunger and exhaustion and fear. The jolly butcher boy was gone.

"I knew you would come," he said.

"Of course I came."

"You have food?"

"All the grain I could load on the ships available to me at such short notice. And I have clothes for the winter, and money. As you asked."

They stared at each other in silence. A wind sent the tent flapping, bringing with it a wave of stench from the camp.

He had always seemed like a giant to her. Now he seemed shrunken, frail even. Fatigue and starvation had wrought some of this damage; but it was not just that. By the look of him, he had lost his faith in himself. She had to shock him out of this.

"Tell me," she said.

"We were betrayed. The Armenian, Artavasdes."

He told her what had happened; the siege engines and the baggage train had slowed their progress through the mountains, so Antony had split his force, left Artavasdes in the rear to guard the supplies and the *ballistae*. But Artavasdes and his cavalry had abandoned the rear guard and returned to Armenia. As soon as they were gone, the Parthians fell on his men, slaughtered them, captured the legion eagles. All the precious siege equipment was burned.

Meanwhile, Antony had reached the Parthian border city of Phraaspa, but without the siege engines he had been unable to capture it. Winter was fast approaching, and without shelter he could not remain in the mountains. He had been forced to withdraw, harried constantly by Parthian cavalry during the retreat. They had fought no fewer than eighteen defensive battles in twenty-seven days just to get out of the mountains. Forty thousand men fell to wounds or cold or disease. Of the sixty thousand veteran legionaries who had begun the campaign, there were just eighteen thousand left.

When he finished recounting the story, he stood by the entrance to the tent, his back to her, staring over the slowly drifting haze of campfires, misery hanging about him like a fog.

So. All of Caesar's plans come to nothing, she thought. Because of Antony's impatience. Was it part of Caesar's plan to split his forces? Was it good military planning to rely on the fidelity of client kings without at least keeping their families with you as hostage to their goodwill? Julius would never have made such mistakes. Much good the treasured legacy had done Antony when he had virtually ignored Caesar's plans and rushed ahead with his own.

Still, it was done. Parthia had been his dream, not hers. Perhaps now she could concentrate his mind on the real business at hand, in Rome. But first she knew she must snap him out of this mood of self-pity.

"Well, Marcus," she said, getting to her feet, "you really made a mess of that."

She saw his shoulders stiffen.

"Here you are, eating gritty bread, scraping scum off your drinking water, and sleeping in the open on some forsaken beach. Caesar would have been in India by now."

He rounded on her. "Don't taunt me!"

"I'm only saying what you're already telling yourself. You're drowning in pity for your own situation. What's done is done. I told you not to go to Parthia. The odds were loaded against you from the start."

"If it wasn't for Artavasdes, we would have won. The Parthians must have been told our plans. He not only abandoned us, he sold us out!"

Or if it was not that, she thought, there would be some other excuse. The truth of it was that it was a pointless war with an inevitable conclusion. For a while he had even dazzled her with his bizarre shyster's dreams.

I wonder what Octavian is doing right now? Eating lampreys and drinking Falernian wine out of jeweled goblets while he fondles his Bithynian dancing boys, no doubt.

"How old are you now, Marcus? Forty-six, forty-seven? It's all downhill from here to the boat across the Styx."

"I am not finished yet," he growled.

"I am relieved to hear you say it. I had thought you had quite given up."

"I will make Parthia mine."

"Forget Parthia!" she snapped. "You have heard the news? About Octavian?"

"That he has defeated Sextus? Yes, I heard it. But it was not his victory. It was Agrippa's."

"A fine distinction that most of Rome seems to have missed. Lepidus has gone, you know. Off to a country estate in a warm climate a long way from Rome."

"Octavian had no right to dismiss him without consulting me."

"Once something is done, these fine points of Roman law tend to be overlooked."

He threw himself back into his chair. "The tide will turn."

"Only if you are prepared to make waves."

He put his head in his hands, sat there motionless as a statue for a long time. "I am relieved you have come," he said finally.

"I would never let you down, you know that. I only wish you would take my counsel as readily as you take my gold."

"I will repay you," he said, but his eyes were hard and angry. A kindness is never forgiven, Mardian had told her once. All men resent a debt, whether it is money or favor. But this was her Antony, and a kindness to Antony was a kindness to herself. She had to get him back on his feet somehow. And point that famous sword arm in another direction, before he had it cut off.

90

THEY LAY IN his tent, listening to the waves crashing on the breakwater, the creaking of the oil lamp as it swayed on the cross beam, the moan of the wind, the whipping of the canvas. The cries of wounded and dying men carried to them on the night.

The camp bed was hard and narrow, their bodies sticky from sweat and the residue of their lovemaking. He had taken her with a fierce and urgent need, something to be endured rather than enjoyed. Afterward he clung to her with a desperation she had never known in him before.

"I have some good news, at least," she whispered.

"I long to hear it."

"You have a new son."

He raised himself on one elbow and his face split into a broad grin. "A son? Is it true?"

"He is plump and healthy. I have called him Philadelphus."

He laughed and hugged her. She was moved that the birth of another child should still touch him so. He had enough children to garrison a small town, by all accounts, not all of them by his wives. But then, a son by Cleopatra was not just a child; it was further promise of a dynasty.

"It is not over," she whispered, stroking his hair. "You have Cleopatra. You have our children. You have Alexandria as your capital and all the wealth of the East behind you. You can build a new and better army. I already have the greatest navy ever seen in the world." His head lay on her breast, and she kissed him tenderly on the forehead. "But you must forget Parthia."

"I could have won," he whispered. "If it was not for Armenia, I would have won."

"I will take your soldiers back to Egypt. You can rebuild and reequip your legions there. You must send Quintus Dellius to Rome and announce a great victory, tell your Senate that you have returned from Parthia with hordes of treasure and you are preparing to invade again. Who will know the truth? Look at Caesar. The whole world thinks he conquered Britain. He confided to me that he got shipwrecked there and fought off a few Celts who tried to raid his tents."

"I will yet ride my horse through Babylon," he said. He seemed not to have heard her.

"Forget Babylon! Parthia is too big, it is too far from the world. Your real enemy is in Rome!"

She wrapped her arms and legs around him, enveloping him in her embrace. She could smell the warm, male scent of him. She had missed that. She was a queen, but she was also a woman. She had not wanted to admit it to herself, but his charm had worked as well on her as it had on any of the slave girls in her palace.

Yet she knew she must not allow her feelings for this man to blind her to what she must do. Julius could not safeguard the future for her or her son, and neither could Antony. So now she, Cleopatra, must seize the day.

"We are over the worst," Antony announced at the morning conference. He and the officers of his general staff gathered around a trestle table, staring at the charts and maps laid out in front of them. "We will regain our strength and then we will take our revenge on Armenia. Then we will begin again our planning for the conquest of Parthia."

The generals looked at each other. None of them had an appetite to go back across those mountains.

"Forty thousand veterans are not easy to replace," Canidius said mildly.

"Octavian still owes me four legions from our agreement at Tarentum."

Ahenobarbus spat on the ground. "You have no hope of getting them from that twister."

"We'll see. Besides, we don't need Octavian. Cleopatra has offered us her full support."

More shuffling silence. "Exactly how much money did she bring?" Ahenobarbus asked.

"She braved the winter storms to come here. She deserves our gratitude."

"She just wants you in her power."

A deadly silence. Antony glared at him.

"Let us take what she offers and extend her our friendship in return," Dellius said, his voice more reasonable. "But let us regroup in Rome, not Alexandria. For this campaign we will need good Roman soldiers, and we will not get them in Egypt."

"You forget," Antony told him. "She is my queen."

"And a useful political alliance it is," Plancus said. By all the gods, even that little toady wanted his say now. "But first of all you are a Triumvir and a Roman."

"What do you think, Canidius?" Antony growled.

The long, mournful face creased into an even deeper frown. "There is no doubt that we need her help right now. But you should not ally yourself too closely with this woman. As things have turned out, you must attend to Rome, or you will leave yourself in an impossible position."

"Because I sleep with Egypt?"

They were silent.

"Rome does not care what their generals do with their nights. A little scandal is good for a man. Look at Caesar. Besides, we have no choice. There are no armies without money, and Cleopatra is my banker. And it never pays, gentlemen, to upset your banker."

"You charter dangerous waters, my lord," Dellius said.

"We all charter dangerous waters. It is the nature of leadership. No, I have made up my mind. We go to Alexandria!" He slammed his fist on the table and walked out.

91

THEY WAITED ON the weather before they started shipping Antony's army to Alexandria, the wounded and the sick, the ragged remains of the greatest army ever seen. It went on over weeks, Antony supervising from his tent on the beach.

One day another ship, a Roman Liburnian, appeared in the harbor. Dellius ran up the beach and announced, breathlessly, that there was a messenger come for Antony from Greece.

The courier had been sent by Octavia. His wife was in Athens. She had arrived there with seventy ships, food and supplies for his army, and accompanied by two thousand of Rome's best soldiers, handpicked from Octavian's personal bodyguard. They were now at his command.

Octavia herself awaited his instructions.

⚜ ⚜

This man. It was impossible to keep the bitterness out of her voice. Surely he would not betray her twice?

"Noble Antonius. You are indeed blessed among men. One defeat and the sea is massed with all your wives, their ships colliding with each other, loaded to the gunnels with soldiers and food for you."

Antony allowed her a tight smile. Oh, he hasn't decided yet, she thought. His word is his bond among men, but when it comes to women he is blown about like a leaf in the wind. I risked the winter storms and the approbation of half of Egypt to come here, and now that he has eaten my food and used my ships and hoarded my gold, he is leaving himself open for offers.

"Two thousand men," he muttered. "That little bastard owes me twenty thousand! He signed the treaty. My ships for four legions."

"If you had the four legions, you would go to her, wouldn't you? He plays you like a flute."

"Of course not. I would not entertain such an idea."

I would like to believe you, she thought. What sort of woman is this Octavia? Her husband marries another woman, has coins minted with his likeness alongside hers, yet still she braves the ocean in winter, chasing after him. Was she milk and water, as they said? Octavian's hand was behind this.

"I am not going to Athens," he repeated.

"You give me your word?"

He was silent for a long time. "Two thousand men!" he murmured.

"I must know what you intend! Come to Alexandria and I will make you master of the East. Or go back to Athens and be the Triumvir's brother-in-law."

She waited for his answer. He hesitated.

"Don't do this to me," she whispered.

"You have to trust me," he said, and enveloped her in those massive arms. Oh, I'm so weak, she thought. I just can't think straight anymore. This is just politics. Why, then, does it hurt so much?

CITY OF ATHENS

Quintus Dellius was ushered through the great villa into the Lady Octavia's presence. As he waited for her chamberlain to announce him, he looked around. He noticed that the mosaic beneath his feet depicted the god Dionysus, holding a thyrsus rod wrapped with ivy. There was a naked maenad at the god's feet, and vines and grape leaves entwined around Doric columns in the background. An unfortunate allusion, Dellius thought.

There was a mural on the wall, painted in deep blues and greens: Aphrodite, mistress of the sea, her sea nymphs darting in and out of the waves around a three-masted galley. The goddess was cool and fair, her eyes like blue chips of ice. She more closely resembled the woman who now received him in the golden chair with its clawed feet, than her rival, Cleopatra. Yet it was the Queen of the Orient who they said was the incarnation of the goddess of love.

"So, Quintus Dellius. You have news of my husband?"

"The noble Antonius sends greetings to the Lady Octavia."

"He is well?"

"The campaign in Parthia was . . ." He searched for the right word. "Rigorous. He is tired but otherwise in good health."

"We received news in Rome that he won many victories there."

Well, if you call a successful rearguard action a victory, if there is glory in somehow extricating yourself from certain annihilation, then we are covered in laurel wreaths. "It was only the weather that drove us back." That much at least was true. If not for the certainty of winter, Antony might still have us sitting outside the city of Phraaspa, dying by degrees and waiting for siege engines that would never come.

"I await my lord's instructions," Octavia said. "I have brought with me from Rome cattle to feed his army, as well as clothes for his soldiers and reinforcements from the Palace Guard."

"My lord is grateful to you for that. But he wonders also why your brother has not sent him the four legions he promised him at Tarentum."

A moment's hesitation. What was that expression on her lovely face? Was it shame? "Octavian campaigns in Illyria. He needs the soldiers there."

"Four legions from the forty-five legions he has at his command seems not too much to ask."

"That may be true, I do not understand military matters. But I know my brother means my husband no ill will. My presence here is proof of that."

Your presence here is proof of the opposite, Dellius thought. A clever little bastard, your brother. We shall all have to watch our step.

"But you have not answered my question," Octavia said. "Do you have instructions from my husband on how I should proceed?"

Dellius took a breath. "My lord is most concerned for you, to be abroad without suitable protection. It is his wish that you return to Rome immediately, where you will be safe."

The blood drained from her face, and for a moment he thought she might faint away. She turned to the harbor, composing herself. Her fleet rode at anchor there. Among the flotilla was the Liburnian that had brought Dellius from Syria.

"I am hardly without protection. I have two thousand of my brother's best soldiers."

"They are my lord's instructions."

She nodded. Pointless to argue with the messenger. "I shall return as he asks, if that is his will." Dellius watched fascinated as a single tear tracked down her cheek and fell on the collar of her pale blue *stola*. Yet her face remained as still as marble. "I shall leave the soldiers and the stores for him here in Athens, to do with as he wills. Thank you, Quintus Dellius."

He bowed and left, his commission fulfilled. He spared her a parting glance and felt for a moment unutterably sad for her. Octavian for a brother and Antony for a husband. It was hardly reward commensurate with such beauty.

PART V

Festina lente—hasten slowly.

OCTAVIAN

92

ALEXANDRIA-BY-EGYPT

THE MUSEION WAS so named after the nine muses of creative thought. The great Library was part of the same building, and was said to be the largest in the world. The collection had been commissioned by Ptolemy II, and now comprised a massive inventory of *voluminas,* each wrapped around a dowel and arranged on shelves, or in pigeonholes, a wooden name tag dangling from the nob of each scroll to identify it. There were halls upon halls of them, each containing hundreds of shelves and hundreds of thousands of books.

It was like a cave, the vaulted, dusty rooms each connected one to another. Yellow sunlight filtered through high windows that were cut into the walls just beneath the ceilings.

This morning Canidius and Ahenobarbus strode through the galleries, ignoring the collections, searching each room in turn for their Imperator. At last they found him, hunched over a marble bench, reading an opened scroll, his brow deeply furrowed in concentration. There was an old Jew in mantle and hood on one side of him, an Arab in a voluminous robe on the other.

"Marcus," Ahenobarbus growled.

Antony did not answer.

"What are you doing in here?" Canidius asked. It was unhealthy for a man to spend too much time in libraries. He should be in the Gymnasium or out at the Hippodrome, practicing his skills on a horse, not breathing in dust and living in shadows.

"There is all manner of philosophy here," Antony said. "Plato, Socrates, the Stoics, the Cynics, they are all here. So that a man might explain himself to himself. Or to his gods." He closed the scroll and replaced it in one of the pigeonholes behind him. He put an arm around both their shoulders and began to walk them back through the cavernous halls.

"Why the long faces?"

"When are we away from here?" Ahenobarbus demanded.

"You do not like Alexandria?"

"I do not like to be so idle when there is so much to be done. Your wife is doing you great injury in Rome."

"My wife? Cleopatra?"

"Octavia," Ahenobarbus snapped, without humor.

"What has she done now?"

"She behaves impeccably."

"What a bitch."

The irony was lost on the old bugger. Trouble with these old republicans. No sense of humor. "She is ruining your reputation," Ahenobarbus insisted.

"By being blameless?"

"When you are so much to blame," Canidius said.

"You still have friends in Rome," Ahenobarbus said. "But every day you remain here you lose some of that support to Octavian. And look how you have treated his sister. Do you know she still entertains your friends and supporters at your home? She devotes herself to your children. All Rome sees her being faithful to a faithless man. She is hurting you now with her displays of devotion more surely than bitterness ever could."

"We must go back to Rome," Canidius said. "You must talk to those who still love you, and then you must either divorce Octavia or make your peace with her. But this way Octavian confounds you utterly."

Antony's high spirits of a moment before had vanished, like a vapor. He frowned. "I will think about this," he said. He pushed them away and walked off, his head down.

〜 〜

At night the corridors of the palace whispered with the thunder of the waves on the reef, the air redolent with the salt smell of the sea. Occasionally a sleeper might be aware of the rasp of a sandaled foot outside their door, a slave on his way to or from the kitchen, the Sergeant of the Guards on his hourly inspection.

Otherwise, there was just the muted rhythms of the Mediterranean.

Antony lay beside her in the bed. She could feel the gentle rise and fall of the great barrel chest. He had regained the look of the old Antony since returning to Alexandria; good food and good wine had put the flesh back on his bones. Not that it was the same Bacchic atmosphere as his last visit to her city. There was no Company of Life this time, no all-night revels at Canopus or on Lake Mareotis. The god no longer thought himself immortal.

She thought he was asleep. But he suddenly murmured: "Aheno-barbus wants me to go back to Rome."

That long-faced old puritan. She had no intention of allowing Antony out of her sight ever again. "And what did you say to him?"

"I said I would think on it. He thinks that my friends there—"

She pushed him away and sat upright in the bed, her body rigid with fury. She could not believe she was hearing this. "You have no friends in Rome. Your friends are here."

He rolled toward her in the darkness. "If I can get back to Rome, perhaps a few bribes here and there—"

"You went back to Rome once before and you betrayed me utterly!"

He stumbled out of bed, and she heard him go into the adjoining room, wake up a slave, and demand a pitcher of wine. After a while she put on a robe and followed him. She found him sprawled on a divan. A Syrian slave boy was pouring him a goblet of wine from a mixing bowl.

Antony looked up. "Everyone wants something of me," he said.

"Perhaps that is because you seem content to do nothing."

"It was impatience that cost me Parthia," he snapped, making his point.

"You should never have gone there in the first place."

"Parthia is my destiny!"

And that was it, she thought, that was the trouble. Caesar's dream was Parthia, so Antony had assumed it for himself, a faithful lieutenant to the last.

Caesar's ghost was in this room, even now. He had sat on that same couch, not naked and half drunk like Antony, but in his battle armor, that familiar look on his face, as if the whole world was an endless source of amusement to him. That was where he had taken her that night Apollodorus had brought her here in the carpet.

If only Julius were here now. He would know what to do.

"Will you not listen to me?" she asked.

"I have had advice to last me ten lifetimes," Antony said.

She went back to bed. Why would he not see? Greatness lay within his grasp while he reached for fruit he could never have.

Antony stayed where he was, talking to the wine bottle until almost dawn, haunted and harried, and sometime before morning the slaves carried him back to his own quarters to sleep it off.

93

CITY OF ANTIOCH

Little Cleopatra Selene flopped across Antony's arms like a wounded soldier, dribble rolling from the side of her cheek and down his arm. Alexander had hold of his ears and was trying to pull him backward across the floor. Antony let out a bellow, caught him by the arms, and rolled him over his shoulder. Both the children were shrieking with laughter.

Cleopatra watched him for a long time as he rolled about on the panther skin with them. She felt an unexpected surge of tenderness for him. She was reluctant to break the moment, but her news could wait no longer. She clapped her hands and walked into the room. "Children! I need to talk to your father."

Alexander and Selene both fell quiet, looking around at her with . . . What? Disappointment, that was it. A good mother, she thought, but not fun. Not like Antony.

He looked up at her expectantly. "News of Rome?" he asked.

A part of her did not want to do this, but she supposed, in the circumstances, there was a certain pleasure in it. News of Antony's conquest of Armenia had reached Rome. What would she have done if they had voted him a Triumph? But with Octavian holding the reins, there had been little chance of that.

"Your victory has been announced in the Senate. Armenia has been accepted as province of Rome."

"And?"

"That is all."

"No Triumph?"

"No Triumph."

Selene was rolling about on his lap, trying to put one of her bare toes in his mouth, while dribbling on his bare shin. He picked her up gently and set her aside. Then he untangled Alexander's arms from around his neck and stood up. He signaled to the slaves to take them outside and see to their amusement.

The children went, if reluctantly, sensing their father's mood.

"No Triumph?" he repeated, as if he could scarce believe it. "Did they order no feasts, no procession to celebrate my victory?"

Victory! A looting expedition, more like. Yet she understood how this news must hurt him. Ventidius, his general, had only recently celebrated a Triumph for his successful campaigns in Syria. Even Sosius had been awarded a Triumph for recapturing Jerusalem. His generals had their glories, but for Antony there was nothing. As if Rome had forgotten him. As if they no longer regarded him as one of their own.

"But I have earned it!" he shouted.

He turned away from her, picked up an amphorae of the finest Caecuban, and hurled it at the wall. The jar exploded with a crash, the red wine leaking down the wall like blood.

"I have *earned* it!"

It was all he wanted; he ached for the mob to sing his name as they had shouted Caesar's, to ride in the garlanded chariot, as Caesar had, to have the prisoners of war and the treasure carts precede him through the packed Forum, hear the acclamation of the meat sellers and the carpet salesmen and the tinkerers and bread makers and the rest of the mob.

"You shall have your Triumph," she said to him.

"How?"

"If they will not give you your due in Rome, I will give it to you in Alexandria."

He stared at her as if she had spoken a foreign word. "Here?"

"Why not?"

"A Triumph may only be celebrated in Rome."

"A Roman Triumph perhaps. This will be an *Alexandrian* Triumph."

He seemed to think about it for a very long time. She watched the play of emotions on his face. She could see him thinking: *Why not?* It would be a revenge of sorts. Antony showing all Rome that he could not be ignored or humiliated.

"Octavian will never give you what is yours," she whispered. "Just as he never gave you the legions of soldiers he promised you. He only gave you his sister so that she could spy on you and cripple you. . . ."

"Spy?"

"Did you not realize?"

"You think he gave her to me as his spy?"

"It was never an alliance. He never intended for it to be." Poor Antony. A great general, a great leader of men. But not *mean* enough to be a politician. "You must stop being Triumvir. It is time for you to be the real Autocrator of the East."

Suddenly there was a look in his eyes that she had never seen before. Perhaps finally he really believed he could do it. "I have earned my Triumph," he murmured. "I have *earned* it."

94

ALL THIS FOREIGNNESS is no good, Ahenobarbus thought. These mother-of-pearl screens, these brocaded cushions and gilded ebony footstools, these pillowed couches and alabaster oil lamps, these beaded curtains. We are Romans. This Oriental luxury will eat away at our souls, like rust on a sword.

"Here comes His Highness now," he growled to Canidius. Swanning into the room, with Cleopatra and her nancy boys and pretty little Syrian catamites in tow, the hairdressers and the nail parers and the navel lint removers, a court like a traveling theater. And Antony, at the head of them, in his Syrian gown and silk-embroidered sandals, rings on his fingers like a court procurer instead of a Roman magistrate. Someone has to talk some sense to this man.

"I have heard," Munatius Plancus whispered, "that he plans to celebrate a Triumph in Alexandria."

"He plans to do what?" Ahenobarbus spluttered.

Plancus was pleased to be first with the gossip. He preened himself as he repeated what he had heard. "There is to be a Triumph when we return to Alexandria. For our victory in the war against Armenia."

"It was not a war. We marched in, we looted the place, we marched out again."

"We came, we saw, we took," Canidius muttered, borrowing from Caesar's long-ago acclamation, his long, lantern face making the bitter aside almost funny.

"He cannot celebrate a Triumph outside Rome!"

Plancus shrugged. "That is what they are saying."

Ahenobarbus shook his head. Madness. Complete madness.

95

ALEXANDRIA-BY-EGYPT

A BLEAK DAY, with gray clouds scudding over the rooftops. The critical judgment of the gods. Despite the weather, the whole city had come out to see this, 700,000 people battling for a better vantage point; Jewish merchants and traders packed under the colonnades of the Gymnasium and the law courts; Greek scholars and students crammed at the windows of the Museion; bare-skinned Egyptians in leather kilts shinning the date palms that lined the road, or perched on the limestone walls that surrounded the palace; others had clambered on the roofs of the temples or clung to statues, and crowds a score deep lined the broad marble streets.

Antony set out from the palace in the early morning, his procession skirting the great harbor and the Temple of Neptune, trooping past the palace and the trimmed gardens of the Regia, then out along the broad white Canopus Way past the hill of Pan. From there the pageant was to turn south toward the Soma and end at the great Temple of Serapis.

Cleopatra awaited his arrival on a ceremonial dais of beaten silver that had been erected on the steps of the Serapion. Antony came accompanied by the same roar that had followed Caesar that day in the Forum, the acclamation of a hundred thousand voices, a wave of sound that followed his progress down the Street of the Soma.

Today, she thought, he has the triumph he has always wanted, has always dreamed of. He was king. And she, in the eyes of all Alexandria, was not only Queen of Egypt, but mistress elect of Rome.

It was the moment she had always dreamed of, though not as complete a victory as she had planned. The shadow of Octavian hung over them still. But she had a Roman marching through her streets, not as overlord, but as her ally and her consort. She had raised Egypt from the ignominy her father and his ancestors had brought them to, and her sons and her daughter now had a future—not to compete with each other for one throne, as she had been forced to do, but each as heirs to the world in their own right.

Antony's Triumph was her own.

⚜ ⚜

She was dressed as Isis, the queen of all worlds, and seated on a throne of beaten gold. She wore a silver-threaded gown, a prominent knot between the breasts, the emblem of the goddess. On her head was the *uraeus,* and a diadem bearing the silver moon and the two feathers of justice. The fingers of her right hand had been stained red with henna; her right hand held the ankh, the symbol of divine life, while in her left she had a lotus-tipped scepter.

Directly below her on the dais was Caesarion, nine years old now, but dressed as a Roman, in tunic and heavy woolen *toga virilis,* intricately draped over his thin frame.

Below him were three smaller thrones for the other children. Alexander Helios was dressed as the Persian king he would one day become, with baggy trousers, a flowing cloak over a sleeved tunic, and a white turban decorated with a tiara and peacock feather. Beside him was Cleopatra Selene in a silver gown that reached her ankles, surrounded by ceremonial Greek guards with silver shields. Finally there was little Philadelphus, wearing the purple of a Macedonian king, the *kausia,* the royal diadem, a chlamys, and tiny felt boots on his feet, the *krepides.* He turned and looked up at her, his lower lip quivering. He was only two years old and was quite overwhelmed by the occasion. She gave him a reassuring smile.

Below them were the guests of honor, the client kings that had come to show their loyalty to their Roman overlord; kings and satraps and princes from Cappadocia and Pontus, Galatia and Paphlagonia, from Thrace, Mauretania, Judaea, Commagene. Once they had been provinces of Rome. Now they owed their fealty to Antony and Cleopatra.

And all of Alexandria was here to see it.

∾ ❦ ❦ ∾

The legions marched ahead, their heavy, nail-studded boots resounding on the cobbled street, followed by Gallic cavalry, Egyptian levies, mounted bowmen from Medea, light cavalry from Pontus. Every nation of the empire was represented here. Her empire now, not Rome's.

There was a long train of wretched Armenian prisoners, soldiers and slaves, then a lumbering caravan of wagons, creaking with the treasure Antony had looted from the king's palace in Artaxata. Finally, covered in dust and wretched in his misery, King Artavasdes himself, dragging his chains behind him.

Antony had his revenge for Parthia, she thought. Well, perhaps. Would this one man's pain ever be enough for the catastrophe he had suffered in the Medean mountains? But what was done, was done. From today they must forget that wretched history. They must think only of the future they would build.

Finally there was Antony.

He made his dramatic entrance into the square on a golden chariot drawn by four white horses. Instead of the purple general's cloak and laurel wreath that Caesar had worn for his Triumphs, Antony had on the robes of Dionysus and an ivy crown, his golden robe fastened with precious stones. In his hand he held a thyrsus wand. He was not there today as Roman Imperator, but as a god, their god, Osiris reborn, Redeemer and Liberator. The mob shouted and cheered, the din deafening.

Hard to make sense of her emotions at this moment. She had expected exhilaration, but there was only a feeling of uncertainty. She had put her faith in Caesar; she had given her heart to this one. She wished she did not know his flaws so intimately, did not care for him so much.

He stepped from the chariot and started to ascend the steps of the temple. She saw him look up at her and smile. Marcus Antonius, Autocrator of the East, was finally happy.

♈ ♈

The Temple of Serapis reared into the sky. It had been built on the city's only hill, an architectural glory whose pillars seemed to touch the clouds themselves. Inside, the bearded god of the Ptolemies waited, carved in marble and gold, the huge gilt head and jeweled eyes gleaming in triumph from the darkened shrine.

The mobs fell to awed silence as Antony climbed the marble steps. Abruptly, the only sound was the whisper of the wind through the high colonnades and the rattle of a systrum. The temple priests awaited him at the top of the steps, their scarlet robes flapping in the breeze that whipped across the city from the harbor. He reached the portico, dwarfed by the great columns with their papyrus stem chapters. He paused for a moment by the torches on either side of the portal; the flames flared in the updraught. Then he crossed the loggia and stepped inside the shrine to make his personal sacrifice to the god of the city.

He is mine now, she thought. There is no way back to Octavia now.

He was right, he did deserve this. He had been loyal to Rome, even she could see that. A weaker man would not have married Octavia, would have taken everything Alexandria had offered him and turned his arm against Rome. A weaker man would not have saved Octavian from the mob outside the Circus Maximus.

He deserved this, and she felt not a little pride that she had been able to give it to him. Egypt, at least, appreciated greatness enough to honor a man like Antony. It was a political act; it was also a public betrothal. She could not help but feel a certain pride. This was the man she had chosen, and she wanted the world to see.

Today was her gift to him, the axis on which their lives would turn. It was the realization of their dreams.

And so it was that she would think of this day many times in the years to come. How proud we were, and how blind. On that day we were gods, filled with such arrogance that we thought we could command the mountains to part for us. On that day we were convinced we were invincible. Standing on that high pinnacle of Alexandria, we could not imagine the day when the true gods would bring us to our knees. They were only toying with us after all, and seeing us so puffed up as we were then, must have only added to their sport.

❦ ❦

Antony emerged from the temple and stood on the highest step, looking out over the vast and silent crowds. The new Dionysus. Caesar had a slave to whisper in his ear that he was mortal. Not Antony.

"Queen of Egypt," he said, in a voice that rang around the great square. "Daughter of Isis, Pharaoh of Egypt, Friend and Ally of Rome, we present today this most noble prisoner, the wretched Artavasdes, who has been brought here to face punishment for his treachery, forfeiting his soldiers, his family, and his gold."

Antony paused, searching for the words.

"In respect of the conquests we have made in the East, we now make the following dispositions. To Ptolemy Philadelphus, our son, I give the kingdoms of Syria and Cilicia. He shall also have the lands of Pontus, Galatia, and Cappadocia to rule as overlord when he is of age."

She saw the little boy shiver, hearing his name spoken before such a massive gathering and in such circumstance.

Antony went on. "To Princess Cleopatra Selene, we give Cyrenaica and Crete, and her brother Alexander Helios we hereby call King of Armenia, and Overlord of Medea and all territories east of the Euphrates as far as India."

There was a gasp, a murmur that spread through the crowd like the ripple of a stone dropping into the still water of a pool.

But Antony started to speak again and the crowd again fell silent. "And to our wife, Cleopatra, Queen of Egypt and Cyprus, let it be known that from this day on she shall be known as Queen of Kings, and her true and legitimate son by Julius Caesar shall be her only heir."

There was stunned silence before the crowd burst into ecstatic cheers. What Antony had done was beyond belief, beyond all expectations. She saw Antony's Romans—Dellius, Plancus, Ahenobarbus, Canidius—all staring at her in stunned disbelief. Her own courtiers were pale with awe. Even Mardian.

I promised them all that I would do this one day. I have made the Potter's Oracle my truth. They all believe I really am Isis now.

And perhaps they are right.

96

THE MORNING AFTER. Reality seeping in, Ahenobarbus thought.

Out on the broad Canopus Way slaves were already at work, gangs of them sweeping the streets clean. Alexandria had never seen such a night. Cleopatra had provided public feasting and drinking for the whole city, and if you said nothing else about them, you had to admit these gypos really knew how to enjoy themselves. Dawn ghosted the sky, and a few of the revelers were still stumbling through the streets, singing as they made their uncertain way back home. Wagons rumbled along the cobbles piled high with broken wine amphorae and food scraps. All over the city dogs and cats were at work, licking at discarded scraps of meat.

Around the Lochias palace slaves had been cleaning up the mess long before dawn, busy with their brooms and mops and brushes. In the gray light of morning the flower garlands and rose petals looked sad and dry. Ministers, courtiers, even certain favored servants lay where they had fallen in the corridors, or under tables, others snoring on the marble steps in the gardens. He recognized an actress from a Dionysian troupe, a lewd Greek girl, naked, her arms and legs entwined around the body of one of his own Roman officers.

The celebrations of Antony's Triumph had even surpassed the bacchanalias of Antony's first visit to Alexandria, or so they said. Well, now the party was over and it was time to pay the piper.

Somehow His Lordship thought he could be the husband of the Queen of Egypt *and* a Roman magistrate. He had started to believe the flattery of his friends and the cries of the mob. But this Triumph was a sham; a Triumph could only be celebrated in Rome, it was an honor granted by the Senate, and Antony's sacrifices should have been presented to Jupiter Maximus, the Roman god, in his temple on the Capitoline, not this hybrid barbarian deity.

As for the ceremony that followed it! How could Antony give away Roman territory to a foreign king and think that all Rome would not think he had gone mad? He had even ceded terrritory not under his dominion. *All lands east of the Euphrates as far as India.* He was referring to Parthia, of course, which was yet to be conquered. Is this what good Roman legionaries were to die for, so that the land they bought with their blood could pass into the hands of some gypo's bastard son?

Antony had to be checked. Somehow they had to get him away from this Oriental witch before any more damage was done.

97

CITY OF ANTIOCH

Egyptian month of Epeiph,
thirty-three years before the birth of Jesus Christ

IT WAS HER old friend Apollodorus, now looking more prosperous than ever, thick rings on his fingers, and perhaps a little more flesh around the middle. Fifteen years since he had rolled her in his carpet, saved her life and her throne. The years had passed so quickly, and she had come so far, achieved so much. Yet sometimes she still felt like a frightened girl, although she was more adept at concealing it.

She received him in her private chamber, Mardian lying on another couch at her side. She did not make the old fellow stand anymore. He had trouble with swelling in the ankles, and he was out of breath if he walked more than a few yards. His skin had an unhealthy gray pallor. She hoped he had no plans to allow Anubis to take him to Judgment just yet. Where would she be without him?

Antony had moved his court to Antioch for the summer, and she had agreed to go with him. It was ostensibly to prepare for another invasion of Parthia, but she suspected he had been persuaded to come here by his Roman friends to limit the influence of Egypt on him. That was all very well. You could alter a man's geography, you could not change his drinking and womanizing. Did they really think that was her fault?

Apollodorus made his obeisances and they exchanged pleasantries. She inquired after his health and his business. Apparently, they were both excellent.

"You are just returned from Rome?" she asked him.

"I left on the birthday of the Divine Julius. I arrived in Alexandria just this morning."

"They still talk about me there?"

"It seems, Majesty, they talk of nothing else."

Where would they be without Cleopatra to fuel their fantasies? "And what sort of things do you hear?"

That crooked smile again. "That you have bewitched our noble Autocrator."

"Bewitched him?"

"With love potions and the like. That Antony is no longer himself and has given himself over entirely to vice. That you engage in orgies every night here in the palace. That Antony has become un-Roman, a degenerate."

"Orgies? If only it were true! I have four children and I have to administer a mountain of papyrus every day. Where do they think I find the energy for all this?"

"The other rumor that seems to have taken the fancy of all in the Forum is that Marcus Antonius now uses a gold chamber pot."

Cleopatra stared at him. A gold chamber pot. Who invented such stories? "My noble lord Antony gave himself over entirely to vice long before I met him. His enthusiasms were not my doing. However, I believe they still fall short of a gold chamber pot."

"This is Octavian's work," Mardian said.

"Indeed, that is how it seems to me," Apollodorus agreed. "He works hard to contrast himself with Antony, or at least, the image he has created of him. In public he is the very picture of Roman piety. Yet I know for a fact, through a friend of mine, that he has an insatiable taste for virgins, who are procured for him by his friend Maecenas, and sometimes even by his wife."

These Romans, she thought. Amazing people. Utter barbarians. It was a wonder they had ever managed to contrive a language, let alone conquer an empire. "Who is this friend of yours?"

"She keeps a brothel near the Circus Maximus. We go back a long way, Majesty."

Cleopatra held up a hand. "I do not care to hear the details."

"Neither do I," Mardian murmured.

"And what do the people think of our son of the Divine Julius?" Cleopatra asked.

"He is still not a popular figure. But the people hate him a little less than they once did. No one calls him Octavian anymore; when the name Caesar is invoked, it is hard to know if they are talking of Julius himself or this nephew of his. He endeavors to make the people love him in many ways."

"Such as?"

"Rome is being reborn in marble. Everywhere there are new temples, basilicas, and amphitheaters. Even a library. It would seem to me they are trying to make their city look a little more like Alexandria."

"Where does he get the money for this?"

"Not from his own purse?" Mardian said.

"Indeed, no. He has persuaded his followers to invest in these projects from their own funds. He gives them promises, they give him money."

"He stole that tactic from Antony," Mardian mumbled, but Cleopatra silenced him with an angry glance.

"Marcus Agrippa has even paid to have the main sewer, the Cloaca Maxima, cleaned out. Rome does not seem like Rome anymore without the stink."

"And all that time I was there I thought it was the Senate," Cleopatra said.

"Octavian has ordered free admission to the baths and the theater," Apollodorus went on, "even to the chariot races. And there is a distribution of free oil lamps to the poor. They are decorated with little silver dolphins, to remind them all of his great naval victory over Sextus at Naulochus."

Mardian snorted with derision. "They say he huddled belowdecks like a girl while the battle was being fought. It was Agrippa who won that day."

Apollodorus gave an eloquent shrug. "That is not what the official history records."

Cleopatra spared a glance at Mardian. "He is clever."

"Indeed," Apollodorus agreed. "He is even building a temple next to his house on the Palatine. To his new patron, Apollo."

"Apollo?" Well, of course. Apollo, the god of order. Many upper-class Romans were suspicious of the Dionysians with their theaters and music and drinking. It represented a breaking down of order. The message was clear. And in the legends it was Apollo who murdered Dionysus.

"Does *anyone* in Rome speak well of my lord Antony?" she asked.

Apollodorus seemed unusually reticent. "Since the Donations, they are harder to find. . . ."

"The what?"

"That is what they call them in Rome. The Donations of Alexandria. The declarations that Antony made after his Triumph."

There was a heavy silence. Finally Mardian said: "Perhaps our Roman *should* go there. The tide turns against him."

Cleopatra gave him a cold stare. "When the Autocrator goes to Rome, he will go with his queen, Cleopatra, at his side or he will not go at all."

Both men kept their silence. You did not argue with the queen in this mood.

"Thank you, Apollodorus," she said.

He took his leave, leaving his brother-in-law to face the music. He wondered if he had truly conveyed to her the hysterical atmosphere he had found in Rome this time. They were obsessed with Marcus Antonius and his adventures in Egypt. Any lie was swallowed as truth. Until you had been there yourself, you could not comprehend it. In his opinion, the Romans had gone mad with fear.

❧ ❧

"A degenerate!" Antony laughed when she told him what her spy had said. "Un-Roman? That's rich, coming from a kid who hawked his peachy little bottom around Caesar's bathhouse crowd. They say he sold himself to Aulus Hirtius for 300,000 sesterces."

Cleopatra had not heard that particular calumny before. She wondered if Antony had made it up.

"And what about his *wife*? She was married to another man when he met her, and pregnant into the bargain! And he calls *me* degenerate!" It was clear that Antony was not sure if he should be outraged or amused.

"He means to destroy you," she said.

"You know he has procurers who go out to get women for him off the streets? His wife encourages it. I suppose it takes the pressure off her. Then she doesn't have to sleep with him. Have you seen his teeth? They have more barnacles growing on them than a mud crab."

She let him rant, while she stood at the window, looking down the river Orontes toward the plain. Sunlight shimmered on the water like liquid mercury. Another summer almost gone, a summer Antony had spent painstakingly garnering another army from among his consort princes, planning for another attack on Parthia. All the while, it seemed to her, the real struggle was taking place in Rome.

"You have to do something about this," she said.

Antony shook his head, a grin on his face. "It's really rich, you know. Did you know his father was a money changer? His mother ran a perfume shop."

"He means to destroy you," she repeated. "Young Octavian is a man now. He has grown accustomed to power and he knows how to use it."

And you, she thought. You are no longer a young man, you are almost the same age as Caesar when I first met him that night in Alexandria. "Take this army you have to Italy, not Parthia."

He became suddenly serious. "I have no legal reason to go against Octavian."

"Then invent one." These Romans and their laws! "Listen to me! If you do not destroy Octavian, he will destroy you! That's all there is to it. Rome cannot have two masters, as a woman cannot have two husbands. There is no Triumvirate in his mind. He got rid of Lepidus as soon as he could, now he plans to be rid of you."

Antony laughed. "That kid?"

The laughter died in his throat. He turned away and his face took on a haunted look. She thought perhaps she had finally got through to him. Would he finally do what had to be done?

"Will you do it?"

He scratched his head. "I should never have left the siege engines behind," he said. "Next time, with Medea on our side, it will be different."

It was no good. He was obsessed with the East. Or rather, it was easier than facing the West, confronting Octavian. In the end, she realized, he was too much the Roman. He might be faithless with women, yet in many ways he was the most loyal man who had ever lived. She might have loved him the more for it, if she did not fear that his fidelity to Rome would bring disaster on all their heads.

98

ALEXANDRIA-BY-EGYPT

FROM THE WINDOWS of the Lochias palace she could see her new fleet riding at anchor in the great harbor. There were scores of biremes and triremes, heavily timbered ships with two or three banks of oars and equipped with fighting castles and grapnels. There were perhaps the same numbers of Liburnians, just a single bank of oars but faster and more maneuverable than the bigger warships. But she had also built ships with five or even six banks of oars, veritable floating fortresses with bronze rams at the bow as large as elephants. Her own flagship was a six; she had named it the *Isis*.

Following Agrippa's lead, she had recruited professional oarsmen to man her new fleet. It was cheaper and more effective than using slaves. Oarsmen were skilled and were paid as they were needed, while a slave had to be supported for a lifetime and was unreliable in battle.

It was the treaty she had wrung from Antioch that had made this new navy possible, for its construction had been financed from the profits of the balsam groves she had assumed when Antony ceded her parts of Judaea. The oars for the massive "sixes" had been fashioned from the great cypresses and cedars in her new fief of Lebanon.

This was the fleet she had used to strike her bargain with Antony. Her price for placing this massive force at his disposal had been the so-called Donations. It meant that Antony now had a navy to match Agrippa's fleet of great ships. He was more than a match for Octavian on land; now he was Agrippa's equal by sea.

She turned from the window. Mardian was watching her. "Soon we will be ready," she said. "We can provide our lord Antony with the finest fleet in the world."

"It is a terrible risk."

"Everything I have ever done has been at great risk. But as you see, I have weathered all my disasters and I am still here. What is that face for?"

"Majesty, you would not wish to hear my thoughts."

"Marcus Antonius," she said.

He shrugged eloquently.

She knew what he was thinking, and he was right, of course. Her enemy was Rome, as it had been from the first, and she could only fight Rome through Marc Antony. By giving him her fleet, she would place her trust in a man who had proved himself utterly unreliable as far as her interests were concerned.

"He has sent his friend Domitius Ahenobarbus to Rome. He did not tell you?"

She shook her head. Of course not. Why would he tell her about something so important?

"It seems our noble lord has changed his mind again. He still hopes to avoid a conflict."

"Let us hope he does not succeed," she said mildly, but her hands clenched into fists at her side. Her husband's faithlessness was remarkable and, apparently, boundless. But there was nothing she could do about it.

She turned back to Mardian. "Ahenobarbus will get nowhere with Octavian. Meanwhile the Queen of the Sea is going to break the Romans. You will see."

CITY OF ROME

Rome, freezing its way through another winter.

There was ice in the fountains, slicks of freezing mud in the streets. When you walked among the *insulae* on the Aventine, it was so dark on these gray and freezing afternoons you could barely see your hand in front of your face and you did not know what muck you were stepping in. A bucket of slops tossed from a window high above landed in the street a few feet away and sloshed on his boots. A wagon crunched through the narrow lane, fir tree trunks piled on the back, pressing him against the wall and splashing more unspeakable filth up his legs.

By all the gods, I love Rome. But even I have to admit it is grim after Alexandria.

Ahenobarbus found a *taberna,* sat there among the launderers and the carters and the ironmongers eating hot pies filled with gristle and listening to the talk: how Caesar—for that was what they called him now—was doing so much for Rome, while Marcus Antonius lived a life of ease in the East surrounded by eunuchs and pretty boys, sprawling on gold-encrusted couches and shitting in gold chamber pots. How the Egyptian queen had turned his head with love potions and orgies.

It made his blood boil. Not least because some of it was true.

There were statues of Caesar everywhere now, and the people in the streets talked about him as if he were still alive. In the Temple of the Divine Julius, in the New Forum, there was a statue of him wearing the star of godhead. People brought offerings of fruit and flowers, even prayed to him.

You old bastard, he thought. Octavian's doing, all of this. Truth be told, your nephew hated your guts, still does. But now he has people praying to you and calling you a god. You were just another greedy, ambitious silvertail with a head for tactics. The only thing supernatural about you was how many women you got to climb into your bed, you bald-headed murderer.

Octavian's hand was wherever you looked. There were drinking vessels for sale everywhere bearing a depiction of the Omphale fable. Omphale was the legendary queen who had kept the great Hercules in bondage for three years, wearing the hero's helmets and lion skins and carrying his club over her shoulder while he walked beside her chariot, dressed in a woman's gown and holding a parasol.

The popularity of the caricature, of a man gone soft and enslaved by a woman, was made doubly pointed because Antony had so often characterized himself as the New Hercules.

When Ahenobarbus left the *taberna,* a street hawker followed him, pestering him to buy one, and he told him to jump in a barrel of rancid oil. The man persisted until finally he rounded on him, hurled the proferred cup against the wall, and threw the man bodily into a drain.

Omphale. Cleopatra. Women. Antony's weakness. Who would have thought it could have been turned against him in such a way?

🌾 🌾

Ahenobarbus rose to give his address. He rearranged the toga about his shoulders and looked around the chamber at the hundreds of somber and well-fed faces. He was disappointed to note the disproportionate number of men with trousers and long hair. Gauls, by all the gods. That had been Caesar's doing.

"Conscript Fathers," he began. "No doubt you have heard many reports of the activities of our Triumvir, Marcus Antonius, in the East. I am here today to make a report on those activities, to allay any suggestions that he has acted outside the law in any way. He has been, and always will be, a great Roman. . . ."

He proceeded to outline his case from the beginning. How Antony had won the great battle at Philippi, while Octavian had lain bedridden in his tent.

How the Triumvirate had been ratified for five years.

How Octavian had illegally gained control of Antony's legions in Gaul during that time, and only Antony's forbearance had saved Rome from yet another civil war.

How Antony had signed the Treaty of Tarentum, and given Octavian four squadrons of ships to fight the pirate king, Sextus Pompey, and how Octavian had promised, in return, four legions, which he had never delivered.

How Antony had undertaken the conquest of Parthia, for the glory of Rome, without any support from Octavian, and how this support was quite properly garnered from Egypt, a friend and ally of the Roman people.

How during this campaign Armenia was added to the list of Roman possessions, a fact not commemorated by this Senate.

As for the so-called Donations, they were merely a rearrangement of the powers of his client kings. He, as Roman magistrate, was still supreme governor of those lands, under the powers given him in the original treaty of Brundisium.

Antony, he said, was a great and noble Roman who had remained loyal to the treaties signed by him, but Octavian had attempted to undercut the Triumvirate at every turn. Octavian was solely responsible for the critical state of affairs in which Rome now found itself. Should there be another civil war, he said, the responsibility for it would be at the feet of Octavian, and Octavian alone. The Conscript Fathers of the Senate, he said, had no option in the circumstances but to vote the Young Caesar an enemy of the people.

When he sat down there was utter silence in the chamber.

❦ ❦

Octavian slowly rose to his feet.

"I have listened to the fine words of our friend Ahenobarbus," he said, "and I am filled with admiration at how he has presented the facts in such a favorable light for the noble Antonius."

There were sniggers from his stooges in the audience.

"I see that he has decided to hide the hand of the Queen of Egypt in these matters. Are not the real facts of the matter that he has been utterly seduced by this woman, and all his actions of late are to further her aims, and not Rome's?"

Ahenobarbus felt his face flush hot. He had warned Antony this would happen! His infatuation with this queen had undermined all his supporters' efforts here in Rome.

"Let us look first of all at her claim that her son is actually Caesar's. How many children did my noble father have? He fathered a daughter, Julia, but this was thirty years before he met the Queen of Egypt. Since that time he had three wives, Cornelia, Pompeia, and Calpurnia, and none of them gave him children. But after just one dalliance with his *pelegrina,* she produces a son. A miracle, and a very convenient one for Egypt."

More laughter from the stooges.

"And what of his behavior in the East? He has recently celebrated a Triumph in Egypt's capital, insulting Rome and the Roman people. We all know that a Triumph can only be granted by the Conscript Fathers of this Senate, and is celebrated not as a personal honor, as our noble Antonius chose it to be, but as a proclamation of the greatness of our city and our Republic. To arrogate to oneself a Triumph is unforgivable by men and punishable by the gods."

A murmur of approval around the chamber. In this much, at least, they all agreed with him. Even Ahenobarbus was of a mind on that point.

"It was Cleopatra to whom he dedicated the treasures, and to her gods he made the sacrifices. Are these the actions of a true and noble Roman?"

Octavian was in his stride now.

"Do you wish, Conscript Fathers, to deliver Rome into the hands of Cleopatra? This woman has seduced Antony's body and now rules his mind. What she desires is for Alexandria to replace Rome as the principal city of the empire. Worse even than that, you too will then be ruled by a woman. Is that what you wish, because that is what you will get if our noble Antonius has his way!"

The Senate broke up in disorder, Antony's supporters trying to shout him down while Octavian's supporters rallied and traded insults with them.

Octavian pointed a finger at Ahenobarbus and shouted above the roar in the house. "I will not allow you to desecrate my father's memory. If you try to destroy Rome, your lives are forfeit!"

Bedlam. Ahenobarbus hurried from the chamber. That kid, as Antony called him, might have a weakling's body, but he had the blood and fire of Caesar in him.

99

"HERE COMES THE big lion!" a deep voice said.

Selene giggled from behind the silk hanging. He turned, saw the movement of the drape and the two small feet poking out from beneath its hem.

Antony stamped his feet on the marble tiles as he got closer, heard her giggle again. "Where is my dinner?" he growled.

He stopped next to the drape, drawing out the moment of anticipation. He could hear little Selene draw in her breath. Then he grabbed her through the silk and she shrieked, laughter and terror bubbling up together.

Cleopatra watched, felt a familiar flood of affection for him, as she always did when he was with the children. She wished sometimes she could be more like him, free with the little ones the way he always was. But she had other roles to play in their life, she reminded herself. She watched over their education and was there to instruct them in the things that no one else could teach them; the art of governing, the obligations of their unique position in life. Their responsibilities, in other words.

"Marcus," she said.

She could see the disappointment on both their faces when they saw her. They knew playtime was over.

"Ahenobarbus is back from Rome," she said.

"Ah. I have missed his jokes and his pleasant company," Antony said, straight-faced.

"It is serious."

He let Selene down and told her to run off and find her brother. Cleopatra was afforded another look of reproach from her daughter and then she was gone.

She has to learn, she thought. There will be many such interruptions in her life. She is born a princess, not an urchin playing in the street.

"Well?" Antony said.

"You wanted to obey the laws of Rome, but it seems Octavian does not care for them as much as you."

"What has happened?"

"The day after your Ahenobarbus made his speech in the Senate, Octavian returned to the chamber with his henchmen. They were armed with daggers. There he made threats against your Consul's life. Ahenobarbus and several other of your supporters have had to flee Rome. They arrived here in Alexandria just an hour ago."

He laughed. "I didn't think the kid had it in him."

"No, you didn't. But that's what I've been trying to tell you."

Antony rubbed his face with his hands. He laughed again and then smashed the palm of his hand against one of the marble pillars.

"He's your enemy now," she said.

"It seems you were right," he said, but she could see from his eyes that his heart wasn't in this. He still didn't know where it had all gone so wrong.

100

CITY OF EPHESUS

EPHESUS, ONE OF the great cities of the East, nestled beneath Mount Pion, the teeming mass of the city built around the harbor, the villas of the rich sprawling up the mountain slopes beyond, where the jangle of goat bells drifted on the salt breeze. Riding at anchor below was the greatest fleet that had ever been assembled outside Rome, three hundred merchantmen and five hundred warships, nearly half of them Egyptian. At the heart of this great armada was Cleopatra's flagship, the *Isis,* resplendent with its rich purple sails and gilded stern.

For the first time since the days of Alexander one man alone commanded the entire sea power of the East.

The city had been overwhelmed by this massive fleet and the great army that was to travel with it. The streets thundered to the tramp of boots as armies rolled in from the mountains and plains; from Mauretania, from Cappadocia, from Paphlagonia, Commagene and Galatia, Judaea and Medea. All of these princes owed their thrones to the patronage of the Autocrator, Marcus Antonius, and they knew success was all but assured with an army like this, especially with Egypt's coffers thrown open to him. They came to ensure Antony's continued goodwill, and for a share of the booty.

And to a man they sniffed the blood of Rome in the air.

🙨 🙨

In the great emporium near the docks, the Agora, you could hear a score of languages, see a hundred kinds of uniform. There were Gauls in short leather jerkins, with drooping moustaches and long fair hair curled up on their heads; fearsome Germans with red-blond hair attracting stares everywhere they went; Egyptian oarsmen with huge shoulders, half naked in leather kilts and short white waistcoats; Moors from Mauretania, their bare arms jingling with silver bracelets; Greek archers, Phoenician sailors—some of the finest in the world—Levantine pirates, Bedouin horsemen, wild tribesmen of Medea, half savage at best. All of them were here at Antony and Cleopatra's behest.

Antony had besides these the remains of his Roman legions, as well as 25,000 levies and 12,000 expert horsemen. This was the tide that was gathering to break over Rome and sweep Octavian away.

🙨 🙨

News came that more ships had arrived in the harbor, this time from Rome. On board was half of the Roman Senate. Octavian and his henchmen had delivered an ultimatum to Antony's supporters: *Give your allegiance to me, or get out of Rome.* Three hundred Conscript Fathers had left. The Senate was divided now, its members split between the two factions. Now Antony not only had the military power, he could claim the backing of Roman law.

❦ ❦

Sisyphus, Antony's dwarf, jumped up on the table and started to sing:

"Antony rules in Ephesus
And all in the Eastern lands,
Antony does just what he wants,
If Cleopatra says he can."

They laughed, but not all of them, though Antony laughed loudest of all. He doesn't see how dangerous this game is, Ahenobarbus thought. The joke would be funny, if joke it was. Canidius was there, as well as Dellius, Plancus, and two of the greasers, Bogud from Mauretania and Amyntas. Marcus Antonius seemed to find them good company, but personally, Ahenobarbus didn't trust either of them.

Sisyphus scampered off the table, his stump waggling like a goad. Antony threw him a handful of silver denarii. He snatched them up and scampered over to the wine jug to refill his goblet.

"There is talk," Ahenobarbus said, "that you mean to divorce your wife."

"Cleopatra?"

"Your real wife, your Roman wife."

Antony shrugged good-naturedly. "A man may have many wives in his lifetime. Look at Canidius here. Four wives and still nothing to show for it. Perhaps he's been plowing the wrong furrow."

Canidius's long face creased with embarrassment.

"If you leave Octavia, you will lose what friends you still have in Rome."

"I thought my friends were all here."

"Octavian will make much play of it."

"I only have to fart in Greece and Octavian says I am responsible for the stink in the Aventine."

"Ahenobarbus is right," Dellius said. "Everyone in Rome respects Octavia."

"Then let everyone in Rome marry her. She'll make them stay home at night and keep their noses out of politics."

"She has been courting the Senate on your behalf these five years. A divorce will be seen as a betrayal."

"They never saw it as betrayal when Octavian took my legions in Gaul or when he broke the endless treaties he has made with me!"

"She is a woman," Ahenobarbus growled, "and helpless."

"That has not been my experience of women at all," Antony said. He turned to Munatius Plancus. "What do you think?"

"Of women?"

"Of what these men say about Octavia!"

"I should not test my wisdom against yours."

Antony grimaced. What a greasy little toad. He returned his attention to Ahenobarbus. "There you are."

"You have to send the Egyptian away!" he shouted, his fist bouncing on the heavy cedar table. "Already the other senators are expressing doubts about the wisdom of their actions. They came here expecting to find the Imperator Marcus Antonius in charge of good Roman legions, not this circus of gypos and pansy boys!"

Antony laughed. "Two out of every three of my legionaries are gypos and pansy boys, as you call them. With Octavian denying me fresh recruits from Italy, I have been forced to rebuild my legions with Egyptians and Syrians."

"It is not the foreigners in your army, but who leads them—" Dellius began.

"Our cavalry are all gypos too," Antony went on, "and I have an extra 25,000 pansy boys as levies."

"It is her!" Ahenobarbus shouted. "She is the problem here! She goes with you everywhere as if she is your queen."

"But she is."

"How can a Roman magistrate have a queen?"

"Now we are arguing points of law?"

"We are arguing about what men see and what they perceive! She is a woman and you treat her as your equal! Can you not see the problems you create for yourself?"

Ahenobarbus looked at Canidius for support, but the general could not meet Old Redbeard's eyes. Canidius was inclined to agree with Ahenobarbus, in his heart, but his head told him otherwise.

"We create greater problems if we send her away," Antony went on. "She is paying the cost of maintaining our army as well as her own navy. An army this size, for food and clothing, and to keep our ships supplied . . ." He shrugged. "Twenty thousand talents for the year. A small fortune. More than it cost her father to buy back his throne from Pompey. Can you imagine that sort of money? If it were not for Queen Cleopatra, we would not be here."

"So she is financing you. That does not give her the right to tell you what to do!"

Antony laughed again. "Every woman thinks she has the right to tell you what to do. Even if she is just your wife, let alone Queen of Egypt."

Antony's good humor just infuriated him more. "Her very presence is a goad to every Roman supporter you have."

"She is no different to any of the other client kings who have come here to support our lord Antonius," Canidius pointed out. It seemed Antony's general was being won over by these gypos as well. This soft-headedness was like the plague, Ahenobarbus thought.

"Of course she is different!" he snapped back. "Our lord Antonius has not slept with the other kings who are here."

Antony grinned. "Well, they have not been here that long."

Ahenobarbus's hands opened and closed into fists at his sides. He did not argue with Antony's aims, yet he could not agree with his methods. He shook his head. "I tell you now, this woman puts your whole campaign at risk."

Antony laughed. "Here, you old rascal, have some more wine and don't look so worried. How can we lose?"

But Antony's old rascal was having none of it. He stalked off. Antony shrugged and thrust jasper goblets into the hands of his companions. Canidius stayed. So, too, did Dellius, drinking Antony's wine, laughing all the while at his jokes, but his eyes clouded with doubt, and he felt like a man who has strayed too near the edge of a cliff, waiting for the fall.

Sisyphus sang:

"They called him Octavianus,
Now he's son of a god,
His name's divine

But his bum's all mine,
Said Maecenas—don't you think that's odd?"

101

ANTONY THREW ASIDE the thin blue silk curtains around the bed. He slipped under the coverlet and reached out for her. She let him hold her, but he sensed her lack of response and held back. "What is wrong?" he whispered.

"You want me to trust you, but you don't tell me what's really going on."

That guilty look in his eyes. For a man who had had so many women, he really was a hopeless liar.

"Mardian has told me . . ."

"Your spies have been at work again."

". . . you promised Ahenobarbus that you would restore the Republic. Is that what you plan to do? Conquer Octavian, then become just a Roman citizen once more? Have Rome at your feet and then give it back?"

"Of course not."

"Well, that is what your Romans believe."

He threw himself back on the bed, hands to his head as if he were stricken with some malaise. "I have to tell them something."

"Or is it me who has to be told something? What exactly have you promised your Roman friends, Antony?"

He did not answer her. He tells everyone what they want to hear, she thought. What does he really believe? To which of us is he telling the truth?

"It was my understanding that we were going to Rome to restore Caesarion to his rightful estate. That you would be Master of Rome, and you would then marry me by Roman laws, as you have betrothed yourself to me by mine."

The candle was guttering in the rose-colored glass lantern beside the bed. Its flickering lent him the look of a cornered animal. "That is what I intend to do."

"But it is not what you told Ahenobarbus."

"He would not support me otherwise."

"How can I be sure which of us you are playing false?"

Antony tried to take her in his arms, but she rolled away from him. So like a man. They thought their embraces and kisses solved everything. "Look, I am balanced on a knife edge here," he said.

"And I am not?"

"You have to trust me."

"You have given me precious little cause over the years," she said. I want to trust you, she thought. I want you for my husband and my consort. I want to think you are as bound to me as I am to you. But I am not a wide-eyed girl anymore. Are you going to betray me or are you just wasting my time and my money?

"It is not as simple as you would believe," he said to her.

I know I behave like a shrew, she thought. But what else can I do? My future, my children's future, the future of my country, all now rides with you. "No, it is not simple. It seems you are captain to every man. Your friends talk of democracy and a new Republic, the kings of Galatia and Cappadocia and Syria talk of freedom from the Roman yoke, you whisper to me of restoring Caesarion to his estates. We are all off to war, and none of us knows what it is we are fighting for."

She got out of bed, slipped a robe over her white tunic. Exasperating. This man was as slippery as an eel, his intentions never absolute.

"My dove—"

"I am not a dove! I would *like* to be your dove, but the Queen of Egypt must have claws if she is to remain queen. Or even to live through a single night." She drew a breath. "Divorce Octavia and I will take you at your word. But if you do not, I shall take my fleet and my war chest and return to Alexandria! "

❦ ❦

She walked out of his bedroom and back to her own quarters, calling for Charmion and Iras to come and attend her. Antony was left staring at the door. In the name of Jupiter. Perhaps she meant it.

What am I to do? he wondered. She is right, as usual. I am like one of those jugglers in the square. I juggle with choices, with futures, with possibilities. I must keep them all in the air at once, my Roman friends, my client satraps, Cleopatra herself. My life at the moment is merely to juggle. I please the crowd, I stay alive. If I drop even one, the crowd will turn away from me in disappointment.

She wishes me to choose. But I cannot. And so I juggle, the crowd laughs, I stay alive.

102

CITY OF ATHENS

THEY HAD BEEN housed at the palatial villa of the Roman legate. It had wide corridors tiled with red porphyry and black marble, murals of fauns and cherubs playing among Dionysian arbors, the gardens a riot of apricot and bloodred rosebushes. There was a dark indoor pool in the east wing, the *impluvium,* and niches had been cut into the marble for a collection of statuary, copies of the great masterpieces such as Leichares's Apollo, which Antony immediately had taken down, and Phidias's Dionysus, which he had moved to a place of honor.

The *triclineum* had been converted to a map room. It looked out over a fountain and a grassed courtyard, which was surrounded by a roofed colonnade. With the doors open, the warm breeze brought with it the heady scent of rose trees and afforded a view of the white columns of the Parthenon.

But they were not here today to admire the Acropolis. A chart had been unfolded on a great table in the center of the room, and it was on this that Antony and his generals now focused their attention. Cleopatra was there also, enduring the cold reception from the others.

The force at the disposal of these gentlemen was massive. To command the seas, they had Cleopatra's fleet, as well as

Roman squadrons from Rhodes, Crete, and Cyprus; on land Antony had at his command nineteen legions, with eleven more in reserve in Alexandria, Cyrenaica, and Syria.

"Why do we not invade now?" Canidius was saying. "All Rome is in uproar over the taxes Octavian has imposed, his army is underpaid and unfed, the people are heartily sick of him."

Dellius shook his head. "We cannot invade Italy with Her Majesty Cleopatra in our army. It would be construed as an invasion. All of Italy would rise up against us, even though they despise Octavian."

"Then let us cross now *without* her," Ahenobarbus said.

These Romans, Cleopatra thought. Betrayal and ingratitude is fed to them in their mother's milk. "If you cross to Italy without me," she said, "you will also have to cross without my fleet and my war chest. Then let us see how far you get."

There was a long silence.

"It would be too difficult anyway," Antony said finally. "There are only two harbors, at Tarentum and Brundisium, and if Octavian closed the sea gates against us, he might prevent us from landing altogether." He stabbed a finger at the map. "No, I plan to move our armies here, to Patrae, in the Gulf of Calydon."

Ahenobarbus shook his head. "And surrender the Via Egnatia to Octavian? It is madness."

"I agree," Dellius said. "We must hold the road."

Antony shook his head. He seemed distracted. "We don't need it."

Ahenobarbus was astonished. "We don't need the main road between the Adriatic and the East? Caesar himself said it was the key to Greece!"

Cleopatra grew impatient with Antony's reticence. Could he not even explain to his own generals his intentions? "The fleet will be stationed here to the south," she said, "at Actium, Corcyra, Patrae, and Methone. The islands offer safe harbors for our fleets, and we will be supplied from Egypt, not from Greece. So, maintaining our forces on the Via Egnatia is impractical and unnecessary."

Everyone was staring at her, the Romans, Amyntas, Bogud, Archelaus, the other kings and nobles. They were unaccustomed to having a woman present at a war council, even less comfortable with a woman who spoke her mind and dictated tactics.

Ahenobarbus looked at Antony, as if waiting for him to overrule her. "Imperator?"

But Antony had gone to stand by the window, and was watching the swallows swoop and dart under the colonnades. And he was drinking. The fifth hour of the day and already there was a goblet of wine in his hand. "It is decided," he said, and he dismissed them.

The others reluctantly filed from the room.

103

SPRING IN GREECE, and Antony had grown weary of preparing for the war, leaving Athens with his retinue of musicians and actors, bound for the island of Samos. The other kings had followed him there, and were competing with one another to provide the most lavish entertainments and the richest gifts. Mardian reported to her that the theaters were filled to overflowing every night.

Antony had had a scaffold of green branches erected in the gardens of his villa, and tambourines and fawnskins and vines had been hung on it to make it resemble a satyr's cave. It was said he lay in it from early morning, drinking with his friends, Munatius Plancus and Sisyphus the dwarf and the rest, entertained by musicians and actors from Dionysiac guilds from all over Greece and Asia. He had attracted a vast retinue of Pans and maenads, and every day the whole island resounded to the shouts of the revels, and the music of flutes and pipes and cymbals.

And every night Dionysus himself, forty-six years old now and running to fat, presided over the orgies that followed.

My noble Antonius. In a young man such excesses could be excused as youthful exuberance. But what can we say, she asked herself, of a man in his middle years who refuses to let go of his yearnings and cloaks them in the name of his religion?

Or was it something else? Might it be that in going against Rome, both victory and defeat were equally abhorrent? Did the noble Antony now wish for his own destruction as much as his enemies'?

She wished she understood him better. She knew that he loved his ease more than any man should yet had accomplished more in his short life than any of his peers save perhaps Caesar. At heart he was still a boy, but stood as a giant among other men. He shunned responsibility as if it were a leper, and his vanity was boundless; all of that, and yet he had burst into her life like a warming sun, and when he had left her, the halls of Alexandria were empty as a tomb without his laughter.

How this would be resolved she did not know. They had a lion by its tail, and they could not release it now until it was vanquished.

PALATINE HILL, ROME

Octavia had been hoping that with the passing of time her husband's infatuation with the Egyptian woman would fade, as indeed his interest in every woman seemed to pass with time. She could not rely on her hate; there were days when it failed her and she almost forgot that he had humiliated and abandoned her, had even denied her after she braved the winter storms to go to him after his defeat in Parthia.

Indeed, her hate failed her time after time, and continued to disappoint her until the day a messenger arrived to tell her that she had been divorced.

From that moment she had no choice but to do what Octavian had for so long been urging her to do; by law, she must leave Antony's home and remove herself and the children once more into the care of her brother.

Octavian, of course, turned the occasion into a public event. It could have been done by night, in private, to preserve her dignity. But that would not have served his purposes. Instead he came for her at the fifth hour of the day, and ensured that notice of his intentions had been relayed around Rome. As she emerged from the villa on the day of her departure, there was a huge crowd gathered under the pine trees to witness the spectacle. They watched in dumb fascination, as if attending a public execution.

Octavian had provided no carriage for her; she was forced to leave on foot, the children and her slaves trailing behind her as she trudged through the Palatine to Octavian's home. What a pathetic spectacle we present, she thought. My brother has staged this eloquent testimony to my former husband's fall from grace.

Oh, I have had enough of men for this lifetime. If Antony has used me, my brother has used me more. Even in my misery he finds time for politics. I hope Hades will open his gates to both of them and may they both suffer, there in the shades. For myself, in the hereafter I shall consort only with women.

104

CITY OF ATHENS

He was an awkward boy, he seemed both too thin and too tall. He had a long face with a jaw like a horse and teeth that were too large for his mouth. Was this really Antony's son?

Antyllus was the only one of his children who had chosen to leave Rome after the divorce and come and live with his father. It seemed to Cleopatra that Antony, who had not seen him since he was a small boy, was ill-prepared for this show of filial affection.

"Antyllus," he said. "My boy." He tried to embrace him, but the adolescent kept his arms at his sides like a statue. He mumbled, "Hello, Father," and continued to stare at the veins in the marbled floor.

Antony, red-eyed and shaking, had not yet recovered from the previous night's excesses. He sat down on a silk couch, and needed two hands to guide the jade goblet to his lips. Cleopatra, Caesarion, and the rest of the children were all in attendance, to welcome their new half brother to Athens. They all stared at Antyllus, puzzled and embarrassed. As if they had all been sitting down to eat and someone had thrown a skinned dog onto the banquet table.

"He curls his hair," Caesarion sneered, breaking the silence.

"These are natural," Antyllus stammered, shocked at the directness of this insult.

Caesarion sniffed the air. "And he's wearing perfume. By all the gods, he looks like a Syrian dancing boy."

"Enough!" Antony snapped, but Cleopatra could see that the barbs had hit home.

"You will apologize," she said to him.

"I am sorry," Caesarion said, sullen. "I am sorry for calling you a 'Syrian dancing boy.'"

Antyllus's bottom lip quivered.

Antony was clearly embarrassed by this outburst and tried to recover some lost ground with his son. "How are your sisters?" he said, ignoring the tear that was tracking a course down his lost son's cheek.

"They are well."

Another awkward silence. "Octavian treated you kindly?"

"Very kindly. But I told him my place was here with you."

Antony nodded. "Just so."

"And besides, I suppose he has dancing boys of his own," Caesarion said. "Prettier ones."

Cleopatra nodded to Caesarion's tutor. "Take him away and thrash him," she said. Caesarion glanced up at her, his eyes glittering with anger. He was sixteen years old now, too old to thrash, perhaps. But such behavior would not do.

The eunuch she had assigned to him dragged the boy away. Too old and too feeble to do the boy much damage. Still, it would teach him a lesson, perhaps.

Antony sat there, completely at a loss. A perfect father to Alexander and Selene and little Philadelphus, but with this creature he seemed completely befuddled. Perhaps it was guilt, for he had all but forgotten about the boy these last few years. Or perhaps it was because Antyllus reminded him of his marriage to Fulvia.

Antyllus was finally led away and shown to the apartments that had been prepared for him. Cleopatra sent the three younger children off with their tutors.

"I am sorry for Caesarion's rudeness," she said when they were alone. "Perhaps my son regards Antyllus as a rival."

Antony nodded. "All brothers are rivals someday."

"And sisters, too," she said, thinking of Arsinoë.

The scene between Caesarion and Antyllus had shocked her. We place such value in our heirs, she thought, as if we can continue our own short lives through them. And yet, did either of these boys resemble her, or their fathers? Caesarion had become a sneering, ill-tempered youth, though she hoped that this would pass with age. Her immediate impression of Antyllus was that he had spent far too long being fathered by women.

She left Antony, resigned to his gloom. No doubt he would seek solace for this new problem in a wine cup.

105

THE SUN HAD warmed the marble bench. The bees and insects were busy gathering nectar from the roses. Purple wisteria climbed the wall behind her. Cleopatra listened to the play of the fountain, let the gentle zephyrs of summer play on her face. Two servants stood beside her, brushing away the insects with gold-handled ostrich fans, but she dismissed them so that she and Mardian could be alone.

The old eunuch fanned himself furiously, sweat staining his voluminous gown, making his skin shine like copper.

She knew he had bad news. And on such a beautiful day. A disaster deserved grimmer weather than this. She breathed in the perfume of the garden, delaying the moment a little longer. Finally, she said: "So, Mardian. You have heard from our friend, Apollodorus."

"Indeed, Majesty." Her chief minister mopped at the sweat on his face with an embroidered silk handkerchief.

"Munatius Plancus is ensconced in his new home?"

Plancus, one of Antony's most trusted generals, had left Athens for Rome, there to pledge his allegiance to the Young Caesar.

"Octavian always has room for one more toady."

"I am sure he found his conversations with him of great interest. After all, he knew the exact number of our forces and their intended dispositions."

"Indeed."

She studied the eunuch for a moment. She wondered how his life would have gone if he had not bowed to his parents' wishes when he was a boy and submitted to the operation that allowed him entry into the royal service. "So, I am prepared. Tell me what has happened."

"When you were in Rome, Caesar showed you the Temple of Vesta in the Forum Romanus?"

"Indeed."

"Then as you will know, it is customary for Romans of noble birth to lodge their will with the virgin priestesses, for safekeeping. The persons of the Vestal Virgins are of course considered inviolate."

"I know of the custom."

"So you can understand how all of Rome was shocked to wake one morning to discover that the temple had been invaded, the priestesses manhandled, and certain documents carried off by armed men. It was—it is—a crime of unthinkable proportion. But then, the next day, Octavian rose in the Senate to declare that he had taken possession of the will of Marcus Antonius Imperator. It was clear from that moment whose henchmen had perpetrated the outrage."

Cleopatra blinked in confusion. Surely, this was good news? Not even Octavian could violate the Temple of Vesta without the severest punishment. But why would he profess to steal something that was not there?

"Octavian read the will to the Senate. It named Caesarion as Caesar's natural heir, named you as his wife, in denial of Roman law, and stipulated that on his death he was to be buried not in Rome, but in the royal mausoleum of the Ptolemies in Alexandria. Apparently, this has caused such uproar that even the crime that brought this document into Octavian's hand has been overlooked. Antony's villa on the Palatine was immediately burned to the ground by the mob."

Cleopatra was silent, trying to think her way through this.

"Was there such a will, Majesty?"

She nodded. "But it is lodged with the priests of Isis at Brucheion."

"Plancus, then," Mardian said, his suspicions evidently confirmed. "He told Octavian about this testament. The document Octavian read to the Senate is a fraud."

"It was supposed to be secret," Cleopatra said. Suddenly she understood. "He raided the Temple of Vesta to make it appear that the will was genuine."

"Indeed. Who would risk such a terrible crime if the stakes were not of the highest?"

The sun dipped behind the clouds for a moment. She shivered. She remembered the callow boy she had met that night at dinner at Caesar's house. Octavian's greatest strength was that everyone discounted him too quickly as a weakling.

Twenty years of struggling, for herself, for her son, for Alexandria, for Egypt. Still she remained in jeopardy as great as on the day she took the throne.

But soon it would be decided. At least now it would soon be over.

106

OCTAVIAN GOT SLOWLY to his feet. The Senate chamber was filled to overflowing. Antony's divorce of Octavia, the reading of his will, had galvanized them.

He waited until the coughing and shuffling of feet had subsided.

"Conscript Fathers. Today we face a threat such as we have not known since the days of Hannibal. Not just another civil war, as we have had to endure between my father and Pompey, and the subsequent rebellions by Pompey's sons and followers, but this time a threat to Rome itself.

"For make no mistake, my argument here is not with Marc Antony, but with the woman who now commands his every move. For if we do not take arms and act as men, we shall find our affairs are ordered likewise by this Cleopatra . . ."

PATRAE, GREECE

A huge map of Greece had been unfolded and lay on a great chart table. Canidius was bent over it, Dellius beside him, their staff officers in attendance. Sosius, who had been placed in charge of the Roman naval squadrons, was pointing to the map.

"Antony's plan is to station our navy so that we may intercept Octavian's forces before they cross from Italy in the spring," he was saying. "Our deployment is like a shield extending along the whole of western Greece. Wherever Octavian tries to cross with his army, we will be able to attack him, while protecting our own lines of supply from Egypt."

"As our Imperator pointed out," Canidius added, "it is imperative, politically, that Octavian attacks us first. We have to make this war on neutral ground. Time is on our side. Why take risks? We have food from Egypt, and Cleopatra's unlimited treasury to draw from. Our army is bigger, our navy superior. Meanwhile, Italy is starving and Octavian is broke. His army is on the point of mutiny, so there is a chance we may not even have to fight at all."

Dellius nodded. He was sure they were right. Octavian was no general. This time next year they would be ensconced once more in their villas in Rome.

❦ ❦

". . . For us, Romans and lords of the greatest and best portion of the world, to be trodden underfoot by an Egyptian, by a woman, is unworthy of our fathers, unworthy also of ourselves. Should we meekly bear the insults of these Alexandrians, these gypos, who are slaves to a woman and not to a man? Who would not lament at seeing Roman soldiers acting as bodyguards of this queen? Who would not groan at hearing that Roman knights and senators fawn upon her like eunuchs? Who would not weep when he both hears and sees Antony himself, the man who was twice Consul, often Imperator, calling her children the Sun and the Moon, and finally taking for himself the title of Dionysus, and, after this, making presents of whole islands and nations to her, as though he were master of the entire earth and sea?

"So why do we fear him at all? Because of the number of people with him? No number of persons can conquer valor. Because of their nationality? Surely these gypos and Asians have more practice carrying melons on their backs than weapons. Because of their experience? They know better how to fish than how to fight at sea. For my own part, I am rather ashamed that we are going to contend with such creatures, for in vanquishing them we shall attain no glory at all. Whom do we really fight against? Who are Antony's generals? There is Mardian the eunuch, and Iras, Cleopatra's hairdressing girl, and Charmion, her wardrobe mistress. Those are your enemies—to such depths has the once noble Antony fallen!

"If he wishes to die and be buried in a foreign land, let him have his wish. While he lies embalmed like a pharaoh, I, Imperator Caesar, will lay my bones in the family tomb I am even now constructing beside the Tiber. Even my dust will not forsake or abandon you, Mother Rome!"

"I don't like it here."

Caesarion stood at the window with a scowl on his face and watched the storm. She had invested so many of her hopes in the boy. In profile now he even looked a little like his father, but there was so far little else to commend him. He had shown a certain aptitude for horse riding and had had an affinity for language, but that was all. She hoped other talents would develop as he grew older.

"You have to be here," she said to him. "This war is being fought for you."

"As long as I don't have to go on the ships anymore. I get seasick."

One trait he had inherited from her at least. "We will stay here for the winter. After that, we will have to see."

"It's too cold. There's nothing to do."

"You have your lessons. You should practice your rhetoric and your numbers."

"Why?"

"Because you are a prince!" she snapped at him, and his eyes went wide at her sudden and unexpected anger.

"You let Antyllus stay in Athens."

"This war has nothing to do with him."

He said nothing. He continued to stare out of the window at the gray sea. Such a dismal boy. More like my brothers, in fact, than Caesar. The irony of it; he was all she had left of Julius.

⚉ ⚉

Octavian marched to the Field of Mars in solemn procession with his generals, in full military attire, wearing a leather cloak and decorated breastplate, watched by all the *boni* of Rome, dressed in their ceremonial purple. The Rite he was about to perform was one of the most ancient of the Roman tribe, and had never been witnessed by any of those present.

Octavian stopped at the doors of a temple, dedicated to Belona, Goddess of War. Inside the shrine he dipped a lance in fresh human blood and, after making his offering to the goddess, he stepped outside, in full view of all.

His voice rang on the cold morning air.

"The Egyptian queen, Cleopatra, has her sights set on Rome and wants to rule us, and we solemnly declare her our enemy. This harridan of the House of Ptolemy, who has trodden our general Marcus Antonius underfoot and made him her slave, this Egyptian who worships reptiles and beasts as gods, must be vanquished."

He turned to the southeast, facing the direction of Egypt, and hurled the lance into the air.

"With this action we declare *justum bellum,* a just and righteous war, against this foreign sovereign who threatens our state. We must allow no woman to make herself equal to a man!"

And with that Rome was at war with Egypt.

107

PATRAE, IN THE GULF OF CALYDON
Roman month of Mars,
thirty-one years before the birth of Jesus Christ

By FATEFUL COINCIDENCE it was on the Ides of March that the news reached them from Methone. The winter was not yet over, and Octavian, as some had predicted, had indeed been goaded by circumstance into acting with uncharacteristic haste. Or rather, his admiral, Marcus Agrippa, had demonstrated that with his back to the wall he was the most vital and dangerous foe of all.

He had flanked the great shield Antony had put around Greece, sailing far to the south with half of his fleet to attack Methone. The Roman squadron there had been caught by surprise. They were not expecting to be attacked; like most of Antony's force, they did not even think they would be called upon to fight.

The fortress was captured, and Bogud of Mauretania, one of Antony's most enduring allies, was killed in the action. It was a numbing blow. Methone had been their most southerly outpost, guarding the supply routes from Egypt.

Antony and his generals were confounded. They had not anticipated such a move. What did it mean? Did Octavian plan to land his army there and march on them from the south?

Events compounded swiftly after that.

Before Antony and his generals had a chance to react, Agrippa fortified Methone with his own soldiers and set out to harass Antony's southern flank while the rest of his fleet attacked Corcyra to the north. Beset now on two fronts, news reached Antony that Octavian had successfully landed his army at Panormus, one hundred Roman miles north of the Gulf of Ambracia.

In just a few weeks the initiative had been wrested away from him, and his plans lay in tatters. His own legions were still brawling and drinking in the dockside taverns of Patrae, unprepared for a long campaign, thinking they would be fighting a weakened and dispirited enemy, if they had to fight at all.

What had gone wrong?

Corcyra fell to a determined assault from the sea, while in the south Agrippa's ships sallied out of Methone to ambush every wallowing merchantman on its way from Alexandria with corn for Antony's army.

Antony gave the order for the army to be ferried from Patrae to the mainland, where they would force-march northward to meet Octavian. They would camp at Actium on the Gulf of Ambracia, and there, Antony decided, he would destroy his tormentor once and for all.

108

ACTIUM WAS PERCHED on the southern tip of a shallow inland sea, subject to tides, which at the ebb left behind vast expanses of marsh and lagoons, and a few small low islands covered with mud. The surrounding hills were limestone, dotted with sparse shrub, and by day the only sounds to be heard there were the mournful cry of waterfowl under a lowering sky.

Cleopatra's fleet lay at anchor on the flat, lead-gray water, the masts silhouetted against the mountains of Akaramania, the peaks hidden in cloud. Beyond the mouth of the estuary, the great cliffs of Leucas loomed over the sea.

Skeins of smoke drifted into the sky from the camp. Moats and wooden fences had been constructed around the perimeter and all seemed in order. But as they rode past the guards at the gate, Cleopatra was disconcerted by the looks on the sentries' faces. They stared back at her, eyes dull with exhaustion and hunger. What a long winter it must have been in this dreary and depressing place.

It was the classic dilemma of any general, she thought. What seemed so secure on a map was quite different in reality.

The charts never gave off the stink of death or the air of futility. A pall of lethargy and dread had settled on her on the long march from the Gulf of Calydon, and now it threatened to overwhelm her. Coming here was like crossing over to the Shades.

❦   ❦

Antony's purple cloak was splashed with mud, his face and arms grimy with sweat and dirt from the long journey north. Eros, his equerry, brought him fresh water in a ewer, and he quickly washed his face and hands, then settled himself on a stool while Eros removed his boots. He called for wine to be brought.

Cleopatra studied him. The swagger had gone from him, utterly. And just last summer he had thought this was going to be easy.

Is it too late to seduce Agrippa? Mardian had wondered it aloud to her the night before they left Patrae. She had scolded him for his insolence, but he was right, of course. If one thought only in terms of politics, she had allied herself with the wrong man. But Octavian had never been a viable alternative, even if she could have trained herself to ignore the spots and the bad teeth. Not only because of Caesarion, but because the kid, as Antony still referred to him, would never have been persuaded to share his power with anyone. As Antony had discovered.

The truth of it was, Cleopatra the queen had few equals in the world, and her choices for a consort had always been limited. She had counted herself fortunate to have found not only a man she found attractive, but had even loved. Once.

Cleopatra's nose wrinkled. The air in this place was putrid. "I don't like it here," she said.

"You don't have to like it," Antony growled. "We will not build our capital here."

"I mean, for my fleet. They have been anchored in that stinking swamp right through the winter. The timbers will be riddled with worms."

"There's nothing we can do about that for now."

"Everything, it seems to me, relies on us maintaining the island of Leucas. Are you sure your Marcus Grattius has enough men maintained there to defend it?"

"Who is the general here?"

She shrugged. "So far in this campaign? I should say Agrippa."

The barb stung him deeply. Sometimes, she thought, my tongue is a little too quick. "Let me worry about the campaign," he said. "I have done this sort of thing before, without your assistance. Perhaps you should leave. Your servants will be eager to attend you in your own quarters."

It was pointless to argue with him. As she left he already had a wine goblet clenched in his fist and was calling for another jug of wine.

109

CANIDIUS ARRIVED BY forced march with seven legions from Patrae, along with Antony's Asian allies and their contingents; now there was an army of 100,000 men camped on the peninsula. Antony held his first war council in a flimsy wooden pavilion that was to serve as the *principia*, the headquarters. Everyone had crowded in, kings, senators, and generals, around the large chart that had been unfolded on a trestle table.

The map showed the dispositions of the two armies. Their enemy had occupied the high ground to the north, Agrippa's fleet anchored nearby in Gomaros Bay. Octavian had fortified his position with trenches and stockades right down to the sea.

But Octavian was not their only enemy, as became clear when Canidius turned to Cleopatra and asked her about the preparedness of her fleet.

She hesitated. "We lost ten thousand oarsmen to disease during the winter."

There was a sharp intake of breath from the men around the table.

"Ten thousand!" Canidius shouted. Grattius had told them there had been a plague. But so many?

"Well, it's hardly surprising," Ahenobarbus said. "Most of Grattius's men are Asians and Syrians. They use the same latrines month after month. Then they wonder why they get sick."

Cleopatra saw Amyntas and several of the other princes exchange a glance across the table. They were not accustomed to being so blatantly insulted.

"We'll recruit more rowers from the local population," Antony said.

"The men I lost were Phoenicians and Egyptians who had spent months in training before we left Athens. Professionals. They will not be so easily replaced." Her forthrightness obviously bothered him. But he had to be told. "It also worries me that we seem to be bottled up here."

"We are not bottled up. Our fleet is well-protected. It is Agrippa's that is in danger. He has no storm harbor."

"He can come and go as he pleases. We cannot."

"I agree with my lord Antony," Ahenobarbus said. "We are impregnable here. We thank Cleopatra for her opinion, but we also wonder how many campaigns she has fought."

Cleopatra. This piece of Roman donkey dung dared to address her by name. She fought to hold her temper. "I have no battle experience to guide me, as you well know. Just common sense."

"As we are not planning to fight a sea battle right now, I do not see the point of the argument," Antony snapped, stifling the exchange. "Octavian is camped here," he continued, "on the Hill of Mikhailitzi. We cannot attack him directly, so we must try and force him off his perch. His water supply appears vulnerable." He stabbed a finger on the map. "If we can capture these springs here, he will have to leave the fortress to fight. Agrippa will not be able to save him then."

Cleopatra kept her silence, but she knew what he was doing. He wanted a land victory so he could dispense with her and her fleet. What irony. He had invested so much in Egypt's sea power, and now it seemed he would allow the best cedars of Lebanon to rot in the bay.

❦ ❦

The next morning Cleopatra woke to find a pall of smoke hanging over the island of Leucas. Mardian rushed into her tent to inform her that Agrippa had launched a surprise attack on the island at sunset the previous evening, that he had sunk or burned the squadron stationed there and overrun the fortress. Survivors were still staggering up the shore.

Another disaster. From now on, all their food, clothing, and weapons would have to come overland from the Gulf of Calydon on the backs of mules. They would have to force the battle or starve.

110

Eros helped Antony with his armor, tightening the straps at his shoulders and waist, fastening the breastplate over his purple tunic. It was armor fit for an Imperator, the enamel decorated with scenes from the legendary exploits of Antony's claimed ancestor, Hercules. He will need a little of that fabled strength and courage today, she thought.

Next he put on the heavy bronze helmet with beak and cheekplates, accepted a great double-edged sword, as long as Cleopatra's arm, and fitted it in its scabbard. Eros adjusted the hand strap on the curved rectangular shield, and finally he put on the purple cloak that identified him as Imperator, commander of the Roman army.

As Eros dressed him, Antony kept glancing through the door of the tent toward the sea, where the island of Leucas filled the horizon, whitecaps breaking at the base of the limestone cliffs. Agrippa's ships patrolled there now.

"I have prayed to Isis for your success," Cleopatra said to him. She had established a small shrine beside her silk pavilion, where a marble statue of Isis Pelagia, lit with candles, accepted the offerings of incense and wine. She now prayed there every day.

Antony ignored her reference to the goddess. Perhaps he thought to revert to his stern Roman gods now that Fortune had deserted him. There was no talk of Dionysus now. "It is good to be strapping on armor again," he said. He looked at her and grinned, and for a moment it was the old Antony again.

"The council yesterday. I am sorry if I offended you. But you must remember I am a queen, not one of your serving girls."

"It creates a bad impression with the others," he said.

"That I have opinions?"

"That their Imperator may be taking direction from a woman."

"I am not a woman. I am a goddess."

He stared at her. Perhaps he thought she was joking.

"I have never understood the workings of gods or women," he said.

"I doubt if they have ever understood you."

He grinned again. "No doubt you're right." He kissed her lightly and strode out of the tent. There was a mist of camp smoke in the air, mixed with the smell of leather and horses. The army was assembling by ranks on the plain, the endless rows of levies and legionaries shimmering in the still, hot air. Roman eagles were held aloft by the standard-bearers and the morning resounded to the sounds of hooves and trumpets.

Canidius and Ahenobarbus were waiting for him, mounted on horseback. Antony pulled himself onto his own giant bay. At that moment the drink and the defeats and the years of revels seemed to slough away from him. He gave her a nonchalant wave and then the three men rode down the gentle slope to join their army.

❦ ❦

They returned just before evening.

Antony galloped his horse almost to the doorway of his *praetorium* and stamped inside. From her pavilion a hundred paces distant she could hear him raging and calling for the wine bottle.

The next person she saw was Ahenobarbus, sitting on his horse, his beard crusted with blood from a sword wound on his cheek. He had removed his helmet and held it under the crook of his arm. His shoulders sagged with exhaustion.

"You were defeated?" she asked.

He gave her a look of disdain. "No. We were not defeated."

"Then what went wrong?"

"The walls are down, we took the springs. Pissed in the water myself, just to spite them."

"Then why this gloom?"

"We had encircled the walls, as the Imperator had planned, and we were preparing to attack their main camp. The battle was going with us. Then one of your greaser friends, Deiotarus, took his cavalry and rode over to the other side." Deiotarus, King of Paphlagonia, installed on his throne by Antony himself. This was his unique way of showing his gratitude. And that was that. "Without his cavalry it would have been suicide to continue the attack."

"He betrayed you?"

He frowned. "Perhaps it was you he betrayed."

"Me?"

"I believe he thought you were planning to add Paphlagonia to your empire after Octavian was defeated. He did not balk at being ruled by Rome, but he did not care to be ruled by a woman."

Cleopatra felt her anger rise. She did not like the offhand manner in which he addressed her, or how casually he blamed her for all and any of their defeats. "You blame me for his treachery?"

He did not answer her directly. "By all the gods, I have never served in such an ill-starred campaign." He grunted and slowly dismounted his horse.

She watched him deliberately turn his back on her and walk away. Antony was still throwing things in his tent, shouting at Eros to hurry and get his armor removed and where, by all the gods, was the wine?

PART VI

Freed from a tedious life, I lie below,

Ask not my name, but take my curse and go.

111

SUMMER IN ACTIUM.

A white haze hung over the gulf, the marshes shimmering in the breathless heat, a miasma of stench clung to the air, the stink of mud and stagnant water and the filth of a hundred thousand men. Disease had taken a hold among them again. Cleopatra's oarsmen were still dying by scores in the camp; every day corpse wagons lumbered through the lines of tents, bodies were thrown in the carts like scraps and hauled out to the brush to be burned on dump fires.

Her ships rotted in the water. The timbers had not been tarred during the winter to protect them from the sea worms, and now many of them were no longer seaworthy. They were down to six squadrons, and even those were undermanned. Every trireme needed a crew of 170 rowers, and in an effort to replace those who had died, Antony's soldiers were now kidnapping Greek laborers from their fields, or ambushing mule drivers in the mountain passes. Desperate measures, and perhaps futile as well, for the men were farmers, not seamen, and it would take months, if not years, to teach them to maneuver the ships as skillfully as the Phoenicians and Egyptians they had lost.

The greatest fleet Egypt, or any nation in the world, had ever built, dying of neglect.

Disease was not the only curse. The salt grasses were infested with snakes, and at sunset the mosquitoes swarmed from the reeking lagoons to make their lives even more miserable. The only creatures that seemed to thrive in the dismal place were wild fowl, crane, duck, and heron, but even those were gone now, trapped for food by desperate soldiers.

The heat and hunger frayed men's tempers. Every day there were fistfights in the camp, over food, or possession of one of the camp followers. Soldiers died in dagger fights, others were crucified by their commanders for disobedience or mutiny. Day by day the tension and frustration grew.

Octavian and Antony were deadlocked. Agrippa had blockaded their fleet in the gulf, Antony had invested Octavian's army in its fort. Octavian was still receiving corn from Italy; Antony, though with more difficulty, was being supplied from the Greek hinterland. Both waited for the other to make their move.

Antony led another raid on Octavian's water supply, and yet another of the satraps, Amyntas, took the opportunity to defect to Octavian with his cavalry, two thousand of the finest horsemen Antony had.

A hot and desultory wind stirred the dust around their feet. They sat under an awning that had been erected outside the *praetorium,* hoping for some cool breeze. Cleopatra was fanned by servants with huge ostrich fans. Days such as this, there did not seem to be enough air to breathe.

Antony sat with his hands on his knees, staring out to sea. He wore just his red woolen undertunic and high-strapped sandals, a red scarf around his sunburned neck. At times like this her heart bled for him. Antony may have fallen in love with the East, but the East had proved to be as faithless a lover as he. First Artavasdes, then Deiotarus, now Amyntas; these puffed-up princes with their greased ringlets and jewels on their thumbs were as trustworthy as carpet salesmen. He must be wondering who will sell him next.

Me perhaps.

"If it were not for the King of Armenia," he murmured, "I could be sitting in Babylon now."

"Marcus, how long are you going to sit here day after day, mooning like this? You have to do something."

He ran a hand across his face. "I never wanted this war."

"But you have it. And now you must do something about it."

He nodded, as if he agreed with her. And then he said, his eyes fixed on some future that was forever gone: "I could have won, if it were not for that greaser. I know I could have won."

112

AHENOBARBUS LOOKED ILL. There was a sheen of sweat on his face and the grizzled face looked gaunt. His eyes had retreated into their sockets. Never the most handsome of men, now he looked like a cadaver. He stood there in the doorway of Antony's *praetorium* with Canidius and Dellius, swaying slightly on his feet, but determined to make his point. As always.

"You have to give her up," he was saying. "Hand her over and negotiate with the bastard. It's the only way out."

"What about my honor?" Antony said quietly.

"What has honor got to do with it?" Ahenobarbus said bitterly. "Every other bastard's out to save his own backside. Why can't you?"

"I would not stoop so low."

"Oh, that's fine to stand on your high moral principles, but look at the shit pile you've led the rest of us to!"

"I did not ask you to come here. You stood with me against Octavian of your own choice."

"I did not say I supported your relationship with that woman!"

"She has proved a more faithful supporter than many of these other allies we have!"

"That's not hard!"

Antony was silent.

"Look, old friend, we've known each other a long time," Ahenobarbus went on, his tone gentler. "You've got to listen to me. If you ditch her now, you've still got a chance. His soldiers won't face you in a battle. A lot of them have served under you and most of them hate Octavian's guts. They'd rather fight for you than against you, if only you'd give them a damned good reason. It's this gypo that stands in your way—"

"Don't call her that," Antony growled, and leaped to his feet.

But Ahenobarbus was not in the mood to be intimidated. He stood his ground. "What's the sense in this?" he shouted back.

"You said we needed her for her war chest and her navy. Well, frankly, they're both fucked now."

The obscenity reverberated in the low-roofed tent. A gust of wind stretched the seams of the canvas, and the *praetorium* creaked in the rush of wind.

"She is still Queen of Egypt."

"If she were *king* of Egypt, all would be asking why you have favored her so much more than all the rest. Is it because you are sleeping with her, is that what she holds over you?" When Antony did not answer, he went on: "Every one of these greaser princes is jealous of her, don't you realize that? That's why you lost Amyntas and Deiotarus! As well as that, all of your generals and every single one of the senators in this camp think she is a danger and wants her gone!"

Antony looked for confirmation at Canidius, who hesitated, then nodded his agreement.

"You see?" Ahenobarbus said.

Antony stared at them. Ahenobarbus, Dellius, Canidius, they had been his most trusted generals and supporters. Perhaps on this occasion they were right.

But it could have worked, he told himself; his dreams of adding Parthia to the empire and founding a dynasty on Egypt's wealth. It had been Caesar's plan all along. All he was doing was following the old boy's plans. And he had come so close.

But they were right. It was all coming apart. There really was no choice now. He would have to do something. "I will talk to her," he said.

⛧ ⛧

Cleopatra's silk pavilion had been erected near Antony's headquarters, the enclosure manned and patrolled by her Nubian guard. Antony was ushered in by her chamberlain and stood in the doorway, looking around her pavilion as if startled by the luxury; the thick Cappadocian carpets, the marble-inlaid tables, the yellow jasper wine cups, the throne inlaid with coral and pearls. These Romans had not lost this opportunity to criticize her, of course, but surely even they understood that for a queen, such accoutrements of power were as important as their legions or their giant catapults. Would they have her sleep on a cot, like Antony, with only a talking raven and a map table for decoration?

He looked troubled. She could guess what was on his mind. "You have been talking to your republican friends," she said.

"How did we come to this pass?" he said. "I don't understand it."

She was in no mood for this. Too many revels in Ephesus and Samos had turned his spine to jelly. "Marcus, you have your privates caught under a rock. It is pointless worrying how they got there. You just have to remove them."

"Some of the others are saying that *you* are the rock."

"Ahenobarbus."

"Everyone."

She regarded him from her ebony throne, hands on his hips, eyes like stewed grapes. What a waste. "What is it I have done to disturb you, my lord Antony?" she said. "Is it my money, my fleet, my corn ships? Have they all stood in your way?"

"Your presence here makes this campaign impossible for me."

"Because I am a woman?"

He flopped into one of the jeweled sandalwood chairs she had brought with her from Ephesus. "Please, dove," he said, his voice like warm honey now, "we might yet break the blockade and land in Italy. It might be done. It could save the day for me, for all of us. But you must remain behind if it is to succeed."

"I remained behind once before. Do you remember? The next I heard of you, you were married to Octavian's sister."

"That was politics."

"So is this."

"Octavian has declared war on you, not me. If you were to go to Italy with me, the whole point of the plan would be lost."

"And if I do not, I am just another vassal. I am not that, and I shall not be that."

"You have to go back to Egypt!"

You bastard. You have used up my money and my warships and now you want to cast me aside, like an empty wine flagon. If you did go to Italy, once you were away from me you would let these Roman friends of yours persuade you to toss me aside completely. Caesarion and his cause would be forgotten. I would be in the same position my father found himself in twenty years ago, just before he died.

She sat there, staring at the mental and physical wreck that was her husband and consort. "My lord Antony," she began. "In Antioch, you asked for me to come, I came. In Leuce Kome, when you were on your knees, when your army was starving and you were desperate, you sent for me, I came. I have denied you nothing. Now you will not deny *me*."

"Trust me."

"Trust you? How can I trust you?"

"We both want the same thing. I shall not desert you this time."

She stood up and walked toward him. He looked hopeful.

On closer inspection she could see that he had not visited his barber recently and the famous curls were tangled and unkempt. Signs of age on his face these days, too, the lines around his eyes deeply etched by weather and by care. "I know you will not desert me this time," she told him, "because I will not give you the chance."

He stood up and walked slowly out of the tent, without another word. That it should come to this. She thought of that day in Alexandria when she had given him the Triumph he said he so desired. They had been gods then.

How his Jupiter and Apollo must be laughing at us now.

☙ ☙

"Well?" Ahenobarbus said.

He had seen Antony leave the queen's quarters, followed him back to the *praetorium* where he now sat on a camp stool, his head down, hands limp between his knees. "She will not go," he said.

"Then send your messenger boy, Quintus Dellius, over to Octavian and bargain with him. Put her in chains and you can yet talk your way out of this."

Antony stared at him, considering this perfidious, if tempting, proposal. But there comes a time, he thought, when you have to stop talking your way out of things. It seems to me it is all I have ever done. Since I was a boy I have been talking my way out of trouble, and for a long while it seemed to work. Shall I make another treaty with Octavian and seal it with Cleopatra's blood? It could be done. Octavian might even let me keep the Ironclad and the Old Fifth and have Syria as a province. Within the year I could be back to the revels and the all-night orgies, fighting off a few Parthian invaders for the sake of self-respect.

"Well?" Ahenobarbus said.

"No," Antony said.

"But there is no other choice for you now!"

"There is always another choice. That is why the gods gave us death. It is a gift for when life becomes too unbearable."

Ahenobarbus shook his head. "I never thought to hear you talk this way."

"I never thought that spotty boy and his pansy friends could bring me to this. Life holds surprises for us all."

Ahenobarbus seemed to deflate. He threw himself down on a stool beside him, partly from despair, but also from sheer physical fatigue. The plague is on him, Antony thought. He could smell the fever, feel the heat coming out of him. He should be in his sickbed.

"Marcus Antonius," Ahenobarbus murmured, his voice flat, "I have known you many years. I number you among my dearest friends. I beg you, do as I ask. There is no dishonor in it. She is a *pelegrina,* and a woman at that. It is not treachery, for you are not betraying a fellow Roman. There would be no stain on your precious honor. Have done with this charade. Negotiate. Save yourself. Save us all."

Antony met his eyes. What he said made sense. "No."

Ahenobarbus got slowly to his feet. He was trembling; the fever. "I have loved you, my lord. I had thought you could rescue us from this petty tyrant. It grieves me that I was wrong."

"It grieves me also," Antony said.

And those were the last words they spoke to each other.

⚜ ⚜

After he had gone, Antony sat for a long time staring at the floor. If only men did not fear death, he thought, there would be nothing to life at all.

It would be so easy.

113

"AHENOBARBUS HAS GONE," Dellius said.

Antony was in morning conference in the *principia.* Cleopatra was there, as were Sosius and Canidius and several other of his commanders. As usual, they were gathered around their charts discussing possible strategies, future deployments. Perhaps this will finally spur him to actually do something, Dellius thought.

He handed Antony the note the old redbeard had left. It had been scratched onto a wax tablet with a stylus. There was a deathly silence as Antony read it. They all knew what this meant to their Imperator.

"He rowed across the gulf during the night. He took Sisyphus with him," Dellius added.

Antony nodded. He seemed dazed. He laid the tablet aside.

"He has left all his possessions behind. They are in a brass-bound trunk in his tent. Shall we burn them?"

"No, of course not. Arrange to have them sent after him."

"My lord?"

"If he is finally going to have a proper dinner, instead of the poor bread we have here, I would not have him go to Octavian's table dressed in the same rags every night. Send them after him."

"But he has betrayed us!" Dellius said.

Antony laughed. "Don't be so sour." He returned his attention to the charts and the war council. And that was the last he ever spoke of it to them.

〽 〽

It broke up an hour later, and as usual, nothing was decided.

Cleopatra lingered after the other officers were gone. "That was generous of you," she said.

Antony stood at the doorway of the *principia,* his hands on his hips, staring across the gulf toward Octavian's camp, watching the greasy fingers of smoke rising from behind the palisades and earthworks. "Nothing was ever lost by generosity. That was what my father always told me. He broke us, you know, my father. Almost everything the family had, he gambled away or gave to his friends. My mother had to give orders to the servants to hide the ceramics and our silver. Once, a friend came to the house, asking for money. My mother would not let my father keep even a few coins on him, so—I don't know if he did this to save himself from embarrassment or because he wanted to help his friend—he told one of the servants to bring some fruit. The man brought it to him on a silver platter. My father took the fruit off it, gave the platter to my friend and said: 'Here, this should pay for your debts.'"

"It wasn't just generosity that made you send Ahenobarbus his trunk."

"No, that was sentiment. I am sure he did not want to leave us. It was weakness. We all of us have our weaknesses. His . . . is he's afraid to die."

"And you?"

He made no answer.

She touched him lightly on the shoulder. There were times still when she glimpsed the old Antony and it stirred something in her. He was so nearly a great man.

"If you wish to come to my tent tonight," she whispered, "I will be happy to see you."

He said nothing, so she left him and returned to her own quarters. She waited for him that evening, but he did not come, and she supposed she had not expected him to.

⚒   ⚒

Julius dragged itself into the month the Romans called Sextilis, white and oppressive. The stink that crept from the dead waters of the gulf became unbearable. Cleopatra watched Antony's great coalition disintegrate, worn down by heat and fear and the slow rot of disease and stagnation. Every day the death carts carried yet more bodies to the corpse fires. Her navy rotted in the brown waters, seabirds nesting in the yards, green scum settling around the waterlines.

Every day there were more desertions. The King of Thrace soon joined the number of Antony's allies who had defected to Octavian. The greasers, as Ahenobarbus called them, might owe their crowns to Antony, but many of them now decided that to keep their thrones they should court his rival.

Antony's council of war stood around the trestle table in his headquarters, staring at the charts, a familiar fresco. For all the good it does us, Cleopatra thought. We have looked at these maps so many times I dream them in my sleep. Sosius was there, Antony's admiral, as was Quintus Dellius and Canidius, brushing angrily at the flies. A canopy shielded them from the worst of the sun. The officers' tunics were stained with sweat and dirt, their faces masks of exhaustion and despair. The drowsy heat seemed to have paralyzed them all. There was a pitcher of wine on the table with some jeweled cups, jasper inset with pink coral and carnelian, such opulence incongruous in this hard and desperate setting.

Quintus Dellius picked up the pitcher and poured himself some wine. He put it to his lips and almost immediately spat it out again, into the dirt. "I'll wager Octavian is not drinking this vinegar," he said.

Antony would have made a joke of it once. Now he just glared.

"He has corn for his bread too," Dellius added.

It was true. Octavian might have impoverished Italy, but he made sure he kept his army supplied with grain. For his part, Antony had all but exhausted his own supply; Greek peasants staggered down from the mountains in ragged groups with sacks of wheat on their backs, their shoulders striped from the whips of their Roman overseers.

"You can try Octavian's bread if you wish," Antony said to Dellius.

There was deadly silence. Dellius's face flushed crimson. "That is not my desire, Lord Antony. You know I shall serve you until the day I die."

Antony turned to Canidius. "What is the state of our army?"

"I still have seventy thousand fit fighting men," he said.

It sounded impressive, Cleopatra thought, until you did your mathematics and concluded that their army must have then lost thirty thousand men to disease. You might not lose so many in a pitched battle.

"And the fleet?"

Cleopatra looked at Sosius. Let him answer. She didn't want to upset delicate Roman ears with her woman's voice. "The fleet is badly undermanned," he said. "We have lost another ten thousand of the crews to sickness and the ships are badly in need of repair. We can man no more than three hundred ships with the crews we have left."

Three hundred! The previous summer they had five hundred warships and three hundred merchantmen, from Corcyra to Methone.

Antony turned to Canidius. "What do you suggest?"

"I say we abandon the fleet and retreat over the mountains to Macedonia. King Diocomes is friendly toward you. We may then count on his aid and draw Octavian into a land battle where Agrippa's genius for the sea is of no use to him."

Oh, this was too much. "You are again going to rely on the good auspices of one of your allies?" Cleopatra hissed. Antony blanched. The barb had found its mark. How many times had he counted on the support of princely friends?

She felt them all staring at her as if she had uttered an obscenity. She would never understand these men. She was a queen. Did they expect her to stay silent and fetch them their wine like a Syrian slave girl?

She turned to Canidius. "Our army has been weakened by hunger and disease. How many more will we lose force-marching them over the mountain passes?"

"Better than losing everything at sea."

Cleopatra could see Antony waver. Yes, she thought, he is quite capable of burning my entire fleet here in the gulf and running off into Greece. "Have you forgotten how many men died in the mountains of Parthia during your last retreat?" she asked him, and even Canidius paled at that memory. "You wish to trust this Diocomes? Like you trusted Artavasdes?"

"At least we can fight on land!"

"And if you lose?"

"We can withdraw, as Pompey did."

"Pompey had ships to withdraw on, Canidius. Besides, look what happened to him."

Dellius could keep silent no longer. "But we can win the land battle," he said.

"If I were Octavian," she said, "why should I let myself be drawn into such a contest? Surely you understand this man by now? He has never won a battle for himself. He lets time or other men's foolishness play his part for him. If you withdraw to Macedonia he will buy off Diocomes, and then, when you are forced to flee to the east, he will have Agrippa's ships waiting for you at Hellespont and you will be in this same dilemma you are now. But this time you will have lost another thirty thousand to desertion and disease and treachery. Is this a familiar picture for you, my lord Antony?"

Antony looked stricken. Yes, he could see what Octavian had planned for him. His own gullibility was clear to him now.

"While the army marches north, what happens to me and my fleet?" she asked.

"You break the blockade and return to Egypt," Canidius said.

"How can we break the blockade if there are no soldiers to fight on the ships? You are consigning us to our doom."

"There is no other way," Canidius said, his face bleak.

"While you are here," Dellius said, "victory for us is quite impossible."

She sighed. She had hoped it would not come to this. "Very well, then," she said. "I shall leave."

They all stared at her.

"My plan is this. We man what ships we can and burn the rest, so Octavian cannot lay his hands on them. Leave me sixty of my fastest triremes for my war chests and my retinue and personal guard. You take your best legions on board the rest and break the blockade. You will lose some ships, but surely not all. Better than losing your legions in the mountains and abandoning the entire fleet to Octavian. Those ships that get through will go to Italy and march on Rome. Meanwhile I shall return to Alexandria." Better than staying here and seeing my navy rot in this accursed swamp. This way I may escape with my ships and my treasure intact. I can start again. I have always known how to weather the storms, I have been doing that all my life. But if I am to survive I must have my fleet.

Dellius was getting red in the face. "We cannot entrust our legions to the sea! We cannot win against Agrippa!"

"You do not need to win," she said to him. "You only need to break the blockade. There is as much risk as trying to cross the mountains to Macedonia. But the rewards are much greater. Get to Italy and you win everything."

Antony was hunched over the table. He stayed that way, eyes squeezed shut, while the flies buzzed and the generals' faces shone with sweat.

"Cleopatra is right," he muttered finally. "I have had enough of foreign princes and mountain passes for a lifetime. We must finish this. One battle shall decide it. We go by sea."

"But noble Imperator—" Dellius began.

"Enough, it is decided," Antony roared, and pushed his way past them.

Afterward, they heard him in his tent, calling for his musicians and his wine jug.

❦ ❦

Quintus Dellius watched the black smoke billow into the sky. The holds of the ships had been flooded with pitch and oil to make them burn better. Orange flame crackled along the wood, turning the hulks into pyres that blazed briefly then sank into the foul mud along the banks. Most of the ships now being sacrificed were triremes, but there were even some sixes among those picked out for destruction, hugely expensive warships that were no longer of any use, because they were too far beyond repair or there were not enough oarsmen left to man the great banks of oars.

Men ran along the line of ships now beached in the mud, throwing brands from the shallows. Soon the entire bank was thick with clouds of roiling, foul-smelling smoke. The air was rich with the smell of burning cypress pine and cedarwood. So much for the great forests of Lebanon.

Sosius had been generous with his estimate of the size of their navy. In fact, there were just 230 ships left from the massive armada that had sailed from Ephesus a year before. Dellius sighed and shook his head. Such a waste. Like Marcus Antonius. It was a pity to abandon him, too.

But abandon him he must. Apart from the obvious impediment of the queen, the omens were all bad. He had heard from one of the messengers that in Athens a violent storm had knocked the statue of Bacchus from its pedestal, and at Patrae the Temple of Hercules had been struck by lightning. It was clear that the gods had ranged themselves against their noble Imperator, probably because he had taken up with a *pelegrina*.

It was time to leave, before he got caught up in the bloodletting. Besides, he was sure he would be welcome in Octavian's camp, now that he had Antony's battle plans in his head.

114

INDEED, THE PANTHEON of the gods is against me, Antony thought.

The storm that blew in from the north had lasted now for four days. The camp had become a quagmire, rain running in channels along the paths between the tents, flooding the latrines, bringing the stink of the swamp right up to their feet. Down by the shore the hulks of the ships they had burned looked forlorn in the gray sheets of rain, like blackened skeletons rotting on a battlefield.

After so many months of inaction, he had made his decision to move, and now the weather forced him to stand still and mark the hours. As if the gods were mocking him. Any advantage of surprise that he might have gained was gone. Quintus Dellius had defected to Octavian the night before the storm, and now Agrippa knew his plans and had four days to prepare his fleet. At least the gale had given them one advantage: Without a storm-water harbor, Agrippa's galleys had been forced to row against the wind for four days and nights to keep from being wrecked against the shore. Perhaps it would count in their favor.

But if it did not, and the day went against him, he would accept the judgment of the Fates. If he could not break through the blockade, then he would die with his men on the ships rather than run to Egypt. He would not spend the rest of his life like Pompey's sons, forever in exile, becoming a pirate and brigand like Sextus, or a refugee living under the good graces of the queen. He would have Rome or he would have nothing.

Once the queen had escaped through the blockade, he would have kept his word to her, as he had always kept his word to Octavian. After that, let the gods decide.

~ ~

The next morning, after four days of gales and rain, the dawn broke to clear skies. At first light, Antony gave the order to board the ships.

Spars and sails were usually beached before a battle, as they restricted movement on the decks and took up valuable room that could be used to board extra soldiers. But today Antony ordered that all his ships take on their full complement of rigging and canvas. It would put him at a slight disadvantage, but the object was not victory, which was unlikely, but to break through Agrippa's lines and race to Rome.

While the pick of his legions were boarding his war galleys, now divided into three squadrons, Cleopatra's flotilla—her flagship, the *Isis,* and sixty triremes—were being hastily prepared for the voyage back to Alexandria. The Conscript Fathers who just days ago would not even share a meal with Cleopatra were now only too eager to accept her hospitality on one of her ships. They waddled like geese up the gangplanks, their baggage and retinues in tow. Hypocrites.

Meanwhile, Cleopatra's eunuchs and courtiers, flapping in their long gowns, oversaw the loading of her furniture aboard the *Isis,* the slaves slipping and struggling through the mud. Of course, the queen could not go anywhere without her rosewood couches and ivory tables. Her great iron-barred treasure chests were already aboard, containing fortunes in gold plate, lapis, emeralds, and silver coin. Another fleet there, another army, if it could be rescued from Actium.

After so much lethargy, the camp was suddenly alive with movement, as if someone had kicked over a nest of ants. Canidius's officers were hurriedly forming the legions and levies in his own command into ragged ranks for the march into Greece. Meanwhile, other tribunes were down in the camp, rousting out the camp followers, who shrieked and scurried away from their boots like seagulls. Baggage was being hurriedly loaded onto mules, trumpets blared all around the plain. Soldiers ran through the camp with brands, torching the wooden palisades and barracks so they could not be used by Octavian. For the second time in four days smoke spiraled into the skies above the gulf.

It was the second day of the Roman month of Septembris. Out on the sea the sky was a washed blue, white mare's tails pointing the way to Rome. A good day to die, Antony decided. If death it must be.

Cleopatra was dressed today not for splendor or seduction, but for battle, in a fireproof cloak and bronze helmet. The mud squelched under her boots, her cloak dragging in the puddles. She was escorted through the camp by her Nubian guards, but went alone into Antony's *praetorium* for the final farewell.

He received her in the uniform of Imperator: a cuirass of silver and brass, with the Hercules relief on the breastplate, over a kilt of leather strips, heavy sandals laced halfway up his calves, and heavy purple cloak.

They stared at each other in silence for a long time. "I do not know when we shall ever see each other again," he said finally.

"Then perhaps I may speak frankly."

He looked at her as if he now wished he had kept his bodyguard present.

"Neither of us can be sure how this will turn out. You may still win the day, my lord."

He shrugged his shoulders. "We cannot know what the gods have in store for us."

"We were gods once ourselves."

He raised his chin. The old Antony. "Today you shall escape this trap, on that I give my word. I shall see you and your ships safely through the blockade. After that let Fate roll the dice. I shall have Rome or I shall have death."

"Every vintner in Greece and Italy shall be holding his breath."

"You know," he said to her, "I have always been fascinated by you. Politics aside. From the first moment I saw you I was possessed by you. After Tarsus, wherever I was in the world, even in Parthia, when I never knew if an arrow from some high ridge might end my life at any moment, I thought only of you. Of all the women I have known in my life, you remain . . . unknowable."

Oh. She had come here intending not to waste her final words to him, if final words it was to be. She had planned to deliver her last reproach to him for his drinking and his womanizing and his neglect of this, the most important campaign of his life, of all their lives. Yet now she heard herself say to him: "I shall pray to Isis that this is not the last time we shall meet."

"I have wronged you many times," he said.

"All debts are paid, my lord Antony." She turned and left the tent. There was a burning in her eyes and she thought she would choke upon her grief. She really did not understand it.

She thought she had married him for politics.

115

THEY ROWED PAST the promontory, in single file, out of the hated gulf. In the distance they could make out the dark line of Agrippa's ships on the horizon, waiting. They formed into four squadrons, right, center, and left, with the Egyptian flotilla behind and protected.

Then they halted in double line, in a great arc almost a mile and a half long, extending from the northern promontory to the sandy shallows off Leucas. Antony commanded a great four-deck warship, a crocodile emblem carved on the prow. He stood by the helm, his hands gripped on the rail. The sun hurt the eyes, reflected on the lapping water, the sea flat as a lake. There was a sour taste in his mouth, familiar to any soldier, raw fear. His helmet was fiery hot and he could smell his own sweat.

"Come on, Marcus Agrippa, come in and fight," Antony murmured under his breath, but he knew it was a vain hope. Agrippa was too clever to be drawn into a battle in these waters. There was no room for strategy here. He would wait until they were farther out to sea, where his smaller Liburnians would hold the advantage. With the heavy sails on board, Antony's ships would be slower and heavier for the oarsmen to maneuver during the battle. Moreover, some of their galleys had less than half their complement of rowers; most of those at the oars were vagrants, diseased farmers, or underage mule drivers. Hardly a navy to make Agrippa quake in his boots.

But if just a few ships could break through . . .

And so they waited on the wind. An eerie silence fell on the fleet, broken only by the cries of the gulls overhead. Men waited side by side on the iron-reinforced decks, sweating in their heavy armor, their eyes screwed to the horizon, each alone with his own thoughts.

⸙ ⸙

The sun reached its zenith and whitecaps appeared on the ocean. The wind arrived from the southwest, as it did every day at this time, the fair breeze that would take Antony to Rome if the gods allowed.

Antony gave the order to advance.

To the beat of drums, the lines of oars began to dip and sweep, water streaming from the long blades, arrowing the fleet toward open water. Antony watched Agrippa's ships retreat before them. Agrippa knew he had them penned, and he wanted them well out to sea before he began his attack. He had set the killing ground, had waited too long for this moment to rush in. His ships outnumbered them more than two to one, and he would want ample sea room to take best advantage of that superiority.

The breeze started to swing around to the northwest, the wind that would fill Cleopatra's sails and speed her past the mountains of Leucas and away from the trap. Agrippa had halted his line, and the masts of his battle fleet began to loom large on the horizon. Archers and slingers clambered up the towers fore and aft, in readiness, while the centurions patrolled the decks, ordering their men to stand to.

The legionaries, many of them grizzled veterans with skins the color of leather, drew their swords and lined the rails, preparing themselves for whatever the Fates had planned. Surely they had not survived Philippi and Parthia just to die on some wretched ocean?

❦ ❦

It began with a rain of arrows and lead pellets from the slingers and arrows in the towers on the great warships, some clattering harmlessly onto the deck, others finding their targets, to shrill screams or bellows of pain, leaving men writhing, suspended in the yards, or rolling on the decks in their own blood and vomit.

Later there was just a tangled confusion of memories, without chronology or significance. Hours passed like minutes, a single second might go on forever. He remembered seeing a firebrand arcing into the sheets, men scrambling up the rigging to smother the flames with wet hides.

. . . the gleaming bronze prow of a Liburnian bouncing off the iron hull, then a great boulder crunching through its deck from the catapult mounted on their stern castle, men screaming as their ship broke up in front of their eyes, before they were sucked into the roiling gray sea and under their hull.

. . . an archer falling from the forecastle, to be crushed between their six and an enemy trireme, the man splitting apart in the water like a ripe tomato, the water blossoming red.

. . . another trireme ramming them broadside, smashing the oars on the starboard side like twigs. He looked below and saw a Greek muleteer staring up at him with blood on his teeth, the splintered handle of an oar impaled in his chest.

. . . and once he saw Agrippa's own great six, broadside, perhaps no more than a stadion distant. He thought he saw his tormentor then, for just a moment, standing quite still on the stern castle of his ship, and it was as if they were looking into each other's face. And then a pall of smoke drifted across the sea and Marcus Agrippa was gone.

There was one moment of lucidity when he knew it had all gone wrong. The smoke trails that had marked the perimeters of the battle were no longer clearly defined, his squadrons broken up and hopelessly outmaneuvered. Agrippa's smaller Liburnians were harrying his bigger ships, his terrified and inexperienced rowers unable to evade them, the gleaming bronze rams smashing into the hulls of his triremes and sixes time after time before they had the chance to dump heavy stones or fireballs on them from their castles. The enemy's biremes were armed with grapnel hooks that were fired from a catapult and ripped through the ropes and rigging of his own ships, making the sails that were to carry them past Agrippa virtually useless.

Now, many of his ships were so closely grappled they could not escape. Their carefully planned breakout had dissolved into a battle just for survival.

Acrid black smoke drifted across the ocean, stinging the eyes. It parted for just a moment and Antony glimpsed a flash of purple as the *Isis* hoisted sail before the wind. He saw Cleopatra's ships heading south, shielded by his embattled squadrons. She was safe. He had kept his word to her, at least.

He experienced a brief flaring of hope.

Later—how much later?—his flagship was beset by smaller Liburnians and biremes, like a pack of dogs around a bull. Their rudder was smashed, and a fire had taken hold in the forecastle, the black smoke from the burning pitch suffocating many of their oarsmen or driving them up onto the deck. Without oars or sails, they were virtually dead in the water. But Agrippa's Liburnians could not ram them, for their six was well-protected with bronze spikes, so the battle had taken the form of a siege.

Javelins thudded onto the deck and a fireball bounced twice before rolling over the stern and into the water. Antony heard the thud of grappling irons landing on the deck. A boarding bridge had been thrown across the rails and now there was hand-to-hand fighting among his veterans and Agrippa's legionaries.

Sosius's face hung there in front of him, as if disembodied, blood streaming from his cheek. "You have to get away from here!" he shouted.

Antony stared at him, could not believe that Fate had engineered his defeat once more. He started to run to the aid of the veterans who were battling to repel the boarders, and slipped on a slick of blood underneath his feet. By all the gods, the stuff was everywhere. The air was rank with the metallic smell of it.

As he tried to scramble to his feet, there was a deep, booming shock as their six collided with another warship, sending him sprawling again. He struggled to his knees, his fingers clinging to the rail. Below him the sea was littered with corpses, slicks of burning oil, wounded sailors clinging to broken spars, smashed rigging, floating timbers.

He heard Sosius screaming in his ear, "Save yourself while you still can! While you live, we still have a chance!"

A bireme had pulled alongside. Its captain was shouting for him to jump.

Antony thought of Canidius and his fifty thousand men even this moment marching toward Taenarum, of his legions in Syria and Cyrenaica, the shipbuilding yards in Alexandria and the Red Sea. It doesn't have to end here, he thought.

While you live, we still have a chance.

He had always thought he would never fear death when it came, that it would be easy for him. Yet at that moment something in him shrank from that final dimming of the light. He wanted one more Triumph, one more revel, before he went to the Shades. He could not accept this defeat. Not from that boy. That bitch.

He turned away from the fight and launched himself through the billowing smoke toward the lurching deck, landing on his feet, as he always did, rolling to soften his fall. The fall winded him and for a moment he lost consciousness.

He came around in time to see his flagship receding through the smoke, one of his veterans, a centurion he had known from Philippi, pointing his finger at him from the rail. "You bastard!" he yelled, and then the point of a sword appeared in the center of the man's chest and he rocked forward and somersaulted into the water.

Cleopatra lay belowdecks, in her cabin, stricken, as always, with sea-sickness, oblivious to everything but her own misery. Charmion was bent over her, clutching a silver bowl. They were speeding south on a following sea, the timbers creaking as the ship tossed and bucked. Mardian had to cling to the paneling of the stateroom to keep his footing.

"Majesty, my lord Antony has come aboard!" he said.

She barely raised her head. Antony on board? Surely that was impossible. He had told her himself that he was bound for Rome or for death. But she was too ill to make sense of such news.

"Are we . . . defeated?" she managed.

"The sea is shrouded in smoke and we are too far away for me to tell."

"What does . . . my lord Antony . . . say?"

"He will not speak. He sits alone at the bow with his head in his hands."

Cleopatra shuddered and closed her eyes. How had he gotten on board? They must have surely lost their gamble. But they were at least free from Actium. They would throw the dice again.

Three days later they reached Cape Taenarum, a small fishing harbor at the southern tip of the Peloponnese, a white village clustered around it. Aside from Cleopatra's sixty ships, forty others had escaped and joined them in their flight south.

The Conscript Fathers they had brought with them were all safe, along with nearly two legions of soldiers. The lords of Commagene and Cappadocia had remained loyal, as had Polemo of Pontus. They were out of the trap and they had fifty thousand men marching to meet them from Greece.

"Now it begins again," she told Mardian.

But it was not to be.

When Canidius arrived at Taenarum three weeks later, he was alone, save for a few of his staff officers and his personal guard. She received him in the stateroom of the *Isis*, Antony beside her. He was covered in dust and grime from the long ride, the lines on his face etched with dirt and misery. He relayed his news in a few sentences. His army of fifty thousand was gone. They had surrendered to Octavian without a fight.

"The Asian and Syrian levies just wanted to go home," he said, "and our own troops thought you had deserted them. He offered them money and land settlements to lay down their arms. I had to flee for my life."

Antony's face was ashen.

"I should have died at Actium," he said, and went back to sit in the prow of the boat, alone and inconsolable through the long night.

116

THE LONELIEST PLACE imaginable, as desolate a place as she had ever seen. Its name was Paraetonium, 150 Roman miles west of Alexandria, a small fort perched on a narrow cliff, baked by the unrelenting *khamsin* that blew in from the surrounding desert. Heat phantoms danced along the white rim of the coast.

Antony maintained a small garrison at the fort, which guarded the western approaches to Egypt. They had made landfall here rather than sailing directly to Alexandria so he could obtain reports on the readiness of his troops in Cyrenaica. But when they arrived, a messenger was sent out from the shore on a small boat with a letter from him. It was from the commander of the fort, informing him that his four legions in Africa had all deserted to Octavian.

Cleopatra watched his face as he read the letter. His army had evaporated, like a mirage in the desert. How many more blows did the goddess of Fortune have in store for him? She had been extravagantly generous with Antony over the years, which made her sudden abandonment of him even more inexplicable. Or perhaps that was just the humor of the gods.

All that night, Antony stayed in his cabin belowdecks, emerging the next morning in his armor and general's cloak, Eros behind him. They had barely spoken to each other on the nine-day voyage from Greece, given each other neither encouragement nor comfort. What was there to say?

His friends and supporters had evaporated like his armies. Antony had given the senators who had supported him free passage to Corinth to negotiate with Octavian. His remaining generals he had freed from their pledges and given them gold enough to secure sanctuary in the barbarian lands to the east. Of his senior advisers, only Canidius remained faithful. Even his fool, Sisyphus, was said to now be in the employ of the Young Caesar.

A boat had rowed out from the fort to take Antony and his freedman ashore. Antony stood at the port rail, watching it come, his face set like iron, staring into the sandy shallows. There was not a breath of air to stir the cloak around his shoulders. He looked old now, his eyes dull and flat, his brown face deeply lined.

The Roman soldiers on board had their eyes averted; humiliation was worse than death to a Roman. Even the Phoenician sailors looked away. Painful to see a man fall so far.

"Marcus."

He turned around. The look on his face was hard to witness. "Don't do this," she murmured. "Come with me to Alexandria."

"I should put you in danger."

"Whatever happens, he will come after Caesarion now. Nothing you do will encourage or prevent him."

He shook his head. "I have seen Alexandria for the last time."

She touched his arm, lightly, with her fingertips. "It doesn't have to be this way."

"It is the only honorable thing to do. There is nothing left now. I will finish it here."

A good Roman. Open a vein, fall on your sword. There was a part of her that understood that; there were some defeats too painful to be borne. But there was another part of her that could not let him go.

"We can still win," she said.

"Do one thing for me," he said. "When you return to Alexandria, see to it that the greaser Artavasdes is dealt with. He is the cause of all my troubles. That, and Fate. Lady Tyche has deserted me utterly."

She wanted to grab his arm, but others were watching and it would only be further humiliation, for him, for her. He climbed down the rope ladder and jumped into the rowboat below. Cleopatra stood at the stern and watched the boat row toward the shore. Marc Antony did not look back. She saw him stride up the empty beach toward the fort, and then he was lost on the horizon, utterly out of reach.

⨯⨯ ⨯⨯

Alexandria was like a white heaven, blue and bright and glittering in the sun, the illusion of sanctuary after the long and dreary months at Actium, the numbing despair of her defeats. But it was hard for her to raise her spirits. She felt as if there was a lead weight in her chest. A part of her had died with Antony.

Yet she would not accept defeat. There had always been an avenue of escape before. And so she ordered the *Isis* decorated with garlands, the purple sails cleaned of salt, cheering crowds arranged for their arrival the next morning. Have them throw flowers as we enter the harbor, she told Mardian, as if we had a won a great victory.

"Theater," she said, "the world is a theater. People will believe what they see. If we slip into the harbor under cover of night, all Egypt will be in rebellion by morning. Better to give them a show and dare them to call you a liar."

⨯⨯ ⨯⨯

She met with her *dioiketes* and her ministers under the shimmering marble pillars of the Hall of Audience within an hour of her return. There, dressed in a sheath-tight gown of golden silk, wearing a collar of carnelian and lapis, and seated on a throne of beaten gold inlaid with emeralds, she announced that Octavian had been dealt a devastating blow at sea. She had now retired for the winter to oversee the administration of Egypt while her fleet wintered at Pelusium and Antony reviewed his forces in the West. She saw the looks of confusion and bewilderment on all their faces. No doubt they had all heard the rumors from Actium. Well, that should keep them off balance for a while.

There was at least some good news. Her ministers informed her that the last season had been the most bountiful harvest from the Mother Nile in living memory. The Treasury coffers were overflowing. Which was just as well, for the project she now had in mind was likely to be hideously expensive.

〜 〜

After the audience, she returned to her quarters for a private consultation with Mardian. "A magnificent performance," he said to her when they were alone.

She looked suddenly like a young girl, complimented on her beauty. She grinned back at him. "You think so?"

"Even I believed we had won at Actium. And I was there."

"It is one of the great privileges of my position, Mardian. No one has ever called me a liar. Now, tell me, what have your spies to report from the bazaars?"

Look at her, he thought. She is positively radiant. Defeat inspires her. She feeds on a crisis like a child on its mother's teat.

"While we were absent there was the usual horde of Ptolemies laying claim to the throne." A phenomenon; even though Julius Caesar had displayed Ptolemy's body in the marketplace in Rhakotis after the battle of Alexandria, there were still men coming forward claiming to be Cleopatra's long-dead brother. They fomented rebellion whenever there was a crisis.

"We must assert ourselves quickly. If anyone has spoken against me in our absence, have them dealt with immediately. What are they saying in the marketplace?"

"Octavian's gossip has arrived here on the ships." He hesitated.

"Go on. Tell me the worst."

"They say you fled the battlefield as . . . as one would expect from an Egyptian and a . . . a . . ."

"A woman," she finished for him.

"They are saying that Antony was blinded by passion and abandoned his men to follow you. That it was a victory for Roman virtue over Oriental despotism and debauchery."

A long and painful silence. Octavian had a way of working around inside the truth, like a worm eating along the grain of the wood, probing for weaknesses in the grain. He had claimed it as a great naval victory when the truth was it had not been a battle but a containing action. They had been trying to escape from Actium, and Agrippa had been trying to stop them. Only forty of their ships had been sunk. Many more had returned to Actium, where they later surrendered, but only after Sosius and the other captains discovered that Antony was gone. Over a quarter of the fleet had reached Taenarum, a creditable result in the circumstances.

In fact, Octavian's greatest accomplishment had been achieved away from the battlefield, when he had bought off Canidius's centurions with promises and gold. Antony had not been defeated until then. But like the queen, Octavian knew the value of a bold lie.

Cleopatra bit her lip. "And do we have news of Octavian?"

"He is in Athens, Majesty, where I am pleased to report that he has his own problems. The veterans in his army are back in Italy and rioting. They want their money and the land settlements he promised them. It is said he is preparing even now to sail back to Italy."

"But it is almost winter."

"The situation is so dire he is to risk shipwreck."

"Perhaps the Fates will yet save us."

"Perhaps," Mardian said, but he thought that was unlikely. Octavian had been shipwrecked twice in his life and had yet to come to harm. Pompey and his sons had always claimed Neptune as their patron, but it seemed to him that if anyone was favored by the god of the sea, it was the Young Caesar.

"He has financed his whole career on promises, Mardian," Cleopatra was saying. "The only way he can pay for them is to appropriate Egypt's treasury. His problems only make our situation more dire."

"Yet it buys us time."

"Indeed. For we are not beaten yet. I have a plan."

A remarkable woman, Mardian thought. Amazing. "A plan?"

"We cannot just sit here in our palace and wait for him to come to us. As you say, the Fates have given us a little time to prepare. We should use it well."

"We will defy Octavian?"

"How? We do not have an army to defy him with. Without Antony, we cannot rely on those legions he left here in the city to defend the crown. I now believe Alexandria to be lost. But Alexandria is not the whole world."

Mardian blinked. Surely Alexandria was the center of the world?

"But first our friend, Artavasdes. I will not see him restored to his throne by Octavian, as he assuredly will be if he lives. I gave my word to Antony that he would have his reward for his treachery, and he shall. I want his head pickled and sent to Medea."

"Medea?"

"The King of Medea is Armenia's enemy. He will be delighted with such a gift. We will send along with the head a proposal that my son Alexander marry his young daughter when they are of an age. If he assumes his guardianship, at least one of my sons will be shielded from the cataclysm."

"And the rest of us, Majesty?"

"We will have to go into exile. Come now, Mardian, don't look like that, we have done it before, when Pothinus plotted against us. We survived then, we shall survive again."

"I was much younger then."

"You may stay behind if you wish. Your life is not in danger."

Mardian was appalled that she could even suggest this. "My whole life has been dedicated to you. That is unthinkable."

A suggestion of a smile. "I am relieved to hear you say so. For a moment I thought you wished to retire."

"This time the desert is not an option, I hope."

"I am not as young as I was either. No, I thought India. Or perhaps even Parthia."

"Parthia? They are our enemy."

"An enemy is a place in time, Mardian, not a place in the world. Think about it. It may be over for Cleopatra, but it has occurred to me that if my daughter should marry a Parthian prince, one day she can lay claim to the throne of Egypt and have her husband's armies make that claim real. Such a future the Parthians may well see to their benefit, especially with Selene's brother on the throne of Medea and in a position to help them in their ambitions."

The woman was breathtaking.

"India and Parthia are both a long way from Egypt."

"We still have a navy."

"Which is locked in the Mediterranean."

"Not quite. You have not read the histories, Mardian."

He stared at her, his face blank with incomprehension.

"Five centuries past, the Persian king, Darius, conquered here. He built a canal between the Red Sea and the ocean through the lakes of Balah and Timsah and the Bitter Marshes. The old canals are now buried under the sands, but I believe they can be located and restored. It would make a passage from the Mediterranean to the Red Sea possible. To that end we will have the ships dragged ashore at the narrowest point of the isthmus on rollers and hauled to the Delta."

"That is a monumental task. It will drain the Treasury."

"What else do we wish to do with the money. Hand it to Octavian?"

Mardian was astounded. Alexander himself would have applauded such audacity. "I shall call a council of the *strategioi* immediately. We will set to work."

"Mardian, you know what will happen to me if Octavian takes me alive?"

He nodded. He had been at Caesar's Triumph, in the viewing gallery when Arsinoë trudged through the Forum Romanus dragging her silver chains. Arsinoë had been treated with a sort of grudging respect by the mob; after Octavian's propaganda war, Cleopatra was as feared and hated as Medusa herself. The crowds would pelt her with rubbish and worse, spit on her, jeer her every step, and at the end of her last procession she would be strangled by the state executioner and have her body thrown in the sewer. "I know," he said.

"I cannot ever let that happen," she said.

〰 〰

Caesarion was no longer a boy. He was sixteen years old, almost a man, taller than she by a head, long-boned and stoop-shouldered. He looked hauntingly like his father; there could be no doubting his paternity to anyone who remembered Julius.

Even more reason for Octavian to want him dead.

But the expression on his face this morning was not Caesar's; the intelligent, black eyes, the cruel, ironic smile, the trademarks of her

Julius, were quite absent in this lad. Cleopatra took his habitually sullen demeanor as personal reproof. Perhaps she had invested too much in him, had even spoiled him. Not that it was all her fault. She guessed that what his character had needed was the stern hand of a father, not these fawning time-servers in the palace, the eunuch tutors and simpering advisers.

She had summoned her son to her private chambers along with his tutor, Rhoddon. The morning was cool and the sandalwood braziers had been lit by the servants, filling the room with their sweet scent. Cleopatra shivered inside her cloak. Outside, a gale swept the streets of the city, moaning around the palace walls. Her last winter in the Brucheion.

"We have to leave Alexandria," she said to him.

His lips curled into a sneer. "It's true, then. You lost. Antony was just a bag of wind after all."

She felt a flaring of anger. She had sent him home from Patrae instead of taking him with her to Actium. Perhaps she should have allowed him to taste a little hardship. The boy had been cosseted all his life. "When you have fought in as many campaigns as the lord Antony, you may criticize him. Until then, you should hold your own counsel."

"I heard he was drunk right through the summer at Actium."

For a moment his impudence left her speechless.

"You've really made a mess of things," he said.

Her tutor looked as if he would faint. She got to her feet and Rhoddon took a step back. Caesarion just glared back at her with a look that let her know he thought himself inviolable. "Get out of here," she said, trembling.

After he had gone, she leaned against the windowsill, waiting for the blood to stop pounding in her ears. Caesarion was and always had been her future; and now the future itself mocked her.

And what of Antyllus? A nice enough boy, harmless in his own way, and quite without spite. She had given him shelter for his father's sake, yet as Antony's successor, he was also her son's natural enemy. If she were to help him survive the cataclysm, he could claim a part of Caesarion's birthright, now that Rome was no longer Antony's estate.

Something must be done with the boy. But what? While her children yet lived, Octavian could never have his final victory.

❦   ❦

Cleopatra had commissioned more ships to be built in the docks on the Red Sea, while the remainder of her fleet—except for the *Isis,* and her surviving sixes, which were anchored in the great harbor—were hauled across the sands near Pelusium on massive wooden frames mounted on log rollers.

Mardian still could not comprehend how such a massive undertaking could be achieved. The isthmus separating the ocean from the Red Sea was 160 stadia at its narrowest point. Tens of thousands of fellahin were put to work digging out the old canals first built by Darius five centuries before. They had been restored three hundred years ago by Ptolemy Philadelphus but were now buried once more under the desert sands.

The backbreaking work went on through the long winter, the heat of the desert still formidable even at this time of the year. But as the Nile rose, the ships were hauled along the newly rebuilt canals to the lakes of Balah and Timsah.

The *oeconomi* came to Cleopatra and protested that even Egypt's vast treasury might not have the funds to complete the work. Cleopatra immediately levied a tax on the temples and Alexandria's wealthiest citizens to raise more money.

Finally the flotilla reached the Bitter Marshes. This was the way the Jew, Moses, had come in his flight from Egypt in the time of the pharaohs. It had been a tidal swamp then, and the tide had turned and drowned the pursuing soldiers. Now the estuary was far inland, and the fellahin were forced to drag Cleopatra's navy through a stinking, snake-infested swamp.

Finally they reached the last few sections of the old canals and the ships were dragged along the narrow waterway into the Red Sea. The fleet was finally safe from Octavian and ready to carry Cleopatra, her family, her treasury, her bodyguard, and her government into exile. Mardian wept when he heard the news. It was an astounding achievement. It seemed Cleopatra's instincts for survival were right again.

117

CLEOPATRA WAS IN the Audience Chamber in the palace when the news came. She was dressed in silver robes, in the head-dress of Isis, the silver disk with horns of fertility and feathers of justice, enthroned under the high gold-fretted ceilings, hearing a case concerning the legality of a marriage between a woman from Alexandria and a wealthy merchant from Memphis. At dispute was the income of an estate on Mareotis, and the custody of six children.

The great tortoiseshell doors were flung open and Mardian shuffled in, puffing from exertion, his gown stained with sweat. The moment she saw him she knew the Fates had toyed with her again.

Everyone had stopped and was staring in his direction. "Malchus," he said.

Malchus was the chief of the Nabataean Arabs. He had harbored a grudge against her ever since the treaty she had made with Antony at Antioch when the Imperator had granted her land that formerly belonged to him, including some bitumen-rich waters along the Red Sea.

"What has he done now?"

Mardian could not get the words out.

But she knew, even before he said it. "The ships," she said.

He nodded. The ships.

The story came out, slowly. The Nabataeans had staged a raid on the navy in the Red Sea from their capital at Petra. The fleet had been torched. The ships that had been dragged across the desert, at so much cost in gold and human life, as well as the new biremes she had commissioned, all gone. Malchus had gained a sweet revenge indeed. The bitumen fields she had won at Antioch had realized enormous profits to the Egyptian treasury. But what they had finally cost her was incalculable.

She had been careless, she realized, too busy congratulating herself on the brilliance of her strategem in getting her fleet to the Red Sea, giving too little thought on protecting it once it was there. Malchus would not have dared harm her while Didius, the Syrian governor, remained faithful to Antony. But Didius had recently defected to Octavian, with three more of Antony's legions, and Malchus would have known that not only did he have nothing further to fear from Egypt, but that his actions would be well-rewarded by the Romans.

Things had gone Octavian's way again. She was trapped in Alexandria.

All her dreams were dust now. Her plans for Caesarion, for Selene, for her own survival, vanished in an instant. It was as if she had swallowed stones. How could the Great Mother have allowed this to happen to her?

"Leave me," she said, "leave me, all of you."

⚜ ⚜

When Mardian returned, just before evening, she was still alone in the great marble hall, and even in her splendid robes she appeared a small and lonely figure beneath the great columns of purple-veined porphyry. She was gazing out of the window toward the island of Pharos and the great lighthouse. It was a gray evening, and overcast, and the beacon seemed to throw a comforting glow over the harbor. An illusion, for there was no sanctuary now, not for the Ptolemies.

"Majesty," he said. "Are you all right?"

"Is there any news from Paraetonium?" she whispered, her back still toward him.

"Antony has gone to Cyrenaica to try and persuade the legions there to rejoin him."

"He still lives, then?"

"Apparently."

"His sword must be blunt. Poor man. He loves life too much. He really is not like a Roman at all."

The way she spoke of him; in contrast to her words, the tone of her voice was gentle, almost fond, even now. A difficult woman to understand. Not a goddess, of course, as the mob in the street would believe, but remarkable for all that. She should hate him as bitterly as she hated Octavian after all the disappointments he had led her to.

"What can we do?" he wondered aloud.

"Perhaps Antony will return after all."

"I do not think we can look to Antony to save us, Majesty."

"No, but it might be pleasant to see him again. Don't give way to despair, Mardian. I will think of something."

My poor, valiant queen, he thought. She does not yet know when she is beaten.

Egyptian month of Phamenoth,
thirty years before the birth of Jesus Christ

Mardian kept a palace on Lake Mareotis, to the south of the city. The villa was set among vineyards and apple orchards and had a landing stage for his own personal houseboat. His quarters rivaled Cleopatra's in their opulence; there were tables fashioned from hardwoods in Damascus, inlaid with pearl, camphor-wood chests from the Indus, Coan silk hangings. Apollodorus looked around appreciatively. His brother-in-law had done well for himself in the queen's service. There were rings of emeralds and lapis on his fingers, he wore silk clothes, ate the best foods from embossed silver plate, drank the best Falernian wine from jeweled cups. But the price had been high, not one he would like to have paid.

Mardian's mood was subdued. He had a wine goblet in his hand, which was out of character for the old fellow at this time of day. Not yet noon and he seemed almost bleary from drink. And depressed. Apollodorus supposed that was to be expected. These were gray days for Egypt. To a landless mercenary like himself, it was difficult to appreciate how hard it must be for these Greeks to give up their beloved city.

"Apollodorus," Mardian said. "It is good to see you again. Would you like some wine?"

He allowed a slave to pour him a cup from the krater and he settled back on one of the silk couches.

Mardian flopped his great bulk down on another couch. "So. How do the Fates treat you? Has this war with Octavian affected your trade?"

"Men still want good carpets under their feet, they still need spices for their food. War is for soldiers, not for merchants." Apollodorus sipped his wine. "You have lost weight. Did you suffer terribly at Actium?"

"I tell you now, there is nothing worse for a eunuch than to go hungry. Still, as you can see, I did not quite waste away."

"And how is our lovely goddess after her recent travails?"

"She remains indomitable."

The Sicilian smiled. "Have you ever wondered what it would be like . . . no, you could not . . ."

"I know what you are going to say, and let me tell you this, you have listened to too many of Octavian's lies. She has had just two lovers in her whole life. Neither of them deserved her, or appreciated her."

"A man must have his dreams. I look into Her Majesty's eyes sometimes and . . ." He shook his head, the thought going unfinished.

"Men think her eyes are mysterious, but let me tell you this now. She thinks of nothing except politics."

"You have shattered my illusions. I do not know if I shall ever forgive you."

Mardian did not smile. "To be honest with you, these days she does not think of politics anymore. She thinks of her survival."

"I heard about the attack on her fleet in the Red Sea. That is why I wanted to see you. What is she going to do?"

"I do not know. Escape is impossible now."

"Not impossible. I can get her away from here. Spain perhaps. Or down the Nile to the elephant country. She could find refuge there."

Mardian shook his head. "She is too proud. She could not live as the guest of another ruler. She would rather die. She needs her servants, her bodyguard, her army, her treasury. Do you have ships enough to transport all that? Do you have a navy to protect her when she leaves Egypt?"

"I rescued her once before."

"Yes, but then there was hope of a crown. Without her fleet, her bodyguard, her retinue, she would be at the mercy of any who wished to trade her life for profit with Octavian."

"What about her son?"

"Caesarion? A wheedling boy. He farts and thinks it is incense. But his mother loves him, and while he lives, Octavian will hunt him to the ends of the earth, even down into the underworld."

They were silent with their own thoughts for a long time. "I have heard this Antony has returned to Alexandria," Apollodorus said finally.

"What you have heard is true. He has built himself a tinker's hut on the waterfront. The poor man shuns all visitors and thinks to shut himself away from the world. He thinks Octavian might forget him. This the man who called himself the New Dionysus!"

"I thought he would certainly fall on his sword like the rest of his breed."

"Perhaps in the end he lacked the courage. You would think he would have grown tired of life after the way it has used him."

"I cannot ever imagine growing tired of life. No matter what it did to me."

"He returned to Alexandria in stealth and did not even go to the Brucheion to visit the queen. What kind of man is this? She has not given up. How can he?"

Apollodorus leaned forward. "You must tell her," he said. "My fleets travel everywhere in the world. I can hide her and her family, I can find her safe refuge. Tell her."

"Why would you take the risk? Octavian would have you crucified if he discovered what you had done. Do not tell me you would do it from sentiment?"

Apollodorus looked affronted. "I would expect to be well paid," he said.

Mardian allowed himself a smile. "Very well, then, I will pass on your offer. But I tell you now, she will not accept it. I fear the queen is hatching another plan of her own."

❦ ❦

The mausoleum had been built alongside the Temple of Isis on the eastern side of Lochias, and the final stones were laid while she was at Actium. The main door was of heavy Lebanese cedar, decorated with frescoes of the goddess Isis. It was reinforced with iron bars and could be sealed with giant bolts. It opened into a hall with pillars of polished black porphyry supporting the black granite ceiling, the walls lined with marble. This hall led to an inner shrine where two sarcophagi, made from pink Aswan granite, stood side by side. These were the tombs of Marcus Antonius, Imperator of Rome, and Cleopatra VII, Philopator, Philopatris, Queen of the Two Lands.

Cleopatra ran a finger along the smooth stone of her own grave. She wondered what Julius would have thought of this. He had always said Egyptians were too absorbed with thoughts of their own deaths. She allowed herself a grim smile.

Beyond the sarcophagi there was another chamber, a much larger one, and from here came the curious but overpowering aromas of spices mixed with the stench of pitch. She walked through two great pillars with papyrus bud capitals and was confronted with the most astonishing sight she had ever seen.

Before her lay a mountain of treasure, perhaps the greatest ever collected in one place, the last unplundered wealth in the world outside Babylon, and worth many times the annual income of Rome. The base of the pyramid was made up of solid slabs of black ebony, resting on a bed of pitch. Ingots of gold had been stacked on top, and then a fortune in ivory tusks from the southlands, to the height of four men. Next came sacks of spices, cinnamon and nutmeg and fenugreek, as well as bales of silks that had been carried across the Eastern deserts from Cathay and India. Sacks of priceless Arabian pearls lay atop this great mountain like rubble, as well as countless emeralds and blue lapis stones with fine golden veins, the gemstones glistening wet and visceral in the gloom.

A single torch applied to the bed of dry tinder and bitumen beneath the ebony wood and the spices would burn up in the conflagration, the pearls and emeralds would crack and explode, the ebony and ivory burn into ash. Octavian might be able, after much labor, to rescue the gold ingots from the ruins.

Would the Young Caesar risk losing all this? She doubted that he would. Perhaps she might still use Egypt's wealth to barter for her throne and her life.

118

THE RELENTLESS PASSAGE of the seasons, the gradual erosion of time. Winter passed to spring, Octavian returned inevitably to Greece, then sailed to Syria and began his inevitable march south. Thus began the counting of the days, the cadence of destiny, its limits marked in hours.

A bright day, the sky swept with mare's tails. The *Isis,* her stern painted with fresh gilt, rode at anchor in the harbor. Nearby, a rude hut of limestone blocks had been constructed on the end of the breakwater to the west of Antirrhodos, close to the white porticoes of the Temple of Neptune. Mardian dragged his bulk along this jetty, sweating in the cool onshore wind. He could make out the distant thunder of the sea on the reef and the cries of the gulls as they wheeled over the fishermen's nets in Rhakotis.

Mardian screwed his eyes against the glare, saw a giant come out of the hut, hands on his hips, blocking the way.

He barely recognized him. He had lost weight since he last saw him, and was bearded and unwashed. He was dressed in a ragged tunic, his hair matted like a beggar's.

They said he had built the house himself. He called it his Timonium, after the renowned Timon of Athens, another hermit who blamed mankind for his miserable life. He had been living there for several weeks now, and spoken to no one since his unexpected return to Alexandria. He had not even gone to the Lochias palace to see his children. Now he glared at his unwelcome visitor and his lips curled into a snarl. "I want nothing of you, you fat pansy," he said.

"Greetings to you also, my noble lord Antony."

"You are not welcome here. Nobody is welcome here."

"A few moments of your time. Out of the sun, perhaps?"

"You can stand there and fry for all I care." Antony turned to go back inside his hut.

"The queen wishes to see you."

Antony turned around. "I no longer have any wish to share the company of any man or woman. I have been betrayed by my friends, shunned by fate, and wronged by women. I spit on all of you." And he did, there at Mardian's feet.

"It is about your son, Antyllus."

Was there a flicker of interest in his eyes? Mardian wondered.

"I have no son."

"You have a son and more children besides, here and in Rome. And as much as you shun the world, you will surely not shun your own flesh and blood."

Antony seemed to hesitate. "Is he well?"

"He is a man now," Mardian declared.

"What do you mean?"

"The queen has held the traditional rites for her son's arrival at manhood. He has been awarded the *toga virilis*. She has likewise awarded one for your son, Antyllus."

Antony's shoulders slumped. So, this belligerence was just pretense, after all. This Antony was as transparent as glass.

"Does she know what she has done?"

Of course she knows, Mardian thought, the crafty little minx. She has made Antyllus into a man, and now he is as much target for Octavian as Caesarion. Now you have to come out of hiding and do something. "She knows."

"The bitch," Antony said.

"Yes, she is. Shall I tell her to expect a visit?" Mardian said, and smiled.

To the Imperator Octavianus, divi filius.

Salutations. It seems your star has risen over the world, and our conflict has left you resolved to remove me from my throne. So be it. But perhaps we can avoid further bloodshed to both our supporters and friends. This I ask: that you turn back from our borders on the receipt of twelve talents of gold, which should prove adequate to recompense your costs of war and pay for your soldier's happy return to Italy. In return I shall relinquish the throne to my son, Ptolemy Caesar, and retire into exile. As you know, he took no part in the battle at Actium, and my sins are not his. As for my

*lord Antony, he has resigned himself to a hermit's life and is no
further threat to you. As a mark of my good faith I send with this
missive the gold diadem and scepter of Alexander. Do this, and
you shall hear no more of me again.*

*Cleopatra Philopater Philopatris, Queen of the Two Lands,
Chosen of Osiris, from the loins of Amun*

The wide stone steps led down from the palace gardens to the
water's edge, where Philadelphus was busy collecting starfish and
anemones in the shallows. The dolphins had returned with the
spring and could be seen playing in the eastern harbor between the
anchored ships. Dolphins were the natural companions of Isis,
Queen of the Sea. A good omen, perhaps.

Cleopatra watched the child playing in the sand. *The poor boy. I
wonder what will become of him.*

She turned to Caesarion, waiting beside her with his tutor, Rhoddon, a predictable scowl on his face. "I am sending you away," she said.

Caesarion bit his lip. "Where?"

"We do much trade with the prince of Bharukaccha, which is a
land across the Arab ocean. I have sent letters to him and he promises to receive you as an honored guest. You will go there with your
tutor as guardian and jewels enough to buy you your ease until the
day you can return."

"What about you?"

"I shall stay here."

"Here?" He seemed to be thinking about this. "What about that
fat drunken Roman down by the harbor? You're not looking to him for
protection?"

She felt herself color at this unflattering description of Antony.
But she held her temper. "I may yet be able to negotiate with the
Roman Imperator."

"Like you negotiated with my father?"

She slapped his cheek, hard. He flinched and his lower lip
trembled. There was a livid red mark on the side of his face. They
stared at each other. She had thought he would cry, but he held her
eyes. Perhaps there was something of Julius there after all.

"Octavian wants you dead," he said.

"No, he wants *you* dead. He just wants me out of the way. That is why you have to leave."

"When can I come back?"

"Octavian is in poor health; they say it is a miracle he has lived as long as he has. He has no son and his marriage to Livia is barren. As soon as he dies, you can return."

She made it sound so simple. If he died. If Livia did not bear him a son. If, *if*. Antony had been prophesying his death for years and it had never happened. Octavian had survived not only his habitual poor health but two shipwrecks and numerous rebellions. Sometimes she wondered if he was indestructible.

"I don't want to leave," Caesarion said, pouting.

"You have no choice," she said. Losing patience with him, she turned and made her way back up the steps to the palace. She turned around once and saw him standing by the water's edge. He appeared to be crying. Because she had slapped him or because he had to leave her? Or because he was frightened?

She supposed she would never know.

To the Queen Cleopatra, greetings.

I have received your tokens of submission and accept your surrender to my will. However, the question of the succession of the Egyptian crown cannot be resolved in these present circumstances. It is not a diadem I require of you but the head of Marcus Antonius. Send it to me and we may talk again about your son's claim to the throne of Alexander. Do as I ask, and I shall look kindly on you.

Octavianus Gaius Julius Caesar, divi filius, Imperator.

119

BY THE END of the Roman month of May, Octavian had marched south from Antioch. He was now less than five hundred Roman miles from the border. Alexandria was a city on the edge. The bankers and *oeconomi* and court secretaries and merchants downed their expensive wines as if they were water, doused themselves with long-hoarded ointments and perfumes, and argued with each other at hugely expensive *commissatia*, debating whether they should sell everything and go into exile or if they could buy immunity from past loyalties with judiciously placed bribes; in other words, would it be business as usual?

Would there be bloodshed? Would Cleopatra take them all down with her in fiery conflagration? Would Octavian order wholesale slaughter?

And then one day Antony strode from his hut on the breakwater and marched up the hill to Brucheion.

✺ ✺

"My lord Antony," Cleopatra said.

He stood there, on the marbled floor, the Antony of old. He had lost weight; the months spent in his spartan confinement on the wharf had burned away the flab around his waist. His eyes were clearer than she had seen them for some time. It seemed misanthropy agreed with him. He was dressed in the purple chlamys of a Greek courtier, his face freshly shaved, the thick curls cut and attended by a *tonsore*. And he was smiling.

"Majesty," he said.

She returned his smile. "We thought you were lost to us."

"For a time I blamed the world for my misfortunes. Now I see that I have no one to blame but myself."

"We are glad to have you back with us in court."

"I am glad to be returned here. Why is everyone so miserable? Is it the end of the world?"

Polite laughter at that. The Jews were indeed predicting an apocalypse, and the coming of their Messiah. Recent events had only added to the hysteria in the Jewish quarter.

"Some say it may be the end of our world," she said.

Antony looked around the Audience Hall, at the bright-colored gowns, the ringleted greasers in their jewels and their pomades. Alexandria. No, the only Alexandria he had ever known was Cleopatra. It would end with her. "Bankers and merchants," he said softly. "For them, the world never ends. They will lend their money to Romans instead of Greeks." And then he turned around and announced, in ringing tones, "I plan to hold a symposium tonight, in my quarters in the palace which your queen has been kind enough to furnish for my use. I invite all the former members of the Company of Life, all my good friends from my first winter in Alexandria those many years ago."

"We are truly glad to see your spirits so restored," Cleopatra said.

"A man may learn much from solitude."

"So I am told."

"Besides," he added with a grin, "after all these months, I am thirsty again."

❦ ❦

Once he had called it the Company of Life. Now they came together again as the Company of Death.

The chamber was filled with the city's brightest and best, in their finest silks and jewels. Slaves carried chaplets of willow leaves decorated with nightshade berries and poppies, all plants associated with the underworld, and handed them to each of the guests as they arrived, to much brave talk and forced merriment. A Dionysian actor arrived dressed in the black cloak of Hades, Lord of the Underworld; another came as jackal-headed Anubis.

Antony himself wore a double-faced mask, well known to the Greeks among them, Comedy with its mate, Tragedy. "We will have need of both in the days to come!" he told them.

Everywhere there were bowls of gold coins, and the guests were invited to help themselves to as much as they wanted. Then slaves rushed in with couches and tables, and the guests were invited to take their places for the feasting and the wine.

Antony had made it a rule of the evening that no one there speak of Octavian and the advancing Roman army. The talk, he said, must be of fashion and food, theater and music. While harpists played from the alcoves, platter after platter was brought from the kitchens; there were cutlets of deer, gazelle in a spiced sauce, squill patties, roasted meats of hippopotamus and crocodile, cranes stuffed with quail, peacock wings, flamingo tongues, and each dish served with amphorae of the best Chian wine; for dessert there was melons, grapes, dates from Jericho, sweet figs, and honey cakes, all washed down with sweet raisin wine.

"I thought you were lost to me," Cleopatra whispered into his ear as the revels went on around them.

"Would you have missed me?" When she did not answer, he said: "When I was at Paraetonium, I received a delegation from Cyprus, from the wine growers there. They begged me to reconsider." He made light of it, but she saw in his eyes that he was haunted by the sword.

"We can still win," she said.

He turned and looked into her face. "You are truly a remarkable woman."

The servants had brought out the Falernian wines and the toasts had begun. Each man and woman had to drink thirteen toasts, the maximum number allowed, before the dancing could begin. Antony thrust a cup into her hand. "No more talk of this," he said. "Tonight is ours, at least."

Hades led them in their dance of death, around and around the chamber to the music of flutes and harps and drums. Everyone joined their hands in an endless chain, and as the music increased its tempo, the pace increased, the dancers crossing their steps, bowing their heads, moving faster and faster until the tempo reached frantic crescendo.

Finally, drunk with wine, exhausted, replete, they fell laughing on the carpets or the couches, or into the garden beds outside, the men pursuing the serving boys or the laughing slave girls, as their taste allowed, the revels ending in frantic couplings.

Cleopatra and Antony, too, found their refuge together. She helped him blot out the dark days of Actium in her garden, both of them drunk with wine and pleasure and the joy of simply being alive on that hot Alexandrian night. Antony opened his mouth greedily for grape and nipple, licking the sweet juice from her breast, taking his pleasure with her, letting her straddle his thighs as she took a mouthful of rich purple wine and passed it to him with her kiss.

"I thought I had lost you forever," she whispered, her voice husky with drink and surfeit.

"You made me the love the world too much," he said, and perhaps it was true.

She brought him to his pleasure then, the glimpse of soaring view, the little death that mimicked for one moment the great death, that final second that now haunted his every waking moment.

Brother, I ask no mercy from you, for I know what sort of man you are. Yet we have been brothers and we have shared the same table and are conjoined in love and respect for your sister, Octavia. I only ask now that you turn away from Egypt and return to Rome. It was I that stood against you, Cleopatra was merely an ally and client monarch, as Amyntas and the rest, and you have pardoned them. Give me your word that she and her children will live and I will fall on my sword and end it straightaway. I am your enemy, not they. Deny me this and I still have legions and a fleet and I will fight you to the last. Let her live and it is over. Let there be no more blood but mine now. Let her live.

    Marcus Antonius

120

THE SEARING MONTH of Julius and Octavian was almost at Joppa, just three hundred miles distant by sea. Alexandria was choked with dust and the city rippled with heat. Only the sea breeze, the *meltemi* from the north, made life bearable.

Antony and his Club of Death resumed their rounds of the city. Theirs was a defiant gaiety, for an eerie waiting had gripped Alexandria. Would there be fighting, a siege, a massacre? Or perhaps just the name of their ruler would change; perhaps they would become a Roman province like the rest of the world and life would go back to normal? People hoarded food in their houses, made wills, mended quarrels, wrote final letters to friends and family over the sea.

And waited.

Their queen had saved herself from certain disaster countless times before. They suspected she might yet do it again.

❧ ❧

Cleopatra stared at the great lighthouse of Pharos. She remembered when Caesar challenged the forces of Achillas that had been stationed there during his Alexandrian war. It seemed like yesterday. Now she was nearly forty years old and her life was coming to an end.

Too soon, too soon! Give me back that time! Where did it go? Let me live it again!

Mardian was watching her.

She turned away from the window, uneasy that he had seen her in an unguarded moment, that her face might have revealed her thoughts to him. She did not want anyone to know how desperate she had become.

"My spies tell me, Majesty, that Antony has sent missives secretly to Octavian."

"Do your spies know what they say?"

He shook his head.

"Do you think he yet plans to betray me?"

"It is possible. He has been heard to say to his Roman friends that all he wishes now is to retire to private life in Athens and live out the rest of his days as a country gentleman."

"A country gentleman," she murmured. A bizarre notion for those who knew him. Octavian would never believe it. Even if he did, he would never allow it to happen. He had always shown himself to be utterly ruthless in the past, and she saw no reason for him to have a change of heart now, with the whole world in his grasp.

"And what of us, Majesty?"

She felt suddenly tired. "We will barter with Octavian one further time. Send him a letter, Mardian. In the usual forms. Tell him that I shall abdicate my throne and live in banishment if he wishes. I shall also send him everything that is in the Royal Treasury, a sum beyond his imaginings. In return, he is to name Caesarion as my heir. If he fails to do this, tell him I shall immolate myself and the Treasury together, and he will lose everything he seeks to gain."

Mardian looked up from the wax tablet on which he was noting her instructions. His eyes were mournful. "This is a deception, Majesty?"

"No, Mardian."

"But you cannot!"

"It is the Treasury he wants more than anything. If he thinks he will lose it, he will bargain."

"And if he does not?"

"It is the last great treasure of the world outside Babylon. If he thinks he will lose it, he will barter."

"You cannot play the Roman! I will not allow it!"

She smiled. "I am touched by your concern for me, but you forget yourself. I take orders from no one. Not even my former tutor. You have not ruled me since I was fourteen and you will not again, old friend."

"There is another way, Majesty. My brother-in-law Apollodorus can guarantee you safe passage to Spain—"

"The lady Isis flees the Nile for the end of the world?"

"Majesty, this talk of Isis—"

"I do not wish to listen to your blasphemies. I am yet the spirit of Egypt, Mardian. Say no more about it. If I go to Spain, Octavian will pursue me there. Should I swim to the bottom of the ocean, I daresay he would send his minions after me. I must reach an accommodation with him now or I shall confront my death. Either way, I shall have some peace. Finally."

She left the chamber, did not see the expression on her eunuch's face. Even if she had, she would not have been persuaded to change her course. For the woman she was, for the dice the Fates had rolled, there was no other choice for her.

> *To the most noble Antonius*
> *Greetings.*
> *We are distressed to hear you talk of death. We have no desire to see you dead, and that you should believe so grieves me deeply. This quarrel between us, I believe, has at its root just one cause and her name is Cleopatra. All that needs be to end this war is for you to deliver her to us and we shall again talk of peace between us.*
> *Imperator Gaius Julius Caesar, divi* filius.

His name was Thyrsus and he was a freedman, sent by Octavian himself. Cleopatra received him formally in her audience chamber. She spent many hours preparing herself for this interview. She wore a purple gown banded with gold at the hem and shoulders, and gold sandals. There was a heavy gold necklace at her throat, and on her head a gold diadem with the royal *uraeus*. A golden snake, artfully fashioned from gold, was entwined around her right upper arm, and she held a scepter in her left hand.

"Your Majesty," the man said, bowing, "I bear a message from Caesar."

The name echoed like blasphemy around the red-veined marble pillars. She fidgeted on the golden throne, struggling with her temper. "You have spoken to him?" she said. "From beyond the grave?"

The man appeared confused.

She settled her gaze on the unlikely creature at the foot of the dais. "There was just one Caesar," she reminded this boy, this freedman, this *nothing*, "and he is father to my son. Your lord is one Gaius Octavianus, and he is neither Caesar nor the son of a god. Talk plainly to me or I shall have you thrown to the snakes."

He turned pale. It was an insult, she thought, sending this tanned and handsome boy to her as his ambassador. Octavian must believe his own stories of her depravity, if he thought to seduce her with this pretty herald.

"What is your message?" she snapped.

"Caes— The noble Octavian says that he was alarmed to receive your letter and it grieves him to hear you talk of death."

"Or rather it grieves him to hear me talk of destroying the treasure he covets so dearly."

"Indeed not, Majesty. I was there. He wept openly for you."

This impertinent boy. Does he think I am so foolish as to believe his nonsense?

"He has asked me to entreat you that if you will throw open the gates of the city and send him the head of the traitor, Marcus Antonius—"

"What?"

Thyrsus swallowed hard. He had doubtless expected a queen cowed and timid from defeat, ready to bargain for anything.

"The Imperator said . . . said that . . ."

"Tell him if he wants my husband's head, he will have to break down the walls and come and get it himself! He will not even have to get it pickled for the return to Rome, for Antony has done the job for him. Should he decide on such a course, remind him of what lies in my mausoleum and tell him again that Cleopatra does not say she will do something that she cannot do. Now get out of here! Now!"

Her Nubian guards dragged the boy bodily out of the door. She looked down at her hands; her fingers were clamped, white-knuckled, around the arm of her throne. Antony had suffered enough betrayal for one lifetime. He would not find another at the hands of Cleopatra.

121

THYRSUS WAS RECLINING in the chamber they had given him, in the south wing of the palace. It overlooked a garden winking with bright flowers and a dark pool where palace slaves tended the lotuses that floated on the surface. Beside the sumptuous couch where he lay was a bowl of ripe figs and oranges, set on a table of priceless carved ivory. There were vases of alabaster and basalt ranged around the room, and silk hangings on the windows. They had even arranged entertainment for him, a troupe of Syrian acrobats. He had decided to ask the youngest member of the troupe, a young boy with buttocks as hard as apples, if he would like to earn some extra denarii after the performance.

He thought he might like the life of ambassador to the great Caesar.

But he had to admit, the interview with Queen Cleopatra had rocked him. He had heard much about this depraved queen, and everything he had seen and heard during their brief audience confirmed the rumors. She was indeed beautiful, with eyes like burning charcoal and a temper to match. Terrifying. They said she tortured prisoners for amusement on dull afternoons, and slept with one of her bodyguards every night, only to have him put to death the next morning.

It would make a fine story when he returned to Rome. He would say he saw it with his own eyes, because it was doubtless true.

He chose another fig and peeled away the skin to the sticky, sweet flesh underneath. Ripe to bursting, he thought, smiling. Like this gypo queen.

His repose was rudely shattered.

He yelped in fear as the door burst open and a mountain barged in, the bent-nosed gladiator's face twisted with fury, a horse whip in its right hand. A massive paw grabbed him by the throat and lifted him bodily from the couch.

"You piece of camel shit," this apparition breathed into his face, and then hit him under the jaw with the handle of the whip. He fell on his back on the floor, stunned.

He lay there senseless for a few moments and then tried to get up and run. But the giant grabbed him and flung him against the wall. The breath went out of him. He heard the whistle of the whip and a hot agony burned through his tunic, searing the flesh of his back.

"What did she say to you?" the man screamed.

The pain was so shocking, he could not speak. The giant grabbed him by the hair and twisted his head back. He saw one of the Nubian guards staring over the giant's shoulder, too terrified to intervene, though he had a sword and the man was unarmed save for the whip.

"What did she say to you?" the man yelled at him again.

He tried to say *Who?* but the sound came out as no more than a sob deep in his throat.

The man shook him, like a dog tearing meat from a bone. "What message did the queen give you for Octavian?"

"She said . . ." His voice came out as shrill as a girl's. He barely recognized it as his own. "She said that . . . if he . . . wanted . . . Antony's head . . . then he . . . he . . . he should . . . come and . . . come and . . ."

The giant grew impatient and dropped him onto the floor like a sack of wheat. The whip whistled three more times while he cowered on the floor, trying to crawl into a corner, away from the terrible burning lash. Disgusted, the apparition threw the whip at him and stormed out.

Thyrsus curled into a ball on the floor and wept.

Dearest Brother,

Please find your freedman Thyrsus here returned to you, soundly thrashed. I found his face displeasing and his general manner a provocation. My temper is short these days, due to my current circumstances, as I am sure you will understand. Should you wish to

revenge yourself on me for these actions, I believe you have a freed-
man of mine in your hire, one Sisyphus, a short fellow with one arm
whom I once employed to make up filthy jokes about you. You have
my leave to give him a thrashing in return. Then we'll be quits.

Marcus Antonius

122

CHARMION HAD SPENT the last half hour combing through her mistress's silky hair. Now she held it out like a rope in both her hands and twisted twice, before fixing it on top of her head with gold pins. As she worked on Cleopatra's coiffure, Iras, the queen's dresser, worked from a little ebony box, darkening her eyes with malachite, painting her hands with henna. Cleopatra watched them work in a polished silver mirror that a slave held in front of her face.

Mardian's face appeared around the ivory screen. Of all her servants and ministers, he alone was allowed access to her at any hour of the night and day. "A messenger from Octavian, Majesty," he said, handing her the leather-covered metal cylinder.

She took it from him and broke the seal. "Where is he now?" she asked.

"Raphia, Majesty. On the border."

Octavian had made the forced march through the terrible heat of the Sinai in just two days. Two days without water in unbearable heat, she thought. He must be impatient for my blood.

She read the letter through, twice, as if there were a sentence that might have been overlooked, something to offer hope when there was none.

To the Queen Cleopatra,

I fear there has been a misunderstanding between us. I have
no quarrel with you; but while you continue to harbor an enemy
of Rome, what choice do I have but to send my army wherever

this man chooses to hide. If you expel him from the city, and send
him to me in chains, you will find me gentle and understanding to
your situation.

Octavianus Gaius Julius Caesar, divi filius, *Imperator*

She held the letter to the candle flame until it was well alight and
then tossed it on the floor to burn to ash on the marble.

"The priests still support you," he said. "In the *chora* they have
vowed to raise armies to fight the invaders."

"Why would they do this?"

"Because you stored grain for them when there were famines.
Because you revered the Apis bull and helped restore their temples.
Because you are Isis."

She shook her head. "Tell them to send their fellahin back to the
fields. Why waste more lives?" She handed Mardian a sealed papyrus
scroll. "Here are my instructions for my children. Selene and
Ptolemy are to be hidden in tunnels under the palace. Their hiding
places have already been stocked with food, lamps, and water. The
Captain of the Household Guard will escort them there."

"What of Antyllus?"

"He is his father's responsibility."

"And Caesarion?"

"He is to leave with his tutor, as we discussed. Tomorrow. Is Apollodorus here?"

"He is waiting outside, Majesty."

"Send him in."

⚜ ⚜

Important in these last few days for people to remember her as invincible. When she emerged from behind the screen she was perfectly
made, in a golden gown, with the sacred knot of Isis between her
breasts. There were pearls set in gold at her ears and a heavy collar of
lapis and gold at her throat. Her hair had been braided with pearls,
and there was a golden serpent curled around her right upper arm.
Its eyes were carnelian stones.

Apollodorus waited for her in the antechamber. A little older, a
little grayer, a little thicker around the girth, but with that same
expression she always remembered, as of a man vastly entertained by

the iniquities of the world. She remembered their first interview all those years ago, in her exile's tent at Mount Kasios. She had been frightened then, too.

"Majesty," he said.

"So. You are to come to my rescue once more."

"That was a long time ago. Do you still have the carpet?"

"The carpet was Caesar's. He took it to Rome. It is lost now."

That impertinent smile. Apollodorus was much too familiar with her, but that was part of his charm and perhaps also why she trusted him.

"There is no profit in this for you. If Octavian discovers what you have done, it will make an exile of you also."

"I am rich enough to run."

"But why do it?"

He drew breath. "Majesty, my family have all made our living from the sea. I did it from trade, by robbing others by legal means. My younger brother, however, became a brigand. The Romans crucified him. It took him three days to die. Caesar ordered it."

"Julius?"

He nodded. "I hate these Romans. I have always prayed that one day you would triumph. If not you, then perhaps your son."

She experienced a flicker of doubt. Should she entrust her son to this man, knowing what she now knew?

"He is Caesar's son," she said.

"No. He is your son. I would protect him with my life."

"I hope that will not be necessary."

"I have made the necessary arrangements. I shall escort him on a felucca as far as Coptos. From there we will join a caravan to make the desert crossing to Berenice on the Red Sea. One of my ships will be waiting there to give us safe passage to India. But we must wait for the summer monsoon, as it is the only time ships can sail eastward safely."

"Do not fail me, Apollodorus."

He grinned boyishly. "Have I ever let you down before?"

He bowed and was about to leave. "What about your wife?" she said.

He turned, and there was an expression on his face she had never seen before. He drew a long breath. "My wife was a leper these twenty years, Majesty. I have not seen her in that time. She lived on an island in the Nile south of Coptos. Between Mardian and myself, we ensured she was well cared for." He shrugged. "She died last year."

"Mardian never spoke of this."

"I imagine his sister's misfortunes were not relevant to the affairs of state."

She felt somehow chastened. Other lives had always been so remote. Yet she was intrigued by this man, had been in truth ever since Mount Kasios. "Is there no woman then, in all that time, who has been fortunate enough to receive your affections?"

"Only you, Majesty," he said, and proffered that familiar crooked smile before being ushered away.

123

PELUSIUM HAD FALLEN. There was nothing standing now between Alexandria and Octavian. She could wait no longer. She resigned herself to her duty as a mother and as a queen.

Caesarion was dressed in the coarse and common clothes of a tribesman from the desert, his Roman features darkened with dirt. At least he has the manner of a fellahin, Cleopatra thought. That scowl suits your disguise perfectly. Rhoddon was with him, dressed in similar fashion. He looked ridiculous. That great gawk of a scholar isn't going to fool a blind man, let alone a Roman soldier.

The barge was pulled up to the landing place in the royal harbor. A common barge, as the hundreds that plied the Nile every day, so as not to draw attention to its precious cargo. Caesarion's bodyguard, who would escort him as far as Coptos, were hurried aboard and hidden belowdecks. Rhoddon followed them, slaves carrying two trunks of books.

The barge would bear them across the royal harbor and through the Heptastadion into the Harbor of Good Return and into Lake Mareotis through the canal under Rhakotis. Caesarion would hide belowdecks with Rhoddon, so Octavian's spies might not see him.

This, she supposed, was her real parting from Julius, for Caesarion was all she had left of him. All her hopes for the future were invested there and went with him today. She held him to her, but felt no answering pressure in return.

"Good-bye," she whispered.

He said nothing, but turned and went down the great curving marble steps of the landing to the waiting barge. Impossible to know if he was choked with sorrow or fear. She never knew his mind. In that, at least, he was very like his father.

She had left a mountain of offerings in the Temple of Isis for his safe delivery to India.

Apollodorus came last to make his obeisance. She cast one doubtful look at the Sicilian. Even after what he had said to her, was she right to trust him with so much?

"I will look after him," he said, reading her thoughts. She watched the barge slip away across the harbor. She knew she would never see her son again.

≫ ≫

Antony had made his chart room in the same chamber that Caesar had used during his Alexandrian campaign, and it was here he held his final war council. Canidius was present, with a handful of officers who had been with Antony from Actium, as well as her Phoenician admirals, the commander of her Egyptian levies, and the captain of her Guard.

Antony was in armor, a Roman once more, the ornamented gold and ivory breastplate polished and gleaming, a purple Imperator's cloak around his shoulders.

"My lord Antonius," she said as she entered.

He grinned at her.

"I did not expect to find you here."

"You thought I would play the drunkard while there is a battle to be had?"

"I do not know what I thought."

She came to the table. This was a different Antony from the man who headed these same conferences at Actium, bowed and blowsy with drink. Now his personality held the room transfixed. If only she had had this Antony then.

He pointed to the chart, pointing out the disposition of Octavian's forces and the location of their own defenses. "We still have four legions," he said, "along with our Egyptian troops and Nubian Guard. In the harbor we have the big warships that survived the battle of Actium, an impressive fleet on its own."

Octavian, perhaps through overconfidence, or perhaps for once through undue haste, had brought just seven legions and a small navy of biremes and Liburnians.

"Our army is well fed and well paid," Antony said. "His are tired, thirsty, and have not been paid for months, perhaps years. And this time his navy does not have Agrippa. So perhaps the fight is more evenly matched than we thought.

"His vanguard was sighted yesterday at Canopus, just over one hundred stadia from where we stand. I have drawn up our legions outside the Gate of the Sun, here, facing east. I will command the cavalry, Canidius the infantry. Publicola here will command the navy."

Publicola. Personally, I wouldn't have him in charge of my chamber pot, she thought. But after the recent defections, centurions have become generals overnight. Antony's dresser might soon find himself at the head of a legion.

"You think we can win?" she asked him.

"We can turn the tide. If Octavian is defeated here, perhaps I can persuade the garrison at Cyrenaica to think again. If they come over, others will mutiny. And his new Asian allies will only support him as long as they think he can win. We are in better shape than I thought."

She looked at Canidius. He seemed to believe it also.

"Then let us do it," she said.

❦ ❦

He came to her quarters late that night. He stood awkwardly by the door, still in his armor, no longer young, ravaged by wine and decadence and misfortune. But still, in his way, Antony, the Inimitable.

"Husband."

He smiled.

"Why are you here?"

"You are my wife."

"We have children. There is no sense in making more. In our current predicament."

"This is not politics," he said, and laid his crested helmet on the long cedar table. The yellow light of the oil lamps glittered on the brass trappings of his armor. Over the silence between them came the familiar sounds of the Lochias palace, the gentle rhythm of the sea; and through the windows the beacon in the tower of the Pharos turned the waters of the royal harbor the color of fire.

"I am sorry," he said.

"Sorry?"

"For everything." He fumbled with the buckles on his breastplate. "Will you help me, please?" he whispered finally.

She got up and helped him out of the heavy armor. Then he put his arms around her and kissed her. For a moment she was lost. He pulled off her clothes, tearing the fine silks. Worth a fortune, but then she supposed it no longer mattered.

She braced herself for onslaught, but then he stopped and held her, his face buried in her neck. He stayed like that for a long time, and then, when he kissed her again, he began to make love to her with a sweetness that reminded her of their first time together, in Tarsus.

"I have missed you," he murmured.

"You miss no one."

"You are wrong there."

He lifted her by the arms, perhaps to prove to her still that he was as strong as always, and she gasped as he entered her. I have missed this, she realized. I have missed being loved by this man. He is cloaked in frailties, as Julius never was. Yet in a way I love him the more for it.

Was it minutes or hours? There was no sense of time. Afterward she held his head in the circle of her arm, his cheek pressed against her shoulder. She could feel the drumming of a pulse at his throat. A droplet of perspiration trickled between her breasts.

"Did you ever love me more than Julius?" he whispered.

She did not answer him, and he did not ask the question again. They listened to the silky cadenza of the sea, everything done now, everything forgiven.

PART VII

Not heaven itself upon the past has power

But what has been, has been, and I have had my hour.

124

First day of the Egyptian month of Mesore

CLEOPATRA STARED AT the great lighthouse, the flame, she knew, visible for hundreds of stadia across the ocean, magnified by the polished bronze mirror shield in its lantern. Even today a slave clad in thick leather armor would be turning the shield in its groove around the fire, so it could be seen far out to sea.

The lighthouse had become as much a part of her life as the sun in the morning, the moon at night. Strange that this would be the last time she might ever gaze on it.

Antony's soldiers had their first skirmish today. His cavalry routed Octavian's vanguard as they tried to make camp near the Hippodrome. The real fighting would take place tomorrow.

She heard the sound of Antony's revels from the halls below. If it was to be his last night on the earth, the New Dionysus had given himself one last night to remember. He gathered his generals and the Company of Death, and called together every Dionysiac player, every acrobat, every fire eater in the city for one last great entertainment.

It was impossible to sleep anyway. Tonight the ghosts were walking the corridors, slipping along these halls of filmy curtains, and the whispering of their feet on the marble tiles kept her from her rest. There was Julius, watching her from the desk where he wrote his Gallic memoirs, that sardonic smile still poignantly remembered after all these years; her brother Ptolemy, his face creased with tears as he begged Julius not to send him out of the palace; and Arsinoë, proud and haughty in filmy white silk, her beautiful face framed by a sneer.

And finally there was little Antiochus, staring accusingly at her from the couch, his face shrunken and pale. She closed her eyes. "I had no choice," she told him.

You cannot nail a shadow to the floor, she thought. As a queen, as a goddess, I am all things to all the world. If they would label me cruel, I would recite my kindnesses and mercies until dawn. If they should call me kitten, I could have my executioners pull the bodies from their resting places in the sewers and the swamps. No one is both good and great. How is it possible? Humility and charity might sometimes be found in any king or queen, but so must strength and aggression.

So what shall they say of me tomorrow when I am gone? Octavian will make a whore of me, when I have had just two men in my bed and have lived chaste half my life. He will label me torturer and wanton and temptress with his lies and half-truths, when all I have done is only what a ruler must, and often with reluctance.

I am not cruel by nature and I do not revel in death, yet I have done things that make me shudder still; but I should do them again if my duty asked it of me. Is the murder of a few members of a family worse than the slaughter of millions of foreigners in a war? Ptolemy led a rebellion against me, as did Arsinoë. We were not brother and sister as humbler people understand brother and sister to be.

With young Antiochus, pale child that he was, what choice did I have? Pale children became sallow adventurers like our friend Octavian, and if I had Olympos poison him, it was to prevent greater bloodshed later. And Fulvia; that was just good statecraft, and no one could truthfully say that she was missed.

Yet their ghosts come to haunt me tonight. They are waiting for me to join them in the Shades, their spirits watching me from the darkened corridors, taking their revenge in my anguish tonight. In that, at least, they will not be denied.

⚜ ⚜

And so the searing month of Julius came to an end.

She stood on the terrace and watched Antony take his leave of the children. Selene clung to his neck as if she were drowning and would not let him go. Little Alexander tried to be brave for him, standing ramrod straight like a sentry, but his face was creased with tears. Unlikely he would marry into the house of Medea now. After the Nabataeans rebelled and Antony lost Syria, it was too dangerous to send him east. Everything had been lost with her fleet in the Red Sea.

Antony scooped Philadelphus up in his arms and kissed him. He was too little to understand, but he was crying because his brother and sister were crying. Antony laughed and was putting a brave face on it, of course, as Antony would. Perhaps he could not believe himself that it might really be over.

And then there was Antyllus, standing apart from the others. An awkward boy, he had a stricken look on his face that was painful to see. He and Antony looked at each other as if they were complete strangers, which in many ways they were.

Then he turned to her. "My queen," he said.

"My lord."

She wondered what he would do. She had braced herself for this final battle, and she feared that sentiment might break her resolve.

He gave her a lopsided grin. And suddenly there he was, the old Antony, golden, larger than life, spoiling for a fight. "I shall see you at our victory celebrations," he said, and gave her an extravagant salute.

She watched him ride off toward the Gate of the Sun and the flat, sun-beaten reaches around the Hippodrome. A plume of dust trailed into the sky, Octavian's legions taking up their positions.

We can still win this.

125

IT WAS QUIET, an unearthly stillness had settled over the city. This morning the docks and the markets were silent, there was no rumble of cartwheels from the streets, and inside the palace walls there were no gardeners bent over the flower beds. Cleopatra stood on the terrace with Mardian, watched in utter silence as her navy rowed out past the Pharos to meet Octavian. She appeared outwardly calm, but her heart was hammering against her ribs so hard it was almost painful.

From here she could watch the great sea battle take place. As the fleets approached each other she waited for the great stones and fire baskets to arc through the sky. Instead, as soon as they were in the open water, Publicola's vanguard boated the oars and turned broadside to Octavian's ships, in the universal signal of friendship.

She realized she had been holding her breath, and she let it out slowly. Another defection. Octavian's ships sailed past her own without hindrance and made for the harbor.

It was over.

She turned to Mardian. "Let us take a walk in the sun," she said.

❦ ❦

Antony leaped from his bay and threw himself inside the tent that had been erected on the Hippodrome as his *principia*. He took off his helmet and hurled it across the tent. All he had asked of the gods was the chance to die on the battlefield with some honor, and now they had denied him even that. A few minutes before, he had watched his cavalry desert him once again, wheeling away from the ranks and leaving him alone on the battlefield. When his infantry saw what had happened, they, too, turned and fled back to the city.

Faithless bastards. *Eaters of shit!*

Eros, his dresser, ran into the tent as Antony struggled to remove the heavy breastplate, helping him unfasten the strappings. When it was free, Antony tossed it into the dust along with the curved rectangular shield with the emblem that designated him Imperator of the Roman army.

He gripped the edge of the map table and tossed it on its side into the dirt, trampling the charts and battle plans under his boots.

"Fucking useless gypo fucking bastards!" he screamed.

Eros stood in the corner, trembling.

Antony pulled out his sword.

He tossed it at Eros. "Do it!"

"My lord?"

"We're fucked, finished. Understand? Do it!" He tore open his tunic. "Finish me!"

"I can't . . ." Eros stammered.

"You have to! That's your job!"

Eros stared at the sword in his hand and then at Antony. His eyes were goggling in his head. Just a boy, an addle-brained country turnip who had never known any other life but putting on and pulling off his tunics and his armor and fetching him bowls of water to wash his face in the mornings. He was shivering with fright.

"But I love you, lord," he said.

"Just do it!"

Eros looked as if he was about to cry. He took the sword, his hands shaking so hard Antony thought he might drop it. But then, without any warning, he turned the point of the sword around, braced the hilt on the tamped dirt, and launched himself on the blade. It was over before Antony could stop him.

And then Eros lay there at his feet, whimpering with the pain, his guts in the dirt, vomiting up blood.

"You bastard," Antony grunted. Weren't things bad enough?

Antony tried to free the sword, but it was lodged deep in bone and gristle, and when he attempted to pull it clear, he succeeded only in lifting the poor boy a foot off the ground.

He found another sword in his armor chest and drew it from its scabbard. Eros was still taking his time about dying. Not an attractive proposition. His loyalty was touching, but it was not what Antony needed right now, a glimpse of the ugliness of his own death, this keening agony, the purple and yellow viscera oozing onto the floor.

He laid his cloak on the ground. Don't want to get dirt on my liver, he thought, and laughed hysterically. He braced the point of the sword under his rib, aiming upward. I hope my aim is better than his, he thought, hearing his dresser's last gasping breaths.

And then he hesitated. Long minutes dragged by. He looked at Eros. His eyes had glazed over, like a hooked fish that had lain too long in the bottom of the boat. Dead.

By all the gods, I thought it would be easier than this.

Twice now I have failed myself. First at Actium, when I leaped to safety from the deck of my flagship. I told myself that it was just common sense, that a general has to save himself for the sake of his army. But in my heart I knew I was afraid. My valor had failed me.

And then it deserted me a second time, at Paraetonium, when honor demanded sacrifice. How many times did I sit on that desolate beach, with my sword, delaying over necessity?

I have grown too fond of life. I am too little the soldier now, and too much the god. But gods are immortal, men are not.

He felt the point of the sword pierce the skin, felt a trickle of blood leak down his stomach. Dionysus had promised him redemption in the afterlife, but he feared the promise was a lie. This act, now, was his only redemption, and he feared that even now he could not do what must be done.

Do it, Antony, do it now!

But still he hesitated.

❦ ❦

Cleopatra made her last offerings to Isis, kneeling among the swirling plumes of incense. To her dismay, she found that her hands were shaking. Give me strength to do what I must, she prayed. Let me be faithful to Egypt till the end.

She heard the hammer of hooves in the paved street, heavy boots on the cobbles. A messenger brought the news. Antony's legions had run and his cavalry had deserted to Octavian. The harbor was filling with Octavian's ships. There was little time left now.

"We must hurry," Mardian urged her from the doorway.

She rose to her feet and followed him along the quiet and shaded paths outside the temple to the doors of the mausoleum. Charmion and Iras were already there, waiting for her. As soon as she was inside, they leaned their weight against the great cedar doors, which slammed shut with a deafening crash. They slid back the heavy bolts.

❦ ❦

Why was it so hard to die? Antony wondered, staring at the billowing purple silk of the pavilion. Like a reluctant guest, death stands there on the threshold, undecided still, even after I have so effusively invited him in.

There was blood everywhere, on his hands, and his clothes, and thick gobs of it on his cloak. His limbs were numb with pain and he could not move. He was shivering with cold.

By all the gods!

Visions coming to him. Aphrodite sailing down the river at Tarsus, purple sails billowing like the silk of the tent; he saw a spotty schoolboy with bad teeth, and then heard Caesar's voice, *Marcus, this is my nephew, Octavian;* the memory faded to the mountains of Parthia, cold and capped with snow.

He heard a peacock screech, saw the sun disappear behind a cloud. Then he heard Octavia's voice. "You will find my loyalty is worth far more to you, Marcus."

Loyalty. Where would a man ever find loyalty in this snake pit?

Faces swam in and out of his vision: Canidius, slaves, servants. He heard someone say: "He's botched the job." Another vision or was it real?

"Cleopatra," he said, his voice dry as grating metal, the coppery taste of his own blood in his mouth. Now, at the very last, he found himself guilty of the crimes Octavian had laid at his feet. He did not wish to leave the Egyptian queen.

❧ ❧

The rich and heady smell of spices, the gleam of lapis lazuli and emeralds from the dark vault. Beneath them the pyre was ready. Torches flickered in their sockets on the walls, the flames reflected in the buttery stacks of gold.

Mardian could hear the shouts of Octavian's soldiers very close, centurions shouting orders in rough Latin. Soon they would be at the doors of the mausoleum itself.

Cleopatra stood by the casement window on the upper floor. She had dressed like a queen for this, her final performance, an Egyptian pharaoh queen, the golden *uraeus* on her brow, her body sheathed in a golden gown, bangles on her arms and ankles. So composed, so still.

Mardian saw that a ladder had been placed against the sill. "You must go now," she said to him.

He experienced a bewildering surge of emotion, hope and disappointment and fear all battling each other for his attention. "But I do not want to leave you," he said.

"Charmion and Iras have made their choices. I accept them here. They are servants, and it is right that they should die here with me. Not you, Mardian."

He hesitated, trapped between loyalty and love. And he *did* love her. After all these years, first as her tutor and then as her adviser, he could not imagine a world without Cleopatra in it. And he discovered, to his astonishment and against his every expectation, that he no longer wanted to live.

Someone was hammering on the heavy doors. The Romans had found the mausoleum, were attacking the doors with their fists and swords. "Go, quickly," she said.

Still he hesitated.

Someone was shouting to them from below. He looked down. Windows were built high into the casement, overlooking the sea on one side and the courts of Isis on the other. A cart had drawn up at the marble steps below, and he recognized Canidius, still in his general's cloak, and several other of Antony's Romans. They and a knot of servants were clustered around a figure that lay on a litter on the back of the cart, wrapped in a bloodstained cloak. For a moment Mardian did not recognize him.

"You must help us!" Canidius shouted up to them.

Cleopatra seemed to sag against the wall. "Oh," she murmured.

Canidius did not wait for their answer. He had tied a rope to the four corners of the litter and now he was climbing the ladder. As he reached the sill he tossed the leading end to Mardian.

"Quickly," he shouted.

Octavian's soldiers were attacking the doors with a ram now. So little time.

Down below, the slaves were helping the Roman officers hoist the litter into the air. Canidius was straining at the rope. "Help me!" he shouted to Mardian.

"What good does it do?" Mardian groaned.

"He wants to die at the queen's side. After everything, he should have that, at least."

Mardian just stared at him.

It was Cleopatra who moved first. She pushed past him and began to drag on the rope, tearing the pretty manicured nails and soft pampered skin of her hands. An astonishing sight, for he had seen her lift nothing in her whole life heavier than a scepter. And there she was, dragging on the rough hemp like any peasant girl hauling at a well in the *chora*. The sight galvanized him, and he threw his weight at the rope, too, Charmion and Iras beside him.

The battering at the doors reached its crescendo.

The litter swayed and scraped against the wall, and with every jerking movement Antony cried out in pain. Finally they had it hauled up to the casement, and while the three women strained at the rope, holding it steady, Mardian and Canidius hefted the litter into the room. Antony shrieked with agony. There were bloody drag marks on the stone sill and the marble flooring.

Cleopatra threw herself across his body.

The great doors trembled under the assasult of the Roman rams.

"We must hurry!" Charmion said.

"Wait, wait," Cleopatra said.

Ah, so you are a woman after all, Mardian thought. You do love him. All this time you told me it was just politics.

Cleopatra was staring at the blood on her hands and arms as if she had never seen such stuff before. It was everywhere. It seemed impossible for one body to contain so much.

Antony was gray, his eyes staring. He tried to say something, but the words would not come. His hand clawed ineffectually at the air.

"Majesty," Mardian said.

She stared up at him, her face transformed by grief and pain. He had never seen her this way before, even as a child.

"Majesty, we must hurry! Give the command and we will light the pyre!"

Antony convulsed again. She held his hand and stroked his curls, and then she started to weep.

There was a commotion at the window. Octavian's soldiers had found the ladder. Cleopatra seemed to realize, too late, what had happened. Canidius ran to the window to throw it down, but it was too late.

A dagger appeared in Cleopatra's hand. She was about to plunge it into her breast, but one of the Roman officers was already inside the room, and he leapt at her and wrestled it from her.

Three other legionaries had leaped in through the window. Canidius was captured. Mardian grabbed one of the torches on the wall. Not too late to light the pyre. But a soldier tripped him. He fell on the granite floor, the breath knocked out of him. When he looked up, the man was standing over him, a sword held at his throat.

Mardian looked over at the queen. She was held tight by the soldiers, as any common prisoner. Antony lay at her feet, eyes glassy with the death that had finally accepted entrance to his riotous but noble house.

126

BERENICE, ON THE RED SEA COAST OF UPPER EGYPT

A BREATHLESS NIGHT, too hot to sleep. A full moon floating above silky clouds. Apollodorus stood on the deck of his felucca, staring at the dim lights ranged along the shore, listening to the gentle lap of the black water against the hull. So. It was almost done. Caesarion was a tiresome boy, but Apollodorus felt he had fulfilled his part of the commission, as the queen had asked. Now there was nothing to do but wait for word from Alexandria. If the queen reached an accommodation with Octavian, everything would be well. If not, they would take the sailing across to India.

The deck creaked. He turned around and saw that it was only the tutor, Rhoddon. A weak, feminine creature. Well, he was a eunuch.

He turned back to the water. "A nice moon," he said to Rhoddon. "Isis is watching over us."

There was a single shock of pain as the dagger plunged deep between his ribs, followed by a moment's utter incomprehension, and then he felt himself falling toward the water. The blackness swallowed him up before he realized that the weak, feminine creature had teeth.

ALEXANDRIA-BY-EGYPT

Almost a week now she had been held prisoner in her own palace. Octavian had imprisoned them, insultingly, in the guests' quarters in the south wing. She, Charmion, Iras, and Mardian had all been locked in together. There were just two small rooms, four beds, a washstand, narrow windows newly fitted with bars. A chest of her clothes had been delivered, and each day they were given some bread, fruit, and water.

There was no word from Octavian, but every night she could hear the soldiers drinking and swearing and laughing in the gardens.

Antony had been buried, as he requested, in the mausoleum. She had watched the funeral procession from the barred window. His gilt coffin had been borne through the palace on a golden carriage to a solemn dirge of cymbals and drums. In death Octavian could afford to be magnanimous.

Octavian sent a messenger, his freedman, Thyrsus, who preened himself in front of her like the palace cat, enjoying his exalted commission and the fact that she could no longer afford the imperious manners of their last parley. He seemed to take particular pleasure in informing her that Alexander, Selene, and Philadelphus had been found in their sanctuary in the catacombs and taken prisoner; Antyllus had been murdered by Octavian's orders after he was found hiding in the shrine of the deified Caesar.

But still no news of Caesarion.

She had eaten nothing since the fall of the city. She had resigned herself to her bed, speaking to no one. Charmion and Iras sat with her, in attendance, but she would not let them dress her or attend to her hair or her cosmetic.

Finally, on the eighth day, he came.

He was as unappetizing as ever, she thought. His skin had been burned by the desert wind, and his lips were cracked and dry. He had on a ridiculous broad-brimmed hat to shield his face from the sun, and his homemade tunic was badly fitting. To look at him you would not think him any more than a halfway successful laundryman. And now he ruled the world.

He sprawled on one of the couches.

"You look thin," he said. She knew her appearance must shock him. In Rome she had been a much younger woman, painstakingly primped and coiffured for state occasions. Now here she lay in her bed, pale and sallow, her hair lying in tangled bunches around her pillow.

"I seem to have lost my appetite," she said.

"So I have been told."

She wondered what he wanted. To see her beg? Or perhaps he was contemplating a taste of Egypt, as Julius had once described it. Did he think she might try to bargain with him in that same way, offering herself along with her throne as part of the same trade?

"Are you here to amuse yourself?" she asked.

"No, indeed. I find nothing amusing in your humiliation."

"Humiliation? I thought it was just defeat."

"They are the same thing."

There was something in his eyes, a soft, gloating expression that told her to be careful. Caesarion! she thought. Why else would he wait so long to visit me? He wanted to be sure his victory was complete. She felt her heart lurch in her chest. No, please, not my son.

"What are your plans for me?" she asked him.

He picked idly at a pimple on his cheek. "You shall return with me to Rome. You shall be the centerpiece at my Triumph. The infamous Queen Cleopatra in chains; the plebeians will love it. You are quite notorious in Italy, you know."

"Thanks to you."

"Well, you did rather play into my hands. Or Antony did."

"Antony may have been naive, but at least he was brave and good-hearted. You were very opposite men."

The barb hurt him. Perhaps not so much the nature of it, for she supposed he was impervious to her opinion of him, but because she still had the gall to confront him. "After the Triumph, I plan to have you strangled in the Tullianum prison and your body thrown in the sewer."

She felt herself blanch. Why did I not take my opportunity when it was offered? The pyre had been prepared, all I had to do was lay the flame. I was a fool to have cried for Antony. Why did I let myself down at the last?

He sat forward. "You *can* save yourself."

He waited for her to ask how. But she would not give him that pleasure.

So finally he went on: "You bestowed your favors on Caesar and Antony. Should you bestow them here, you would not find me ungrateful."

She was right. It was what he wanted. She could imagine how his gratitude would display itself. "I should rather mate with a warthog," she said. There, it was said before she even had time to think. But she meant it.

He leaped to his feet. His face was pale. "You will regret having said that to me. Perhaps you would like to think on those words when you follow my chariot through the Forum, dragging your chains behind you. By then you would have had a year to grow filthy and pale in the Tullianum. You shall be the one who looks like a warthog." As if he would have had her any other way, she thought. If she had agreed to play the wife for him, he would have taken his pleasure and handed her to his executioner anyway.

He made to leave, then turned back. "By the way, I almost forgot to tell you. Your son, Caesarion . . ."

Her head jerked up.

"He is dead."

He smiled, enjoying the look on her face.

"His guardian met with an unfortunate accident at Berenice and drowned. Your son's tutor then persuaded him that it was in his best interests to return to Alexandria. That was a lie, of course. But he has been well-rewarded for it. I am sorry, but it was necessary. It is not a good thing to have too many Caesars."

Rhoddon! And she thought it was Apollodorus who would betray her. How blind she had been.

"So you see," he said to her. "You have nothing left to live for now."

❦   ❦

Octavian regarded Munatius Plancus with both amusement and disgust. He would lick my ass and call it honey, this fellow. Still, an Emperor—for that was what he was now—needed a few bum flies like this. Why be divine if you do not have chaps who call you god?

He sprawled on a couch in Cleopatra's former chambers. They said Caesar himself had used this same couch often when he was in

Alexandria. It was rather quaint to avail himself of the palace where Antony had created so much scandal. It was a pleasant city, it had to be said, the views over the harbor and the astonishing beacon at the end of the breakwater were quite enchanting. And such souvenirs to be had. This table, for instance. Made from a solid slab of lapis lazuli, flecked with veins of gold, supported by sphinxes of basalt, inset with gold and coral. It was said to have been in the possession of the Ptolemies since the time of Alexander and was quite priceless. He had decided to take it back with him to Rome and display it prominently in his home.

"So, Noble Lord. Have you convinced her of the futility of her life?" Plancus asked him.

He returned his attention to the creature before him. "I think so," he said. "I believe it was the news about her son that really sank her." He shook his head. "I would not have this trouble if it was not for that fool of a captain, Proculeius. She was going to stab herself and he took her dagger away. Still, I should love to see her in my Triumph. It would be a pretty sight."

"You remember how they hooted Caesar . . . your father . . . over Arsinoë. It might not be good for your image."

"Yes, I know." He sighed. "Still, it is a shame for all that."

Plancus handed him a scroll. Octavian unrolled it and gave it cursory inspection. "What is this, Plancus?"

"My recommendations for the Senate on your return to Rome. We shall ask them to award you three Triumphs. One for Actium, one for Illyria, and another for Egypt."

"What is this here? You would declare Marc Antony's birthday cursed?"

"I also propose that we pass a law forbidding anyone to use the name Marcus and Antonius together and that we erase his name from every monument. Further, I recommend that we create a new name and title for you, Caesar."

Octavian looked amused. Hard not to like this man. A weasel, of course, but *his* weasel. "Have you something in mind?"

"Augustus," he said.

Augustus: revered one. Yes, it had a certain ring. It hinted at sanctity without being overtly offensive to those republicans who still held influence in Rome.

"Imperator Caesar Augustus," Octavian murmured, delighted with the sound of it.

"As your father Julius had the month of his birth named after him, so I would suggest that the month of your victory here in Alexandria be named for you. The month of Augustus."

"You have done well, Plancus. We shall place these recommendations before the Conscript Fathers upon our return."

"Now we wait only on the queen, Cleopatra, to do what is necessary."

"Indeed. But I do not think we will have to wait long."

127

AT THE END of the month of Mesore, almost a month after Octavian's triumphal entry into Alexandria, Cleopatra was given permission to visit the tomb of Antony, in the mausoleum. That morning she rose from her bed for the first time in almost a month and told Iras and Charmion what she wanted them to do.

A queen and a goddess is a work of art; its creation took time. First she had Iras prepare her bath. Precious essence of lotus and other aromatic oils were added to the water. Afterward Charmion washed her hair and spent several hours brushing it through and attending to her coiffure, arranging it in the plaits and curls of the Great Mother. Cleopatra then sat patiently in a gilded curlicue chair as Charmion painted her face, ashes of antimony to darken her eyebrows, her cheeks and lips reddened with powdered rock lichen, her forehead whitened with chalk. She painted her hands and feet with red henna, then anointed her neck and her wrists with a special blended perfume made from violet and black hyacinth.

At last it was done. Accompanied by her guards and a retinue of servants carrying baskets containing food and offerings for the mourning feast, Cleopatra made her way out of the palace to the mausoleum.

She is decided, Mardian thought. Ever since the defeat, she had been distracted by grief and confusion, but this morning she seemed calm, almost serene. He imagined he knew the reason, and there was lead in his heart and a pain deep in his chest that would not leave him.

"Have you done as I asked?" she said to Olympos once they were inside the mausoleum. The great vault was empty now, dark and gloomy and eerily cool after the heat of the garden. The mountain of treasures, the spices and gold and ivory and precious jewels, had long been removed to Octavian's care.

"I have done everything as you said," he answered. Her physician was dressed this morning as a common slave. A very old, useless one, Mardian thought, but the guards had not thought to challenge him.

"Thank you. You may all leave me."

Olympos seemed about to say something else, then thought better of it. He turned and followed the rest of the slaves through the door.

Cleopatra turned to him. "You, too, Mardian."

"But, Majesty . . ."

"Go." Her tone broached no argument. That imperious chin, those black eyes. What was she thinking, feeling?

He experienced a welter of emotion. "Majesty, I do not want to live now. Let me stay here—"

"You cannot be a part of this. I will not allow it. You have always served me faithfully, and I thank you for it. Retire to your villa and enjoy the fruits of autumn."

Once, that was all he wanted. There could not be many years left to him, after all, but he had wanted every day owed him, hoarding them in his mind as a carpet trader counting coins after a transaction in the market. How tenaciously we cling to life, those weaker of us who cannot abide the thought of our own deaths.

Now he realized the days no longer held value to him. "Majesty, I have enjoyed your graciousness and your wisdom, and as well I have endured your bad moods and your insults to me, and they are all like food and water to me now. All I ask is that I be allowed to die with you here."

"That is impossible. Go."

He wanted to say to her: But my spirit will die with yours. But she had never been one for weakness. He feared she would think less of him for giving voice to such maudlin sentiment. The only other choice was to confess to her what he had done, but that would change nothing, not now, and he did not have the courage to do it. Besides, what was done could not be undone. He turned to leave.

"I was sorry," she said to him. "What happened to your brother-in-law."

He nodded and slipped away, into the light. A bright, hot morning in Alexandria, the city white with heat, dust blowing in from the desert, choking the streets. His eyes were blind with tears.

The guards closed the great doors behind him and she was left alone with Charmion and Iras. The sentries would no doubt be flogged later when it was discovered what she had done, even though he was sure that Octavian was party to it. Another charade, another theater.

It was how things were done.

❦ ❦

Poor Antony, she thought, to die with so little grace. His blood still stained the marble walls of the upper chamber. There was a bloody handprint below the sill, perhaps hers. He had deserved better, for all his faults. She had wept all her tears for him. But those tears belonged to that other woman, the Queen Cleopatra. Today she was here as Isis, and a god.

Four torches, fixed in iron sockets, still flared at the four corners of the chamber. She took flowers and incense and set them on top of the pink granite of the sarcophagus, kissed the cold stone, and murmured a prayer to Isis for his resurrection. When it was done, she surrendered herself once again to the ministrations of Charmion and Iras.

She stood up, and the two girls stripped away her robes and removed from one of the baskets the clothes they had concealed there. Her breasts were painted blue with lapis, and she was dressed in a gown of shimmering blue silk, tied between the breasts with the mysterious knot of Isis. In her left hand they put a gold scepter, and then jewels were placed at her ears and her throat and her wrists, darkly splendid in the gloom of the vault.

A snake armlet of pure gold was placed around both of her bare upper arms, and on her head they put the *uraeus*, the serpent crown of Lower Egypt. Its hood was inflated, rearing above her brow; the cobra was the sacred emblem of Isis and guardian of the groves of Paradise. In the ancient Book of the Dead it was the symbol of indestructible life.

When they were finished, Cleopatra, the Macedonian queen, was gone. In her place was Isis, Mother of Egypt and of the World. She took her place on the gilded chair the servants had carried with them from the palace, immaculate, serene, utterly remote.

Charmion fetched the other basket, the one Olympos had brought for her. She placed it gently on the queen's lap. Cleopatra stared at her for a long time, her breathing shallow and quick, her fingers trembling.

Dust filtered through the shadowed light; above her head the sun's rays were slanted through the upper window. Outside she could hear the muted sounds of Alexandria, returning to its normal rhythms now, the chant of priests in the temple, the distant murmur of voices at the harborside, the silky cadence of the sea.

She opened the basket lid.

The cobra was slow to rouse, not as aggressive as she had expected. It reared slowly from its warm nest, curious more than alarmed, yellow eyes staring. She smacked its head to anger it and its hood rose in alarm, in imitation of the crown the queen wore upon her head. It struck back at her hand in its own defense.

She stared at the tiny puncture wound. It was done.

The snake struck once more, on her arm, then coiled off her lap and slipped away. She heard the soft susurration of its scales as it slithered away across the black granite floor.

The effects of the poison were swift. Already there was tingling in her fingers, and her arm felt numb and heavy. A coldness spread through her limbs to the rest of her body and a steel band clamped around her chest and she could not breathe. She fought down a wave of panic, the instinctive struggle for life. She forced herself to stillness.

She closed her eyes, heard a buzzing in her ears. The black shadows moved swiftly across the room toward her and it was done, as simply as that.

Mardian stared, ignoring the guard's profanities.

He heard footsteps behind him and half turned. It was Octavian.

He was smiling under the ridiculous broad-rimmed hat that he wore as protection against the Alexandrian sun. "So, Mardian. She has done it," he said. He frowned. "You know, it is a pity. I always admired her."

Mardian did not answer. Cleopatra's two maidservants, just flesh and blood, lay on the marble at her feet. The guards searched the mausoleum for the cobra, but found no sign of it.

"You have done well. You will be well rewarded."

"Keep your money. I don't want it now."

"After everything you did for us?"

It was true. After they lost their fleet to Malchus he had lost faith, had thought to save himself from Octavian. After all, he had reasoned, there is nothing more my prodigy can do to save herself. He had been wrong in thinking her beaten, in believing that he still loved life so much.

"I wish I was dead," he said.

Octavian smiled. "Well, anything can be arranged. You only have to ask."

Cleopatra sat quite still, composed in death, on the gilded throne. But no, this was not Cleopatra; it was Isis, the goddess whose earthly death, the priests said, would bring redemption to Egypt and the world. But because she was a goddess, she could not really die; one day she would be resurrected and return to Egypt to lead her people to salvation. Cleopatra had deified her own death, he realized, turned even this her most desolate moment into theater, a promise of hope and of triumph.

EPILOGUE

ALEXANDRIA
October, Anno Domini 1998

THE HARBOR CITY looks tawdry now. The great palaces on the Lochias are lost beneath waters too polluted with sewage and discarded plastic for them to be seen. The mausoleum with the tombs of Antony and Cleopatra are gone, probably forever, though scuba divers using modern technology are out there this morning, part of an international exploration team searching for what may still lie hidden below the murky waters.

The great lighthouse of Pharos was destroyed by earthquakes over fifteen hundred years ago. The fort of Qait Bey, flying the red, white, and black flag of Egypt, now stands at the end of the breakwater in its place, though they say that some of the stone used in its construction once formed part of that great marvel.

Two hours away from here, on an air-conditioned bus, preserved in the Egyptian Museum in Cairo, are the remains of pharaohs ten thousand years old. Everywhere you travel in modern Egypt you are confronted with the country's antiquities: moldering mummies, the tombs of ancients with hieroglyphs as vivid as the day they were painted, the staggering temple complexes of Luxor and Karnak.

Yet of Cleopatra hardly anything remains.

History records that Augustus reigned for another forty-four years, sole master of the Roman world. Emperor in all but name, he presided over an era of peace, prosperity, and cultural achievement unknown in Rome for almost a century. He became known as a patron of the arts and often boasted that he had found Rome in brick and left it in marble. Egypt became his personal fief, and no Roman was allowed to travel there without his express permission. In his lifetime he fulfilled Caesar's dream of empire, and proved himself, finally, Caesar's son, if not in fact then in deed.

But although he won his temporal victory, Cleopatra and Isis did rise again, throughout the Mediterranean. The image of her as Mother, holding Horus to her breast, was imitated by a cult whose religion was based on Judaism and who called themselves Christians. Their icon of a madonna holding a child became a universal symbol for compassion and peace.

The Potter's Oracles had prophesied a glorious child who would usher in a golden age and bring about the downfall of Rome. In Augustus's time that glorious child did come, an Essene revolutionary whose death on a cross was made the staging cry for a religion that proved the death knell for the ancient gods of Rome and Greece.

But the Potter's Oracles were wrong in their prophecy of a perfect age. The long-awaited peace did not come, the Golden Child heralded only more conflict, endless wars and slaughter and death.

And so it is to the madonna that men, tired of war and anger, yet look for peace and for compassion. She is their healer and mother, a religion within a religion, older than time itself. Men and women still light their votive candles at her feet.

And it is perhaps then that we glimpse her, Cleopatra, on her knees before her beloved Isis, peering back at us from behind the dark and velvet shrouds of history, from a time when we were gods.

WHEN WE
WERE GODS
COLIN FALCONER

A Reader's Guide

A Conversation with Colin Falconer

Q: Cleopatra has been written about for centuries, by hundreds of authors with hundreds of different agendas. What motivated you to write about her? Do you like her better before or after you'd researched and written the book? Do you think history has been kind or unkind to her?

CF: I'd discounted Cleopatra as a subject many times, precisely because she has been so widely written about. But then I was astonished to discover that despite this library of literature, almost every fictional account of her is based on myth rather than fact.

History has been unkind: much of what we think we know about her is actually propaganda from the Romans of two thousand years ago. (It would be like people in 4000 A.D. accepting Khrushchev's view of John F. Kennedy.) We think of media manipulation as a recent invention, but of course it isn't.

In short, yes, I did like her better. History has painted her as lovelorn and promiscuous; Monica Lewinsky on the other side of the Oval Office desk. This is a terrible legacy for Cleopatra, a woman who could speak nine languages, was very possibly a faithful wife and mother, and almost achieved the unthinkable and defeated the greatest empire of her day— the Roman Empire.

Q: How did you research this book?

CF: I read every book I could find on her, of course, and there's a frightening amount. Some of it's even readable. I'm a member of the British Library in Bloomsbury and I researched there. Then I went to Egypt; Alexandria, Cleopatra's capital, was frankly a disappointment. There's hardly anything left from that time. The Romans destroyed most of it; an earthquake five hundred years later did the rest. The research was the challenge of separating myth and ancient Roman propaganda from historical fact. A number of scholars have actually done a plausible job of this, but when a fiction writer attempts it, it almost sounds original because no one much reads books written by scholars.

Q: Most people know the broad outlines of Cleopatra's life and have many preconceived notions about her. Is there anything you found in your research that would surprise readers who think they already "know" Cleopatra? Did you incorporate those surprising facts into your book?

CF: Here's a thing: some historians speculate that Cleopatra may have been blonde. As she was part Macedonian, there's a fair chance, so to speak. I toyed with the idea of having Cleopatra as a blonde, mainly so Michelle Pfeiffer could play the role in the film. Or, at least, in my fantasies.

But my wife said to me: you can't do that. (Have Cleopatra be a blonde, not have fantasies about Michelle Pfeiffer.) She said: "Cleopatra is now far too deeply ingrained in our consciousness as Elizabeth Taylor with a bob; it will jar in a reader's imagination to have her be blonde."

I took her advice on that one.

A problem I encountered: there are few existing likenesses of the lady. A coin from the period shows her in profile, a rather terrifying image not unlike Mike Tyson. Accounts of the day take some pains to describe her "pleasing personality," which, as every male chauvinist knows, is code for "plug ugly." But apart from these unreliable and discouraging clues, there's really nothing to show what she looked like.

I have imagined her in the book as she may have looked; her mother, after all, may have been a Syrian princess and Syrian women were, and are, noted for their exceptional beauty. What I took pains to do, though, was explore the fact that this was a princess of fabulous wealth, of unchecked ambition and uncanny expertise in the manipulation of her own image, a woman gifted with intelligence, charisma, and supreme power, who lived fast and died young.

I discovered she was almost certainly not the sexual virago of myth. She did not copulate with crocodiles, for example (it's dangerous), or slaves (beneath her dignity). In fact, it seems she only slept with two men all her

life, and both of those men were husbands. Well, not her husbands ini-
tially, but she did marry them later.

And the other thing—the asp to the breast. There's a strong likelihood
that she did die by a self-administered snakebite—but it was a cobra
almost certainly applied to her arm, not to the plump breast of Renais-
sance fantasy.

*Q: You've written in a variety of genres, including children's books, myster-
ies, and historical fiction. What is the most satisfying—and most challeng-
ing—about writing historical novels?*

CF: The challenge: avoiding the pitfalls of bodice rippers; using language
that makes historical characters sound like you and me; making a world
long gone feel and smell real to the reader, and not like the literary equiva-
lent of a costume drama; combining sound historical research and attention to detail with a thriller element to make history a riveting read.

I also like to use humor; I think it's sometimes easy to forget that wit
and a sense of humor are not twentieth-century inventions.

The extra challenge with Cleopatra is that the sources that chronicle
her life were written after she was dead. They often conflict and are invari-
ably hostile to her. I tried to deconstruct her from what we know she did
and worked back from there: I believe I have created a very plausible
Cleopatra. But no one can ever know if it's the real one.

*Q: You often write about female characters and have been praised for the
strong, intelligent women in your novels. Is it difficult for a man to write
about women's lives or from a woman's perspective?*

CF: For a man to write about a woman is incredibly difficult for all the
obvious reasons. I do not see myself as in any way especially sensitive to
women in a New Age or politically correct way. However, I like to think I
have some empathy for all my characters, regardless of their gender. After
that, though, I get help. My wife, Helen, reads my drafts and is not afraid

to tell me: "Hey, stupid, we don't think that way/feel that way/a woman wouldn't do that." And I was fortunate to have two good female editors on the book, to filter out anything she missed. I think it helps when you *know* you don't understand women and are therefore open to taking advice.

I like to think of it as research.

Q: Some authors say they find writing very easy. Do ideas and characters come easily to you?

CF: No, not easily, and I'm never ever satisfied with anything I do.

However, I'm not the sort of writer to agonize for hours over a semicolon. Writing comes from experience and from people; you don't get much of either if you're stuck in a room with a computer twenty hours a day.

Ideas come to me all the time; it's like a mental barrage. It's structuring those ideas into a readable book that's hard. And characters: well sometimes, like Caesar and Mark Antony, they just write themselves, bless them.

Q: What do you want readers to take away from this book, and from Cleopatra and her world?

CF: I would like, in a small way, to undo the damage done by tens of thousands of stupefyingly boring high school history teachers. I would like readers to discover that history has riveting stories taking place in a fascinating place we can never go to—the past.

And I'd also like my readers to remember that Cleopatra did not have a bob and a beauty spot and look like Elizabeth Taylor; and that Julius Caesar did not talk with a Welsh accent and have a drinking problem.

Reading Group Questions and Topics for Discussion

1. It was pharaonic practice in Cleopatra's time for royal siblings to marry to ensure the "purity" of the blood line. Steeped in this heritage, why does Cleopatra renounce the practice, which she finds barbaric? What are some other examples of Cleopatra thinking outside the prescribed practices of her time and place? Is it this independent spirit that makes her a legend?

2. Cleopatra's first encounter with Caesar is from a position of utter weakness, as she is unwrapped, dizzy and disoriented, from the rug in which she has been smuggled to Rome. Does this first impression— "she looked so small, like a broken bird"—color the relationship between Cleopatra and Caesar from here on? If so, does it benefit Cleopatra, or detract from her power in the relationship?

3. Caesar is genuinely horrified by many aspects of Egyptian culture. What bothers him the most, and why? Does his discomfort exemplify a larger culture clash between ancient Egyptian and ancient Roman philosophies, or is he simply personally threatened by the differences? Does Cleopatra attempt to downplay these differences, or does she use them to her advantage? What aspects of Roman culture disgust Cleopatra?

4. As Arsinoë is dragged into court to face her final humiliation, Cleopatra calmly thinks, "You have gambled and you have lost, sister. I thought you should bear your defeat with better grace." Where else in the novel do we see the theme of gambling with fate, and the various responses to victory or defeat that result? Is Cleopatra consistent in how she handles her own gambles? Is there anything she is not willing to gamble for?

5. When Cleopatra shows Caesar the warehouses at Rhakotis, full of Egyptian treasure, the power balance between them shifts subtly in her favor. Caesar seems shaken, both by her wealth and by the temptation she is laying before him to share it. Why, then, does Cleopatra bite her tongue and submit to his abrupt idea that she wed Antiochus. What point to you think Caesar is trying to make with this plan? Is this diplomacy, or is it more personal than that?

6. In Caesar's final days, he spins a legend of his own invincibility, and he throws all caution to the wind. Has Cleopatra influenced him in thinking that he is divine? Or is he simply exhausted by statesmanship and flirting with death? Are the statues of himself, Cleopatra, and Caesarion that Caesar has erected on the high altar at the Temple of Venus Genetrix a rash, end-of-life decision, or a sign of how he has felt about them all along? How does Cleopatra respond?

7. Falconer provides no lead-up to Cleopatra's murder of Antiochus. It is the first instance we have seen of Cleopatra's ability to be truly ruthless, and it arrives without fanfare. How does this scene affect your opinion of Cleopatra? Are you surprised when Arsinoë and Fulvia meet similar deaths?

8. After Antony's wife, Fulvia, makes a spectacle of Cicero's death, Antony is suddenly fed up with all the bloodshed and the struggle for power in Rome. Why does this change of heart hit him now? Is he big-hearted to spare Octavian—"the boy had only done what any man would have done in the same circumstances"—or is he foolhardy? Do you think Antony has taken his cue from Caesar in this sudden revolt against violence and politics? Why do his thoughts now turn to Cleopatra?

9. "The truth is what people see," Cleopatra thinks to herself as her servants transform her ship into a floating palace for their arrival into Tarsus to visit Antony. Despite the fact that she is seasick, lonely, and terrified, she plays the part of the goddess Isis to perfection and awes Antony's entire court with effortless decadence. In what ways do each of the central characters in the novel display a similar belief that what people see is more "truth" than anything else?

10. Cleopatra's wit never fails her. When, after a four-year silence, Antony sends her an envoy who announces, "Reverend Majesty, I bring greetings from my lord Antony, Imperator of Rome," she responds, "Who?" When do we see Cleopatra relying on humor for survival? Does Falconer do a good job of making Cleopatra accessible as a character, yet believable as an ancient ruler? What motivates Cleopatra in this interview with Antony's envoy: love or politics?

11. After 337 pages of Cleopatra longing for a marriage that will bind Egypt and Rome, the wedding between her and Antony takes place in two understated paragraphs. Why?

12. The concept of what it means to be Roman is so salient in the novel that it is almost another character. The burden of Roman-ness weighs heavily on both Caesar and Antony, guiding nearly all their decisions, and continually confounds Cleopatra with its inscrutable intricacies. Can you think of any national identities as pervasive today?

13. Why is Octavian's campaign to clean up Rome—including the creation of a library, the distribution of free oil lamps to the poor, and the building of a new temple to Apollo—so clever at this point, after Cleopatra and Antony's marriage? What does it symbolize? Is Antony threatened by it? Why does he immediately turn his attention back to Parthia? Is his dogged persistence in the Parthia campaign a tribute to the goals of Caesar, or just a strategy to avoid the troubles brewing in his own backyard?

14. Cleopatra is dangerously stubborn in her refusal to allow Antony to march on Italy from Actium without her. If she lets him go, there is a good chance that Octavian's troops will refuse to fight against Antony and will defect to his side. But with Cleopatra at his side, his own supporters are divided, and he will face animosity in battle and almost certain defeat. Cleopatra has plenty of reasons to distrust Antony based on past events, but is she too stubborn here? Is she sacrificing good politics and war strategy for proof of personal loyalty?

15. Cleopatra asserts that "An enemy is a place in time . . . not a place in the world." What does she mean? How does this belief allow her to continually adapt and renew her plans for Egypt and for her family?

16. Antony knows that Octavian is ruthless. So why does he bother appealing to Octavian's reason and sensitivity in asking him to spare Cleopatra's life at the end? Is Antony hopelessly naive, or simply infused with an undying belief in honor?

17. Why does Cleopatra refuse to allow Mardian to die with her? Does she know something about his secret?

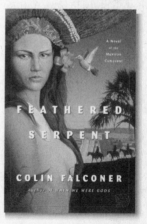